*W*hat the critics are saying...

Sarah McCarty

Conception
THE OTHERS

ELLORA'S CAVE
ROMANTICA PUBLISHING

An Ellora's Cave Romantica Publication

www.ellorascave.com

Conception

ISBN # 1419953990
ALL RIGHTS RESERVED.
Conception Copyright© 2005 Sarah McCarty
Edited by Pamela Campbell.
Cover art by Syneca.

Electronic book Publication August 2005
Trade Paperback Publication February 2006

Warning:

The following material contains graphic sexual content meant for mature readers. *Conception* has been rated E–rotic by a minimum of three independent reviewers.

Ellora's Cave Publishing offers three levels of Romantica™ reading entertainment: S (S-ensuous), E (E-rotic), and X (X-treme).

S-*ensuous* love scenes are explicit and leave nothing to the imagination.

E-*rotic* love scenes are explicit, leave nothing to the imagination, and are high in volume per the overall word count. In addition, some E-rated titles might contain fantasy material that some readers find objectionable, such as bondage, submission, same sex encounters, forced seductions, and so forth. E-rated titles are the most graphic titles we carry; it is common, for instance, for an author to use words such as "fucking", "cock", "pussy", and such within their work of literature.

X-*treme* titles differ from E-rated titles only in plot premise and storyline execution. Unlike E-rated titles, stories designated with the letter X tend to contain controversial subject matter not for the faint of heart.

About the Author

ജ

Sarah McCarty published her first book with Ellora's Cave, Inc. in the spring of 2004 and she hasn't looked back. She published four books her first year and received twenty awards. Among her many accolades, Sarah received multiple Best of 2004 awards and was voted by reviewers as the Best New Author Romance Erotic. A long time member of Romance Writers of America, she has published three popular romance series and one novella.

Sarah has traveled extensively throughout her life, living in other cultures, sometimes in areas where electricity was a concept awaiting fruition and a book was an extreme luxury. While she could easily adjust to the lack of electricity, living without the comfort of a good book was intolerable. To fill the void, she bought pencil and paper and sketched out her own story. In the process, Sarah discovered the joy of writing.

Sarah writes what she loves to read; fast paced stories with vivid dialogue, intense emotion and well developed characters. Her attention to detail in her stories continues to earn her awards and a reserved spot on Keeper shelves everywhere.

Sarah welcomes mail from readers. You can write to her c/o Ellora's Cave Publishing at 1056 Home Avenue, Akron, OH 44310-3502.

Also by Sarah McCarty

&

A Bit of Sass
Mac's Law
Promises Linger
Promises Keep
Promises Prevail

Conception

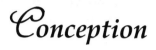

$\mathcal{D}$edication

$\mathcal{F}$or Kelly...the truly innocent one (wink) with a gift for gab

and making people feel good about themselves. May your icons
always be your favorites and your smile find you at the end of
the day.

~ Trademarks Acknowledgement ~

The author acknowledges the trademarked status and trademark owners of the following wordmarks mentioned in this work of fiction:

Barbie: Mattel Inc.
Mack Truck: Mack Trucks, Inc.
Cheerios: General Mills, Inc.

Chapter One

හ

There would be no escape.

The realization slashed through pain, through despair, and most devastatingly through the hope that this was all a horrible nightmare. That she wasn't suspended above the floor in her kitchen, hanging by her wrists, blood dripping from her back onto the old wooden planks below. That her grandfather wasn't the one who'd ordered the whipping that was draining the life from her body. That it wasn't her loving uncle wielding the whip. That her whole world hadn't disappeared because she'd dared to fall in love.

Her uncle grunted, the whip whistled and the now familiar agony exploded throughout her body, racing faster than she could gather her determination to endure. She screamed. Again.

"Where is he?"

The question snapped out with the force of a blow, striking deep into her fear. She dug her nails into her palms as agony rolled through her body. Oh, God! It hurt so badly! She couldn't take it. Couldn't take any more. She needed something to hold on to. Something to get her through. She couldn't fail Dusan again. She wouldn't.

Swirls of mist seeped into her consciousness, delicate tendrils wafting up through the red haze shrouding her mind's eye, blurring the edges of her vision. The mist built and grew into a fog, and as it did, the agony lessened.

Was she losing her mind? The fog thickened, beckoned, offering a miracle to a nonbeliever. The whip dragged across the floor, the sound seeming to come from far away as reality tucked behind the thick fog. Without further resistance, she allowed her mind to sink into the comforting haze, welcoming the oblivion it promised.

Ice-cold water hit her face with the force of shattering icicles, yanking her back into the horror. Fingers sank into her hair, jerking her chin off her chest. "Damn it, girl! Just tell us where he is and we can stop all this."

She opened her eyes. Her grandfather's face swam in and out of focus, distorted beyond recognition by his rage and the knowledge that she'd betrayed him. He shook her and the room jerked out of focus. She didn't fight his manipulation of her head, accepting his dominance over her body.

"Answer me!"

She summoned the remnants of her strength and remained mute. They couldn't make her do anything anymore. Least of all make her reveal where Dusan was. Not when it was her fault he'd been captured. Not when his only hope for escape was her silence.

Retaliation was swift. The blow jerked her body high in the chains. Blood filled her throat and the world swirled red and black.

"Jesus, Clay. Ease off." Her uncle's shout was a dim echo of her own silent plea. "If you kill her we'll never find the bastard."

"We'll find him." The conviction in the statement jarred with the rattle of the chains. "I've waited too long, worked too hard for this to fall apart now."

"Maybe another dose of the drug?"

"The drug isn't working," her grandfather retorted.

"How the hell can it not be working?"

"I don't goddamn well know, but any more and she'll die." Anger and disgust colored the outburst. Metal rattled against metal. The sound was just as discordant as the truth her grandfather spat out. "But she won't die before she tells us where she put that damn vamp."

Water hit the bottom of the bucket in a roar of sound that masked Eden's soft gasp. He meant it. Her grandfather really didn't care if she lived or died. Somewhere inside her the scream started, swelling, pushing against her throat, the last of her innocence wailing to be heard. She bit the inside of her lip, the stab of pain snapping her back into control. No matter what her grandfather did to her, revealed to her, she couldn't lose it now. She had to hold on a little longer.

"How badly do we still need the vamp?" her uncle asked.

"Without him, we're nowhere."

"We've got his DNA."

"We need *him*."

"I thought we needed her, too."

They wanted her? Why?

"We do, but if I have to sacrifice her, I will."

"And what will we do then?"

Eden knew the answer before her grandfather said it.

"Go to Plan B."

Her grandfather always had Plan B. Plumbing clunked a protest as the water was turned off.

"Did you stop to think that maybe she doesn't know where the vamp is?" her uncle asked, disgust putting an edge on the question.

Eden didn't fool herself that the disgust came from concern for her welfare. No, Uncle Henry was disgusted because her grandfather had left him out of the loop. Something he should be used to by now. No one, not even her, had ever been able to gain Clay Lavery's trust or approval. The nearest she'd ever come was when she'd dated Deuce. And now she knew why. Somehow, her grandfather had known what he was, had predicted his interest in her, and had used her to lure him into a trap. She'd just been the lovesick fool who thought it had all been real. The start of a new beginning. Instead, she'd dragged the only person who'd ever loved her for herself into a deathtrap.

"She's the only one who had access to his cell," her grandfather snapped.

"He could have escaped."

"Not without help. As long as he's on that drug he can't move, twitch or summon help."

"Theoretically."

There was a disbelieving snort from her grandfather and the sound of the metal bucket scraping the counter. "If the creature could have moved, he never would have allowed the sampling." Heavy footsteps approached, slightly uneven in rhythm. "Therefore, if he's been moved, she's the one who moved him."

Viciously cold water hit her face and chest again, filling her nose and mouth. Eden couldn't prevent the rasping cough that jerked her body. She couldn't preserve the illusion of unconsciousness. Once again, her head was hauled up. "Isn't that right, Ladybug?"

She said nothing, refusing to respond to the harsh parody of the familiar endearment. Her grandfather let her head drop. In her mind, the cloud appeared again, hovering just past her reach. Waiting. For what? If the damn thing was going to show up, it should sure as shit do its job.

"Maybe we'd better lay off for a while," she heard Uncle Henry offer cautiously. Uncle Henry was a brilliant man, but he lacked her grandfather's hard edges.

Oh, please, she prayed, straining for the cloud, *lay off for a while*. She wasn't proud. She'd take whatever respite she could get.

"There's no time." The metal bucket thudded to the floor. "He's already an hour late for his injection. In another two, he'll be free of the drug entirely."

"Shit!" Uncle Henry gasped, horror lacing his tone. "It'll be full dark in two hours!"

"Exactly." Two more steps and she heard the slither of leather sliding off wood. The shift of air across her face, the flicker of interrupted light against her closed eyelids, indicated the gesture she couldn't see. "So stop mollycoddling the traitorous bitch and let's get this over with."

Two hours. She just had to hold on for two more hours. She could do it. What was two hours when it meant Deuce's life? Eden fought back the writhing fear as she heard the rasp of the whip dragging across the floor. Two hours was just one-hundred-twenty minutes. Seventy-two-hundred seconds. That wasn't so long. She'd heard of POWs who'd hung on for twenty years. Surely, she could hold out for two hours. She owed Deuce that much.

The whip snapped on the backswing. Her gasp was instinctive. Unpreventable. She hated herself for the fear. The weakness. The desperate prayer for something to save her. But nothing could save her now. There was no turning back. Even if she told them where he was, it wouldn't save her. She'd betrayed her grandfather. He'd never suffer her to live. But hanging on could save Dusan. That's where she needed to hold her focus.

Eden braced herself, knowing it was pointless. There was no preparing for the agony of the lash cutting through flesh and muscle, but a small kernel of stubbornness demanded she try. She stiffened in anticipation as the lash whistled its approach. The cloud swelled and gathered. As if straining against an invisible wall, it hovered and bulged and then exploded forward. She threw herself into it, hoping against hope it wasn't a mirage, imagining that it came from Deuce, needing for the moment the illusion that he cared for her and his attention hadn't been part of some sick war he and her grandfather fought. The wet slap of the lash hitting flesh reverberated around her. Her body jerked, the chains rattled, but no corresponding burst of agony detonated in her flesh. It was as if she floated in a protective space where nothing could touch her.

She huddled her spirit deeper into the cloud. She panted, breathing in the acrid odor of her own sweat, tinted with the metallic scent of blood. She had her miracle. Now, if the powers-that-be were willing, she just needed one more. Just one.

It came in the form of a horrendous crash and a rapid succession of small explosions.

Gunfire!

The cloud disappeared in a puff. Eden raised her head and forced her swollen eyes to slit open. She was just in time to see her grandfather and uncle slip through the wine cellar door. Two seconds later, the room filled with huge, broad-shouldered, khaki-clad strangers. One of whom bumped her. She couldn't suppress her gasp as she swayed.

"Oh God!" That hurt. Her voice was a slight gasp of air, barely sound, but it was enough to immediately make her the focus of a pair of golden eyes.

"Shit."

She must look as good as she felt.

The hard-faced man spoke into the mike on his shoulder. "We've got life here."

She waited for the man to help her down. Shoot the chains. Pick the lock. Any number of the things she'd seen on TV. Instead, he grasped her chin in his gloved fingers and tilted her gaze to meet his. "Where is he?"

Oh Lord. Not another one. If she'd had the strength, she would have jerked her chin away. Instead, she settled on the tried and true method of resistance. She sought her cloud.

It failed to come. Violence hummed beneath the skin of the golden man holding her. His grip on her chin tightened. His strange eyes narrowed. "I'm only going to ask you one more time, lady. Where is he?"

Or he'd do what? Beat her? She closed her eyes and didn't dignify his threat with a response.

"Nick," golden man barked. "Can you smell him?"

"Hell, there's so much blood here, I'd be lucky to pick out anything but her."

"Try."

"It'd be easier if the Chosen weren't so elusive."

"It'd be easier if the humans would just leave us alone."

"No argument there."

Humans? Did that mean the man holding her wasn't human?

Eden forced her eyes open again. Only one would open enough to see through clearly. The man wasn't looking at her. He held her chin almost absentmindedly, his attention on a dark-haired man across the room. He certainly looked human, but there was a certain cast to his profile, the way his hair swept off his forehead that lent him an otherworldly aura. Was it possible?

"Who are you?" The clear demand she intended came out as a hoarse, dried-up croak of sound.

The golden man turned back to her. "I'm the man looking for Deuce."

"Why?"

His right eyebrow went up. "Because his brother asked me to."

"You're not human."

"What makes you say that?"

"Something you said."

He exchanged a look with the others in the room. With a curt "Secure the area" he turned back to her. His demeanor was noticeably softer. His grip on her chin gentled.

"Deuce's family is very worried about him."

He was going to have to do better than that. "What are you?"

"What do you think I am?"

Her left eye throbbed and her back burned. She was dangerously close to losing consciousness, and he wanted to play games? Was she cursed? "Are you one of them?"

His gaze sharpened. "I'm one of the Lyons. Dak Lyons, to be precise."

"You're on his list," she breathed, weighing the information and what it might mean.

"Whose list?"

"My grandfather's."

She ignored his small start at that piece of information. It didn't necessarily follow that just because Dak Lyons was on the same list as Deuce that he was a friend, but it was the only hedge she had in what was a pretty dismal situation. Bottom line, trusting Dak Lyons was the only chance Deuce had.

"You've got to get him out of here," she told him.

"Where is he?"

She stared into his golden eyes for a minute, looking for something, anything that would tell her if she was doing the right thing. There was nothing for her to see, however, except the level assessment he was making of her in return.

Across the room, the little green light on the alarm panel started to flash. Oh God, they were out of time. "Under the floor."

"Where?"

She closed her eyes on a brief prayer and said, "Under my feet."

All eyes fell to the blood-spattered wood.

"Hell. Get a crowbar over here!" She sensed, more than saw, movement at the edge of the room.

"You've got to hurry," she whispered. "He activated the defenses."

Dak whipped around. "Who did?"

"My grandfather. He's always been worried about someone stealing his research."

Dak's lips twisted, derision clearly evident. "I'll just bet."

Two of the heavily armed, heavily muscled men made short work of the nails she'd pounded so deep to keep Deuce safe. Nails squealed as they were dragged free, wood groaned and thud after thud, two beats slower than her heart, built into a clatter as the floorboards were tossed aside. No one made a move toward her. They weren't even going to get her down, Eden realized. Not until they were sure. And maybe not even then. She was the granddaughter of the head of the Coalition. She was the enemy. Though she'd been late coming to that understanding, she had it now. The minutes stretched like hours as the men worked beneath her. Then with a "Got him", the agony of wondering if she'd done the right thing was over.

"Jeez, Deuce," a big man with a bandanna tied around his head asked, no small amount of horror in his voice, "what the hell did they do to you?"

That horror in his voice dug deeply into her fear. Had she been too late? Had something happened while he was down there? "Is he all right?"

No one spared her a glance, let alone an answer.

A hammer went flying past her field of vision before landing with a bang in the pile of discarded floorboards. "He's not moving, Dak."

Dak turned her face to his. "Why isn't he moving?"

"It's a drug," she whispered. "He can't move or talk. It'll wear off in a couple hours, but you've got to get him out of here now."

Not a flicker of expression touched his face. "Nick, bring the body bag."

"He's not dead!" she gasped, struggling in a futile effort to see for herself. He couldn't be dead. All she got a glimpse of was her chest and a set of wide male shoulders.

Dak's hands on her hips put paid to her efforts to see. His "He needs protection from the light" was almost gentle. There was a faint stiffening in his arms as he stepped aside for the men to work. He took a breath, paused, and lifted her weight off her arms. "You're hurting yourself."

Her struggles had reopened the wounds in her wrists. It didn't matter. She craned her neck to see. "Is Dusan okay?"

His gaze held hers, puzzlement pushing aside the anger. "I can't tell."

There was a snap that had her flinching before she realized it was the heavy vinyl bag snaking out, and not the whip.

Nick reached down for Deuce, bumping her legs as he did. "Damn," he muttered as he hauled him out, grunting with the effort. "He's going to be pissed at someone when he wakes up."

Dak got a better grip on the sides of her hips and lifted her out of the way. The agony wrenched the scream from her throat against her will. Hard curses from Dak and Nick swayed in tandem beneath the echo.

The urge to succumb to the haze that immediately appeared was almost overwhelming, but she couldn't take advantage of it yet. Not now. They had to understand.

"Get her down," Dak barked again, his grip on her hips tightening.

"Who the hell did this to them?" bandanna man growled, stepping forward.

She had, with her blind stupidity. But she wasn't admitting that now, to these men. Eden forced her right eye open. The left lid refused to move. Across the room the lights on the panel started flashing in ever increasing patterns. The time for atonement was at hand. She met Nick's gaze through his sunglasses as he zipped Deuce's bloody body into the bag. She redirected his gaze to the panel on the wall. She forced her ravaged lungs to fill with air. With everything she had, she ordered, "Run!"

She saw realization dawn in the men's eyes as the last consonant faded.

Nick threw Deuce over his shoulder. "Get the hell out of here. The whole damn place is going to go."

As one, the sea of khaki made for the exit. Eden was only concerned with Nick's progress.

Her body was jerked relentlessly as Dak and the other man tested the metal restraints holding her in place. Bandanna man pulled out his gun and fired. The agony of the percussion tore through her wrists and down her arms, so intense she could no longer scream. Dak's curses came as fast as her heartbeat, just as frantic and just as useless. The chains held.

Her gaze followed Nick as he cleared the door, his image blurring out of clarity. As he passed through with his burden, she turned her attention to Dak and the other man. She knew the instant he recognized what she'd known from the moment she'd chosen to save Deuce. She wasn't getting out of here alive.

"Get out of here," Dak ordered bandanna man.

"Just as soon as you do."

"You're in charge of getting Deuce to Bohdan."

Bandanna man glanced at her, at the chains, and finally at Dak. With a sharp nod, he sprinted for the door, long hair whipping behind him.

"You need to go, too," Eden told Dak. She couldn't have any more lives on her conscience.

"Just as soon as I have you down, I'll do that very thing."

"There's no time!"

Dak's expression turned to stone and his eyes glowed with defiant determination. She shook her head as he picked at the locks with a piece of metal. With the last bit of strength she had, she pulled up her leg, placed her foot on his chest and pushed him away. He stared at her, fangs showing, face morphing as she swung in the chains, past pain. Past everything.

Explosions began in the outer compound, the impending violence vibrating down the chains straight to her soul. She was going to die, but he didn't need to.

"You can't save me." The gold of his eyes changed to deep amber with uncertainty, and then regret. His fingers brushed her cheek with the lightest of touches. She closed her eyes against the reality and found the strength to do one last thing right. "Get out of here."

Chapter Two

ఞ

"This had better be good," Deuce growled, tossing his battered backpack on the chair in the main security room. "If I do not leave soon, Dak will have all the fun rousting those spies by himself."

"Oh, it's good." Nick leaned back in his chair and folded his arms across his chest. "And I don't know what the hell to do about it."

"Do what we always do with journalists." He shrugged. "Scare them off."

"Tried that."

"And?"

Nick fiddled with the camera controls. "She didn't scare."

She? Deuce's curiosity piqued. Not many women came this far into the wilderness. Let alone in the bitter cold following a raging storm. "Who did you send?"

"Harley."

He moved toward the screen. Harley was a big nightmare of a werewolf and one of his top security experts. "Hell-bent-for-leather Harley didn't send her screaming?"

Nick's chair creaked beneath his shifting weight. "Nope."

"Did he forget his biker regalia?"

"Nope. He even took along Luke and Shiva."

Which meant the three had been hanging around waiting for him to get back, and boredom had driven them out to scare off the pretty little journalist.

He looked at the monitor. In the darkening twilight, there was only a faint stir of movement. At times, the limits of human technology frustrated him.

"She's between cameras," Nick apologized.

Deuce scanned with his senses. The only people on the mountain, according to his senses, were those who were supposed to be there. Which was impossible. He was staring at evidence to the contrary. A prickle of unease went down his spine.

"What happened when Harley performed his badass biker routine?"

Nick's smile was full of admiration. "She shot him."

"What?"

Nick laughed. "She warned him to get out of her way, and kept on walking."

"What did he do?" Deuce leaned his hip against the desk and watched the screen as the woman trudged closer.

"Harley went full testosterone and dared her to make him."

"And she shot him?"

Nick tilted his head to the side, his long brown hair falling between Deuce and his view of the screen. "Didn't even break stride."

Deuce stepped to the side, keeping the woman in view. "Was he hurt?"

Nick snorted. "It'd take more than a flesh wound to the thigh to slow Harley down."

That was true. Deuce studied the screen more closely. There was a familiarity in the way the woman moved. A bone-deep determination in the way she held her body that he recognized. He touched the screen, his fangs surging into his mouth, fury summoning his power. "Did Harley retaliate?"

"Hell no." Nick fiddled with the zoom, sharpening the focus. "But Luke and Shiva hightailed it down her back trail to make sure she wasn't being followed.

"Good." He would hate to have to kill the Pack leader. Deuce fought back the darkness beating at his calm.

"Said he wasn't having any part of scaring a momma and her baby," Nick added with a flick of his brow.

"What?"

He motioned to the screen. "She's got a baby under that coat."

Anger mixed with hope. She'd betrayed him. That he could deal with. But she'd let another touch her. That he would not be forgiving. "Where is Harley now?"

"Keeping an eye on her."

"Tell him to wait on my arrival."

Nick murmured into the transmitter. Deuce did not need to wait for a reply to be relayed. Harley's "If she falls one more time, I'm just carrying her and to hell with the rules and that peashooter she's packing" reached his ears just fine.

Nick arched a brow at him. "You get that?"

"He will not touch her," Deuce stated calmly, as he left the room.

No one but he would ever touch her for as long as it took for his demons to exhaust themselves.

* * * * *

Deuce dropped silently to the ground beside Harley. As if part of the increasing storm he slid between the flakes. To anyone but an Other, he would have been invisible.

"She's about played out," Harley murmured, not taking his eyes off the slow-moving figure. Snowflakes caught on his hair, collecting on the shelf of the deep blue bandanna he used to keep the long brown hair out of his eyes.

Deuce watched as Eden slogged through the heavy, knee-deep snow with muscles long since exhausted. She slipped, went down on one knee, and caught herself on a sapling. Her "Son of a bitch" reached them clearly on the crisp evening air. One hand clasped her middle protectively. For the space of a minute, she stayed bent over, slight shoulders heaving beneath the huge parka with the effort to draw a breath.

Deuce strained, but he could not detect her energy or that of the baby.

Harley smiled slightly. His canines gleamed in the purple of twilight. "She's got quite the colorful vocabulary when she gets going."

"She has a tendency to do everything well." Including setting him up. "You saw a baby?"

"I can't sense it any more than I can sense her, but yeah, she's packing a little one."

Deuce absorbed that information as Harley continued. "Got it in one of those little chest carriers."

Deuce could feel the wolf's eyes on him as he asked, "What do you want me do with her?"

That was a loaded question. What did he do with a ghost? Deuce sighed and ran his hand through his hair. Every instinct in him demanded that he protect her, shelter her from harm, while his baser self remembered all that she'd been part of and demanded vengeance. In spades.

"Damn it!" The woman threw her head back as if she sensed him. The blue pom-pom on her knit hat bounced with the gesture. "Dusan Knight! If you don't show yourself in the next three minutes, I am going to fall down here in the snow and die. Come the thaw, you'll find my body, but by then it will be too late. Not only will I be stinking up your precious mountain, I'll be a spirit, and by God, if you let that happen, I'll haunt you from here to eternity."

From what he knew, she was a spirit now.

Harley interrupted his thoughts. "Hard to tell with the way she's bundled up, but is she the type you want hanging round your neck through eternity?"

Deuce shrugged and straightened. "At this point, I am not sure."

"So what do you want to do with her?"

Eden heaved to her feet. The thin wail of a hungry infant pierced the cold silence. A forlorn, painfully sad sound. Deuce stepped through the flakes toward the woman and child. "I will go see what she wants."

* * * * *

He comes.

The whisper drifted through her weary mind in that female voice she neither trusted nor understood. A warning or an alert? Not that it mattered. She'd been following that voice's instructions since she'd hauled herself off the operating table five minutes after they'd finished the C-section. It had gotten her this far. She just needed it to guide her a little longer. Deuce was coming.

She glanced up. In front of her was row after row of tall pines rising starkly from the smooth white blanket of fresh snow. The trunks blended with the shadows of the approaching night, standing as dark sentries to the fathomless corridors burrowing between. Eden dragged her foot out of the snow and moved it forward, heading toward the one set just off of center.

She didn't even know if she was going in the right direction anymore. She just kept her head down, slogging forward, believing somehow, some way, this harebrained plan of hers was going to work for the simple reason that it had to work. She wouldn't let those monsters have this baby. Hers or not, Deuce's or not, she wasn't going to let it be part of the Coalition's hellish pursuit of immortality. Her foot snagged on something, and she went to her knees again.

"You are exhausting yourself."

The simple statement resonated deep in her being. Beneath her exhaustion, beneath her fear, a tiny flutter of excitement pulsed to life.

"Deuce." It was more of an exhalation than a word. Still, she shouldn't have been surprised he heard. His hearing was extraordinary.

"Yes."

"You're alive."

"I believe that should be my line." Nothing in his voice let on how he felt about her, about the past, and what he had to believe she'd done.

She looked up. He stood twenty feet away, separate from the gloom, yet somehow part of it—lean hands on his hips, his long black hair blowing about his shoulders, his shirt pressing against his torso outlining muscle cuts a bodybuilder would love. He looked as wild and untamed as the wilderness around him. She blinked. She'd forgotten how big he was. "I'm sorry."

With a short incline of his head, he acknowledged her apology. He started toward her. She took a breath and held it. Dusan didn't look happy. The flat evening light played across his high cheekbones, shadowing the slant to his black eyes, accentuating the thrust of his square chin, lending a hard edge to a face already devastatingly masculine. She took a breath as he got closer, dropping her eyes, staying where she was, ignoring the instinct to run. The only thing running would accomplish would be to release against her all that seething energy shimmering around him. And she so wasn't going there.

His boots came into view. Black like his shirt and pants, they were strangely bereft of the snow accumulating on everything else. The breath she'd been holding rushed from her lungs. Her pulse pounded in her veins. One heartbeat, two, three. He didn't move and didn't speak. Just stood there. She clenched her hand into a fist, forced a ragged breath into lungs too tense to accept it, and made herself meet his eyes. If he wanted revenge, he was going to have to look her in the face while getting it.

It was a long way up and when her gaze got to his face, his expression didn't give her any clue as to what he thought. His eyes, however, said everything. They glittered with red flashes of emotion, belying his calm. In their depths, where she'd expected to see anger and hatred, she saw…reproach?

"Why did you not contact me?"

She almost collapsed into the snow with relief. At least he was going to give her a chance to explain. She tugged at her foot. Instead of freeing herself, she wedged it deeper. Damn! Her day only needed this. "Things were complicated."

"How complicated?"

"Very." She yanked harder. The pull on her abdomen sent pain knifing through her gut. Without thinking, she doubled over, squashing the infant. The baby wailed a protest.

Immediately, Deuce was on his knees beside her. "You are hurt."

It wasn't a question. He paused before clearing the snow from her short boot with an elegant wave of his hand. "You bleed."

She rubbed the baby soothingly through her coat with numb fingers. "Right now, that's the least of my problems." She shot him a wry glance. "Unless it'll send you into some vampiric psycho moment?"

His hands were huge against her ankle. He could snap her leg with a flick of a finger. His strength had always drawn her. Along with his gentleness. He carefully extracted her foot from the fallen tree limb. There was no change in his expression as he said, "I will endeavor to resist."

She bet he didn't have to try hard. The last year had been hell, pure and simple. She no longer looked the pretty little naïve thing he'd claimed to be in love with.

"Where are you injured?" he asked, those sharp black eyes running over her body, head to toe. Even though his examination was clinical, her nipples tightened and her pussy clenched in anticipation.

She waved away his concern. "It's not important."

She touched his shoulder before he could stand, refusing to let her gloved fingers linger on the hard muscle like they wanted. He wasn't hers anymore and never would be again. "I need your help."

"We will talk of that later."

She shook her head as she took the hand he held out. She didn't know how long she had. She just knew that the foreign sense of urgency that came from *her*—that unknown woman who spoke to her—remained strong. "We need to talk now."

He eased her to her feet. "Later. When you are well, I will have explanations."

She was as good as she was ever going to be. The constant experiments her grandfather had performed in the pursuit of immortality had made sure of that. His hand stayed on her elbow. She leaned on it, needing the support. He seemed to understand, because his other arm slid around her waist.

At least one thing hadn't changed. The old-fashioned manners that had first entranced her still existed. She could only hope that the old-world chivalry did, too, and if this wasn't his daughter that he would still feel compelled to offer protection to the child.

The muscles in Deuce's forearm shifted against her coat as he frowned. "You are too thin."

It sounded like an accusation. She shrugged. "I prefer to think of myself as fashionable."

He stared harder at her, his frown deepening. "I thought you dead."

She shoved her hat back on her forehead. "You and me both."

"But you live."

If you could call it that. She batted the snowflakes away from her face. "You sound disappointed."

"I am confused as to how you could live, and I could not know."

She bit her lip as the baby kicked her incision, breathing through her nose until the urge to cry out had passed. "Just chalk it up to one of the great mysteries of life."

"I think I would prefer to simply know how you have managed this." He eased her forward with the same calm with which he spoke, for which she was very grateful. Just standing upright was taking all her strength. She couldn't ever remember being this weak. Even at the beginning of her grandfather's tests.

She tightened her grip on Deuce's arm, feeling a pang of envy. If she had half his muscle, the success of the second part of her plan would be a given rather than a huge question mark. She dragged her foot out of the snow. "Do you mean how did I survive the explosion?"

He nodded, supporting her. "That would be a start."

She caught her breath and her balance, gathering her strength for the next step. "My grandfather came up and took me down the stairs as soon as Dak left the room. There was some sort of bunker down below."

Another one of her grandfather's Plan Bs.

"I am grateful."

"I wasn't."

The bitterness in those two words pulled Deuce up short. He looked down into Eden's set expression and the lines of strain etched into her face. Her features were as familiar to him as his own, from her big blue eyes to the softly rounded cheeks beneath. Everything about her was soft. Giving. At least, it had been when they'd first met. She was outwardly harder now. Wherever she'd been the last year had changed her.

Another wail came from the depths of her coat.

"Sssh, baby," Eden whispered in her soft voice, ducking her head to peer inside the coat so all he had to look at was the bedraggled pom-pom flopping on the top of her knit cap. He suppressed an urge to snatch the hat off her head so he could see the bright yellow curls he knew were hidden beneath. He didn't like the changes in her. The mystery that shrouded what once had been clear. She was his. There could be no secrets between them.

She rubbed her hands over the bulge in her middle. "It's going to be all right," she whispered to the fussing baby. "We're here. You'll be safe now."

Deuce did not need a psychic connection to hear the desperation in her voice. He doubted the baby did either as it continued to wail. Anguish and guilt clouded Eden's scent as she stood in the frigid night, rubbing the baby's back, collecting snowflakes and bravado with every second that passed, managing to look fragile and strong in the same breath. His path became clear. She was his, given to him by the Maker. His to protect. To cherish. To pleasure in this life and the next. He could not turn away from her any more than he could stop his next breath. She was his mate, and she needed care.

Deuce forestalled Eden's effort to walk by simply sliding an arm under her knees and lifting her up. The scent of fresh blood immediately intensified. As she threw an arm around his neck for support, the underlying taint of infection mingled with the soft scent of woman. He frowned, gliding quickly over the snow to where Harley waited. Before all else, her injuries needed to be tended.

The wolf said nothing as he approached, though the amused lift of his brow had Eden stiffening in Deuce's arms.

"He's one of yours?" she asked, blinking at him as a snowflake landed in her eye. Her weight shifted as she reached into her pocket.

"Yes." He tipped her against his body, using her imbalance to remove the small handgun from her grip. He tossed it to Harley who caught it easily.

Eden glared at Harley as he deftly emptied the bullets out of the chamber and tucked the gun into his pocket. "I should have aimed higher."

Deuce forestalled Harley's response with a slight shake of his head. "I would have been displeased had you hurt him," he advised her softly, turning slightly to shield her from the wind when she shivered.

Eden's wry "As if that would ruin my day", dry with sarcasm and weariness, was muttered into the pad of his chest. The words breathed through the silk of his shirt melted hot and sweet against his skin, triggering memories of when she'd teased him with her wit as well as her body. After a year of deprivation, his flesh welcomed the incidental caress. He shifted her higher in his arms, so her next breath drifted past the open collar of his shirt, gliding across his throat in a moist promise of what could be.

Beneath the veneer of civilization, all Chosen were prone to baser emotions. He more so than most, apparently. He wanted nothing more than to lay her down in the snow and stake his claim, despite her injury, the baby, or Harley's assessing gaze. Maybe more so because of the other male's presence. There was too much admiration in the wolf's eyes when he looked at Eden.

The baby cried again, drawing his attention. The faintest tickle of its scent touched his nose. Female and…familiar? He frowned as the cry warbled higher. There was more anger in the cry, but its timbre was weaker, as if the little one also suffered. It was not the way of his people to harm children. As much as he resented what this child represented, he could not resist the high-pitched plea. With a thought, he sent the zipper of Eden's yellow parka down just enough to slide his finger through. All he could see was a round head covered in delicate blonde peach fuzz. The touch to the baby was meant to be soothing, calming, but as soon as his finger connected with the downy cheek, all hell broke loose inside him.

Pain. Hunger. Loneliness.

The torrent poured over him in an unrelenting wave. The depth of the rage that swelled in response shocked him. His fangs exploded into his mouth as the child's scent encompassed him. His grip on Eden tightened to the point that she grunted in protest. He closed his eyes and summoned the calm he normally took for granted. He turned to Harley who watched him in wary confusion, all indolence gone from his posture, no doubt scenting his loss of control.

With a jerk of his chin, Deuce directed Harley's attention to the broken path in the snow. "Remove all traces of her approach."

Harley pulled to his full six-foot-three-inches of height beside the snowmobile. He was one of the few Others tall enough to look Deuce in the eye. "Are we expecting company?"

"Yes," Deuce responded, touching his mind to the baby's, soothing her tears with a thought, struggling to cope with the emotions overwhelming him. "But no harm will come to my daughter."

He ignored the wolf's shock along with Eden's startled protest, and launched into the air. As soon as he had his mate and daughter to safety, he would have answers.

Chapter Three

ဢ

"Are you feeling better?"

Eden bit her tongue on a "Hell no" and ignored both Deuce's question and the imperious knock on the bathroom door that followed it. She pulled up from leaning over the toilet, and rested her cheek on the cool porcelain tank. She'd just been picked up by a man who leapt into the air, seemed to change into a giant bird with a flex of muscle, swooped her over hill and dale before landing in front of a brick monstrosity of a house, whereupon he pronounced them home. The memory alone made her stomach roil with a new set of dry heaves. She rolled her forehead against the cool porcelain. She'd thought she was immune to everything, but this was going to take some getting used to.

The knock came on the door again. It wasn't hesitant. How had she ever thought Deuce anything but arrogant?

"Do you need assistance?"

"No thank you. I can handle vomiting all by myself."

There was a pause, as if he were circling her answer. "I would help you."

He'd said that before and she was just as vehemently opposed now as she had been ten minutes ago. "Sorry, Deuce, but there are just some things a woman insists on doing for herself."

The door swung open as if she hadn't locked it firmly behind her.

She put as much effort as she could into her glare. "I locked the door."

He shrugged uncaringly, the baby snuggled in the crook of his arm. "It was necessary to see to you." He stood huge and tall in the doorway, a mouth-watering vision of aggressive masculinity holding his child tenderly in his big arms. The baby contentedly stared up at his face, as if fascinated by the way all those planes and angles came together in such a compelling package. She knew exactly how her daughter felt. She'd reacted the same way when she'd first seen him. Deuce was strong, fascinating, dangerous and gentle. Everything she'd ever dreamed of, but he was no longer for her.

She had to remember that. As soon as she assured herself that the baby was safe, she was going back. And she was going to make sure that her grandfather was never a threat to anyone again. She shoved to her feet, bumped her shoulder on the edge of the sink, and fell back to her knees.

Deuce came forward, his shadow gliding over her. "If you had waited, I would have helped you."

"Thank you."

"You are weak."

Eden waved away his concern. "It's a temporary thing."

She didn't look at the baby again. It was too bittersweet to see them together, knowing she wasn't going to be part of their future. Her stomach lurched. She refused, absolutely refused, to get sick in front of Deuce. "Go away."

He held out his hand. "It is my duty to care for you."

Great. Just what she wanted—to be someone's duty.

"I don't need to be cared for." She struggled to stand, but she was so wedged between the wall and the basin that she couldn't get leverage.

The quirk of his brow was the only indication that he knew her for a liar. His fingers slid under her arm, sending goose bumps down her spine despite the barrier of her heavy coat. She'd always been way too sensitive to his touch. "I think, maybe this time, I could be of assistance."

She didn't say a word, but allowed his much greater strength to free her.

He kept his hand under her arm as she attained her feet, steadying her. In his other arm, the baby dozed, contented as she'd never been content with her. She blinked back a surge of tears. She'd made the right decision bringing her here. Still staring at that sweet face, with its pale cheeks, tiny mouth and button nose, she whispered, "Thank you."

"You are welcome."

Water suddenly poured into the sink, making her jump. Deuce's grip on her arm tightened briefly, and then he released her to reach for one of the thick blue washcloths. Water droplets bounced off the dry material in a desperate bid for freedom, only to splatter pointlessly against the side of the sink. Her chances of escape were about as good. There was no way out except the window above the toilet or the door directly behind Deuce. And no way to avoid him unless she wanted to step into that huge, totally decadent shower with its multiple heads and unexpected seats.

Deuce placed the cool damp cloth against her cheeks, gently wiping away her sweat and stress. She made the mistake of looking into his face as the cloth curved beneath her chin. His expression was intent, mesmerizing. She found herself wanting to lean into him, to give him what he wanted—her heart, her soul, her body. Her pussy clenched and wept in hope. Her nipples beaded and ached. The fact that she was feeling this way in the shape she was in was a definite heads-up.

"Stop it," she hissed, pulling her gaze from his with tremendous effort. Both she and her hormones needed to get a grip. Falling under his spell was not going to save her daughter. This time both brows lifted above his wickedly sexy dark eyes, sending her pulse tripping along with her hormones, which had long since bolted from the starting gate.

"I am doing nothing."

She took the cloth out of his hand, making sure their fingers didn't touch. "Right."

He paused, a slight smile on his lips. "You cannot be upset because my body calls to yours?"

"Want to bet?" She scrubbed at her face with the now warm cloth.

The smile deepened to real amusement. "That is not logical."

"Logical or not, that's the way it's going to be. Your body can call all it wants. Mine's not answering."

"I can smell your arousal, Eden."

Mortification started at her toes and just kept climbing until she was choking on it. "You're making that up."

He took the cloth from her frozen fingers and ran it under the cold water again. He handed it back. "I have a very acute sense of smell."

No matter what angle she tried, there wasn't a good way to respond. She was trapped. By her past, her body, and her plan. She looked at the baby again. She had to remember her purpose. And to keep her distance.

"Well, good for you." She tossed the cloth into the sink. Keeping her distance was going to be easier said than done. She had to be insane to think the attraction wouldn't be there anymore. To assume Deuce's anger would be a barrier she could count on. "Excuse me."

He stepped aside, letting her pass. She could feel his eyes upon her, feel the questions he wanted to ask. In his way, Deuce was as relentless as her grandfather. She needed a moment to regroup and rebuild her defenses.

"Has your nausea passed?" a deep voice asked out of the darkness of the bedroom. She spun around, searching for the source.

The stranger sat to the left, dominating the upholstered chair he occupied. He was a big man, impressively built with muscles that strained the civility of his cotton shirt and jeans. The angles of his face had been cut with a ruthless hand, emphasizing the raw power that burned in his slanted black eyes. His lips were set in the same uncompromising line as his expression. He was unrelentingly masculine. And scary. Definitely scary. She backed up. Right into Dusan. She immediately took a step forward, and then, realizing she had nowhere to go, braced herself for the confrontation.

The stranger rose to his feet, for a moment blending with the gloom before shimmering into focus. She blinked, not sure she'd seen what she thought she had.

"I startled you. I am sorry."

He didn't seem sorry. He was studying her like she was some kind of bug under a microscope. His speech had the same cadence

36

as Deuce's, but she didn't need that to tell her he was another Chosen. He radiated that same power, that same magnetism, and as she looked into his face, an aura of sadness that struck straight to her core.

"It's all right."

He took another step forward, but when she instinctively flinched back he stopped, his long black hair sliding forward. He quelled the defiance with a sharp gesture. "I am not here to hurt you."

"That's good to know." She'd form her own conclusion in regard to his threat level later.

"The man before you is my brother, Bohdan," Dusan said over her shoulder. She glanced back. She could see the similarity now. Both had the same golden coloring, same strength, same harsh edge to their features. Both were incredibly handsome in a rawly masculine way. Both looked as dangerous as hell. The baby hiccupped. He paused to murmur some nonsense into her tiny ear, and then continued. "He is our healer."

"You are tired." Bohdan stepped to the side, motioning to the chair he had vacated. "Please sit."

Both men watched every nuance of her progress toward the chair. Eden sat cautiously, keeping both of them in her line of sight. The way they held themselves, as if only waiting for the right moment to pounce was not making her comfortable. They wanted something from her. Something they thought she wouldn't give. The two men exchanged glances before Bohdan stepped forward.

"I would like to examine you."

Panic ricocheted through her system. She couldn't tell if it came from within or without, whether it was hers or the strange woman's who'd helped her, but it didn't matter. She grabbed the wooden arms of the chair. "No."

"You are injured."

"I won't die."

"You have an infection," Deuce countered quietly, as if softening his speech was going to soften her resistance. "We cannot allow your health to deteriorate."

She wiped the perspiration from her face. It was hot in the coat and the hat but as long as they were in the room, she couldn't take it off. If they touched her skin, her defenses would crumble. She couldn't allow the Coalition to find her before she was ready.

"I'm not comfortable with either of you touching me."

Dusan handed the baby to his brother. Not for the first time she marveled at the ease with which he moved, the way he seemed to glide rather than walk. He was pure beauty and temptation. She sighed. And he was watching her eat him up with her eyes. She dropped her gaze to the patterns in the Oriental rug, too little too late, but it was all she had. She was so tired.

His boots came into her line of vision, the scuffed toes surprising her. She remembered everything about him as being perfect. His thigh muscles bunched, straining the fabric of his jeans as he squatted beside her chair, his face tilting up to hers, his black eyes giving away nothing as he said in that quiet voice, "You must be reasonable, Edie mine."

And that fast, he shot past her guard, the old endearment finding her vulnerable spot, the part of her that clung to the romance of his old-fashioned courting, the part that wanted to believe nothing in the last year mattered, that everything wasn't different now, that her daughter's future didn't rest solely in her hands. She blinked rapidly to dispel the memories and the stupid "what-ifs" they conjured.

"I'm fine." She had to be.

"Are you fine in the same way you are not hot?"

"Yes. I mean no." Damn it! How could he rattle her so easily?

"You came all this way to find me." His head tilted ever so slightly to the side, in one of his subtle gestures that said so much more than words. "Would you not look at me now that you are here?"

"No." She couldn't. She couldn't stand to see his face without the love. She wasn't strong enough for that. Not now. She kept her gaze off to the side, over his shoulder.

She was not surprised he persisted. "Are we going to play word games all night?"

She shot him a quick glance, finding nothing but calm, gentleness, and concern in his expression. "Do you have to go into a hole come morning?"

"I will sleep in my chamber, yes."

"Then, absolutely."

Bohdan's laugh caught her by surprise. "You are stubborn."

"And opinionated," she added, not looking up. "It's considered a plus nowadays in a woman."

"You think I would not appreciate your independence?" Dusan asked in that same gentle voice he'd used since she'd met him.

This time she did look up at him, hoping to catch something in his expression beyond that controlled calm, but whatever she'd hoped to find, it wasn't there. "I think you'd appreciate right up until my independence came up against your wishes."

He smiled. Small creases fanned out from the corners of his eyes and melded with the severity of his cheekbones, creating a composite image of rugged masculinity. "Like now?"

"Yes," she agreed, sucking in a breath. Dusan Knight was a very handsome man. "Like now."

The baby woke. Her little arms flailed and her mouth pursed into a Cheerio of displeasure. Bohdan first looked shocked, then awkward, but when a wave of her fist connected with his chin, totally captivated. "The little one is hungry."

As one, the men looked to her to fix the problem. She folded her arms across her chest and stared right back at them. "Then feed her."

Both gazes dropped to her crossed arms, but it was Dusan who responded. "We are not so equipped."

She snorted in disbelief and raised her voice to be heard over the baby's cries. "If you can change into a giant bird then I think you can grow a pair of breasts."

"That was illusion, this is reality."

The baby's cries increased in volume. "I can't feed her."

The shots the lab techs had given her had taken care of that. They weren't interested in the baby's emotional well-being, just her genetic makeup.

Bohdan stepped closer. "She has no milk."

"Is this true?" Dusan asked.

Eden didn't answer, and she didn't reach for the child Bohdan held out to her.

"A woman's milk lets down when her child cries. Hers has not."

Deuce's nostrils flared as he took a breath, as if trying to catch a whiff of her...milk? That was just disgusting.

"Will you two stop sniffing me?" She dug her fingers into her arms and leaned back into the chair.

Bohdan glanced at Deuce before tilting his head to the side and saying in that aggravating, soothing tone, "It is not a problem. Other arrangements can be made."

"Did it ever occur to you two bloodhounds that I may not be her mother?" It was a possibility that nipped at her certainty, and one they should have at least considered.

The look Dusan gave her was pitying. "You are her mother as I am her father. Her scent and thought patterns are of both of us."

"You're sure?" She had assumed the child was hers, but there had been no way to know for sure. Her grandfather's house was huge, a labyrinth of rooms that could hide hundreds of secrets, dozens of victims. God, she hoped she was the only victim, and her child the only experiment.

Deuce paused as the question hung in the air between them, the quiver of uncertainty in the two syllables more telling than words. Eden had not known if this was her child. Their child. Yet she'd risked everything to bring her here.

Dusan placed his hand on her arm. The coat blocked his access to her flesh. He pressed until he could feel the resistance of substance beneath the material, very aware that all he'd need to do to feel the pleasure of her flesh was to extend one talon and slice through the material. He focused instead on matching his mind to hers, to calm the fears that had put that look in her eyes, but all he encountered was that frustrating wall of silence. This could not continue. "I am sure, but I do not understand how this came to be."

Eden sat tall in the chair. Her throat muscles worked. She took a breath and stared somewhere off to his right. "They had the...samples from when you were captured. From there it was just a matter of technology."

"You will explain."

She pulled her jacket tight around her and turned away, shaking her head. The ridiculous pom-pom bounced in his face. He snatched the hat from her head and froze. Eden gasped and covered her head with her hands, her big blue eyes filling with hurt and humiliation as she grabbed for the hat. Anger, an emotion Deuce was fast becoming familiar with, set a muscle in his cheek to ticcing. Her head was shorn as smooth as a newborn babe's.

He stood, unable to believe what he saw. "Who did this to you?" He would kill them. The hat crumpled in his hand, the pom-pom offering no substantial outlet for his rage. Slowly and surely, he would kill them.

Her hands dropped from her head. Her chin came up and those shoulders—those slight shoulders—squared with that indomitable pride that comprised so much of her personality. She held out her hand. "Give me my hat."

He looked at her hand and then at the ugly hat. He tossed it across the room and stood, straining to hold on to his control. "You are beautiful to me in all ways, Edie, but I would know who dared do this to you."

Her chin wobbled as her gaze trailed the flight path of the hat like a lifeline, then firmed. "That was unnecessary."

He hated the hat and all it represented—his failure to protect her, her suffering, his grief at the thought of her loss. "It was very necessary."

A trickle of power filled the room. He glanced at Bohdan as a soft feminine scarf appeared in Eden's hands. Eden gasped and dropped it as if it stung her, looking first at him, then at Bohdan before slowly reaching for it.

"You will tell me their names," Deuce ordered as she picked up the scarf and whipped it into a triangle. He could not believe anyone would dare to be so cruel as to cut off her hair. Those beautiful, wild go-where-they-would curls he'd loved to slide his fingers through.

"It doesn't matter," she whispered, tying the scarf quickly.

Dusan touched a dangling corner with his fingers, unable to express the regret and guilt he felt. She had needed him and he had not been there. "It matters." And he would take great pleasure in handling it. "Forgive me for not protecting you."

She jerked out of his reach. Her elbow hit the arm of the chair with a dull thunk. She grabbed it and rubbed it, but did not look at him. "I was there, remember? You were in no condition to do anything."

That still stung his pride. That he, one of the Chosen, had been so easily tricked. He took a breath before releasing it on a sigh. "I would still ask your forgiveness for leaving you unprotected."

"You're kidding me, right?"

"No."

"You're forgiven."

The words came too quickly. Too easily. "If that is so, you will allow my brother to heal you."

Every muscle in her body pulled taut at the suggestion, until it felt like she'd shatter if he pressed too hard. "I said you were forgiven, not trusted."

"Nonetheless, I must insist."

She flicked her fingers at him in a parody of the humor he remembered. "Insist away."

He did not mistake her words for consent any more than he missed the flare of pain that radiated from her when she lifted her arm. She suffered. The time for humoring her had passed. Because he thought it would scare her less, he used his hands rather than his thoughts to open her jacket. Her response was beyond reason.

She turned on him like a wildcat—teeth bared, hands doubled into fists, her emotions leaping past that wall of silence in an equally wild bid for freedom. Her blows were nothing against his strength, but the impressions that flooded his mind as she vented her fury almost dropped him to his knees.

He caught her arm as her fingers went for his eyes. With a simple spin, he turned her around, arms folded across her chest, hands anchored at her side. He could not let her harm herself. He nodded to his brother.

Bohdan whispered to the baby, sending her to sleep. He placed her on the bed. Even from across the room, Deuce could feel the waves of soothing comfort in with which Bohdan surrounded the baby. He was taking no chances on the little one waking up before they were ready.

"Let me go," she hissed, kicking out at Bohdan who easily sidestepped the blow.

"No." Deuce sat in the chair and pulled Eden down onto his lap. He was never letting her go again. She tried to butt him with her head, but she was so small she only rapped his collarbone. Neither her lack of size nor the odds against her swayed her determination. Her breath came in ragged gasps. Her heartbeat thundered in his ears and still she fought. The scent of blood intensified. Dusan tightened his grip, sheltering her with his body, trying to find a path through her panic. "You need care."

Bohdan approached again, hands at his side, weight balanced on his toes. "You will explain why you fear the healing."

The calmness of his order did not override the battle stance he'd adopted. Bohdan was ready to force the issue. It was pointless to hope Eden didn't know that. She cast one desperate glance over her shoulder, the agony in her blue eyes raising his beast before she wrenched so hard against his hold, he feared she would pull a muscle. Sweat poured down her face as she arched against his restraint. "If he touches me, they'll find me."

"How?"

"I don't know how." The admission strained out between her gritted teeth as she pitted her strength against his. "But if they find me, they find the baby."

Deuce held her until she accepted the futility of her effort. She slumped against him after one last valiant bid for freedom, either accepting the pointlessness of further struggle or simply being too weak to try again. Deuce suspected the latter. The Edie he knew did not understand the concept of surrender. He turned her in his arms.

Chapter Four

෨

He would never let the Coalition have his daughter. "You and our daughter will be safe here."

The distress in her expression puzzled him at his proclamation as much as her "I can't stay" offended him.

He pulled the coat sleeve over her arm. "Nevertheless, you will."

The odors of female sweat and desperation swirled around him, mixing with, but not masking the scent of her injuries. Her lids dropped to over her eyes as she whispered, "I won't."

"You have no option." Deuce tugged the other sleeve. He would simply make the barrier go away, but he feared it might send her into hysteria. At last the coat fell from her body. He reached for her shirt front.

"It's too dangerous." Her voice reflected the tension in her body. She was terrified.

Her hand hovered over his as if she knew she could not stop him from undressing her, yet she was driven to try. She was right to think she could not. He was desperate to see the extent of her wounds. Her gaze bounced off his to check the window, the door, as if she feared discovery. Or attack. It was the behavior of a person who'd learned there was no such thing as safe.

Bohdan put his suspicion into words. "You have escaped before?"

"Yes."

Deuce worked the collar button free of its hole as Eden sank back into his lap. If she were Chosen, she would have disappeared. But she wasn't Chosen, she was human and her only defense was her determination and her wits. It never failed to amaze him how she could do so much with so little. He opened the buttons over her chest. She jerked, her lip catching between her teeth, her breath filling her lungs and staying there. "You were not successful."

With his hands so close to her skin, Deuce could not miss her shudder or how the memories intensified the stench of her fear. Her memories were not pleasant.

"No."

Such a little word to contain so much emotion. It was his right to know her thoughts and emotions. His privilege to protect her from her enemy and the memories that would hurt her. It was not right that he stand on the outside looking in, watching her suffer. "How did you escape this time?"

Edie did not look at him. She kept her gaze locked on her hands, her lashes dark against her cheeks, the pale tips blending with her skin. "I had help."

Deuce nodded to Bohdan who turned away before he pulled the shirt off. "Who?"

"I don't know."

She wore no bra. A flush spread up over her chest, surging over the prominence of her breastbone as he glanced at her breasts. Her embarrassment tainted the air around them along with her stress. She was afraid of, or feared for, whoever had helped her.

"They will not find you again," Deuce said quietly, draping her shirt across her full breasts, preserving the modesty she valued. "And if you give me the name or the image of the one who helped you, they will not harm him either."

She shook her head. Her fingers locked together and clenched until the knuckles glowed white. "I can't."

He would have pressed, but he had fears of his own. One of them being that she was holding onto her sanity by a thread. When she was healed, he would know his enemies and know his debts. He pulled the bottom of the shirt up, exposing the white bandage steeped red with blood that rose above the waistband of her jeans. He reached for the snap.

She jerked back as far as she could. She would have fallen to the floor if he hadn't caught her. "I can't allow you to touch me."

He kept his hands where they were, absorbing the tangle of emotions spilling from her—terror, pain, need and determination. The last was the most disturbing. Now that she had found him, she should be relaxing, not building her resistance. "You will be healed."

She tugged her shirt tight around her middle. The physical gesture seemed to bolster her composure. Her voice was almost normal as she said, "Not if you can't do it without touching."

"Touching is required."

"Then no."

"You like that word too much."

Her glance was wry, with the faintest hint of amusement, giving him another glimpse of the woman he remembered. "Men always say that."

"Men are always right."

"Says the male wanting to get his way." She scooted to the right.

Deuce rested his hands on her hips, keeping her there, blending their shadows into one. "Says the male who *will* get his way. In the matter of your healing, I will suffer no argument."

Another shadow flowed into theirs. Bohdan. "Your fears are unfounded."

Eden straightened to the last fraction of her height, her shoulders squaring as she challenged his brother. "You don't know what I'm afraid of."

"You fear the ones you ran from. You fear for the baby. And you fear us."

This close, Deuce could not miss her start.

"You're reading my mind!"

"It is not necessary to read your mind when logic makes it so simple," Bohdan murmured, coming closer, healing energy radiating from him in soothing waves.

"But you do read my mind."

"We can, yes."

She turned to Deuce. "Promise me you'll stay out of my head."

"I cannot block the thoughts you project when upset."

Her blues eyes widened. She wrapped her fingers in the shirt and twisted. She had not known she projected. Adrenaline raced through her system again. "Fair enough, but I want your promise you'll stay out of my head."

Her fear was greater than his arguments. He stemmed the flow of adrenaline. It would not hurt to give her this promise now. Soon enough nature would make it obsolete anyway. "This promise is given."

She looked at him askance, whether because of the formal Chosen wording or because she was still worried about the ramifications of her projecting, he did not know. Deuce tugged the shirt free of her fingers, smoothing the material across her hips. He could at least address one of her fears. He sent his own soothing energy into the waves with which Bohdan had surrounded her. "I can and will protect you, Edie."

With the hard bulge of Deuce's biceps under her hand and the force of his personality around her, it was hard for Eden to believe anything could defeat him or his brother. But her grandfather had. She'd seen it with her own eyes. And he'd used her to do it. She couldn't go through that again. Be responsible for that again. Risk failure again. Not with the stakes as high as they were. She couldn't take that chance with the baby's life. "What makes you think you're strong enough?"

The smile Deuce gave her was gentle, but the energy that radiated from him shifted, deepened, took on a darker resonance, twisting her resolution into a mixed message she couldn't untangle. "I am Chosen. You are my mate. I will not lose."

Oh God, could anything get more complicated? She didn't need him staking a claim on her. "I don't want to be your mate."

"A mate is determined by birth, not choice."

The certainty with which he said that made argument futile. She couldn't do anything about his delusion that she was his mate, but she could focus on what was important. His ability to protect her child. Was he strong enough?

She looked to Bohdan. The same lethal aura that surrounded Deuce surrounded him. His eyes, as dark as Deuce's, never wavered from hers. "It is true."

She glanced at her daughter, still asleep on the bed. So little and defenseless. So reliant upon her to do the right thing. What if she was wrong? If they were wrong? It wouldn't be the first time someone had overestimated their abilities. "I can't chance it."

"There isn't any chance."

Something hard pressed against the top of her head. Deuce's chin? The sensation of being surrounded intensified, giving birth again to that false sense of security. She squashed it immediately. The scarf slid across her forehead as she twisted until she could see Dusan's face. "They got you before."

The flicker of his eyelashes told her he didn't like to be reminded of that. "The circumstances were unique."

Pain lanced up from her abdomen, grinding through her chest, making it difficult to breathe, let alone speak. "Circumstances are always unique."

The pain was too much to hold the position. She turned back around to find Bohdan shaking his head, his brows lowered in a frown. He was a damn scary man when he frowned. She instinctively leaned back into Deuce. His hand opened over her midriff, pulling her into his chest. The unquestioning way he offered her his support made her want to cry in relief and run in terror. She had no defense against him. Never had, and apparently the last year hadn't changed that. She sat as still as she could, taking breaths to not only control her pain but her instincts. She had to stop thinking of Deuce as her personal miracle and start thinking of him as a man she was about to put in a horrible position.

"You hurt." Bohdan's frown deepened with the observation.

She did not need them making a big thing of her injuries. Even though her grandfather's latest experiments had failed to restore the incredible healing properties he'd initially created, she was still strong enough to do what she had to. She had to be. She didn't have any choice. "I'll be fine."

As if her assessment was a gnat he could wave away, Bohdan motioned to her abdomen with his hand. "We need to tend to your wounds."

She looked at him, and then at Deuce. She couldn't allow that. If they succeeded they would know too much and never let her leave. If they failed, their attempts could make her too weak to do what needed to be done. "I'll live."

The determination in those two words flicked Deuce on the raw. Willpower may have gotten Edie this far, but she was worn out, her energy weak and fading. She needed to be healed. As her mate, it was his duty to see that she was. He stroked his hand over her shoulder, his finger catching on the fold of her shirt. He pressed in, freeing his finger and the trapped air from within the light fabric. The strong odor of blood welled around him, giving birth to a foreign panic. She would not die. "You will allow Bohdan to examine you."

She went stiff in his arms. "No."

"I will force this, mate, if I have to."

"You won't. "

She was badly mistaken in her belief. He would do whatever he had to ensure her survival. He shifted his hands to her abdomen. The waistband of her jeans was wet with blood. They would not slide off easily. He would rather scare her than hurt her. With a thought, he made them vanish.

She grabbed at air as if she could recover what was gone, her shriek echoing in his ears as he stared at the blood-soaked bandage covering her entire lower abdomen. Blood smears spread down her thigh. There was a crudely gouged hole in her upper thigh. The flesh surrounding the seeping wound was red and swollen, obviously infected.

Bohdan took a step forward. A whisper of power and then the bandages were gone. Eden cried out, Deuce swore and Bohdan's breath hissed out between his teeth. He stepped closer. Eden lashed out with her foot. Deuce struggled to mentally contain her panic as it crashed through him. Following the emotion back to its source with the intent to quell it, he ran up against a barrier that should not have been there. He probed it carefully. It was strong. He could not penetrate it.

More emotion poured out of Eden, demanding his attention, blending into the chaos of his own, catching on the primitive edges, dragging them higher, forcing him to turn his mental efforts to controlling his own response rather than hers as he absorbed the reality of what he was seeing.

She had experienced surgery. Recently. Her abdomen was laid open, stitches popped. Blood flowed in a sluggish seep. She was a mess. He did not know how she still lived, yet she'd climbed the mountain with his daughter, struggling with the snow and cold, and injuries — that will of hers carrying her when others would have surrendered to defeat.

"Be easy, mate," he whispered in her ear, keeping his horror to himself, giving her calm. "You are safe now."

His words had no effect. Her panic spilled over into his anger, feeding it. Driving it higher. His fangs pushed through his gums. Red hazed the edges of his vision. His control slipped a notch. And then another.

In the next instant, he felt Bohdan's touch in his mind, controlling the spill of energy, siphoning off the excess so he was free to isolate Edie's emotions and his reaction to them, to bind her anger with his, to pull it back into himself to be sorted through another time. She twisted against him, hands curled into claws, her mind for a brief second unguarded. He pushed into the small opening, and with a thought sent her to sleep. She slumped against him, all that desperation blessedly smothered under a forced veil of unconsciousness.

Chapter Five

ɛɔ

"I cannot heal her." Pale and drawn, Bohdan sat back on his heels, and slowly withdrew his hands from Eden's stomach. Of all the things Deuce had expected his brother to say, that was not it. Bohdan had perfected his skills over centuries of existence for precisely a moment like this. He could not fail now. Not with Eden. He above all others, knew how important Edie was to him, to their people. But one look into his brother's eyes confirmed the words he would not accept.

"I do not understand." The wound on her stomach was closed and the wound on her thigh likewise, but they were not gone like they would be had the healing been complete.

Bohdan frowned. With an elegant gesture he indicated Edie's wound. "Whatever was done to her was done without regard to harmony."

"And?"

There was infinite sadness in Bohdan's eyes. "It is killing her, and I cannot stop it."

Deuce rejected the comforting brush of his mind with a hard shove. He lifted Edie up against his chest so her breath brushed his skin in a rhythmic proof of life. He kept his emotions as contained as his tone. "That is unacceptable."

"I know." Bohdan leaned back and shook his head. "I have never seen anything like it. Her chemistry is unbalanced. Her organs mutated into something I do not recognize and are badly damaged. Attempting to fix anything only causes greater problems elsewhere. "

A sick, unfamiliar knot gathered low in Deuce's stomach. "She cannot die."

Bohdan cut him a glance. "I know her importance."

"Then she will live." He could accept nothing less.

"She cannot live as she is."

Deuce scooped Edie fully into his arms draping her across his knee, baring her throat to his bite. "Then I will bind her."

Bohdan's hand on his arm stopped him with his teeth a hairsbreadth from her jugular. "Binding will kill her."

Logic battled with instinct. "I will not lose her." The knot grew, spreading its cold through his stomach and chest. Whatever it took, she would live.

"I bought us time." Bohdan ran his hand through his hair, letting it drop to his hip as he looked at the sleeping baby and then at Eden. "For now, I have slowed the breakdown of her organs, but how long that will last, I do not know. "

"How much time?"

Bohdan did not answer, just folded his arms across his chest and shook his head.

"How long, brother?"

"Do not force me to say what you will not hear."

"Then do not tell me you have done all you can."

Bohdan stood slowly. "I have done all I know how to do with the information I have."

Against Deuce's chest, Edie rested, her breathing too shallow for comfort. In front of him, Bohdan stood, his face expressionless. The knot in Deuce's stomach exploded outward in an emotion so unfamiliar it took him a minute to recognize it. He tightened his grip on Eden and looked at his daughter lying so helpless on the bed.

Fear. He feared for his family. He did not know such a depth of feeling was possible, but with everything logical and elemental in him, he feared. He brushed his lips over Eden's forehead. He was Chosen. She was his mate. He had not found her again just to let her go. "Then I will get more information."

* * * * *

Eden came awake slowly, hovering above realty and pain on a soft cloud of comfort. The awful burning agony in her body drifted just below her beneath an invisible shield, unable to reach her. She savored the moment of peace. She'd almost forgotten how it felt to wake without biting back a scream.

"It is time to wake up now, Edie mine." Deuce's voice floated over her sweet dream, strong and confident, with those varied timbres that resonated in the core of her being. She snuggled deeper into the dream, into the memory.

"Come, my Eden. Awake."

She groaned and rolled to her side. Even in her dreams, the man was bossy. She tucked her hand under her cheek. Fingertips met hers. Knuckle bumped against knuckle before locking together. The scent of wilderness and man surrounded her. The fingers entwined with hers squeezed. There was comfort and demand in the gesture. This wasn't a dream.

Eden remembered the argument, the command from the "Voice" to fight. Her hysteria. The pain. And then nothing. For sure, Deuce had touched her while she was unconscious, which meant there was no going back. They were all living on borrowed time. She cautiously opened her eyes. Deuce leaned over her, his expression neutral, his gaze meeting hers without guilt.

"The baby?"

"Our daughter is fed, happy and sleeping in the next room." His hand stroked lightly over her head, snagging in the hair at her nape.

Her hair?

She put her hand over his as he worked his finger free of a snarl. Thick silky strands twisted against her fingertips. This time shock had her blinking. "You made my hair grow back?"

Something dangerous flared in his eyes before disappearing behind a wall of neutrality. "I would not leave you so shamed."

"I wasn't ashamed."

His thumb stroked over her cheekbone as light as a feather, as tender as a kiss, sliding under her defenses. He always could say more with a touch than most people could with an hour of speech. "No. You would not be."

He said that as if it were a given. Like she was some sort of wonder woman, taking on all comers with a brave front. Her "Yes" was a partial truth. She remembered the helplessness of being strapped down while the two attendants approached with the razor, their laughter as they'd done their job, feeling like they'd stripped the last of her humanity from her as they'd shaved her head, the horror of knowing she truly had become nothing more than a vehicle for an ongoing experiment sinking in as the last of her hair had fallen to the lab floor.

Deuce's grip tightened as his breath hissed between his teeth and something like satisfaction flared in his black eyes. "I will enjoy making them pay."

He was reading her mind! "Stop it!"

She pulled back into the pillow as far as she could, pushing his hand away before just as quickly letting go. She caught her breath and reined in her panic. "You have to stay out of my head." However slight the chance was, if the Coalition had not found her yet, she didn't need to create a beacon for them to follow.

His gaze searched her face. "That is not possible."

"Why?"

"Mates do not—cannot—withhold secrets from each other."

She pulled herself up higher on the bed and leaned back against the carved headboard, weariness dragging at her. For all that she'd slept, she felt drained to the point of exhaustion. "Maybe we should just drop the subject of mates."

For a second he looked like he was going to argue, but then he shrugged and handed her a pillow. "If that will make you happy, it will be done."

She could get used to that attitude. She tucked the pillow behind her back. She reached up and touched her hair. She didn't know what she'd expected to find, but it felt the same as always—thick, with curls springing all over the place. She squashed one flat. "You couldn't have seen to making it straight while you were at it?"

He glanced at her hand in her hair and what could have been a smile tugged the corner of his mouth. "No."

"You could at least sound regretful."

Strange lights flickered in his eyes as he touched a curl. "I like your hair."

So it would seem from the length he'd given her. It was halfway down her back. She dropped her hand to the comforter. The intricate quilting drew her fingertips. "You said you fed the baby?"

"It had to be done."

She rolled her eyes. As if she didn't know that. "What did you feed her?"

"Bohdan examined her. While there are differences in her physiology, her feeding needs seem to be human at this time."

"Which means?"

"Baby formula works fine."

Thank God. "I didn't know how to care for a vampire child."

Deuce didn't respond, just stared. He stared long past comfortable and just when she couldn't suppress the urge to fidget, he said, "You call our daughter 'the baby' or 'the child'."

"I don't know her name."

"You have not given her one?"

"No."

It hadn't seemed right when she hadn't known if she could save her, if Deuce would accept her, if she was even theirs.

Deuce frowned, pushing her hair off her face, his expression as harsh as his touch was gentle. "Did you fear loving her?"

She counted the stitches in the quilt. They were very small. Twelve to an inch. "Yes."

"Because she is mine?"

She looked up to find him staring impassively at her, as if her not loving a child because it was his would suit him just fine. "No."

"Why, Edie?"

The way he called her Edie, in that deep voice that danced like soft notes over her desire, immediately poked holes in her defenses. She held his gaze and bit her tongue on the shameful truth that wanted to spill out.

"Why did you not name her?" he pressed. His hand slid around her head to cradle her skull in his broad palm. With one gesture, he made her feel small, pampered vulnerable. And valued. Incredibly valued. She didn't deserve his respect. "I didn't want to think of her as real."

"So you did not name her." His fingers stirred the curls over her ears.

Anger shimmered in the air, mingling with her guilt, leaving her feeling completely exposed. "Pretty much."

"And for this you feel guilty."

It wasn't a question. She jerked her face away from his touch.

He shook his head, causing his hair to swing and catch the light from the lamps, and caught her chin on his fingertips. The same lights gathered in his eyes, flashing—red?—in the black depths. He looked at once totally familiar and completely alien.

"I am grateful you were there to care for her when I could not."

His thumb brushed her cheek. She flinched back. "I didn't care for her. I threw her in a sack and ran."

"To me."

"That doesn't make everything okay."

"It does."

She squared her shoulders and blurted out the horrible reality. "When she cried, I covered her mouth until she shut up."

He nodded as if she'd just told him she'd bought the baby a new blanket.

"And in doing so you preserved both your lives. I am grateful for your quick thinking."

Eden closed her eyes and wrapped her arms around her churning stomach. She'd never forget the baby's expression as she'd smothered her cries. The tiny forehead wrinkled above big blue eyes wide with terror. The way she'd fought and struggled. Her baby, and her first memories were of the terror her mother had given her. There was no taking that back.

Light vanished beneath shadow. Deuce's scent surrounded her. When she opened her eyes, his face dominated her field of vision. The sympathy in his gaze told the story. He'd read her thoughts. The warmth of his hand settled over her stomach. The nausea left, but not the guilt.

"When our daughter is old enough to understand," he began in his deep voice, "I will tell her the story of how her mother loved her enough to do what it took to get her to safety. She will know what true courage is, and she will know it was her mother's gift to her. There is no need for your guilt."

A fairy tale. He wanted to spin her daughter a fairy tale. "It doesn't change the fact that at a day old, I taught her fear."

The bed dipped as he pulled her against his side, under his shoulder, in an age-old gesture that screamed protection and comfort. She turned her cheek into the cocoon of his strength because she needed, for one moment, to let go of that pain. As if he understood, Deuce murmured, "It will not matter when weighed against a lifetime of love and security."

She hoped so. She really did. She relaxed totally into his embrace, too tired to fight the lure of his touch. "You have this thing for invading my space."

"If you are stating that I feel free to touch you, this is true. It is my right."

"Are we back to that mate thing?"

His lips twitched. The mattress protested as he turned to lean over her. "Yes."

"I don't suppose it will do any good to reiterate that I am not your mate?"

"No." His head cocked to the side and his smile spread. "I have no doubt you are mine, my Eden."

There was a distinctly possessive edge to his voice. She pushed up higher, expecting him to move back. Instead he leaned in, letting his lips brush down her neck as she rose off the pillow, his hand on her back supporting her as she scooted back. Heat raced over her skin as his cool lips skated her flesh. His laughter puffed over her collarbone as his tongue tested the hollow. Pleasure shot to her core, followed hotly by need. Her pussy flowered as her body instinctively arched into his. His fingers opened on her back in an invitation.

God, he was dangerous.

"Let me go."

"You will fall."

"I don't care."

He pulled back, his dark eyes studying her face so intently that she threw up additional mind blocks. "Stop it."

"What do you fear?"

She feared becoming weak again, of surrendering control, of losing the impetus to do what needed to be done. Of having another person running around in her mind, controlling her emotions, reducing her to a puppet whenever he got the urge. "Just because I don't want to become 'playmate of the minute' does not mean I'm afraid."

"I can smell your panic."

Panic was what she'd felt when she'd stolen the baby out of the lab. Panic was what had driven her up the mountain looking for a vampire who might be dead or might want her dead. This was just a healthy dose of fear. This she could handle. "You need to get your sniffer adjusted."

He blinked, and then the slightest of smiles curved his lips. "I like your sense of humor." He grazed the back of his fingers over her cheek. Sparkling, effervescent bubbles of delight danced through her bloodstream. "But you are still afraid."

She tried to contain those seductive sparkles. "I'm nervous."

His fingers traced along her jaw until they reached her chin. With a nudge, he forced her gaze to his. "You will tell me why."

"Is that an order?"

"Will you obey it?" His thumb pressed lightly on her lower lip.

"No."

"Then it is a request for which I expect an answer." The pressure increased until her lips parted and his thumb slid within. A thrust of pure desire speared through her center. Her womb clenched and her core softened and dampened in anticipation.

"I can't fall under your spell again."

Deuce's nostrils flared and the sharp planes of his face tightened. "There was never a time when you left."

He leaned in. She pressed back into the high headboard, the carvings cutting into her back, the small discomfort mingling with the desire, giving it a harder, more pleasurable edge. Dear God, he was potent.

"Don't," she whispered as his hair fell against her, enfolding her in a prison of his scent and her desire.

He paused. "I just want a taste, Edie mine."

She pushed against this chest, the solid wall of muscle pressing into her palms, not giving under her strength. "It won't be enough."

His hair brushed her cheek as he shook his head. His "No, it will not" whispered against her mouth as he fitted his lips to hers. Edge to edge, breath to breath, he matched their mouths as he matched their respirations. In to her out. Out to her in. His energy swept around her, through her, summoning her response. She resisted, shutting her mind, closing her lips. His broad palm slid behind her head, holding her in place as he slanted his mouth over hers. His tongue teased her lips, lightly flicking at the corners before stroking along the seam in a clear demand. Around her his power intensified, electrifying her nerve endings. His will made mincemeat of hers as his deep voice whispered in her mind, *Come to me.*

Her defenses crumbled with the gentle thrust of his tongue past the seal of her lip. He was seducing her with his thoughts, his touch, his taste. He tasted of heaven and man. Of passion matured to the perfect ripeness. She moaned, opening her mouth to his will, arching into his embrace. He tugged her to him, curving her torso into his, holding her for the thrust of his tongue, imprinting every breath she managed with his essence, claiming her thoughts as his until there wasn't anything left except the sweet hot ache of desire and the need for him to soothe it.

"I assume this means she has agreed?"

The intrusion nudged the corners of Eden's awareness, demanding something, but she couldn't focus on what. Not while she savored, for the first time in forever, Deuce's mouth on hers, the strength of his embrace, the power of his touch. His lips eased away. She couldn't believe the pathetic little whimper that escaped her control. Part of her was horrified that she was clinging to him, straining against his efforts to pull her down against his chest. The other part, the much more dominant part, just wanted the soothing magic of his mouth on hers again.

"Be easy, mate." The murmur echoed in her mind as well as her ears, stroking along her desire. She turned into his chest. Rubbing her cheek against the solid muscle, breathing deeply of his clean woodsy scent. With the softness of down, the agony of unfulfilled desire banked to manageable, fading behind the same wall as her pain, until it hovered just beyond her experience.

Deuce straightened, taking her with him, his chin brushing her head as he looked to the right.

"She has just awakened."

"You need to ask her now."

Eden shrugged off the lingering lethargy and looked toward the door. Bohdan filled the entry, his eyes studying her so intently that she immediately became aware that she was in a bed, locked in an embrace with his brother. Embarrassment chased away desire. She shoved against Deuce. "Let me go."

Beneath her hands, his pectorals twitched and for an instant the pain that hovered became real, then disappeared before she finished her gasp.

"He will not let you go," Bohdan said calmly as he crossed the room. "You only hurt yourself and him when you struggle."

Yeah. Right. Like she could hurt Deuce. His shoulders were so broad, sitting this close, they seemed to stretch forever, and beneath his loose cotton shirt, layers and layers of muscle flexed in a blatant challenge to all who would try. She wrenched again, getting nowhere, but under her hand, that subtle, involuntary tightening happened again, making her pause.

She reached beneath the sheet and placed her hand on her stomach. The wound was closed with only a rough scar left. She pressed. Nothing happened. No pain. Nothing. Not even a sensation of pressure. Had the nerves been cut? She looked up into Deuce's face. There was nothing there except calm. She pressed deeper, deep enough that she should be noticing. Deuce caught her hand in his and pulled it away, turning his wrist so her palm faced outward and brought it against his chest, reconnecting them. And she suddenly knew what was happening.

"You're blocking my pain, aren't you?"

"Yes."

"You promised to stay out of my mind."

"To control your pain, I only need to touch the edge. Your thoughts are deeper in."

"That's still invading."

"It is a compromise."

"I don't like it."

"It cannot be helped."

"Why?"

Deuce tilted his head back and said with complete seriousness, "It is unacceptable that you suffer."

"To whom?"

Bohdan was the one who answered. "To any of the Chosen."

He was very close now, standing by her side, frowning at her and then at Deuce. Eden turned back to Deuce so fast her hair swung out, bouncing into her eyes. She brushed at it impatiently. "Do you feel my pain when you block it?"

Deuce nudged another stray curl out of her eyes, seemingly fascinated with the way it wrapped around his finger on the recoil. "It is of no consequence."

She took that to mean yes. She opened her hands on his chest, stretching her fingers as wide as she could, reaching for patience. "Stop it right now."

He released the curl. The mattress dipped as he hitched himself higher, taking her with him. "It is my duty and my pleasure to care for you."

He had to be in her mind to be blocking her pain, but she couldn't detect anything, which scared the living daylights out of her. One more person in her head and she'd go insane. "I appreciate the consideration, but you need to stop it."

His smile was a slow, satisfied stretch of his lips, completely masculine in nature. And it called to everything feminine in her, with a force as scary as his ability to invade her mind. She knew she would have to fight Deuce to move forward with her plan, knew she'd have to kill her grandfather to secure her daughter's safety, but she had never planned on having to fight herself. She pushed against him. She got nowhere. He kept her locked to his side with the weight of his arm, as he shrugged. "The decision is mine."

He hadn't been this autocratic when they were dating. Eden glanced at Bohdan. "Is he always this unreasonable?"

"Caring for my mate is not unreasonable," Deuce countered before Bohdan could answer. He wrapped his arm around her waist, lifting her a little to the right so she half-sat on his lap. The heat from his body felt so good, she didn't resist, just rested her cheek against his chest while she tried to figure out what to do. Both of his arms came around her immediately. And even though she knew it was a false illusion, for the first time in a year, she felt safe.

And there was the catch. She needed to take care of herself. She couldn't go back to being blindly stupid—letting other people make her decisions and just trusting that they were right. She had a daughter to protect. She pushed away from the seductive comfort he offered, and reached the barrier of his arm before she expected. Her head whipped back then forward. The room spun to the left. A cold, sick wave of nausea welled from deep within.

"Deuce?"

His "Yes?" came from far away. Her vision blurred, tendrils of darkness crept in, blocking out the light. Eden dug her nails into his forearm as she fought the overwhelming weakness, too scared to answer. With a jarring thrust, he was there in her mind. Incredibly powerful. She tried to block him as he roved through her thoughts, emotions. To no avail. He was always one step ahead of her, a gliding alien presence going where he willed with no thought to her preference.

"Bohdan?"

She wasn't sure if Deuce said his brother's name or thought it.

I am here. And he was, less intrusively, but there. She thought her head would explode from the pressure.

Relax. Bohdan whispered the soft mental command.

Eden grabbed her skull and squeezed, putting everything she had into expelling them. "Get out of my head."

A shot of white-hot agony nearly split her brain in two.

Immediately, the pressure faded. In the wake of the debilitating pain came a crippling weakness. She couldn't support her own weight. Deuce caught her, cupping her head in his hand, holding her to him as she battled unconsciousness. Something hot and moist pooled on her upper lip. Her hand shook as she wiped it away. She knew what it was before she looked. Blood. She was bleeding the way she always did when she expended too much mental energy.

"You are very strong." Bohdan handed her a handkerchief.

She took it and pressed it to her nose. "Not strong enough."

"To block us?" Bohdan raised his eyebrow at her before shaking his head. "No."

Deuce lowered her to the bed. The mattress, softer than his hard body, didn't provide the same comfort. He squatted beside the bed, stroking his fingers over her skull while his gaze searched her face. Pain faded until even the memory was gone. She was so tired that she couldn't muster the strength to complain. If he wanted to feel like a Mack truck had just driven into his brain, that was his problem. Her hand fell to her side, the handkerchief forgotten.

"She will not survive that again," Bohdan pointed out as if he were talking about nothing more serious than the weather.

"I know." Deuce took the handkerchief from where it had fallen and folded it before pressing it against her nose.

"We will need her cooperation," Bohdan said over her head.

Eden grabbed for the handkerchief. "I can wipe my own nose." Barely. She was so damn weak. "What do you need my cooperation for?"

"Without help you are going to die."

She suspected she was going to die anyway. "That is not a newsflash. Any clue what's taking me out?"

Bohdan handed her a clean handkerchief. "You do not have enough red blood cells to supply your organs."

A flicker of hope she'd thought long abandoned snuck past her defenses. She took an extra moment to wipe her upper lip. "You're saying all I need is a transfusion?"

"If it were that simple it would already have been done." Deuce took the handkerchief from her, steadying her with a hand on her shoulder as he wiped carefully at her face. Anger simmered around him in an invisible field.

She took the opportunity to put a little space between them. She got as far as the length of his fingers. "Then what are you saying?"

"Your body chemistry has been systematically altered." The smooth linen tickled her lips before Deuce pulled it away.

"To heal you I need to know how," Bohdan added with his soothing calm.

"So you want to draw blood?" She stuck her arm out. "Run amok."

Bohdan was shaking his head before she finished. "Although I have my suspicions, I need to know how it was done."

"I don't know. I don't even know if I could tell you if I remembered." There had been too many experiments over the months. Too many mysterious liquids injected to sort it all out.

"You do not need to remember." Deuce touched her temple. Even that slight touch had her weakened body wanting to lean into him, to let him take over for just a little while. "The memories are in here."

"I need your permission to view them." Bohdan explained very gently. Too gently.

"View them? As in sticking your mind into mine again?" Revulsion tore through her weakness, giving her the strength to resist. She shook her head. "Absolutely not."

Strands of hair bounced into her eyes. Deuce's hand met hers, his fingers entwining with hers, catching the frustration in her gesture, softening anger to affection, his fingertips lingering on her face after hers fell to her side.

"You will."

She snatched the handkerchief out of his grip and crushed it between her fingers "No. I won't." Nothing could make her go through that again.

Deuce tilted her face to his with the side of his hand, his thumb resting against her lips. "You will."

She jerked her chin. He didn't let her go, just held her there, her gaze lifted to his will. As if that was going to convince her of anything. She could match him for stubborn any day of the week.

Instead of reacting, Deuce merely lifted a brow at her. "What choice do you have?"

She couldn't, however, fight the truth. She closed her eyes and drew in a breath. None. She had no choice. Again. More than she hated knowing that, she hated Deuce knowing it. But hating looking like a total failure before the man she'd once thought to impress didn't change her options. It just made them harder to swallow. But, swallow them she would. She needed to live to save the baby. Period. Nothing else mattered. Not her ego. Not Deuce's preferences. Not her grandfather's obsession with immortality. The only thing that mattered was that she survive long enough to kill Clay Lavery and give her baby a chance at life. Which meant she had to let Bohdan try.

Inside, the alien "Voice" that had guided her from her prison, and saved her from the Coalition, stirred in protest. She squashed it. Her chances for survival were caught somewhere between slim and none. Even the most insubstantial of opportunities needed to be explored. She met Bohdan's patient gaze over Deuce's shoulder with an assurance she didn't feel. "Do you really think you can fix me?"

"With enough time and information, I am positive I can."

It didn't take a genius to interpret the glance Deuce shot his brother.

"But you're not sure about how much time I have, are you?"

Bohdan didn't answer. Deuce's finger slid down her jaw until he supported her chin in his palm as he stood. "I will ensure he has as much time as he needs." His eyes were dark, bottomless pools of temptation, drawing her in. Random red lights flickered in the depths, the pattern almost, but not quite coalescing into something she could recognize—understand.

"Thank you."

Inside the "Voice" clawed free of her hold, sending its conflicting message into the mix. *Resist.*

She closed her eyes as its power swept through her, seducing her will. Deuce's grip on her chin tightened. Did he hear it, too? It took all her strength to lift her lids.

Before her Deuce stood, shoulders squared, legs braced apart, head tipped back in that arrogant challenge that was so much a part of him, reeking of more confidence than she could scrounge on her best day, asking for her trust with the steadiness of his gaze and the surety of his grip. Not by a bat of an eyelash did he indicate anything was amiss. Inside her, the "Voice" fought harder, yelled louder, equally determined to be obeyed. Was the "Voice" that powerful, that she could evade detection, or merely crafty?

Eden licked her lips, tasting the remnants of Deuce's touch, the echo of their past flowing through her, full of the subtle nuances that had made their time together magic. The laughter, the love. Oh, how she'd loved him. She wrapped her fingers around his wrist, digging into the muscle and bone, needing tangible proof of his strength. She could either trust an amorphous voice in her head or the strength of the emotion she'd once felt for this man. "Do you really think you can do this?"

"I will not fail." He was so unbelievably, blessedly, recognizably sure.

"Thank you."

"What bothers you, Edie?" His finger stroked along her jawline sending tingles down her spine, weakening her muscles until it was almost impossible to sit upright, dragging the confession past her will.

"I don't know if I can do this."

"You will not be alone."

She caught the promise and held it tightly as another wave of weariness threatened to drag her under. No. He would never leave her alone. The knowledge wove through the cold, empty hollows of her heart, brightening the dark corners, warming the embers of emotions she'd thought dead.

"They might not leave you a choice." Her hand fell from his wrist and her lids grew impossibly heavy. She didn't want to make decisions. She just wanted to lie down and sleep for the next fifty years. She blinked quickly and tried to widen her eyes. She caught a glimpse of Deuce's frown before her lids closed again and stayed that way. The comforter rustled as he sat beside her. Instead of an argument, Deuce gave her his support, one hand moving behind her back while the other slid around to the back of her head, completely taking over the responsibility of her weight.

"You tire."

"I'm sorry."

He stood, taking her with him. The cool air in the room struck her naked flesh as he shifted position, and then he was sitting back on the bed, his chest and thighs offering welcome support for her torso.

The floorboards creaked, and through slitted lids she saw Bohdan lift the comforter from the bottom of the bed and drape it over her. It felt as heavy as lead, too heavy. It slid to the left and her body wanted to go with it, just flow down the path of least resistance.

"Just a little more, Edie," Deuce coaxed.

She didn't have it to give him. She was so tired her body ached with the effort to sit upright. His fingers curled around her shoulder, stroking gently on the tops of her breasts. "Relax. Let Bohdan in."

She cracked her eye. Bohdan stood by the head of the bed. His dark eyes shimmered in the gloom. Energy reached out from him in a seductive pulse. She should be terrified but there was something enticing about that energy field, something good.

Deuce bent his head to hers. His breath stirred her hair above her ear, tickling her nerves. "You will let him in, my mate. I will not allow your stubbornness in this matter."

"It's really not your call."

"Everything about you is my call. You are—"

She cut him off. "I know." She sighed, dropping her head back against his shoulder. "I'm your mate. That's getting old, Deuce."

"Nonetheless, you will do what I say."

"Because you say so?"

"Because it is your only hope."

Yes. It was. She took a deep breath. "Are you sure it's safe?"

"Yes." His lips brushed her forehead. "Lie against me, relax, take slow deep breaths, and all will be fine."

"Relax, Eden," Bohdan echoed in a voice as enticing as the energy he projected. "Your mate is with you. He would never allow a betrayal of your trust."

She took the ordered breath and braced herself for the uncomfortable intrusion. She bit her lip at the first tentative touch of the healer's mind. Inside her head, deep inside, the protest began— only a scream she could hear, only denial she could feel.

"Your fear insults me." The whisper was almost lost amidst the protest of the "Voice".

Eden attempted her first mental response mostly because she was too tired to form words. *Deuce? You're here, too?*

Though her effort sounded garbled and muffled to her, he understood. "I would not leave you alone with your fear."

She caught his finger in her hand and squeezed, unable to express the alien conflict inside that was so much more than fear. "I don't like this."

His hand turned beneath hers, lifted. His lips touched to the back of her fingers softly. Pressed. Lingered. Understanding and sympathy coated his voice. "I know."

"Think back now," Bohdan interrupted in a swirl of color, "as far back as you can. Think of what happened after Deuce was rescued."

Memories rushed at her. Humiliating, painful memories. She held them at bay. "Not with Deuce here."

She didn't want him to see her that way, to know what they had done to her.

Deuce wrapped his fingers around hers. "There can be no secrets between us, Edie."

She had no trouble identifying the probe he sent forth. She shook her head, pushing it back. Pain started at the base of her skull.

Bohdan saved her with a succinct "Leave".

On a hard curse in a language she didn't understand, Deuce retreated. The pain receded.

"He is no longer here," Bohdan murmured in a voice that echoed her heartbeat. "Open your memories."

"You'll keep him out?"

There was a pause and then, "You will not cooperate otherwise?"

"No."

"Then I give you my word."

She didn't know if his word was any good, but as Deuce had so succinctly pointed out, what choice did she have?

Chapter Six

❧

Dusan held Edie carefully. She felt so fragile in his arms, her breath a light brush on his skin, her scent a fragrant enticement. He had wanted to be in her mind with her, shielding her from the memories that jerked her body during the probe, but Bohdan was a man of his word. He would not let him in and he could not force the issue for fear of harming Edie. It had been the longest hour of his life, enduring her emotions without the ability to help, trying to sort through the energy flowing from her, sometimes discordant and wrong, other times clear and precise. He brushed his lips over her bright, springing curls. It was not his nature to sit back and wait.

He wanted to hunt down those who had hurt his Eden, tear into their flesh, hear them scream the way they had made her scream. Only worse. For them it would be so much worse before they died. They had dared to touch the mate of a Chosen. His mate. Their fate was sealed.

Edie whimpered and twisted in his arms, murmuring a protest against the memories he could not protect her from.

"Easy, my mate," he whispered in her ear. "Nothing can harm you. You are a Chosen mate. My heart for yours. My life for yours. My soul for yours, through this time and the next."

The formal joining words spoken aloud, soothed his nerves and reminded him who he was. He was a Chosen in his prime with a mate who needed all his patience and skill.

If Bohdan's findings were correct, the damage to her body was reversible, but they would have to proceed slowly, cautiously, and let the change occur as slowly as it had been perverted. He touched her too cool cheek, the smoothness of her skin a kiss of joy to his senses. No matter what it took, he would not allow Bohdan to be wrong.

"Wake, Edie." He waited for the order to drift through her memories. She came to with a slow twist that knotted his insides with a wrenching lust. He bent to breathe in her sleepy sigh as she turned her face to his bare chest, as if instinctively acknowledging the relationship between them. His cock, already hard, jerked against the confines of his jeans. For a heartbeat he enjoyed the incredible pleasure, before her eyes popped open and she stiffened, pushing away, a frown on her brow and dread seeping from her pores.

"Is it over?"

"Yes." He shifted her naked thighs until his cock nestled into the crease, his fingers curving around the gently rounded muscles as they flexed under his touch.

As tuned in to her as he was, he could not miss her hitch in breathing or the delicate scent of arousal that drifted up in the wake of the move.

"Did it work?"

"Bohdan feels he knows what has happened."

Her big blue eyes filled with a desperate hope. "He fixed the problem?"

He ignored her efforts to shift away and kept her where she was. "The fixing is not under his control."

He rode the edge of her mind, calmed the scared stutter of her heart, caught her fear and tucked it away out of her experience, as always shocked by the strength of the emotions she endured. The Chosen were not prone to so many highs and lows.

"Breathe, Edie." She did, her breath catching until he relaxed the emotion-tightened muscles for her. With a frown, he slowed the rush of adrenaline pumping into her system. "You need to be calm."

Her "I'll work on it" was dry.

A tugging alerted him to the fact that she was trying to get the comforter out from under them. "You are cold?"

She shook her head, sending curls dancing down her back, and her gaze ducking his. "Just feeling a little exposed."

He sighed as she yanked on the comforter and a blush crept over her chest. He stood so she could move it. "You will get used to being unclothed with me."

Her breasts stretched with the pull of gravity, bouncing with the effort she put into covering herself, drawing his eyes and his desire.

He leaned away from the bed, totally freeing the comforter. As charming as he found her modesty, he hoped she would get over it soon. He did not intend to deny himself the pleasure of her beauty. She was a feast to his eyes with that white skin that flowed like rich cream over her lush curves and delicate bones. Her blush intensified to a deep pink beneath his stare. The intriguing color spread across her chest, ending at the paler flush of her areolas and nipples. Nipples that plumped in invitation under his attention. He tightened his grip on her thighs as she curled against him, gathering the excess material up from the floor, her distress palpable.

Deuce nuzzled her hair as he sat, absorbing her scent. She was such a delight to him in all ways, right down to that inappropriate independence and wit that amused him as often as it frustrated him. He ignored her efforts to slide out of his grip, smiling internally as, with a huff, she settled for pulling the comforter over her shoulders until his view was limited to the tumble of curls surrounding her face.

He did not really mind. It was such a lively, beautiful, revealing face, telegraphing her every emotion with vivid clarity. Like how vulnerable she felt in his presence.

"There is no need for the embarrassment you feel. It is right that your body respond to mine.

Her gaze fused somewhere in the vicinity of his chin. "As you see it."

He nodded, conceding her point. "As I see it." Which was the way it would be. Such things were inevitable between mates.

"Was Bohdan able to give me more time?"

"The process can be reversed."

"Thank God!"

He again had to steady her heart, and quell the adrenaline rush that came with the news. No wonder humans had such a short life span. They wore their bodies out with excessive emotional responses.

"How?"

"Your captors tried to convert you to one of the Chosen."

"They tried to make me a vampire?" Her shudder merely confirmed his fear that she would not like what he had to say.

"They tried to make you Chosen."

He felt her hesitation and admired her control as she asked, "Did they succeed?"

"Such a thing is impossible."

She paused, the surge of relief pouring off her making him lightheaded before he contained it.

"You're kidding, right?"

"No."

"You mean hundreds of hours of late-night TV has steered me wrong?"

He smiled, letting one of her curls wrap around his finger. "I am afraid so."

Her laugh was shaky, but there. He felt the weakness still dragging at her. He shifted, leaning back against the bed's headboard, taking her with him.

"I can support myself," she grumbled as he rearranged the comforter to her modesty's demand.

"I am aware of what you are capable."

She finally gave up fighting her body's weakness and allowed her head to rest against his chest. "So what did they actually do?"

"They made a mess."

"What can you do?"

This was not a subject he wanted to plunge into. "A mating between a Chosen and a human is a rare thing."

"How rare?"

"I can only remember one other." He could barely feel her arm through the thickness of the comforter, but with his senses, he was aware of every goose bump, every shiver, the almost imperceptible drop in her body temperature.

"What happened to them?"

"They died."

"Because they married?"

"Not directly, no." Her curiosity built with lightning speed, projecting outward, questions flying about in the blink of an eye, with no discernible order. He did not know how she ever concluded a thought, so pell-mell was her method of analysis. He stepped into the mental melee with the truth. "They were murdered."

"Oh."

Trying to track the spill of speculation that followed that "Oh" was almost enough to give him a headache. He would have to teach her how to shield her thoughts rather than project in moments of emotion.

"By whom?"

"People who wanted to steal what would not be given."

Her sigh was as exasperated as her "That's as clear as mud".

"You cannot learn everything at once." Nor could he reveal everything without overwhelming her.

"I'll settle for what's wrong with me."

"There is a process a Chosen and his mate go through when bonding. It must be completed with all its elements to be successful."

The comforter bunched beneath the tightness of her grip, but her voice remained steady. For such a small, frail human woman, she had incredible strength. "You're saying my grandfather did a halfass job on me?"

"Yes." Likely through ignorance more than design.

"But you can fix it?"

"Yes."

"How?"

He tightened his grip, pulling her close, illogically trying to shield her with his body from the pain his words would bring. He rubbed his fingers over her shoulder, soothing her panic. Even if she never grew completely comfortable as his mate, he could insure she never regretted being his. One would compensate for the other. "By completing the process."

She snapped up straight in his hold, yanking at her arms trapped in the comforter's folds. "I am not becoming a vampire."

"Be calm." He lowered her heart and adrenaline rates again, easing her blood pressure back to normal as she struggled against him. He took the pain from her abdomen into himself as he caught both her arms and turned her to face him. "I have already said that is not possible."

She slowly settled in his grip, her gaze locked to his, her mind taking a subconscious, tentative foray toward his before retreating behind the defensive wall she'd erected. Her eyes searched his face.

He did not know what she saw in his expression that calmed her, but her muscles went lax. She panted against him, her small reserve of strength critically depleted by the emotional outburst. "I'm sorry."

He allowed her to feel just enough of her body's discomfort so she would not try such behavior again. "Do not fight me, mate. You do not have the strength for it."

Depleted or not, she still managed to put enough distance between them so that he could see her frown. Confusion shimmered around her as she asked, "Which reminds me of something that's been bothering me—how did my grandfather know you would think I was your mate?"

That was one of the things he had his people seeking to answer. "I do not know."

The Coalition, which they'd thought weakening, had actually grown more powerful, keeping their increasing strength a secret. He did not like that any more than he liked Eden's phrasing of her question.

He felt the wave of weakness come over her before she leaned against him. Her strength was fading past the point her will could sustain. She needed to get beyond her resistance. She needed to accept their relationship. "We do not have much time to start the process, Edie."

"Is it almost time for you to go into your hole?"

"Yes, but that is not what concerns me." Eden was a strong woman, but he did not know if she could get past her human fears in time to do what must be done. He would prefer to leave her the illusion of choice. Her resentment at the changes being his mate would forever make in her life would be less that way. But if he had to, he would take the choice away. He would not go back to his aching, hollow existence without her. Nor would he deny his claim and leave her unprotected. "The damage to your body is reaching the point of no return."

She shifted on his lap, her legs stretching and retracting as the indecision in her mind moved through her body. "What does being your mate entail?"

"It is a marriage in all ways."

"So this means you'll be off drinking with the boys and fooling around with other women in about two years?"

He shook his head at her foolishness. "You know that is not true."

"I don't know anything about you."

He stroked her hair, offering the only comfort he could. "You know in your heart all you need to know."

"I happen to be a logical person."

She had the least logical mind he'd ever touched. "You did not question the rightness of our union last year."

She hesitated. He could feel the effort to lie in her mind, the wave of loss before she hedged the truth. "Last year was different."

"Last year I was interrupted, or this conversation would not be taking place." Had he had even one more day, she would have been bound to him for all time. Her love treasured and nurtured and nothing, nothing would have harmed her.

As if she sensed the rage inside him, she touched his chest, his throat and lastly his hand where it rested on her thigh, her fingers stroking soothingly. A glance at her face told him the gesture was unconscious.

"How does one of the Chosen see his wife?"

"A mate is the most precious of gifts to one of the Chosen. Not all are fortunate enough to find one." He massaged the tension in her shoulders. "We mate once and only once, for life."

"You live a long time."

"Yes."

Her hand reached over his shoulder and caught his wrist. "A long time to be with just one person."

He knew she could not actually grasp the concept of forever as the Chosen knew it. She thought in human terms with a human concept of bonds. "It is an even longer time to have no one."

Her fingers paused on his wrist, her index finger resting on a life point. Deliberately? Was she asking for entrance to his mind?

"How can you be so sure I'm your mate?"

He opened his mind. She did not take advantage of the opportunity. He brushed his lips over the top of her head. He would need to let her learn to walk before expecting her to run. "All of the Chosen recognize the one meant for them. There is no doubt."

Her "For you maybe" was a mutter of frustration. There was a long pause. He could feel the emotions battering her. He kept the strain from her body, bound by his word, but could do nothing about the turmoil in her mind. "You will trust me in this, Edie."

The muscles under his fingers tensed one by one until he had to stop the massage for fear of hurting her. "I'm not in the habit of putting my life in someone else's hands."

"For this once you must." He stretched his fingers down to the tops of her breasts, measuring the rise and fall of her respiration. "I cannot let you die."

"But you don't normally find mates in humans. Maybe there is someone of your own—"

He shook his head, cutting off that train of thought. "It is rare, but the unions have been happy after a period of adjustment."

"Will your people accept me?"

"My happiness will be theirs."

"What about your parents?"

"They will be happy for us."

"Where are they?"

"They live in the Australian compound."

"They aren't going to like that I'm human." Her fingers clenched on his wrist.

"They will love you."

"You can't guarantee that."

"It is my duty to do so."

Her sigh came from her toes. She shook her head before turning to meet his gaze. "It has never been my life's dream to be someone's duty."

"I have phrased that badly." Her eyes were of the clearest blue with navy flecks in the middle. And they held such worry. He would take her worry from her—shelter her forever if she would let him. He turned her, lifting her thighs across his. Her lack of protest sent a shaft of concern deep. It was not his Eden's nature to be complacent. "As your mate I will care for you always, place your happiness above mine, your health above mine."

"And what do I do for you?"

"You give me happiness."

Her eyes widened. "You expect me to keep you happy forever?"

He leaned down and brushed his mouth across the sun-dusted tips of her lashes. "Your existence does this."

"Uh-huh. Unless vampires are very different from humans, which I severely doubt, this is not going to work."

"Making it work is my responsibility." He tilted her head back with a tug on her hair.

"According to you, everything is your responsibility."

He ran his tongue over the taut cord in her neck, riding the delicate surge of muscle as she swallowed hard. She was so incredibly sweet. "This is so."

He measured the pulse in the hollow of her throat with his lips. Her heart rate was a beat faster than normal with her stress. When he sucked at her skin, it took off racing. He released her flesh and kissed the reddened area softly, enjoying the increased heat against his mouth. "Your worries are groundless."

"I don't see them as so."

"I know." He kissed the soft skin just beneath her jawbone. "But still you must make a decision."

"You could just take the choice away from me…"

He pulled back so he could see her eyes. They were dark with anxiety, and the desire she did not understand. He felt the weakness dragging at her intensify. She was losing her battle to hold onto the life she understood. "Is this your preference?"

There was a long pause in which he knew she was considering it. He could do it easily. Tapping into the primitive side of his soul that screamed for him to secure her any way he could would take no more effort than succumbing. He held himself back, allowing her that last decision. Finally, she shook her head. Her jaw set in that stubborn way he was fast coming to appreciate. "No."

"Then decide."

Chapter Seven

❧

Decide.

To die forever or to live forever. That was a hell of a decision to be making on the fly.

Eden looked Deuce over, from the harsh, uncompromising lines of his face to the broad, heavily muscled expanse of his shoulders. Nothing about the man said easy. And despite her experience that said he could be civilized, everything about him screamed danger. But nothing, nothing said deceit.

"Do you promise I won't become a vampire?"

"I promise."

He watched her with those old eyes. Patient eyes, but beneath her hands, she could feel his impatience humming. The weaker she got the higher the thrum. She tried to imagine how he felt. She'd gone through her whole life knowing she might have multiple relationships over its course, expecting love to come and go, holding back because she never wanted the loss. He'd gone through centuries knowing he had only one, and only if he could find her. And now he thought she was it and he was losing her. A piece of lint tangled in the long strands of his hair. She picked it free, pausing as a dark strand slipped over her thumb, looking very stark against her skin. She didn't know why he hadn't forced her before now. She would have. She would never have risked letting her one chance at happiness slip away. The fact that he would, emphasized the differences between them.

She touched his biceps, letting the hard muscle shape her grip. There was no give anywhere on the man. "I want a promise from you."

"What?"

"I want you to promise to never hit me."

"Done."

"That was awfully fast." Too fast. As if he sensed how hard it was for her to lift her head, he cupped her skull in his palm, his thumbs and fingers gently kneading at the ache in her temples. "You are my mate. It is impossible for me to harm you."

That was good to know. His touch was soothing, healing. The pain in her head faded so she could think. The bottom line was—if she didn't live, she had no more choices. She was a big fan of choices. She took a deep breath. "Fix me, Deuce."

His satisfaction exploded through her in a rush. Hot on the heels of his satisfaction came his pleasure—too hard, too fast. She got an impression of his enjoyment of her scent, the smoothness of her skin, and a flash of worry before it became too much. She tried to slam her mind closed, met the barrier of his strength and felt that knifing pain in her skull that had her crying out just as his mouth met hers.

Immediately, the pain was gone and so was the onslaught. The struggle to breathe eased, and she was able to absorb the feel of his lips on hers. Cool and smooth, they parted. His tongue traced the seam of her mouth. "Open for me."

It was an order, pure and simple. She obeyed because she couldn't help herself. Not with the promise of his taste just beyond her reach, a link between past and present. Not when the memory of that taste had sustained her through hell. When it came to him, her body had a life of its own, wanting his beyond reason and sense. Her lips parted. His tongue thrust past, and his flavor—that uniquely addictive flavor—filled her mouth, sending shockwaves of hunger spiraling downward. She needed more. She dug her fingertips into his shoulders, trying to pull him closer.

The bed rocked as he shifted his weight. His chest dragged across her breasts. She reveled in the sensation, arching her back, offering him more. She was so lost in her sensory feast that it took her a moment to realize he'd removed her hands from his shoulders and relocated them to his chest. A flash of embarrassment had her ducking her chin. His lips brushed her temple, her ear.

"Just let me do this, Edie mine," he murmured. "Just relax and give me the pleasure of caring for you."

"I don't want to relax."

"You do not have the strength to do more."

Her body didn't care. She reached for him. He shook his head. His hair swept her breasts, sending shivers down her spine.

"You may not move."

"I have to."

"You will tell me what you want and I will give it to you, but you must not move."

Her breasts ached. Her nipples strained. His chest was mere inches away. All that muscle and heat denied her. "Why?"

"You are very fragile."

"I feel fine."

"I am glad, but still you will not strain yourself."

His tongue stroked over her lips before sliding within. She wrapped her tongue around his, savoring the flavor, dragging into herself more of the necessity her body craved. He held her close, his arms supporting, letting her take what she needed, his moan a hot encouragement to take more. His mouth opened wider, his tongue sank deeper. She sucked harder. It wasn't enough. He had to give her more. Her hands curled into fists. He pulled her closer, trapping her hands between them, forbidding her movement.

"More," she whispered into his mouth, crying out when he nipped her lower lip.

"More what?"

She didn't know, exactly. She just knew when he kissed her some of the awful hunger was appeased. "Kiss me more."

His laugh caressed her cheek with moist heat. "You are easy to please."

No, she wasn't. His tongue reentered her mouth on a sure thrust, bringing back to her what her body ached for. His big body curved around her, sheltering her even as he plundered her mouth. She inhaled his scent, his strength. Took from him all he had to give, but it still wasn't enough. She was starving. She didn't know for what, but instinct told her he had what she needed. She yanked her fist free and pounded at his chest. He caught her hand. Every cell in her body ached. He'd promised to provide for her, and he was holding back. "Give it to me."

He frowned down at her, something dark and scary moving in his eyes before it was carefully banked. "You will have patience, my mate. I know what you need, but it will be given at my pace."

"No!" If he knew what she needed then he knew how badly she needed it. She turned her face into his chest and bit down, surrendering to the ravenous monster inside.

Deuce's shout was equally primal. His big hands locked her mouth to his flesh, encouraging rather than discouraging her frenzy. Against her hip, his cock surged, hard and hungry. Above her, his growl lingered on the air. The hot, coppery taste of blood filled her mouth. She had no time for thought or repulsion, because under that taste was something else. Something her body recognized on a cellular level.

She drew more of that elusive necessity into her mouth, closing her eyes in bliss as it slid down her throat. Cells that had been shriveled and wasted expanded as she swallowed, pounding at her for more. The need for survival, a primitive driving force too strong to be denied, had her locking her jaw. He caught her head in his hands, to pull her away. She snarled and swung at him.

"Not yet, Edie. Not yet."

"Now!" she screamed through clenched teeth.

With a harsh groan, he tore her free. The loss hit her like a blow, doubling her over with the agony. "Oh God, don't do this to me."

She couldn't take it. Couldn't take another person torturing her with what she needed only to pull it away when it was within reach.

"Edie, you will look at me."

She didn't take her eyes off his chest and the rich red blood pouring down it. She'd done that to him. Bitten him like an animal. And God help her, she wanted to do it again. He cupped her head in his hands and forced her gaze up.

"I know what you need, Edie. How you need it, but it cannot be all at once." His breath caught as he shook his head, his frown a death knell to her hopes. "It cannot."

She wanted to scream, rant and cry. She didn't recognize herself and the beast that prowled her insides, but she couldn't help herself either. She'd do anything he wanted if only he'd give her more. "Please, Deuce. Please."

He swore and shook his head, his thick black hair falling into his face. His sensual mouth thinned.

Tears she hated burned her eyes. "I'll do whatever you want. I'll beg."

His gaze hardened. His thumb brushed a tear from her cheek. For one second, his expression reflected the agony she felt, and then that hard mask of resolve settled over his features. "I cannot give you what you want."

He was punishing her. Had to be. Had to be extracting his revenge for her part in his downfall. "I swear I didn't know, Deuce. I didn't know what my grandfather was going to do. I was so in love."

Oh God, had she really said that? Revealed her weakness? What was happening to her? She raised her gaze to his. "I was so naïve," she moaned, feeling again the burning humiliation of what she'd cost them.

"I would not punish you this way, Edie, but I cannot give you what you think you need."

"Because you think I betrayed you?" She understood that, even as that understanding defeated her.

He shook his head and brushed his lips over hers, the sadness in the touch echoing the sadness in his eyes. "Because the shock would kill you."

"Shock?"

"We need to go slowly," he whispered against her cheek. His tone was incredibly gentle in direct contrast to the violent hunger within her. His hands on the sides of her face were the only thing that kept her from biting him again.

How could he stand to see her like this? If it continued much longer, she knew she was going to lose her mind. "I hurt."

The rough pads of his thumbs grazed her cheekbones, paused and then pressed." I will help."

"When?" *Oh God, when?*

As if he heard her mental cry, he whispered, "Now."

From one heartbeat to the next, his pants disappeared. His cock pressed against her hip, hard and hot. It wasn't what she wanted. She twisted away. He released her face and caught her shoulders. She fought the pressure forcing her back. She needed to stay connected to him. His big body followed her down, his hands controlling her decent. "Slowly, Edie."

She didn't want slowly. She wanted to feel good, the way she had for that brief moment when she'd been drinking from him.

Oh God, she had been drinking from him. Horror built on hunger. She rubbed the back of her hand across her mouth. Her shoulders hit the mattress as the accusation burst from her lips. "You said I couldn't be turned into a vampire."

He pulled her hand free and held it in his. "You cannot."

"Then why do I want to suck your blood?"

His right eyebrow went up. "You really did watch a lot of late-night TV."

"You're avoiding the question."

"Yes."

His honesty surprised her. "Why?"

"Because I do not know if I can make you understand."

"I might have been stupid before, but I am not stupid now."

He fingers on her chin turned her face to his. "You were a woman discovering your mate. You were sweet, sexy and beautifully open, but you were never stupid."

"If I hadn't been so trusting—"

"You were as you should have been."

Being trusting had cost her everything. "I will never be that trusting again."

He didn't argue with her, merely sighed as he pulled her arms over her head, placing the back of one hand into the palm of the other. "You will stay like this."

She shivered under the smooth command. "Why?"

"Because your mate tells you to."

"I have a mind of my own."

Deuce held her hands pinned to the bed with a deceptively gentle grip. "I'm aware of that, but if you wish me to ease your pain, you will not challenge me."

The hunger put an edge on her temper. "You must have confused me with a Barbie doll."

Laughter flared over the concern in his eyes before he pressed her hands into the mattress. "I am not the one confused."

His lips brushed her cheek, his breath wafting over her skin in the softest of caresses. Every nerve ending flared to life, all attention rushing to that one spot. God, she was pathetically tuned to this man.

"Open your mouth."

She did, accepting the thrust of his tongue, arching into him as he penetrated deeper. She wrapped her lips around his tongue and sucked that unique flavor deeper, letting it sink to her core. It wasn't enough. His hand caught her jaw just as she would have clamped down.

"No biting."

She touched the pad of his thumb with her tongue. The hot, salty taste of his flesh spiked the need for more with a roar that sobered her instantly "Why do I want your blood, Deuce, if I'm not turning into a vampire?"

"You do not want my blood so much as to balance your own."

"With what?"

He turned her head gently until her cheek rested on the inside of her arm.

He stood, his thick hard cock stretched before him, the broad head, looking huge and impossibly demanding. A shimmer of moisture graced the tip. His scent reached out to her, primal and musky, like the forest after a rain. Again, that strange sense of recognition surged through her body. She licked her dry lips. Above her, he groaned. She glanced up. His voice was deeper, rougher as he explained. "When one of the Chosen mates with a human, the conversion is done carefully, according to ritual."

"So?"

He released her jaw and her hands, turning slightly as he did. She got a better view of his cock. The way the shaft widened as it extended back toward his body had her insides clenching. He'd stretch her unmercifully if he ever took her all the way. A hot, anticipatory whimper escaped her control, the lust overwhelming her even in her weakened state drained the last of her strength.

"Your grandfather tried to convert you but without the guidance of the ritual, he poisoned you instead."

"So I *am* going to die?" Die with her body aching with an unnatural craving for a man she'd once loved.

Deuce pushed the hair off her face. "I will not let you die, Edie. You need to believe this and trust me."

"Why?"

"Mates are matched in thought and body."

She glanced at that intimidating cock. "Nothing about us matches."

His smile was gentle as he leaned forward, the heavy sac of his balls brushing the mattress in a soft hiss of sound. She shuddered under the implication of his approach. As if on cue, the clamor in her body began again.

"Everything about us fits, my mate." His thumb pressed into her cheek, the touch reinforcing his desire. "You just have to open your eyes."

And her mind, and her heart and her body. He wanted her to lay herself bare before him. But it wasn't going to happen.

She risked a glance down. His cock bobbed between them— hungry, the tip wet with anticipation. As she watched he cupped his cock in his palm, drawing it up and out, milking it slowly, stopping just beneath the flared head, his fingers framing the bulbous tip in a slightly lighter circle. "My blood is not the only fluid in my body that contains elements necessary for conversion."

She blinked. He was talking about his semen. She shook her head. "You aren't seriously going to try and convince me that giving you a blowjob will save my life."

"Conversion is a process, Edie." He said that with a completely straight face.

"I'll give you one thing, that's the most original line a man has ever laid on me for trying to get me to do that."

Above her, he froze, every muscle in that powerful body going taut. "You will not speak to me of other men."

"Why?"

He opened his eyes and looked down. They glowed red with primitive rage. His fangs flashed in the light, adding to the menace sweeping off him. "I do not handle the thought of you with others well."

She cringed back into the bed. She didn't know this man. He blinked, and that fast the vision passed. Once again it was just Deuce staring down at her, his expression calm. He inched her higher. "It does not matter who came before. There will never be another for you."

"That's not your call."

He shook his head. "I will kill any who try to take you from me."

"What if I choose to walk away? What will you do? Will you kill me, too?"

"It is impossible for me to harm you."

Which didn't really answer her question as to what he would do.

She closed her eyes as he leaned over. The mattress creaked and dipped to the right as his hand came down, tilting her slightly away. And then she was tilting back as the mattress on her other side dipped under the weight of his body. "Open your mouth, Edie mine."

God help her, everything inside was ordering her to obey. She started counting back from a hundred in an effort to regain control. She made it to ninety before she realized that when it came to this man, her body simply was not her own. Something hard brushed her lips. His cock? She jumped, repulsed and attracted at the same time. The glancing caress came again along with a softly worded order.

"Open your eyes." She did, seeing it was his thumb that brushed her lips. "Look at me."

All she had to do was lift her lids and she would be able to see Deuce's face, the satisfaction he had to be feeling from being the master puppeteer to her puppet. All she had to do was lift her lids and say goodbye to the last of her illusions. It shouldn't have been so hard to face the truth. With the last of her reserves, she yanked her gaze up, meeting his black eyes with a sense of defiance. The sadness in him shocked her to her core. She searched his expression for the source, once again experiencing that sensation of tumbling into the unknown.

"Know that I did not want things this way between us."

His regret shouldn't have mattered—she was still being forced into a decision she didn't want to make—but it did.

"How did you want it?"

"I would have courted you in the way of my people. Shown you your value to me. Eased you into our relationship."

"Would I still be doing this?"

His fingers at the base of her skull tipped her head back, and he gave her the only thing she'd ever known from him. Honesty. "Yes."

"Then I guess it doesn't matter." His cock loomed huge in front of her as it approached, the slit in the center welling with the fluid he thought she required.

"It matters." His thumb pulled her lip down. "I would blur this for you."

The offer was tempting, but if she let him blur this, where did she draw the line? "No."

"I can feel your distaste."

Chosen or not, he was a good man making the best of a bad situation and deserved more than pretense from her. "I wouldn't call it distaste, exactly."

"No?"

She shrugged. "More of a panic." She brought her hand down to clasp him. His breath hissed through his teeth.

"You were told to keep your hands in place. You are disobedient."

"Get used to it." He was hard as steel in her grip, throbbing with a pulse a half beat slower than hers. "Disobedience is becoming a way of life for me."

"I will allow it this once."

Damn nice of him. If she didn't feel so badly, she'd let him know just what she thought of his "allowing".

His hand glided over her jaw, down the arch of her throat to the swell of her breast. "What has you panicked?"

"If you're to be believed, you've lived for centuries." He rubbed the back of his fingers over her left nipple. Lightning shot through her body, nearly jerking her double. She lay back on the bed, gasping as if pain tore through her, but feeling none.

"I do not lie."

"Well then, I'm far from the first to do this to you, and as this is my first time trying, I can think of about a hundred ways I'm going to crash and burn." A chill snaked down her spine and then radiated outward.

"You are my mate. There is no comparison." The room swam in and out of focus around the edges. His curse seemed to come from far away. His "We are out of time" let her know he felt what was happening to her. He gently removed her hand from his cock and replaced it above her head. "This time, you will just lie there and let me tend to you."

"I don't think I've ever heard a blowjob described quite that way." The room spun harder. She closed her eyes and let the creeping darkness seep into her thoughts. The bed dipped as another curse echoed beyond the veil clouding her mind. The veil that shouldn't be there. He was blocking her.

"No, Deuce."

"You will not remember this as our first coming together." The cloud swirled over reality.

She gritted her teeth and resisted, reaching deep for strength. Pain sliced through her skull. The cloud whipped back to a speck and then was gone.

Deuce yanked the edge of the comforter and pressed it against her nose. "You bleed again."

She glared at him over the puff of white. "I said no."

She could actually hear his teeth grind. With a grunt, he threw the comforter to the side, the streak of red on the white surface was not as bright as it should have been. She stared at that smear a moment, the reality of what was happening slowly sinking in.

Deuce's big hand cupped her cheek. "Let me help you through this, Edie mine."

She shook her head. "I may be weak, dying even, but I'll be damned if I'll play the victim again."

"Letting me ease this for you makes you a victim?"

"No. But running from reality does."

For the longest moment, he stared at her, and then he motioned to the bed. "I'm going to help you turn to your side."

"I can do it myself."

"You will allow your mate to extend this consideration."

He was turning her gently even as he spoke. This close, she had a bird's-eye view of his cock. It was never going to fit.

"Have you done this before?"

She wished she had a list of lovers a mile long to recite, but the reality was, her grandfather kept her too secluded for there have to been much opportunity. There was nothing like being faced with centuries of experience to make a newcomer to the game feel inadequate. "No."

He rubbed the back of his fingers from her temple to her jaw. "It is not a crime to be inexperienced."

"It's nothing to brag about either."

She thought he was going to argue, then he shook his head and cupped the heavy weight of cock in his hands. "I will come in your mouth. "

She waved off his explanation. "And I suck, I get the mechanics. I'm just not sure it's going to fit."

He was shaking his head again before she finished the sentence.

"I do not want you to do anything this time. It will be hard enough as it is to maintain my control. And mate?" He raised his eyebrow. "I will ensure your pleasure."

Once again her hands were anchored above her head. With the same unrelenting gentleness, her face was tipped up. At the same time, his cock surged forward, pressing against her lips. Hard, hot and huge, it demanded admittance.

"Open."

On a deep breath that drew his scent deep into her lungs, feeling like she was stepping off a ledge, Eden parted her lips.

With a steady surge, he pressed in. "Accept me, Eden."

She had thought it would be so easy. Just part her lips and in he'd go, but that wasn't the way it was. He was too big, the angle off. She had to twist her head back and forth, working him in slowly, remembering at the last minute to cover her teeth.

She had expected to be repulsed, at the very least bored, but the feel of the thick stalk sliding past her lips set off tiny explosions in her extremities. Explosions that detonated to the pulse of his heartbeat throbbing against her sensitive lips. She took him a little deeper, accepting the offer of his life and his passion. His flavor, salty and male, spilled through her mouth, and legions of cells leapt forward as if they'd been waiting for nothing more than this moment.

His fingertips grazed her cheek. "Just like that. Just hold still and let me feel that sweet tongue." He worked his cock deeper, in small thrusts, pulling out before the reflex to gag could give birth to action, sliding back in on her next breath. Easily, gently, he fucked her face in a relentless rhythm that caught her desire and spun it taut.

Was she pleasing him as well? She glanced at him from under her lashes. His lips were drawn back from his teeth, his handsome features chiseled with the force of the emotion sizzling between them. With every draw of her mouth something intangible passed from him to her and back again. This was more than sex. This was a bonding. One she didn't know if she could get out of, but she was too involved to turn back. She was so screwed.

Another quick glance showed his black eyes with those swirling hot depths locked on her lips, watching as she took him inch by inch, the lids flicking as the ridge of the broad head caught on her teeth. Another pulse of fluid washed over her tongue, feeding her need and triggering more. She reached for his hips. He caught her hands, holding them in his as he kept up his easy rhythm, shaking his head as she bared her teeth. "Soon."

She wanted it now. Her womb tightened into a knot of expectation, sending shards of agony splintering through her body. Hunger built on need. Demand on hunger. She groaned around him, wanting more. He shuddered and held perfectly still.

"Do you want my come, Eden?" His deep voice resonated along her nerves with the gentleness of a touch. "Do you want me to fill that sweet, tight mouth with my seed?"

The civilized part of her was horrified at the question. The primitive side responded with a resounding "*Yes!*" She wanted him, his seed. She wanted to fill the horrible aching hunger inside, to sate the pain that wouldn't stop, the unrelenting agony that sapped her strength.

He stopped moving, his cock resting on the shelf of her teeth, pressing her tongue flat. His thumb tucked against the corner of her mouth, stroking her and himself in one easy glide as his dark gaze met hers. "Then take from me what you need."

Chapter Eight

ɛɔ

Take from me what you need.

The ancient words flowed easily from Deuce, filling the space between them. This was more than sex. More than pleasure. This was how it was between the Chosen and their mates. She gave him light, purpose and freedom from loneliness, and he nourished her with his seed, his blood, providing all that she needed in all ways. His cock pulsed. His balls pulled up tight. He cupped her cheek, steadying her pulse. She took his first offering with a soft whimper of satisfaction that centered his attention.

"Whatever you desire from me, I am here to provide." His body throbbed with the agony of holding back. And still she lay there, staring at him with those big blue eyes, a seductive combination of pure wantonness and innocence. Another spurt of hot come seared his control, filling her mouth.

Her nostrils flared. Her eyes dilated. Her lips clamped around him like a vise. Her small hands twisted in his. He held steady, enjoying the pull of her lips, the heavy draw of suction pulling his seed to the burn of her need. She took his next offering with an enthusiasm that brought sweat to his brow. He held still, waiting, analyzing her body for signs of rejection. When she did not vomit, he gave her a little more, feeling her body's scream of relief to his soul, resenting the necessity of holding back. He wanted to give her what she cried for, slice an artery, do whatever it took to relieve her pain. Instead he had to give her a just a little of himself at a time, while watching her respiration for signs of distress.

After the fourth swallow, he noted a change in her scent. It was as Bohdan had warned. She could not take much. He needed to pull back, but the hot, wet heat of her mouth lured his inner beast. Her tongue tempted it into dominance with every swirling stroke. His control shuddered under her soft hum of satisfaction when his cock jerked. It went against everything he believed in to deny her anything, least of all his come. She sucked harder, drawing him to the edge of reason. His balls ached and his fangs throbbed. She wanted, and he wanted to give. Eden lunged forward, taking him deeper, her struggles increasing as he withheld what they both needed. He threw back his head and fought for control.

Dusan? You have need?

No.

He did not want his brother here. Not now. He shut Bohdan out and conjured the willpower to yank free of Edie's mouth. His cock jerked in an agony of regret as his come spurted on her breasts and belly, coating her soft flesh in hot cream. She arched beneath him, presenting herself for more. He gave it to her, helpless to do anything else until she was sated. She was his mate. What she needed he provided. He gently pressed her back against the comforter as the last spasm ended. Lamplight glistened on the proof of his possession. He laced her hands above her head. "Keep them there."

Her "Deuce" was a deep moan of distress.

"Be easy." He placed one hand over a warm pool of come just left of her incision scar. His other hand at her hip kept her in place. He massaged the silky liquid into her soft flesh, moving his hands up to her tightly peaked breasts, rubbing his scent into her skin. Marking her as his. He plucked at the plump nipples, watching them harden further. He rested his cock against her cheek. She turned her head, lapping his shaft, cleaning him with little dancing flicks of her tongue. His cock rose again, heeding her demand. He pulled away. "Enough."

She shook her head. "More."

He slid onto the bed beside her. The heavy curtains that darkened the room did not let in a bit of the dawn he could sense behind the windows. But he did not need light to see the agony in her eyes.

She moaned and twisted against him. She hungered. He held her tighter, pressing her face into his shoulder, realizing his mistake when she bit down.

Her sob when he tore her away cut him to the bone. It should not be this way between them. He brushed his lips across the riot of curls at her forehead, anchoring her in place by fisting his hand in her hair until she gained some control. "I am sorry."

"Why?" Her nails cut into his chest. "You didn't do this."

But he had not prevented it. She was breathing too hard, twisting too much, stressing her newly repaired flesh. He lowered her respiration to a more normal level, stopping the pump of adrenaline into her system, holding her as she shuddered under the lash of what was already there. "I would take this for you."

Bohdan's voice broke into his mind. *No! You cannot withstand her need and your own.*

He ignored the order. He was the leader of the Chosen. He would do whatever was required. "I feel your need, Edie. Let me take it from you."

"Can you take it without feeling it yourself?"

Her skin was soft as silk under his lips. Beneath his hand, she was damp with his tribute. In any other circumstance, it would be reason to celebrate. "It is unnecessary that you suffer."

She tilted her head back. Her hair slid through his fingers as she struggled to meet his gaze. "That wasn't an answer to my question."

"I do not feel emotion as you do."

She frowned. "Still not an answer."

He sighed, inhaled her scent, her warmth, memorizing it. "No. I cannot block your need without experiencing it myself."

"Then we'll be leaving things as they are."

A shiver shook her body. He pulled her closer. "It is not your place to be giving orders."

"My place is whatever I want it to be."

He shook his head at her foolishness. Her place was at his side, under his care. Another shudder rocked her frame. A faint clicking alerted him to the fact that her teeth were chattering. He hitched onto his side, turning her so he faced her back before carefully coming to rest against her. She vibrated against him like a leaf caught in a storm. "I will hold you now."

"Why am I so cold?"

"Shock."

"From that little bit?"

"Yes." She was so small in his arms. So fragile compared to him. So easily hurt. He spooned around her, tucking his thighs under hers, easing her cheek onto his forearm. "Do not bite," he warned as she stiffened.

The light chatter blossomed to a clatter, separating her words into fragmented bits. "I don't...think I...could if...I wanted...to."

The violence of her shivers worried him. He pulled the comforter over them while raising his own body heat. She moaned and pushed back. His cock, pleased with her nearness, filled until it lay like a brand between them. Between shudders, she lay unnaturally still as if afraid of setting him off. Did she think he would take her when she suffered like this? "I cannot help wanting you, Edie mine."

Her "I know" was barely recognizable.

"It does not mean I will not care for you or put your needs first."

This time her answer was a nod of her head.

With a sudden move he did not anticipate, she twisted in his arms, curled into a ball, her knees wedged between their chests, and made herself as small as possible, which was very small. He would have to be very careful with her. He wrapped his arms around her and held her against his core.

"When will this stop?" The muffled question came from somewhere in the middle of the shaking.

"Your body is adjusting."

"That's not an answer."

He rubbed his hand up and down her back, his pinkie riding the prominent nubs of her vertebrae. "I do not know."

The violence of her shaking was beginning to concern him.

"Talk to me, Deuce."

The words were almost indiscernible, the syllables lost in her low moans.

"About what?" He upped his body heat, ignoring the protest from his own organs. Her suffering was intolerable.

"Anything. Just give me something to focus on besides how awful I feel."

That he could do. He cocooned her against him, took what he could of her distress from the edges, and rested his cheek on the top of her head. "The first time I saw you, I could not believe how beautiful you were."

Her snort was full of disbelief.

"No interrupting."

"I'm sorry. I wasn't expecting a fairy tale."

Despite the gravity of the situation, she held onto her sense of humor. She was a miracle inside and out. "You were standing outside the restaurant, waiting for your grandfather. Your beautiful hair was wild about your shoulders, almost white in the moonlight."

"Let's keep it believable."

He brushed his lips over her hair. "This is my story. You will let me tell it as I saw it."

"I will?"

"Yes."

Another violent shudder shook her. He suspected her lack of argument came from lack of strength. "There was a moment when I could only stare in wonder, and then I knew I had found my mate."

"Weren't you disappointed?"

Deuce had to ponder for a minute what she could possibly think would disappoint him. "That you were human?" He could not tell if she was nodding or shaking again, but he took the abrupt movement of her head as agreement. He did not know how to explain it to her, the wonder of finding his other half, of knowing she existed, of years of yearning that had faded to despair only to have hopelessness obliterated with the blinding proof of her existence. "No."

Eden moaned and convulsed. He caught her head before it could snap back. He checked her vitals. Her respiration was growing shallower. Her blood pressure dropping.

Bohdan. Come now.

Deuce stroked her back, untangling his fingers from her hair as they caught. He had not allowed her to ingest too much. She should not be reacting this way.

Bohdan entered the room on a glide of power.

He reached for Eden immediately. His hands almost swallowed her rib cage. Edie cried out and flinched away. Her instinctive aversion to another's touch raised Deuce's beast.

"Release her." The words slurred through the baring of his fangs. Whether he was baring them at his brother, or the loss he could feel looming, Deuce was not sure. He only knew that Eden could not bear to be touched by another, so there would be no touching.

Bohdan eyed him warily as he withdrew his hands and pulled away. "I cannot help her if I cannot touch her."

Deuce clenched his teeth, fighting back the need to strike out. He nodded. Bohdan slipped his hands beneath the comforter. Eden's resistance was immediate.

The shake of her head was an extension of her next shudder.

"Do not defy me in this!" He thought she muttered "Bastard". It was hard to tell through the chattering of her teeth. She collapsed at the end of the next shudder, her head rolling with exhaustion. He nodded to Bohdan. "Do it."

Bohdan's face took on the surreal composure it always did when he entered another. Deuce measured the minutes the probe took in the shudders that racked Edie's small frame.

Bohdan pulled back, his hands lingering on Edie's bare back. "She needs blood."

"You said blood would kill her."

"It will, but she does not have enough now to sustain the change that is commencing."

"She will not die!"

The look Bohdan turned on him was sad. More than any other of the Chosen, Bohdan knew the pain that came from losing a mate. He only lived because the union had not been completed. He existed each day knowing his one chance had come and gone. He now faced forever alone. "If we cannot balance her blood, there will be no saving her."

"Then we will balance her blood." There was no other choice. Deuce raked his nail across his chest. Blood flowed freely. Horror rounded Edie's eyes at her body's immediate reaction to the sight and smell. He registered her disgust. She saw her need as something evil. Not understanding the beauty of their union because he had not had time to ease her into it. The hot liquid spilled down over his abdomen, pooling in the hair at the base of his hungry cock before seeping to his thighs. A desperate hunger overrode the horror on Edie's face. Everything in him commanded that he satisfy it. He reached for her as she lunged forward.

Bohdan grabbed her upper arms and pulled her back out of his reach. Edie fought his hold. Her pain and desperation flooded Deuce in a crushing wave. Energy gathered in and around him, seething with the rage coiling within. The growl sprang from his gut. "Let her go!"

Bohdan shook his head, his demeanor calm as always, unswayed by Deuce's rage. "It cannot be that way." He nodded toward Deuce's chest. "Close the wound."

Deuce did not want to close the wound. He wanted to bring his mate to him, strengthen her in the way the Chosen had been making their mates strong for ages. By giving her his blood.

Edie lunged again. Bohdan held her by simply crossing his arms over her chest from above. As he pulled her back against him, his hair fell over her chest, cocooning her in an intimacy that had everything in Deuce tensing in outrage. "Let her go."

Bohdan shook his head, his hair brushed across Edie's breasts in an intimate caress she should know from no one but him.

Deuce bared his fangs. He curved his nails into his palms against the rolling blackness of all-consuming rage. "I cannot promise not to kill you, if you do not."

Bohdan's response was a sweep of calm. *Close the wound, brother.*

The order echoed in his mind, the force of compulsion behind it. From between Bohdan's arms, Edie watched him, her expression frantic, her face ghostly pale against the black of Bohdan's hair. Her breath came in rasping pants, not as deep as they should be. Too fast, too hard. She was dying. She needed help. He had to do what was right for her.

Bohdan's order came again, finding and weaving along a shimmer of logic, *Close your wound or she dies.*

Deuce tamped down the animalistic rage, struggled for, and then found reason. He closed the wound. His instincts howled a protest. Edie moaned in despair.

Bohdan cautiously straightened. "You are yourself?"

"Yes." Barely.

He felt the touch of Bohdan's mind as he ascertained the truth of the statement before he lifted his arms. "Then take her."

Edie leapt for him. Deuce caught her, some of the turmoil inside abating as his flesh made contact with hers. He turned her so her back was to his chest, closing his ears to her despairing moans. They could not both be acting on instinct at the same time. Carefully, he reduced her heart rate and once again the adrenaline pumping into her system as he folded her back against him. Her skin slid across his as she tried to turn. Despite the gravity of the moment, his body sang with the erotic pleasure.

Bohdan reached for the bag he'd brought into the room.

Deuce bent to whisper in Edie's ear. "Be easy, my mate."

Edie showed no sign of quieting. Bohdan pulled a syringe from the bag.

"What are you going to do with that?" Deuce asked.

"We're going to give her blood."

Deuce eyed the needle as Bohdan approached. "Why cannot I feed her as is custom?"

"Because we cannot control the amount she will take, plus this is how they did it, so it is what her body is used to." He jerked his chin at his arm. "I need to get at the inside of your elbow."

Deuce turned his arm. Bohdan wasted no time sliding the ugly needle in. Deuce watched his blood fill the syringe. "The stabbing with needles is barbaric."

Bohdan looked up. "Not to humans."

"So you say, but my mate is looking less favorably on the needle than am I."

Which was true. A new emotion welled beneath the hunger and desperation. It did not take deep delving to define it. Panic.

"Edie?"

She was staring at the syringe with horror. "Oh God, no!"

Bohdan pulled it from Deuce's arm and took her wrist gently in his hand, turning her inner arm up.

Edie tilted her head and glanced at him, the terror in her eyes beyond reason for the small procedure. "Please, don't let him do this."

"It is already done," he whispered, merging his mind to the edges of hers.

Nothing prepared him for the agonizing burn that shot through her body as Bohdan depressed the syringe. The pain swelled in a knot and then spread like acid along her veins. Her agonized scream ricocheted around the room.

The door hit the wall and Harley and Dak broke into the room, guns down and ready to fire. Deuce shook his head and threw up an illusionary wall between them as Edie reared back and screamed again.

Harley's "Son of a bitch!" was as hot as Dak's "What the hell are you doing to her?" was cold. Deuce felt the bite of the anger both projected. The ugly suspicion.

He gritted his teeth against the agony he pulled from Edie to himself. The pain engulfed her, leaving her no strength for defense, facilitating his entry.

"Do not interfere," he warned the approaching Others.

"Unless you speak up fast," Harley countered, raising the muzzle of the machine gun, "I'll do a hell of a lot more than interfere."

Dak, with the calm patience of his Pride ancestry, pushed the muzzle down. "Explanations before threats."

Bohdan retreated from Edie's mind, his expression mirroring the fury Deuce could feel rolling off him in waves.

"What did we do wrong?" Deuce asked, wrestling with the pain, and Edie's efforts to detect his presence. He had to drop the wall between himself and the Others.

Bohdan's expression went carefully blank. He capped the empty syringe. "Nothing."

"She's in agony."

"Yes."

"You said this was how they did it."

"I did not press deep enough for emotional memory for fear of instigating another bleed."

Deuce put it together at the same time that everyone else did. Their curses cut through the last echo of Edie's scream, overriding the whimpered notes as he found the path to block the last of the pain from her consciousness. He closed his eyes as the agony spread to Edie's chest and seized her lungs, taking it into himself. He did not have time for swearing as he fought to keep her heart from stopping at the shock sweeping through her. He felt the touch of Bohdan's presence and then Edie's heart beat again. Once, twice and then steadily.

"I'm calling a hunt," Harley said when he stopped swearing.

Deuce locked Edie's life functions to his, leaving the healing to Bohdan, raising his heart rate to match a normal human one. He opened his eyes. Both men were in battle stance, frustration and rage shimmering around them in a red haze of contained energy.

"The Pride will join you," Dak said with a calm that was belied by the sharp claws extending around the stock of the machine gun. Others only lost control of the change when under extreme emotion.

Deuce lifted Edie's lax body into his arms, balling his rage into a cold, hard knot to be drawn upon later. "The Chosen will exact the revenge on behalf of my mate."

Edie's head lolled to the side as he stood. Her slender neck appeared too fragile to bear what she had. Her pulse shimmered under her skin in a bare thread of life. He would kill them all. His revenge would be long, bloody, and the men who had harmed Edie would suffer well into their death throes. That the Coalition had subjected her to that agony over and over while she lay helpless was inconceivable. He crossed to the bed. How she had survived it, he did not know.

He laid her on the red sheets, away from the bloodstains. He turned the comforter and covered her with a clean section, keeping her unconscious. He would not allow her to wake until the pain was gone. He brushed a curl out of her face, rubbing his fingers over the silken strand as it wrapped around his finger, binding him to her.

"You cannot kill them." As always, Bohdan was the voice of reason.

Deuce spared him a glance as he stepped up beside him. "You cannot stop me."

"You cannot kill them," Bohdan repeated with that same irrefutable calm that demanded attention. Deuce dragged his gaze away from Edie, quelling the panic that said to do so sentenced her to death, that she only lived because he held her here.

What he saw shocked him. Bohdan was at the edge of his strength. Healers were the strongest of the Chosen. They had to be for the effort it took to restore heath. But from the pallor of Bohdan's skin, keeping Eden alive had drained him. As the sun was upon them, he would not be able to replenish until nightfall. Deuce touched Edie's cheek, the agony whipping through her body tearing at him. The situation was bad. Very bad.

"Give me one goddamn reason why we can't gut the whole lousy bunch," Harley snarled, fangs flashing.

Bohdan's gaze met Deuce's, his calm soothing over the violence of the Pack leader's question. "She bore a child of the Chosen. They made it happen. They cannot die until we know how."

It was a very good reason.

Chapter Nine

ဆ

Eden awoke in darkness. Complete and utter darkness. Restrained to the bed, for one horrifying moment she thought she was back in the lab. Except for the darkness. The lab was never dark. It was always lit in sterile white unrelenting light. She tested her restraints. They seemed to be limited to her torso and thighs. Unevenly so. A quick exploration revealed a heavily muscled arm and thigh draped across her. Very heavy appendages that lay unnaturally still.

"Deuce?" She couldn't think of anyone other than Deuce who would dare crawl into bed with her as if it were his right. He probably justified it with his claim of being her mate. He didn't answer. Didn't move. She lifted his arm—definitely dead weight. Eden elbowed him in the side. No grunt marked the impact. Now that she listened, she couldn't hear anything at all. Not even a breath.

She slid from the bed, wrestling free of the covers, her skin crawling with an awful suspicion. His arm hit the bed with a thump just before her feet hit the floor. Was he dead? Was this another of her grandfather's sick games?

Eden backed up a step, disoriented in the dark, and bumped into something sharp. Wood clattered against wood and the corner of something gouged her hip. A table. The unmistakable sound of a lamp teetering had her spinning around. She caught it, fumbling up the curve of the base until she found the switch. With a prayer it would work, she turned it. Soft yellow light filled the room, illuminating the massive sleigh bed that dominated the large space and the lethal looking swords displayed on all the walls. No doubt about it. This was definitely a man's bedroom.

And no doubt about it, it was definitely a naked man sprawled on his stomach on the gleaming burgundy comforter, his cheek resting on his forearm, the long, thick length of his hair obscuring his face. Nothing could disguise who it was, however. There was only one man she knew who had that perfect build setting off the thick ropes of muscle that started at impossibly broad shoulders and flowed inward to the base of his spine in deep, shadowed channels that narrowed until one by one they blended into a single point just above the tight, hard rise of his buttocks. Eden followed the channel below with her eyes as it curved with the angle of his bent leg, dipping into an inviting shadow beneath, finding the darker hue of his heavy balls. Round and slightly compressed, they lay against his thigh and the bed in a tempting display. Her fingers twitched and saliva flooded her mouth. Deuce.

He must have changed the bedding while she slept. The golden cast to his skin glowed against the deep maroon of the comforter, while the stark white sheets accentuated the power in the arm stretched across them, as if reaching for her. Except he wasn't moving. Why wasn't he moving? Between her getting out of bed and the sudden influx of light, he should be waking up. Eden leaned forward and tapped the back of his hand.

He didn't move. She opened her hand over his. His flesh was cold, lifeless, without the vitality she was so used to feeling. She stepped back, black horror devouring hope. No matter how hard she looked, she couldn't see any sign of breathing. That gorgeous back lay as still as the rest of him. Crossing her hands over her chest, she gripped her upper arms. Goose bumps chased over her skin, prickling the flesh under her palms, reminding her that she was naked. Taking another step back and then another, morbidly fixated on his ribs, she waited for them to expand with signs of life. She'd taken five breaths and the man had yet to take one. Nausea welled as she fought back the sickening surety that she'd been sleeping with a corpse. Horror blended with a soul-deep pain. Deuce couldn't be gone. He couldn't. Digging her fingers into her upper arms, she bit her lip. She needed him. Her baby needed him.

Oh God, her daughter.

Eden wiped the tears from her eyes and turned around. She had to find her daughter. Yanking open the biggest drawer of the mahogany dresser, she found a large selection of T-shirts inside. She grabbed a blue one and yanked it on. As the hem fell over her thighs, she hauled open the next drawer. Inside were sweats and shorts. Grabbing a pair of gray sweats, she just as quickly discarded them as they were twice as tall as she needed. Tossing them aside, along with the next three pairs, she settled on a well-worn pair of athletic shorts. She dragged them on under the shirt, tugging the bunched-up folds of the shirt out of the too loose waist.

Eden tightened the drawstring on the shorts before darting to the door. Pressing against the wall, she took three deep breaths, tried to contain the betraying rasp of her breathing, and cautiously opened the door a crack. She peeked through, and immediately gasped. Staring back at her, one brow arched in amused inquiry, was the man she'd seen in the kitchen a year ago. She fumbled for his name. One look at the gun in his hand and she remembered. Dak Lyons.

He pushed the door open with the barrel. She leapt to the side, glancing at the bed. Deuce still hadn't moved. Staying behind the door as it opened, she glanced around hopelessly for a weapon. The swords beckoned in a glint of light. The only ones she'd be able to reach were those on the far side of the room above the small table and chairs. The door stopped moving halfway open. Dak stepped around. His dark blond hair was longer now, but he still wore that lethal arrogance with a natural manner that did nothing to settle her nerves.

Eden glanced at the swords again. She'd never make it to them in time. Clenching her hands, she cast another glance at the bed and blurted out, "I didn't kill him."

Dak's glance followed hers to the bed. A slight smile curved his lips and his left eyebrow quirked up. "It would serve him right if you did."

She took a step back, not liking that gleam of amusement in his eyes. "I woke up and he was like that."

His right eyebrow rose to the height of his left. "You think he's dead?"

"He's not breathing."

"He's sleeping."

"People breathe when they sleep."

"He isn't people. He's Chosen. All their functions slow to near stop when they sleep."

The relief that flooded through her took out her knees. Dak caught her arm. "You're still ill."

She noted that he didn't pose it as a question. "I'm fine."

He steered her back toward the bed. "You need to rest."

Eden planted her feet. She didn't care if she was on her last breath, she was not getting back into that bed with what, for all intents and purposes, amounted to a corpse. "I'm fine. I want to see my daughter."

Dak glanced at the bed. Then at her. "He won't be happy to wake and find you gone."

She didn't really care. Folding her arms across her chest, she said, "I want to see my daughter."

He released her arm and rested the muzzle of the gun in the crook of his arm. "You're feeling strong enough?"

She shrugged. "For now."

"Bohdan will heal you."

Eden wished she had his confidence. "In the interim, I'll just take advantage of the good moments as they come."

Again he stared at her with those piercing amber eyes, then he smiled and stepped back, motioning to the door with his free hand. "She's upstairs. Marlika is watching over her."

Eden gave him as wide a berth as possible, pressing her back to the door as she slid past into the hallway. He made her uncomfortable the way he watched her with those predator's eyes. She waited for him in the richly carpeted hall, the electric sconces on the wall softening the dark wood to a mellow glow. She didn't know which way to go.

"The stairs are to your right."

"Thank you."

He watched her the whole way down the hall as she approached the stairs. When her legs tired on the fourth step, his arm circled her waist, forcing her to lean on his strength. "Thank you."

"You're welcome, though I would feel better if you waited for Deuce or Bohdan."

"What time is it?"

"Three o'clock."

Eden forced herself up another step. "If my vampire lore is correct, I've got another three hours before they're awake."

She felt rather than saw Dak nod.

Turning to meet his gaze dead-on, she winced at the pull in her abdomen. Pain she hadn't recognized before was slowly creeping into her consciousness. "I am not waiting three hours to see my daughter."

She hadn't expected an argument, and didn't get one, which was good since she could be dead in three hours. Her strength wasn't as long-lived as she had hoped. The oversized neck of the too big T-shirt slid off her shoulder. The shorts made a dive for the floor. Stopping suddenly, she grabbed both. Dak didn't comment, just waited. Eden straightened her clothes and breathed a sigh of relief. Two more steps to go.

"Which way?" she asked as she got to the top of the stairs.

"First door on the left."

She tried to slow her breathing as she approached the door, but it was hard. Very, very hard. Up until this moment, she hadn't allowed herself to think of the baby as anything other than a package she had to deliver, but now... Eden paused. The cool metal of the doorknob warmed to her touch as she beat down the hope that popped up. Now was no different than before. The only thing she was to her daughter was a threat. A blur of khaki entered her peripheral vision—Dak's arm. Three sharp raps on the door punctuated the finality of the realization.

Taking a deep breath as the handle turned beneath her hand, she closed her fingers into a fist to cover the tremor that radiated out from the core of her uncertainty. The door swung in and a stunning woman with long, flowing black hair and an air of contentment stood before her. In her arms she held the baby, swaddled in a fluffy pink blanket. All that was visible of her daughter was the wispy blonde of her hair. The woman smiled at her.

"You must be Eden. The Others welcome you."

Was everyone here so formal? "Thank you. I came to see my daughter."

"As you can see, the little one has arisen."

Where she came from babies just woke up. "Oh good."

Dak performed the introductions. "This is Marlika, daughter of Drakor."

"Thank you for taking care of the baby."

"You are very fortunate to have a healthy child." There was an agony of want in the woman's soft voice, putting a face to the desperation of a people battling extinction. A beautiful, gentle face that reflected love for a child, and welcome to a stranger. But no resentment. Maybe this part of her plan really was going to work out.

"She's been well?"

"Oh yes." Marlika kissed the baby on the top of her head. "She's a very contented child."

Eden observed the care with which the other woman held her daughter. It was obvious that the infant's every need was being seen to with total devotion and joy. "Good."

"She's ready to feed." Marlika gently eased the baby away from her chest. The reluctance in her offer to hand the little girl over matched the hunger in Edie's soul to hold her child, for once, just once, without thinking of it as goodbye.

She didn't take the child, but she did touch her cheek. It was incredibly soft. "I've never fed her."

Marlika glanced up, her even features sharpening with her surprise. And maybe just a touch of...accusation? "Never?"

"There was never an opportunity." And she hadn't dared risk the bond.

"You can feed her now," Dak pointed out. Eden glanced at him. It was hardly the kind of advice she'd expect from a man standing by the door, gun at the ready, looking like he was expecting trouble any minute.

"I don't know how."

"I can show you," Marlika offered with a generosity Eden wouldn't have shown if their positions had been reversed. She wouldn't have been able to share her dream that soon, that easily.

Eden hesitated, wrestling with the temptation. She'd brought the baby here to find the family, love and security she couldn't offer her. Nothing in her plans had changed. No matter what Deuce said, the simple truth was, until her grandfather was dead, the baby was in danger. She could not let herself be seduced away from her plans by maternal emotions. "That's all right. I'll just watch."

Only by the slightest rise of her eyebrows did Marlika betray her surprise. She nodded. "As you wish."

As she wished? Who said things like that outside of movies? Marlika cuddled the baby against her, whispering words Edie couldn't hear. The infant sank into the warmth of the woman's embrace with an acceptance that spoke well for her future. Edie curled her nails into her palms and forced back the possessive jealousy that demanded she rip the baby out of the woman's arms. The baby needed a home and safety. Someone who understood her and would understand her coming needs. Marlika was giving her exactly that.

Marlika sat in a large rocking chair, her body curved in a maternally protective way around the tiny child as she tapped the baby's mouth with the nipple. The blanket fell back and Eden was treated to a glimpse of the infant's profile. The softly rounded cheek, pale and perfect, the button of a nose that looked too small to breathe through. She memorized each curve, each flush, each pale tracery of vein. This was her daughter. Her flesh and blood. They'd cut her from her body with the same dispassionate efficiency with which they'd impregnated her, but it didn't make any difference. This was her daughter. And she was going to walk away and leave her to the mercy of fate and the people she'd chosen for her. The howl of agony welled silently.

A snarl of rage erupted amidst the echoes, splintering her calm into shards of primitive terror. Marlika's head jerked up. Eden glanced at Dak. "What in hell was that?"

He smiled and shrugged. "I told you Deuce wasn't going to be happy."

She felt Deuce's rage that she was gone, and his search. She closed her mind, blocking him out. "You also told me he'd be a corpse for three more hours."

Again that aggravating shrug. "He would have been...before he had a mate to keep track of."

"I am not his mate."

Dak stepped aside.

"You are." Deuce materialized in the doorway. His thick, long hair, free of its que, fell over his shoulders, setting off the harsh masculine beauty of his face and the broad set of those naked shoulders. He was pale, very pale, but nothing, least of all paleness, could detract from the perfection of his form. Dressed only in well-worn jeans that clung to his narrow hips and muscular thighs with a lover's touch, he was a sight to sap any woman's mouth dry.

Edie dragged her gaze off his naked torso with its bulging pecs and washboard abs. She intended to stare at his knees, but on the way down her gaze hung up on the way his pants clung to his groin. The telltale bulge beneath his zipper had her womb clenching with hunger and her body flowering in anticipation. God, she was pathetic! It took everything she had and a glance at her daughter to remind herself that he wasn't for her.

"How did you find me so fast?"

Deuce nodded to Dak, and then took the five steps to reach her. "Not everyone is as uncommunicative as you."

Eden expected him to stop beside her. Instead, he stepped behind her. His hands cupped her abdomen over the baby flab of her stomach, directly above her incision. She ducked but he merely used the twist of her body to tuck her buttocks against his thighs. He looked at the other woman. "My thanks for caring for our daughter."

Edie caught her breath as his raw masculinity enveloped her, holding her more firmly than his arm. His fingers pressed into her abdomen, massaging lightly, as if he sensed she ached there. Deuce's head bent. His hair brushed her cheek, and an intake of air swelled his chest against her back, pressing her forward. A muscular arm came up, just under her breasts, and pulled her back against him in a completion her body fully accepted.

"You do not bleed, but you tire."

Through the thinness of her shirt the heat from his skin radiated. As if needing to get closer, her breasts swelled, her nipples peaked. She closed her eyes against the sight and fought the strength of his magnetism. "I'm fine."

"You are not, yet." His lips brushed the side of her neck sending a shiver of pleasure straight to her pussy. "But you will be. I promise."

She leaned away from his lips. He took another of those deep breaths. "Your scent is pleasing, Edie mine."

He damn well better be talking about the soap she used.

His chuckle vibrated against her back. "I am not."

Humiliation and outrage joined arousal. "Stay out of my head."

"You project—"

"When I'm upset," she finished for him. She was really going to have to work on that.

He straightened behind her. "Do you not wish to hold our daughter?"

"No."

His finger on her chin turned her face up. He was frowning at her. She might have been doing a bit of that betraying projecting again. "I might drop her," she explained hastily.

"That is not what you fear."

"How do you know what I fear?"

"I do not, but I do know that is not one of your—"

"She could use a name." The soft interruption came from Marlika. The baby rested against her shoulder. She burped her gently, a frown on her beautiful face. "No child should go unnamed."

Deuce's arm tightened around her, warning her to silence. "Agreed."

Eden ignored the warning. "Maybe Marlika would like to name her?" In front of her, Marlika drew back in shock, shaking her head while cradling the baby protectively. Behind her, Deuce stiffened in disapproval.

"You insult me and our child with such a suggestion."

"What's so bad about Marlika picking a name?"

"A name is a sacred thing, a bonding between past and present, hope for the future. A gift from parents to their child."

"Oh." Obviously, his culture placed a high value on children's names. "Then maybe you should pick it out."

"We will choose it together." The flat delivery left no room for argument. Deuce motioned to Marlika. She got to her feet in a graceful move and brought the child over. Though she held herself tall and proud, there was an aura of deference in her posture when she approached Deuce—a dropping of her eyes as she held the baby out toward him.

Edie would have used the moment to escape, but Deuce kept her within the cocoon of his arms as he accepted their daughter into the cradle of his big hands. The baby started and whimpered for the heartbeat he held her suspended before them, then he brought her against Edie's chest, imprisoning her in a hug that encompassed them both. Eden wanted to keep her hands at her sides, but one look into that perfect little face with its confusion and distress, and her plan fell to the wayside.

She cradled the child instinctively—shushing her with a soft voice, feeling a moment of dread as her daughter looked back at her with deep blue eyes, as if taking her measure. Then, with a soft gurgle, the tension disappeared from the baby's face and her mouth opened wide in an impossibly sweet yawn. Eden rocked her naturally, her weight a precious burden against her trust, just one more incentive to succeed.

"You will let yourself love her, my heart."

Eden couldn't tell whether Deuce spoke aloud or into her mind. In the end it didn't matter. "I can't."

"Why?"

"It's not safe."

"I will protect you, Edie."

"You can't. You don't know how powerful they are. How relentless." She glanced back, catching his gaze with hers. "They won't stop coming after me. They *will* take me back."

His big hands settled over hers, easing their child closer to her heart. Against her back, his pectorals flexed. Cold, deadly energy swirled around them in a restless wave, skating across her skin briefly before flaring outward. "Any such attempt will fail."

"We can't take the chance that it won't." She shook her head as his eyes narrowed and his lips thinned. He didn't understand how committed the Coalition was to discovering the secret to immortality, nor how vital they felt she was to the process. "If they find me here, they'll know about the baby."

His arms wrapped around her and their daughter, turning them so they rested within a shield of his energy and power. For all the comfort of his touch, there was not an ounce of softness in his tone. "I will not allow you to leave."

She had no doubt he meant it. If the decision was left to him, he would hold her here forever. She had no intention of leaving it to him. "No matter what happens to me, Deuce, you need to protect the baby. She has to be your first concern."

"My daughter will be safe." He turned her completely in his arms. "As will you."

She stepped back and ran into the barrier of his hand. Slight pressure from his fingers on the base of her spine moved her forward. She hitched the baby higher and stumbled as weariness made her awkward. His hold shifted, offering her support where she most needed it. He made it so easy to think in terms of giving all her cares over to him. "Thank you."

Some of the energy around them softened. The little girl began to struggle. Deuce touched her cheek. His finger was huge against the small face. But so gentle. So incredibly gentle. "She hungers."

His phrasing reminded her of the differences between them. She had to stop thinking of him as a man and keep in her mind that he was a vampire with an agenda of his own. Before she could hand over the baby, Marlika handed her the bottle. "She has a healthy appetite. She should finish the rest of this."

The rest didn't look like enough to sustain a gnat, but what did she know of babies? She took the bottle. "Thank you."

Deuce's chin brushed the side of her head. A quick glance showed him nodding to Marlika. "Thank you for the care you have shown my daughter."

"I'll be happy to care for her anytime."

"And we would be honored to have our daughter under the care of the Pack."

Pack? Eden's breath caught tight in her lungs. Marlika was a werewolf? Good God, she'd left her daughter in the care of a werewolf? Deuce's palm curved over her shoulder, his fingers stretching down the upper slope of her breast. The knot in her chest eased. Her breathing smoothed out and the shaky surge of energy ceased as abruptly as it had started.

"Marlika is awaiting your thanks," Deuce mentioned in a whisper so soft that she had to strain to hear.

Edie dragged herself out of her shock. Taking a deep breath, she forced herself to smile. "Thank you."

She kept the smile on her face during Marlika's "You're welcome". She had to stop freaking out over things like this. This was her daughter's world now. She wasn't human and the only danger to her came from humans. She would grow up among werepeople and vampires, preternatural beings of legend that Eden had never believed really existed. But it was all right. Here the baby would be accepted, protected, and loved. Here she had a prayer of surviving.

Deuce's arm dropped to Eden's waist as he turned to the door. "We will care for her in our room."

"You'll need her bag."

Eden looked over her shoulder. The bag Marlika held looked big enough for a weekend stay. "There should be enough in here until morning."

Eden blinked. "Are there instructions in there?"

Marlika laughed, obviously not taking her question seriously. "No."

Eden glanced up at Deuce as he took the bag with his free hand—diapers, bottles, creams and cloths overflowing the top. To think she'd managed with nothing but a carrier for a day. "Do you know what to do with all that stuff in there?"

He arched a brow at her whispered question. "No."

She shook her head. "We are so screwed."

Deuce pulled her into his side as Dak opened the door for them. "We will figure it out."

Chapter Ten

ဆ

Deuce was apparently as serious about the naming as he was about everything else. He'd started nagging her about it four steps out of Marlika's room with a question about her preferences. A simple statement that she didn't have one only led to questions designed to narrow the options to areas she would like. He was like a dog with a bone when he got something in his head, and he now had it in his head that the baby would be named. And that she would participate. She sighed, admired the way the muscles splayed out from his spine and the flexing of his tight butt beneath the jeans as he opened the door to their apartment. Naming their daughter clearly topped his to-do list.

Eden followed Deuce into the dark apartment, flicking the light switch as she passed through the door.

The baby squealed.

"Damn it!" She pushed her hair back from her face, the lingering echo of the infant's cry cutting into her like a knife. "I can't see in the dark like you," she explained as Deuce turned, pulling the baby's face protectively against his chest.

"It is fine, Eden."

It wasn't fine. She wasn't doing anything right. She motioned to the grunting bundle in his arms. "Is she okay?"

"She was but startled. No harm was done."

"This time."

"New parents are not expected to know everything." He motioned her to him.

She stayed where she was. "But this is different. This baby is not like others."

"She is of her parents. There is no difference."

"But she's half vamp — Chosen."

"This is what you fear?" He eradicated the distance between them in three long strides. His free hand skimmed up her neck, curling along the underside of her chin, tipping her face up to his. "That because her blood is of both worlds, somehow she does not need her mother?"

"I can't do anything for her." It came out as a whine, and she hadn't meant for that to happen.

The pad of his thumb pulled her lower lip free of her teeth. "You will love her, my heart."

His words were as much of a lure as his touch. She stiffened against the temptation. "You can't make me."

His hint of a smile was the gentle one he usually reserved for the baby. "I would if it were necessary."

She blinked. Could he control her emotions to that extent?

His thumb slipped down the inner curve of her lip, gliding smoothly on the moist lining, sending spiraling trills of pleasure dancing down her spine. "But there is no need, is there?"

She didn't answer, just squared her shoulders and matched his smile with a glare, increasing the intensity as his amusement spread to the corners of his mouth. He dropped his hand to her shoulder and turned her toward the bed. "Come."

Like he gave her any choice. The hand on her shoulder was insistent. She didn't know if he was projecting or if she was supposing, but she had no doubt he'd pick her up and carry her if she planted her feet. "You are way too bossy."

His "You like it" was completely unconcerned.

She planted her feet at that. "What makes you think that?"

He took the last step to the bed, laying the baby down before tossing his hair out of the way and looking back at her over his shoulder. "Your pleasure flows when I give you an order."

He could not mean what she thought he meant. She crossed her arms over her chest, mortified to her soul. "It does not."

He cocked an eyebrow at her. "You are wet now." There was no way she could call that relaxation of his facial muscles anything but satisfaction. "It pleases me."

It was a hard choice whether to pray for a hole to open up in the floor and swallow her, or to brazen it out. She settled for the latter. "I'm getting you a set of nose plugs."

"You may spend my money as you please."

He said that with a nonchalance that she took to mean no matter how many nose plugs she bought, he wouldn't be wearing them. The muscles on his back moved under his skin, the golden flesh gleaming darker in the low light, the hollows beckoning her hands, her tongue. Mindlessly, she took a step closer. And then another, until she was close enough to touch.

Deuce reached back and caught her hand, pulling her into his side, linking their fingers as he rested his arm across her shoulders. "Look at her."

It wasn't what she'd expected him to say. She looked down. While she'd been admiring him, he'd been undressing the baby. The little girl lay in the pink blanket, arms and legs akimbo, her dark blue eyes wide with wonder as she stared up at them.

His arm tightened across Eden's shoulders in a hug that lingered as softly as his proclamation. "Our daughter is perfect."

Tears burned her eyes. How was she supposed to keep a strong front when he said things like that, with all the love he felt for his child just hanging out there for the world to see? She blinked the tears back. "I'm glad you like her."

The baby kicked her feet, and froze, as if the ensuing jerk of her body came as a surprise.

Amusement joined the pride in his voice as he tickled the bottom of one tiny foot. "She is learning about the world. She will find many surprises." The stroke of his fingers on Eden's upper arm punctuated his chuckle as the baby jerked away and then promptly pushed her foot back, as if searching for the sensation again. "She will need the love of her father and mother to guide her through them."

He made it sound so easy, so imperative. "You can't make me do this, Deuce."

"She already loves you."

"She doesn't know who I am."

He shook his head, his hair brushing her cheek as it fell forward. She blinked once, twice, fighting the breakdown that battled for release. "She feels your love and your turmoil, but mostly your love."

She bit her lips and took a stabilizing breath as his cheek rested on her head. If they were any other couple, this would be a tender moment, rather than just a painful one. "You can talk to her?"

"Yes."

"With your mind?" The baby looked too innocent to be telepathic.

"Yes."

This time, she had to blink long and hard to keep from embarrassing herself. "I didn't know she could do that."

"She is very intelligent."

From the amount of paternal pride packed into Deuce's tone, their daughter could be a blithering idiot and he wouldn't care. To him, she was a miracle. What more could she ask? "I'm glad."

It was too much to hope that he would miss the catch in her voice. There was no fighting the pull of his arm, the kindness in his touch, or his power as he pressed her cheek to his chest, enfolding her in his strength. "I promise you it will be all right, my heart. You were strong enough to survive, to bring yourself and our child to me. You did what you had to, but you need to let go now. I am your mate, your strength, your voice." His finger under her chin brought her face up. She didn't know black eyes could be so soft. "You will entrust to me the safety of yourself and our daughter."

He made it sound so easy. Beneath her palm his heart beat with the same surety in his gaze. But he didn't know what he was up against. "I can't."

His hand traveled the length of her spine with excruciating slowness, reaching the base of her skull, stroking the nape of her neck before tangling in her hair. He pulled her head back, fully exposing her vulnerability. "You will."

"I know you think you're strong and can take on anything, but—"

He shook his head, brushing his lips over her cheek and finally her nose. The kisses were so light as to be chaste. There was no reason for her pulse to kick into overdrive or her breath to get caught in her lungs. "You will not deny me my pleasure."

"Getting killed gives you pleasure?"

"Having you and Jalina does."

She was beginning to accept it really was that simple for him. That straightforward. She kissed his breastbone where the bulge of his pectoral muscles carved out a seductive channel. Overwhelmed and grateful to God or his Maker, to whoever had chosen him to be her daughter's protector. "Thank you."

He held her mouth to his skin, moving it a little to the right, the hard flesh under her lips swelling with his indrawn breath. "I would prefer your thanks without sadness."

She propped her chin on his chest to meet his gaze, running her tongue over her lips, her senses delighting in his lingering taste. "I'll work on it."

His eyes narrowed and his nostrils flared as his hand opened over her right buttock. His fingertips lid into the crease, riding it down before snagging on the slight indentation of her anus. Her knees buckled. He caught her weight on his middle finger. Shock and a dark desire held her immobile as her muscles parted the tiniest bit. Red lights flashed in his dark eyes. He tugged her up against him, so the hard ridge of his cock bit into her stomach. "See that you do." The baby whimpered. He stepped back, his hand gliding away from her ass. Eden grabbed the bedstand to steady herself.

Deuce cast her a knowing smile as he reached for the infant. "She chills," he explained as he picked her up.

The fog around Eden's brain cleared. "You called her Jalina."

"I apologize." He tucked the infant against his chest. The baby immediately snuggled in, her fussing quieting.

"It's a pretty name."

He paused, his hand on the baby's back freezing mid-rub before slowly resuming. "There are many choices."

But he liked this one. From the sudden poker face Deuce had adopted, he'd probably been calling their little girl Jalina in his head for a while. "What's it mean?"

"The best translation would be the light of hope."

"I like it."

"It is a strong name, signifying the hope she brings to the Others and the Chosen, and the hopes they have for her." Still that too careful tone.

She put her hand on his arm. "Deuce?" For the first time ever, he was slow to look at her. Could he be embarrassed? She squeezed his arm. "It's a good name."

"You do not object?"

How could she? It was perfect. "Not at all."

"It is decided then." He held the baby away from his chest, cradled on her back in his big hands. "Step into my arms."

"Why?"

"It is custom."

She knew how strongly he felt about custom. She ducked under his arm.

"Turn your back to me and hold the baby as I am."

She tried to do as he ordered, but her hands weren't as big as his. Jalina wobbled. Her limbs jerked out straight, and her face screwed up as she teetered. Oh shit, she was going to drop her!

The thought didn't reach completion before Deuce was there, his hands under hers, lending his support to hers as naturally as breathing. Jalina settled, her breath pushing her little ribs against Eden's hands, her skin the softest thing she'd ever felt. Deuce pressed up with his palms, raising her hands and the baby until they were face level. His voice flowed into Eden's ear and over her skin, into her mind, becoming more than sound and less than substance. Becoming part of her. "The Chosen welcome you, Jalina Knight. May the Maker smile upon your existence and rejoice in your life as we do."

The edges of the room shimmered with an ethereal glow. Power radiated inward, raising the hair on the nape of her neck. The shimmer turned to a pulse and then exploded. Eden staggered under the flood of energy that surged into the room, falling back against Deuce, who stood solid against the wave. Even Jalina didn't move, as if she were too in awe of what was happening to fuss. Deuce held them within that incredible field until it slowly ebbed, and then with a flash, it winked out as fast as it had appeared.

"What was that?" she asked when she could catch her breath.

"The Chosen have welcomed our daughter."

Eden straightened cautiously, half afraid the tremendous energy would come back. "Humans just send a card."

She glanced up quickly enough to catch what just might have been a smile on Deuce's mouth. "Chosen ways are different."

"I'm beginning to see that. So what was…that?"

"A greeting."

He lowered their hands, bringing the baby against Eden's chest. The baby's face worked. She was either trying to smile or pass gas. Eden gave her a smile, surprised when the child stared as if fascinated. "That was more than a greeting."

"All Chosen recognize Jalina's energy now. She can never be alone or lost."

It was the nicest thing he could have said to her. Eden tugged her hands free. As soon as she was sure Deuce had Jalina, she turned and wrapped her arms around his lean waist and hugged him with all the relief she felt. Nine months worth of worry rolled off her, leaving her lightheaded. She could trust her child to this man. Her baby was safe. Jalina was really safe. "Thank you."

Deuce didn't move for a heartbeat, then his lips brushed her head. "You are welcome." He raised his arms so she could duck under. "When our daughter is settled, I would not object to a demonstration of your gratitude."

Eden bit back a grin and shook her head. "You just had to go macho on me again, didn't you?"

He shrugged. "It is the Chosen way."

"That must be a damn handy excuse to have on hand to trot out."

His head tilted ever so slightly to the side and he smiled. She supposed she should take that as an answer.

* * * * *

Eden watched from the bed as Deuce lay the satisfied, sleeping baby in the crib Dak had brought. She was thinking about nominating him to sainthood. He'd handled changing a diaper with his usual calm efficiency, demonstrating none of her disgust. He'd even praised Jalina for the size of the deposit, rebutting her shock with the calm truth that it indicated a healthy digestive system.

She shifted higher, smiling when Deuce glanced over. She didn't know how much longer she'd be able to hide her weariness from him, but she wanted to try. He was so pleased with his daughter that she hated to do anything that would ruin this moment.

As soon as he looked away, she closed her eyes briefly and leaned back against the headboard, fatigue beating at her resolve. She pushed it back with the ease of long practice, again meeting Deuce's gaze with another easy smile. Deuce frowned as he straightened, his black eyes raking her from head to toe and then back up again. When his gaze stopped at her chest and a purely predatory smile turned up the corners of his sensual mouth, she looked down. The neckline of his too big shirt had slipped again and damn near half her breast was exposed. She yanked it up, ignoring the hot flare of interest her body expressed at catching his eye. "Pervert!"

His laugh was a seductive blend of low tones that skated along her nerves in a tangible caress. "A man noticing a beautiful woman is normal."

"But you're not a man, are you?"

He stalked toward her—at least she thought he stalked. She had the impression of being stalked but in reality he seemed to glide with an effortless grace that was hypnotic to watch. In the time it took to blink he was in front of her, his hand cupping her cheek, his thumb tilting up her face, locking his gaze to hers. "Chosen or man, however you choose to think of me, I am all you will know from here on out."

That was just too much. She caught his wrist and pushed. "Who I date is my business."

She should have saved her strength. Her hand slid down his arm, but he didn't budge. He was incredibly strong. Physically and mentally. But she was no weakling. She'd blocked him before. She could do it again.

"As long as you date only me, our future will be harmonious."

"Maybe I have a thing for someone else." The effort of keeping him out of her head was making it ache.

His touch softened and his gaze rested on her mouth. "You do not."

"There's no way you can know."

His thumb came to rest on her lips. "I know."

She didn't know if he was reading her mind or not, but she knew there was one thing he could never know for sure. "You can't know about the future."

She felt his start in his touch. At last a weakness. "'You can force me now all you want, but eventually, I'll be strong and when I am, I'll make my own choices, which may or may not involve another man."

His expression went from fierce to calm. His thumb pulled her lower lip down. Fire pooled in her belly. His smile broadened as her breath caught. "Determining your preference will be my responsibility."

"You can't control everything."

"I can control you."

"Like hell!" Pain shot through her temple. The good old-fashioned kind that came when she tried to do too much on too little food and too little rest.

He frowned. "You tire."

"I'm fine."

His fingers skimmed up her cheeks. "Your head hurts."

"I'm hungry."

"I will have food brought." His fingertips brushed her temples, once, twice and then settled into gentle soothing circles. She didn't bother to protest or pull away. Healing a headache was no doubt high on his mate to-do list and she didn't need another argument right now.

"What would you like?"

"You have food here?" Saliva flooded her mouth. Her heart picked up its pace and her breath shortened in breathless anticipation. "Real food?"

"This surprises you?"

"I just don't think of vampires as eating."

"Chosen do not, as a rule, but the Pride and Pack do." He smiled. "An inordinate amount of food."

His fingers pressed a little deeper, drawing her pain and discomfort away.

All the cravings and dreams she'd had over the eight months she'd been on the feeding tube rushed her defenses and spilled into that zone.

"Do you think I could have a salad?" She tried to keep the hope down to a minimum. Paranormal critters were probably big into meat. "And maybe some fruit?" Oh God, it had been so long since she'd had fruit. She curled her fingers into a ball to hide the shaking the thought of eating again brought.

Deuce's fingers on her temples missed a beat, and then resumed. "You will have whatever you desire."

"I'd like a salad, then."

His lips brushed her forehead. Her breathing eased and the shaking stopped, but she still wanted that salad with a vividness that defied belief.

"Then you shall have it."

Her "Thank you" didn't begin to convey what she felt inside.

He smoothed her hair away from her face. His expression was set in that neutral pattern she couldn't decipher. "There is no need to thank me. It is my duty to see to your needs."

She sighed as his dismissal of her appreciation pricked her nerves. "You make it very easy to dislike you sometimes."

"That was not my intent."

"Well, intent or not, that's what you're accomplishing."

He leaned her back against the headboard. "You will sit here and rest while I order your dinner."

Pressure from his palms gave her no choice but to do as he said. He crossed the room in that easy mouthwatering glide that emphasized the masculine beauty of his form. His hair fell in a thick skein of black to just below his shoulder blades, swinging with his movement, giving her intermittent glimpses of the carved muscles above. She followed that flow of strength as it gathered on either side of his back down to the hollow of his spine, licking her lips as it disappeared beneath the waistband of his jeans, tracing an imaginary path until she came to his ass. The well-worn jeans clung in all the right places to emphasize how that part of him was as perfectly cut as the rest. He paused at the intercom, legs slightly spread. If she looked really closely, she could just detect the bulge of his balls.

He pushed his hair back as he spoke into the intercom, allowing her a view of his profile. The slight hook to his nose and the full set of his lips added to the impression of wild, untamed masculinity. When he'd courted her, he'd tamed that side of his personality, but here in his home environment, he looked every inch what he was. A leader. A warrior. Chosen.

She sighed. It was amazing how love could blind a woman. And not in a good way, though truth be told, if she had to make a choice between who she'd thought Deuce was and who he actually was, she'd choose the man turning to her now.

"Your food will be here soon."

"What about you? Don't you need to…eat?"

"I will feed when Bohdan returns."

He just had to use that terminology. Just like he had to come back to her. The man didn't seem to be able to function unless he was touching her. The mattress sank as he sat beside her. She leaned away, countering the pull of gravity. He made mincemeat of her efforts by putting his heavy arm around her shoulders and tucking her into his side.

"Haven't you heard of respecting a person's space?"

"You are cold and tired."

And bitchy. He forgot to add bitchy. "It doesn't matter what I am." She pushed at his arm. "You need to wait for an invitation."

He left his arm where it was, slid the other under her thighs and draped her across his lap. His sigh of satisfaction was a lot more subtle than her hiss of disgust. "What is it with you and manhandling me?"

"I have a need to hold you." He withdrew his arm from under her thighs and settled it across her hip. Beneath her thighs, his were rock-hard. Against her shoulder, his equally hard chest rose and fell with his breathing. Around her, the muscles of his arms flexed as he turned sideways on the bed.

"Why?"

"It is hard for me to believe that you are real."

Just like that, he took the wind out of her sails. How could she be angry with a man who thought of her as a miracle? Deluded or not, it was sweet. "I'm real, but we are definitely going to have to talk about this notion you have that I'm your mate."

His hand worked around her shoulder, the fingers sliding across her breast, nestling into the valley between, making them swell, and the nipples peak. "You *are* my mate."

She yanked his hand off, and because she was afraid he'd just put it back, she held it in hers. A good five inches away from her flesh which strained for the contact. "Just because my hormones do a jig when you're around proves nothing."

"I agree." His fingers curled around hers. Instead of restraining him, she was now, in essence, holding his hand.

She leaned her head back. His arm immediately shifted to provide her support. "You do?"

"Human women have always been susceptible to Chosen men." His fingers moved up her hip a couple of inches.

"So you've just been screwing your way through the population the last few years?" The thought left a bitter taste in her mouth.

His fingers inched beneath the waistband of her shorts. His hand shifted on her hip, lifting her. "Your jealousy has no justification. I have known no other since our meeting."

"I am not jealous."

"You are, but there is no need. You are the only woman I will know from here on out. In this life and the next." His fingers dipped lower. Which didn't help with the mental images of all the women he'd known over the course of his lifetime.

"How old are you exactly?" The last syllable hit a high note as he brushed the crease between her thigh and buttock.

"I was born over six centuries ago."

She couldn't suppress her moan as he palmed her buttocks, his fingers grazing the crease between, sliding on the proof of her arousal farther down. For over six hundred years he'd been bedding human women. She couldn't calculate fast enough to figure out the average number of human rumps he'd fondled just as he was fondling hers, but she got far enough that the cold shock of disgust dimmed the hard clench of desire. "Get your hands off me."

The infuriating smile at the corner of his mouth made he want to slap him, but she couldn't. The only hand she had free was trapped in his. He raised it to his lips. Those firm, sexy lips that had kissed a thousand, maybe even two thousand hands before hers, brushed her palm. "You do not want them off."

She did, with everything in her that was feminine.

She yanked her hand free and twisted off his lap. She would have landed in a heap on the floor except for his quick reflexes. He held her suspended in front of him, his brows pulled together in a slight frown as he studied her face. "You are upset."

No shit. "Let me go."

He did, steadying her as her feet touched the floor. "You will tell me why."

When hell froze over. "I don't want you touching me."

"You do not lie." Surprise colored the rich tones of his voice. His fingers pressed into her flesh, holding her to him as he searched her expression.

She closed her eyes. It didn't help.

"You do not like that I have known women before you."

"Get out of my head."

"I am not in your head." His lips brushed her forehead and lingered. "I am sorry you are offended."

"But not sorry you were a dog?" It was just a guess, but she was reasonably sure Deuce's bed hadn't been empty often.

He shook his head, the smoothness of his lips rubbing across her skin in a gentle glide. "You took a long time to enter my life."

"And that's an excuse?"

"No."

She opened her eyes, finding nothing in his expression except regret and remembered pain.

"I hungered for you as if you were here, but you were not." His hand under her chin tipped her face up. "There were times when I sought refuge in illusion but it was never enough." His thumb pressed gently into the corner of her mouth. "They were never you."

Well, hell. What was she supposed to do with that? "I can't help how I feel."

"They were nothing to me."

She jerked her chin free. "That's just disgusting!"

"You will tell me what offends you."

"You used those women!"

He nodded, his facial muscles settling into the complete neutrality that she was beginning to realize indicated that he was hiding his feelings. "Yes."

The agreement landed wrong. She caught his wrist in her hand, wrapping her fingers around the solid muscle and bone. Deuce might be vampire/Chosen, but he had a code of honor that went bone-deep. And a protective streak just as strong. She just couldn't see him blithely leading women on and dumping them century after century. It just wasn't his style. She tried to imagine how he felt. How she would have felt in the same position. She couldn't. It was simply too overwhelming to contemplate. She couldn't imagine living with that intensity of need and at the same time knowing it might never end. "I have no right to question your past."

"Mates are allowed their expectations."

"Do you resent my past?"

Cold fury replaced the neutrality of his expression. Flickers of red swirled in the depths of his black eyes. Emotion just as dark surged around them. "Yes."

Fear rose right alongside empathy, choking off her breath. Deuce was as scary as hell when riled. Immediately, his expression gentled and his thumb stroked over her throat. The tension there, left. She took a deep breath. "Then I guess we both have some things to work through."

"I would make you forget."

Forget what? His past, or her objection to it?

"I cannot change my past."

She closed her eyes, counted to five, and then opened them. "I was projecting again?"

"Yes." His gaze searched hers, delving into her insecurities. She pulled back, breaking the connection.

A sharp knock came at the door, saving her from the discussion. Deuce looked at her, then at the door, and sighed. In a coordinated move that indicated incredible strength, he lifted her as he stood. She clutched his neck as he turned. He set her down very gently with a shake of his head, chiding her for her lack of faith. With that smooth glide, he crossed to the door. She had a split second to see a dark-haired man with a broad, handsome face and a gun hanging off his shoulder standing there with a tray in his hands, before Deuce stepped into her line of vision. She recognized him. The man she'd shot in the forest.

There was an edge to Deuce's "Thank you" that made the hair on the back of her neck stand on end.

The man—werewolf—Harley leaned around Deuce. "I'm glad you are feeling better."

She pulled the covers up to her neck. "Thank you."

Harley's step back was too fast to be voluntary. The door slammed hard in front of him. When Deuce turned, there was nothing unusual about his expression. It was as calm as always. The explosion of sound and small burst of violence might never have occurred. No squeak of the floor marked his progress. She would have commented except when he set that laden tray across her lap, she couldn't do anything but stare. There was a steak—a huge steak—and tossed salad loaded with vegetables, and beside it all sat two perfect oranges. Oranges! Oh God. In front of it all, a glass of milk so cold that beads of condensation clung to the surface. She forgot all about her anger, his age, and how many women he might have screwed.

"Oh God." She hadn't meant to say it aloud. She braced the back of her hand against her mouth and just stared at the food, embarrassed by her body's reaction, half afraid to reach out in case it disappeared.

Deuce knelt beside the bed. His hair brushed her thigh as he pushed hers back from her face. She hated the stupid tears that spilled from her eyes. "You will eat."

"In a minute."

He pulled her hand away from her mouth and caught a tear on his thumb. "Why?"

She sniffed and scrubbed away the next tear. "It's been awhile since I've had real food, that's all."

He caught a persistent curl as it fell into her eyes, holding it back. "They starved you?"

It was a question and a statement at the same time. "No. They fed me through a tube. They didn't trust me not to run away."

Because she'd tried. Over and over. Killing one man in one attempt. Breaking her leg and arm in another. They'd finally taken care of the matter by injecting her with a paralyzing drug, caring for her as if she were in a coma when in reality she had been vividly alive, imprisoned in her body, unable to do anything to help herself and the baby that grew in her every day. Nothing except dream and plan.

"You have much to forgive me for."

She reached for the knife and fork. The steak looked good, the salad divine, but if he hadn't been there, she probably would have fallen on the oranges and eaten them whole, skin and all. "It wasn't your fault."

"It was, and will always remain, my fault." He reached toward the tray.

He was going for her orange. She clenched her fingers around the fork, fighting back the urge to stab the back of his encroaching hand. The sweet tang of citrus filled the air as he peeled it with a wave of his hand. A tap of his finger and it fell open, each juicy section lying like the petals of a flower in his hand. She couldn't take her eyes away from the sight. Couldn't move. He lifted one of the orange segments and brought it to her lips. "I can feel your hunger."

She parted her lips. The segment slid between, the smooth skin and gentle ridges caressing her lips. His gaze held hers. "Bite down, my Eden."

She did. The incredibly tangy sweet flavor immediately flooded her mouth. She chewed, closing her eyes, her soul rejoicing in the moment, her taste buds crying out for more. And something inside her, something she'd built to be strong, shattered. The first sob took her by surprise. The second ripped from her chest in a painful gasp. The tray disappeared and Deuce wrapped her in his arms, holding her tightly against him, saying nothing, just stroking her hair and her back, seeming to know she needed to cry just this one time. Just this once. She turned her face into his chest and twisted her fingers into his shirt as the sobs tore at her lungs. They hit so hard, so fast that she couldn't breathe. Deuce's palm spread open on her back, heating her flesh, and the tightness lessened, her breathing eased, but the tears didn't stop.

"They will not hurt you again." The flat delivery implied nothing more than the truth but she could feel his anger swirling around them, the violence wildly primitive, scaring her even though it wasn't directed at her.

She shook her head. It didn't matter. Not his anger and not her fear. As long as she accomplished her goal, nothing they did would matter. The scent of citrus intensified as something nudged her lips. She opened her eyes. He held another piece of orange to her mouth, tapping her lower lip gently with the fat underside of the section, pressing down lightly, commanding her attention. "From here on out, you will have no more tears."

"You can't promise that." She bit into the orange, ducking her head, savoring the flavor as another stupid tear spilled down her cheek.

"It is my duty to ensure it."

She sighed, keeping her head down as she chewed. The one thing she wasn't was a pretty crier. She had a tendency to swell and blotch that defied any semblance of attractive. She swallowed the orange, focused on the snap on his jeans and said, "Deuce?"

"Yes"

"This whole courting thing would go a lot better if you stopped reminding me what a burden you find me."

"A mate is not a burden." He pressed another section of orange to her lips.

She took it in her hand, running her fingers over its familiar shape. "I've got news for you. When you fall back on words like responsibility and duty all the time, you're talking about a burden."

"How does a human talk when courting?"

"He talks of love and beauty and softer emotions."

His hand slid up her spine, wrapped in the fall of her hair and tugged. Through her horror that he would see her blotchy face and swollen eyes, she had to admit to a thrill. There was something fundamentally erotic about the implied mastery in the gesture.

"Pretty words do not keep a mate safe and happy," he informed her.

"Safe isn't all it's cracked up to be, and happy is a relative concept."

"It will be a very relative concept for you."

She could tell he meant that. The first thing she'd noticed about Deuce a year ago was his single-mindedness when he wanted something. Her grandfather had come home many times from business deals swearing at the man's stubbornness. Deuce's dark eyes roved over her face. He frowned, clearly not happy with what he saw.

"You will not cry anymore."

"Excuse me?" She'd just admitted to herself that she wasn't a pretty crier, but she'd be damned if she'd have someone point that out to her. "I'll cry whenever I damn well feel like it."

"I do not like that you swear, and crying damages you. You will not do it anymore." He leaned down. She pressed back into the unrelenting wall of his shoulder. His lips brushed her lids with the delicacy of a butterfly. Immediately the hot burning ache left her eyes. She touched her under-eye area. It was flat and cool rather than puffy and hot. "What did you do?"

"I removed the irritation."

She should have been mad, but what woman wouldn't want a cure for the "after-cry uglies"? "Thank you, but next time, ask."

He shook his head at her, his black hair shimmering with shades of blue in the lamplight. She took that to mean he did not agree that he needed her permission.

"Your food grows cold." He set her back on the bed. The plates rattled on the tray. The delicious odors brought her hunger back with a vengeance. She reached for the tray but he beat her to it. Settling it over her lap, he arranged the sliced orange to the side, in the perfect spot to be aesthetically pleasing. In another of those graceful moves that defied logic, he plumped two pillows behind her back. He was fussing over her like she was an invalid. "I'm not helpless."

He cocked an eyebrow at her as he took the throw off the bottom of the bed and draped it over her feet and legs below the tray. "You are not strong."

"Yet."

He paused. "You will never have the strength of the Chosen."

She picked up her knife and fork again. "I've managed to survive this long without it. I imagine I'll make another fifty years or so."

Again, that shake of the head. He motioned to her plate. "Eat."

Her knee-jerk reaction was to say she was done. She resisted because that would have been counterproductive. She stabbed her fork into the salad instead. The fork hit the bottom of the bowl with a clank.

Deuce sighed. "You are angry again."

"I don't take well to being ordered around."

He nodded. "So you have said. Eat please."

She would have told him that tacking a please onto the end of an order didn't really change it from an order, but she was too hungry and there wasn't any point in arguing with him.

About one-fifth of the way through the meal she was full. A truly depressing state as her taste buds weren't nearly done with their orgy. She put her knife and fork down and wiped her mouth with her napkin.

Deuce frowned at her. "That is all you want?"

"No, but it's all that will fit right now."

There was a pause and then he nodded. The tray was removed and set on the floor. Deuce held his hand out for the napkin. She very deliberately held it high before dropping it into his palm.

"You are still angry."

"I don't like being treated like a child."

"I was not aware I was doing that."

"Really?"

"Really." He stood there beside the bed, so big and disgustingly strong that he made her aware of every weakness, every pain. Every way she wasn't what she needed to be.

"Don't you have friends to visit, feeding to do?"

"My first priority is to see to my mate."

"Consider me seen to."

Between the food and the fluids he had given her last night, she felt revitalized. Not her old self, but stronger than she could remember. Strong enough to do what needed to be done.

He folded his arms across his chest. "I do not understand your mood."

The muscles in his arms bulged enticingly. She licked her lips and dropped her gaze, only to be seduced by his washboard abs. She knew exactly how he'd taste if she ran her tongue over those hills and valleys, explored the depression of his navel, followed that trail of hair as it disappeared beneath the waistband of his jeans.

"It's not necessary that you understand." She dragged her gaze to the safety of his. "It's only necessary that you respect it."

"I cannot respect what I do not understand."

"Sure you can."

She could tell his patience was wearing thin by the furrow growing between his brows. "No. I cannot."

Apparently Chosen men were no better than human men when it came to catching a clue. "I want to be alone, Dusan. I just want five minutes of blessed privacy."

"You want me to leave?"

"Yes!"

It might not have been the most polite of answers, but she needed the man — vampire — and his smothering ways gone.

"And if I grant you this privacy, you will be happy?"

"At the least, happier."

"Then five minutes you shall have."

"Five minutes was a figurative term."

His brow arched in that way that suggested she was trying his patience. "You want more?"

"A half hour at least."

"Why?"

She had to think fast. "I want to use the facilities and bathe."

His expression didn't relax but there was a lightening of the energy around him. "That sounds reasonable."

And if he didn't find it reasonable, did that mean he wouldn't allow it?

He flicked the throw back and slid his big arms under her thighs and back. His scent surrounded her as he lifted her up. She refused to throw her arms around his neck and further his belief that she was helpless. Instead, she wedged her elbow into his gut and folded her hands across her chest. "What are you doing?"

The smile that twitched the corner of his mouth was about as irritating as the arrogance he wore as easily as others wore clothes. "Carrying you to the facilities."

"I could walk."

"Yes."

"But?" There was always a but with him.

"I would not have the pleasure of you in my arms or," his gaze dropped to her bunched arms, "the delightful view of your breasts."

She looked down. Her breasts were all but pushed out of the loose neck of the shirt. She yanked the material, swearing when it wouldn't budge, ending by relying on the stretch of the soft material to keep covered. "Pervert."

He laughed, a soft chuckle that bounced her lightly. "No male, human or Chosen, would look away from such beauty."

Her body, always on high alert with him, pulsed an invitation. His eyes seemed to see right through the shirt to the flesh beneath, and he licked his lips. Her nipples peaked and ached. Her breath came up short. She closed her eyes and thought of all the women that tongue had touched. As a cooling agent, it was only mildly effective. This close to him, her body only cared about one thing. "Oh for heaven's sake!"

She didn't know if she said that aloud or was projecting, but the smile he'd been teasing her with burst to full bloom, drenching his handsome face in a sexual flood of promise as he let her slide down the length of his body.

She could only stare as her feet hit the floor. It simply wasn't fair that any man should look like that. With his finger, he tipped her mouth closed, male satisfaction tingeing the humor in his grin. He put his big hands on her shoulders and turned her toward the bathroom. "I will be outside if you need me."

Her brain finally clicked back into gear. Outside? That was never going to work. She ducked from under his hands and turned around, one hand on the door to steady herself.

"Do you have hearing that matches your sense of smell?"

He reached forward, brushing a long spiral curl from her cheek. "Yes."

"Then no way in hell does standing outside the door constitute privacy."

"Why?"

"Because all I'll be thinking about is what you're imagining as you listen."

His finger traced down the line of her jaw, over her collarbone, between the swell of her breasts to the bottom of her breastbone before pausing. He held her gaze with his as the pressure increased. His fingers folded, turned and then opened under her breast, lifting it up and out. "You could imagine instead that it was my hands on you instead of yours." He squeezed her breast, letting it glide back until he caught the tip between his fingers. "I would like to bathe you."

Heat flooded her cheeks, her knees went weak, and that fast, she was wet and ready for him. He did nothing more than hold her breast suspended by the nipple, letting the weight and her movement determine the stimulation. She leaned back, her breath catching at the stab of pleasure that shot straight to her groin. His smile faded. Lust filled his expression and the air around them. His and hers. His grip tightened. Fire chased the pleasure as she gasped, "I don't think I'd get much bathing done."

"But your pleasure would be great."

It already was. She bit her lip and closed her eyes against the potency of his allure. "I really want a bath."

He released her breast but not her gaze. "You are strong enough for this?"

She glanced into the bathroom at the decadent shower stall, and lastly the window between the toilet and the stall. "Absolutely."

"And you will not be able to relax if I stand outside?"

She shook her head no.

He hesitated, brushed his hair back off his shoulder with a sharp movement and then nodded. "Then I grant you your privacy."

Relief washed through her in a wave she had to struggle to contain. "Thank you."

"But—" He frowned at her, clearly not comfortable with leaving her alone.

"What?"

"You will promise to call if you have need."

"You just tell me what button to hit on the intercom and you've got a deal."

His eyes lit with humor and the stern lines of his face softened. He was laughing at her. She just knew it. She was absolutely certain when he tilted her head up and brought his down. His breath hit her cheek, then her lips, before his mouth settled over hers. Hunger rose between them, fast and furious. His mouth mated with hers, his soul reached for hers. He pulled her hard against his groin, the thick edge of his cock digging into her hip. His mouth separated a hair from hers, leaving her drowning in a wave of longing that threatened to pull her under.

"You have only to think of me, and I will come."

Chapter Eleven

∞

You have only to think of me, and I will come.

The promise lingered long after Deuce left the room, hanging on the moist air like a threat. Eden put all the energy she could into blocking her thoughts as she turned on the shower jets. The last thing she needed was for him to come in here any sooner than they'd agreed. She could only hope the baby didn't wake, and that Deuce took her mental block as a sign she didn't want him doing a peeping Tom routine during her shower.

Steam fogged the room. She threw the switch for the fans. They came on with a satisfying rumble. She needed as much noise as possible to cover her escape. She glanced up at the small window. Assuming she could get it open. The basement windows at her grandfather's house looked similar and those could be popped out. If luck was with her, so could these. She just needed enough height to get leverage. She tossed a towel on the toilet seat and grabbed the stainless steel trash can. The only thing in it was a couple of tissues she'd used the day before. She dumped them on the floor and flipped the can upside down on the toilet seat. She almost knocked it off twice before she found her balance, but once high enough, she checked for wires around the outside of the window. As absurd as it sounded for something as all-powerful as a vampire to have a security system, she could see Deuce investing in one. He had that intensity that suggested he'd be a stickler for all the little details.

To her surprise, there weren't any wires that she could see. She held her breath as she turned the locks on the window, wincing as they clicked. No alarm went off. No warning cry rang out. So far so good. She eased the window open. A cold shot of air blew into the bath, sending the whorls of steam retreating for cover. She unhooked the restraining chain and popped the window free. A stronger gust of winter air followed the first, sprinkling her face and arms with a dusting of snow as she pulled the window out of the frame. Holding onto the casement with her left hand, she braced herself as she lowered the window to the floor. The garbage can teetered on the toilet. She froze, letting her arm take most of her weight for a moment while she adjusted her stance. Nervous sweat dampened her underarms and face, spreading to her hands. She tightened her grip, not needing a slip at this moment. Her heart pounded and her breath fought to clear the clench of her throat. She had to do this. She had to escape. Jalina's life depended on it.

Slowly, she straightened. Adrenaline was rushing through her system so fast she couldn't catch her breath. Every nerve ending stretched taut, waiting for the slightest clue that she was about to be discovered. Indecision took advantage of the hesitation, wiggling between conviction and possibility. Maybe there was another way. She shoved it aside on the next gust of winter cold.

This was the only way. Deuce would never let her leave. He'd fight to the death to keep her safe, but he didn't know what he was up against. Didn't know her grandfather or just how sick he was. Clay Lavery would do everything in his considerable power, use every one of his high-placed Coalition connections to get her back, because he thought she held the secret to his immortality. She could work with that. As long as she could keep his focus on her, convince him that Jalina had died due to an inability to feed, she could adopt the role of discouraged prisoner, convince him that she'd exhausted her last hope before recapture. And in time, get far enough below his radar so that she could kill the son of a bitch.

She shifted her weight cautiously. Standing on tiptoe, she dug the snowdrift away from the opening. The fluffy white flakes melted on her hands. She didn't fool herself that killing her grandfather would stop the Coalition, but it would end the Coalition's path to her daughter. Lavery was a suspicious, cautious man. He hadn't let anyone know she was pregnant. She didn't know if that meant he'd been planning on double crossing his cohorts or if he was holding out for a grandstand moment, but she was willing to bet that, after her escape, those who'd cared for her during her pregnancy were now dead. Clay Lavery did not tolerate humiliation or failure.

The cold air on her wet flesh bit deeply. She ignored the pain as long as she could, but eventually she was forced to tuck her fingers under her arms to bring back the circulation. Precious seconds ticked by as she warmed them, seconds she couldn't spare but had to, or risk triggering Deuce's ability to feel her distress. She did not need him swooping in to cure what he'd regard as a "need" in his mate. Not now.

As soon as the pain left her fingers, Eden hooked her arms over the edge of the sill and pulled herself up, ignoring the flash of guilt at deceiving him that stabbed her conscience. Deuce's ability to ignore the truth was only exceeded by his determination to cure her. But the reality was, she was dying, and no amount of hope or determination was going to undo what had been done. Her body was about finished. But no matter what, she wasn't going to die with her daughter at risk. Which meant she had to leave now. Before Deuce shared "fluids" with her again. Before she weakened further. Not only in body but in determination. The man was a master at illusion. His biggest illusion being that they had a future.

Now. The soft feminine whisper broke into her mind out of nowhere, sliding under her defenses like an old friend, reaffirming her belief in what she was doing.

Eden pulled herself up to the sill, gasping with the effort, hooking her elbows on the outside. She forced more of her body through the narrow opening, for once grateful she'd lost so much weight this year. It was going to be a tight fit. She almost didn't make it. Her hips hung up at their widest point. The cold stung her cheeks and numbed her hands. She pulled harder. The thin jersey of the shirt and shorts were no match for the cold metal. Pain sliced up her side as she pushed herself forward. More than she thought she'd be able to mask, but as her groan welled, a cloud appeared before her, still containing that feminine touch.

She slipped into it, grateful for the protection. One more heave, and then she was free. She landed facefirst in a drift. She lay in the snow, enjoying the blessed peace that came between leaving the heat, and her body recognizing the cold of the outside. It was going to be a hell of a walk down the mountain, but she wouldn't die. She knew that. Not of cold or exposure, at least. If the cloud stayed, it would be a cakewalk. If it didn't, well, all she had to do was survive the pain until she got close enough to her goal to end the game. If she was lucky, her grandfather's men were as close as Deuce feared.

She crawled to the hedge and crouched behind it to get her bearings, standing on the hem of the shirt to protect her feet.

The night was cold, colder than it had felt when she'd left the bathroom. Cold enough to have trees creaking as they swayed in the slight breeze. The moon was nearly full, casting a clear, pale light over everything. As far as she could see there was nothing but black sky carpeted with a sprinkling of stars. It was a beautiful night, damn it all to hell. She really needed to work on timing these escapes better. Either that or make sure she had access to a weather channel. With such clear weather, and a moon hanging so brightly in the sky, it was going to be a bitch and a half getting across the yard without being seen.

A bitter wind blew. She shivered, but otherwise held herself perfectly still. This wasn't going to be as easy as getting out of her grandfather's compound. She'd known every aspect of that security system, known what to watch out for. Her primary role as his hostess for his influential friends, before everything changed, had demanded it. But here, everything was an unknown and all it would take was one wrong move and her plan would be over. She couldn't let that happen. Jalina had to be protected at all costs.

Eden worked her way down the hedge line until she reached the corner of the house, just behind the porch railing. She risked a quick peek at the porch itself. Empty. Thank goodness. She'd definitely take that as a positive sign. Dropping to her hands and knees, keeping her shoulder as close as she could to the latticework bottom, she crept along the edge of the porch until she reached the end. Tucking herself as small as possible under a cedar hedge, she parted the branches and looked out. And promptly swore.

An entire compound fanned out in front of her, straddling a main road which branched off into many smaller ones. Small wooden buildings dotted the snowbanked roads at regular intervals, spilling warm pools of welcoming light into the cold night from some of the windows. It was like a scene from a Norman Rockwell painting. If she discounted the fact that the occupants of those houses were more associated with horror than with cozy. In front of many of the houses were powerful-looking SUVs. She was going to need one of those.

The house to the far right of the first side road had a nice SUV in front of it. There was no light streaming from the windows and the house on the left only had a light on in the back left corner, which hopefully meant no one was home. It was her best shot. The only question was, how was she going to get to it? There was no cover between here and there. Just snowdrifts bathed in moonlight. She could cut back behind the house and try to follow the tree line down, but that would take time she didn't have. She'd already used up ten of her thirty minutes. No. She was going to have to follow the road and try to use the high snowbanks as cover. She untucked her feet and scouted her course.

"You're not going to make it."

The comment came from above her. It was made in the calmest, most conversational tone she'd ever heard and when she looked up, she knew why. Dak stood on the porch leaning against the railing as if he didn't have a care in the world, his gun over his shoulder. The only hint that this was more than a casual conversation to him was the intensity with which he watched her.

"I could if you pretended you never saw me."

He nodded as if acknowledging her point as she stood. "But that's not going to happen."

She kind of figured he'd feel that way. Desperation welled out of resolve. She couldn't fail. She had to at least try. She glanced at the road, and all those SUVs—so close yet so far.

The porch creaked as Dak shifted his weight. "If you bolt, I'll run you to ground, and Deuce wouldn't like that."

"Believe it or not, I'm not overly concerned with what Deuce likes."

He nodded. "Seeing you out here in next to nothing has a way of driving that point home, but that will change."

She followed his gaze. Her shirt, wet from the melted snow, was clinging to her breasts. She folded her arms across her chest. "No, it won't."

He smiled, revealing strong white teeth and larger than normal canines. "I believe you mean that."

Keeping his amber eyes locked on her, he ducked his chin and spoke into the small mike on his shoulder. "I've got her."

There was a pause as he listened to whoever was on the other end. "Will do." He braced the rifle against the rail. "Deuce is on his way."

He shrugged out of his coat and passed it to her. "If you're going to run, you might want to do it now."

She took the heavy leather coat. "Would there be any point?"

"No." He watched her as she shrugged it on. "But sometimes I find humans have a need to indulge in pointless efforts."

The coat was warm from his body. His scent clung to the material. It wasn't unpleasant, but it struck her as wrong. The desperation inside her rose to tears. She clenched the excess leather sleeves in her hands and tried the truth. "I need to leave."

"Deuce will never allow it."

"Why? Why does this matter to him so much? He's got his daughter."

He nodded toward someone behind her, his "You'll have to ask him that" coincided with the "Voice's" scream of *Run!*

She knew it was too late for that even as she turned. At first she saw nothing, but then the night seemed to shimmer and Deuce was there. Twenty feet away and closing fast, his dark gray shirt and black pants blending into the shadows, striding across the snow without sinking into it, grace and anger in every step. His long hair fanned around his shoulders, whipping in a wind that surrounded only him.

"Oh shit." The cloud winked away, leaving her alone with her fear, and one unhappy vamp.

Dak picked up his rifle. "That about sums it up."

"How does he just appear out of midair like that?"

"Illusion."

And then Deuce was there in front of her, no illusion, his anger pounding her like blows. She took a step back. He caught her arm and pulled her toward him. She closed her eyes and braced herself. The politeness of his "Thank you" when she expected violence had her opening her eyes. He was speaking to Dak, who nodded and said, "Any time."

Eden tugged her arm. Deuce didn't release her, and when he turned to her, his anger pummeled her again. Though his face remained impassive and his demeanor calm she had no doubt she was dealing with one ticked-off Chosen.

"Take off the coat."

She looked down at his hand on her arm. "You'll need to let me go first." She was rather pleased with how calm she sounded, when in reality she was scared spitless.

His black eyes held hers a long moment. His grip lightened on her arm. "If you run, I will catch you."

She didn't doubt that. In the flowing shirt and tight black jeans, the man's muscles were very evident. With or without super powers, she had no doubt he'd catch her. She pulled her arm free. "I'll keep that in mind."

She shrugged out of the coat. Deuce tucked her into the shelter of his side before she could miss the warmth. The coat was yanked from her hands with a rough jerk and tossed to Dak, who stood on the porch with a strange smile on his face. And then they were moving. At least Deuce was moving. She was more or less hoisted along in his wake. She tried to put her foot down as they rounded the corner, but landed on a stick. The pain made her gasp. Deuce swore and without breaking stride lifted her into his arms. She grabbed for his neck as he took the first step, expecting to be jostled. She should have known better. Men who glided didn't jostle. Deuce flowed over the steps the same way he glided over the ground. The front door opened. She had a glimpse of Harley's darkly handsome face and then they were moving through the interior with blurring speed. There was only time to gather a brief impression of high ceilings and dark wood before they were heading down the stairs. There was less light there, the atmosphere darker. More in tune with Deuce's mood.

Fear began to overwhelm Eden's bravado. If her aborted escape had taught her one thing, it was that no one here would interfere with Deuce. At least when it came to her. The second door on the left opened. The deep maroon and muted golds of Deuce's apartment beckoned like a haven. She turned her face into his chest and waited. Once that door closed behind them, anything was possible.

The door clicked shut.

She could hear the shower running. Deuce didn't stop. The sound grew louder. Another door opened and she was surrounded by warm steam. She took a steadying breath, and noted that the bathroom window was now closed.

"We're in the bathroom."

"The scene of your crime." Deuce lowered her feet to the floor. It was damp and warm from the prolonged running of the water.

"I can leave whenever I want."

"No," he anchored his hand in the hair at her nape, tipping her head back, locking his gaze to hers the same way he locked her body to his, "you cannot."

The urge to accept his decree pounded at her. "Then I'm a prisoner and have a perfect right to escape. Either way, it's not a crime."

"You played on my trust."

"I did what I had to."

"You will not try again."

The statement echoed in her mind. He was influencing her. She yanked her gaze free of his and put more energy into blocking her thoughts. "I'll do what I have to."

"We will talk of this later. "

"There's nothing to talk about."

"You abandoned your mate and your child and went practically naked and defenseless into the night." His grip worked deeper into her hair. "We have much to talk about."

"The only person potentially harmed was me, and as an adult, I have a right to do what I will with my body."

"You are wrong."

His free hand slashed down. Warm air struck her midriff. She grabbed for the edges of her sliced shirt. "What are you doing?"

His hand, with that elongated nail, slashed down again. "You have his scent all over you."

Her shorts slid down her legs. She made a grab for them and missed. "You have got to be kidding me."

The hard edge to his "No" silenced her protest. She didn't know much about Deuce, but that hard edge packed into that one syllable was a language anyone could understand. This was one pissed-off vamp. She tried placating. "You want me to shower?"

"No."

Between one blink and the next, his clothing was gone, and she was left gaping at the sheer perfection of his chest. Padded with muscle, topped by broad, equally muscular shoulders, the view was any woman's dream. Her pussy flooded with moisture. She had a thing for men with hair on their chests, and Deuce had just enough to tempt a woman to explore to see how it would feel against her palms, to wonder how it would feel against her sensitive nipples as he came over her.

She visually traced the path of that hair down over the hills and valleys of his washboard abs, rimmed the edge of his navel and stopped dead at the solid jut of his cock. Despite the danger of the situation, despite her determination to hold her own, a needy whimper slipped past her control. He was hard. Heavy with the strength of his desire, his thick cock stretched down his thigh. The broad head darker than the rest, shiny with the first drop of pre-come. She knew exactly how he'd fill her mouth if she just bent down. How he'd taste, how he'd feel. How he'd satisfy. Dear God, she wanted him.

He caught her hand before she clasped his cock. With a shake of his head, he dragged her into the stall.

"What? Now you're going to tell me mates don't touch?"

His big body blocked the jets from hitting her front, but three of the showerheads had a free-for-all on her back. He reached over her head. "That would be a lie."

"Then why can't I touch you?"

He looked down at her, his black eyes swirling red flames and emotions she couldn't name. "You have not earned the pleasure."

"Earned the pleasure?"

"Yes." He stepped forward, crowding her back. Warm water poured over her head. She held her breath until he allowed her out of the flow.

"I'm supposed to be grateful to you for the pleasure of touching you?" There was a clunk of plastic against plastic.

"Yes." He rubbed his hands together. Foam appeared and then he was working it into her hair. Though she could feel the violence swirling through him, his touch was nothing more than efficient.

"I'm not some little plaything for you to amuse yourself with."

He crowded her back into the spray, massaging water through her hair as he said, "If you were, it would be much more convenient."

"Go to hell!" She even halfway meant it.

He tipped her chin up. She knew she looked like a drowned rat with her hair plastered to her head and her too skinny body. "Only if you go with me."

"You take this togetherness thing too seriously."

He turned her around. This time when he reached over her head, he retrieved the shower gel. A scent reminiscent of the ocean filled the stall. "The choice was yours."

"So maybe I'm having trouble with some aspects of it."

"Then this should be discussed."

Like she didn't already know how that would go. "You'll just tell me that's how it is between mates."

He turned off the upper shower jet. "Brace your hands against the wall."

"Why?"

"Because I have told you to." His fingers traced a random series of lines down her back. Her scars. He was retracing her scars from her grandfather's whipping.

"And that's enough?"

"Yes."

She did, but not because he told her to. She did it because when he started the gentle massage on her shoulders, she needed the support. He had wonderful hands. "Why are you being so nice to me?"

"You are my mate."

"Whom you are very angry with."

His hands paused in their soothing motion. "Yes."

"So?"

"It is my duty to care for you."

"Even when you're angry?"

He worked the tight knot of muscles between her shoulder blades. "At all times."

She couldn't conceive of that. "Are you trying to tell me that even if I get you screaming at the moon angry, you won't do anything about it?"

"Something will be done."

"But you won't fight with me?"

"Mates do not fight, any more than the Chosen get 'screaming at the moon angry'."

"What do they get?"

"Displeased."

She had to see his face. She turned. His expression left her no doubt. He was completely serious. He really thought he could have a relationship with anyone, her even, and never get angry. "Dusan?"

His brow rose, while his hands rested heavily on her shoulders. His eyes stayed on her face. She had his full attention. "What?"

"You are so setting yourself up for a fall."

He blinked the water away from his eyes. "I do not think so."

She brushed his hair off his shoulder, feeling his anger and his determination to control it. He flinched. She pulled her hand back, curling it into a fist against her hip. She shouldn't be hurt that he didn't want her touch anymore. She had tricked him and betrayed his trust. But she was. Which just went to prove that everything about her having a relationship with him was irrational. "Holding all that emotion inside is bad for you."

He reached up and squeezed more soap into his hands. "The Chosen do not get emotional."

It was her turn to blink, and not because water was getting into her eyes. He was a very intense man and intense men had intense emotions. "You're sure about that?"

"Positive. Turn around."

When she didn't immediately respond, he turned her, his hands sliding pleasantly on her upper arms.

"Aren't we done yet?"

"No."

"We're going to run out of hot water."

"It heats on demand. Now, stay."

"Why?'"

"I can still smell him on you."

"And that upsets you?"

"Yes."

"But you aren't emotional."

"No."

She reached up and took the gel from the shelf. What a crock. "It will go faster if I do it myself."

He took the bottle out of her hands. "I will finish what I started."

And he did, starting at her shoulders and working down, massaging the soap into her skin, his touch sure and soothing, lingering in those areas where the most sensitive of nerves hid, bringing them to vivid life.

She braced back against the wall. "How do you do this to me?"

He palmed her buttocks, his big hands easily encompassing each globe. "We are mates." His thumbs slipped between, riding the soap bubbles, skating the tight bud of her anus before coming back to rest against it. "It is right that we enjoy each other."

She twisted away from the wall and his touch. "Not like this. Not when you're angry." Not with her as some sort of helpless puppet to which he held the strings.

As if her denial flipped a hidden switch, his calm disappeared. His "Yes, now" was a primitive growl. Almost as primitive as the hunger that narrowed his eyes and thinned his mouth. He yanked her against his chest. His lips met hers. Hot and demanding, calling forth her own hunger. Equally primitive. Equally demanding. She wrapped her hand in his hair, pulling him closer, arching into his chest, rubbing her nipples into the delightful abrasion of his hair, moaning when he caught her ribs and took up the motion.

"Yes." He pulled his mouth from hers to kiss her eyes, her cheeks. "Moan for me, Edie mine. Let me hear your desire."

As if she had any choice when he cupped her buttocks in his hands and ran his lips down her neck, nipping at the skin as he went, pressing his lips hard against the pulse at the base of her throat, summoning everything feminine and needy in her to screaming attention. He arched her farther over his arm. The pain in her abdomen blended with the wave of pleasure. One hand supported her head as he took the hard aching point of her nipple into his mouth. The tiny culmination pulled the moan he listened for from her lips. Water ran off his shoulders and slashed her face. The pounding of the shower was lost in the pounding of her heart. She needed him. So much.

She yanked on his hair. His laugh buffeted her breast. She fought his hold, his restraint. He merely gave her more, torturing her with his calm in the face of her desire. She let go of his hair and wedged her hand between them as he tortured her breasts. His cock bumped her fingers. She twisted her wrist. He felt so good in her hand. Hard, strong pulsing with life. Promise. She milked him slowly, the catch in his breathing music to her ears. Pre-come spilled over her hand. He was as affected by her as she was by him.

"Do you hunger, my heart?" Deuce asked in a voice that breathed through her mind, her body, caressing her nerves with the ache of a touch.

She did. She needed him like she needed the other half of her soul. It didn't make sense and it wasn't comfortable, but it was true. However, she wasn't a helpless puppet he was going to control by the strength of her desire. She tossed her wet hair out of her eyes, asking in a voice she wouldn't have recognized as hers, so husky was it with want. "How about you? Do you want me, Dusan?"

His teeth grazed the upper curve of her breast. His cock throbbed against her thigh. "Always."

"Show me how much."

He froze. She tucked her chin and looked. He was looking back up at her. His eyes flared with something wild. His lips drew back from his teeth, exposing the fangs she'd never before seen clearly. Her heart leapt. She wanted to be fucked, not sucked. She cupped his face in her hands. "Or better yet, let me show you."

He didn't let her go, or otherwise move. He seemed quite content to keep her as she was, bent backward with her breasts thrust up for his delectation. Or bite, she realized as he scraped those scary fangs over her breasts.

"Deuce, let me up."

"I like you like this."

She had no doubt he did. And so did she on one level, but she also believed in starting as she meant to go on. And she did not intend to be any vamp's sex toy. "You said it was your duty to give me whatever I need."

He very slowly, very deliberately licked a drop of water from the slope of her chest. "It is."

"I need to touch you," she squeezed his cock as best she could, "taste you."

He shuddered and closed those wild eyes. "You hunger." When he opened them, some of his control was back.

"Yes." And it was true. Every cell in her tired, battered body ached for him. His scent, his touch, it all seemed to fuel the need for more. Part of it was desire, but part of it was so much more, as if her very cells needed the touch of his. That bonding he'd spoken of.

He slowly eased her upright, dragging her body down his, letting her feel every ridge and hollow of his well-honed muscle, his forearm across her back a band of steel. Everything about him was pure, primitive male, but not once did he hold her too hard. And she knew that it would be very easy for him to do so. As soon as she got close enough, she leaned into his chest, testing the resiliency of his pecs with her teeth, smiling at his muted groan. His hands caught in her hair. "Do not. You will make me lose control."

She liked the idea of that—of him losing control and her being in charge of it. "We wouldn't want that, would we?" she murmured against his skin. She lapped at the light red mark she'd left. His fingers in her hair twitched. The sense of urgency surrounding them increased. She didn't know if it was his need or her need, but as the aura built, it was as if there was a third party in control, urging them on, fanning the flames of their desire.

She bit Deuce again, harder this time, wanting to laugh as his head fell back and his groan swirled through her mind, expanding into the room. She definitely liked him like this. She tried to suck more skin into her mouth, wanting to mark him as hers, but it was stretched too tightly over the muscle beneath. She poked experimentally. Damn, there was no give to the man. She rested her fingertip on the ledge of his collarbone and looked up, way up to his face. The heat and hunger in his gaze burned the pithy remark she'd been going to make right off her tongue.

Oh God, no man had ever looked at her like that. Like he'd die if he didn't have her. Like she was the one thing that stood between him and hell. His gaze followed the path of her tongue over her lips with the intensity of a touch. Her lips tingled and her womb clenched as her pussy unfurled and ached with a desperate entreaty. The scent of her arousal floated on the steam. Deuce's nostrils flared. The skin over his cheekbones tightened as he used his grip on her head to urge her down. "Take from me what you need."

He'd said that to her before, with that same cadence, as if it were part of a greater ritual.

She followed the urging of his hands, knowing what he needed, what they both wanted. She nipped her way down his chest, enjoying the jerk of his skin under each little caress, letting her nails drag over the ridges and valleys of his abdomen. Water sluiced off her back as she knelt. As she slid down, the broad head of his cock slid up over her stomach, and between her breasts. She paused with her lips just inches from the tip, letting her breath slide over him like the rivulets of water pouring over her shoulders. His heavy shaft pulsed, a bead of fluid appeared at the tip, centering the hunger within her. One of his hands slid around to cup the back of her head while the other grasped his cock, angling it for her pleasure.

"Take what you need."

The rasp of his deep voice wrapped around her desire, drawing her with the force of his hand toward that single pearly drop, knowing there would be more, as much as she needed. She touched the tip of her tongue to the tip of his penis, closing her eyes as his incredible taste hit her system. So good. So damn good.

He pushed forward, she pulled back into his hands, teasing them both with the tiny connection, knowing he wouldn't allow it for long.

No sooner did she have the thought then his grip on her skull tightened and he pulled her forward, holding her steady for the brush of his cock over the sensitive surface of her lips. The first touch was barren of what she craved, but as more of his come welled, his cock slid easier, painting her mouth with the flavor of desire. He pulled his cock back until it pulsed just out of reach, stroking it as he ordered, "Lick it off."

She did, keeping her movements as delicate as she could, wanting to please him, but also herself.

His cock was right before her, fat with lust, heavy with need. "Put your hands at your sides."

"Why?"

"Because I want it."

He always felt that was a reason. "Maybe I don't."

His rhythm faltered. "Do not challenge me."

"Why not?" She slid her hands up the inside of his thighs, dragging her nails to see if he enjoyed that as much as the other. His whole body shuddered and his fist clenched on his thick shaft. Oh, he definitely liked that.

His "I cannot maintain control if you challenge me" was a guttural testament to how tenuous his control was.

"Maybe I don't want you controlled." She caught the tip of his penis with her lips and sucked delicately as she rasped her nails across his heavy balls. Deuce swore in a language she didn't understand. He was losing it. To her. She cupped his balls and squeezed as she kissed the fat head. "Maybe I want to see you wild."

His growl was as wildly primitive as she could have wanted. The air swirled with power and lust and then his cock was pushing at her mouth with relentless pressure, demanding admittance as he tugged her hair, forcing her head back. She gasped at the dual assault, every nerve ending leaping with an ecstatic "Yes" as his shaft pushed past her lips. The force of his thrust drove her back. His hand caught her head, protecting her as his body followed hers into the shower wall. His free hand slammed against the tile above her head, catching his weight as his penis spread her lips. Water sprayed his chest before rebounding into her face.

She had only a second to catch his expression before the spray forced her to close her eyes. Without sight, her other senses surged forward into the almost forbidding mantle of power that welled off him. She caught his thighs with her palms, trying to push him back as he overwhelmed her. Immediately, that sense of power surged against her resistance. She jerked back into the shower wall so hard she could feel the individual tiles biting into her back. She wanted him wild, but this was more than wild. This was Deuce at his most primitive...and this was scary. Through the violence of his need came a stroke of calm.

"Take what you need, my mate." The familiar command caught her panic and gentled it. She opened her mouth, accepting his dominance as he thrust his cock within. Immediately, the aggression she feared tapered off into the urgent drive of desire. His hand slid lower, applying pressure at the base of her skull, tilting her head back. His cock slid easier, deeper. "That's it. Take me."

She didn't have any choice. He leaned in as he pulled her forward. Her lips stretched painfully around the thick shaft as she struggled not to choke. His hand brushed her neck and the tight muscles relaxed. She took him more easily. "More now."

More? She opened her eyes and looked down at the thick cock buried in her mouth and the whole lot left over. She couldn't believe she'd taken what she had. She shook her head, her teeth grazing his shaft as she did. He thrust to the back of her throat. The water pounded on them, around them. There scents mingled in the moist air. His cock pumped in and out of her mouth with a relentless rhythm, demanding something from her. She brought her hands up to his thighs and pushed.

His index finger traced the line of her cheekbone before drawing over the curve of her cheek to trace the corner of her mouth. His hand dipped to wrap around her throat. The gesture was at once intimidating and possessive. "Open for me."

He couldn't mean what she thought he meant. He leaned forward. She dug her nails into his thighs and pushed back. He groaned. Before she could blink the water out of her eyes, he had her hands trapped above her head. He held her there, half-kneeling and half-suspended while he stood above her, his hair hanging in wet ropes around his massive shoulders, looking down at her with pure satisfaction on his starkly handsome face. Her body jerked with the sensual pleasure of being helpless in his arms.

"I like you like this even more." He withdrew his cock slowly until just the tip rested on the shelf of her lip. She didn't move, didn't dare breathe, waiting in an agony of anticipation for what he'd do next. His foot worked between her legs. Something hard and round nudged her labia, working forward.

"Hold still now. " Her very womb wrenched within her body as he worked his cock back into her mouth at the same time his toe nudged her swollen clitoris. His cock hit the back of her throat and panic struck through her desire, yet even that seemed to egg on her lust. She tried to turn her head, but couldn't.

"Hold still," he repeated.

It took everything she had to obey. His hand cupped her throat while his toe rubbed delicately on her distended clit. "You will submit to me, Edie."

It wasn't a matter of submission—it was a matter of physics, and this was never going to work. She lashed his cock with her tongue. Sucking as best she could, trying to rush him to completion. His deep groan told her it was working. Through the spray she glanced at his face. His features were hard with desire. His eyes glittered with intent, the black depths swirling with red lights. His toe flicked her clit again. Too quickly, too lightly. She stretched to make a deeper connection. His laugh swirled through the mist. When she looked up again, he was waiting for her.

"Make me want to give it to you." It was a dare.

Did he think she couldn't? She tugged at her hands. He shook his head. "With just your mouth."

She narrowed her eyes in a glare that just added a hint of a smile to his challenge.

"Giving up already?"

Not likely. She bobbed her head on his cock in tiny increments, before frowning up at him.

"You want me to play fair."

She nodded.

He sighed as if it were some hardship and pulled back until his cock head rested just inside her mouth. "Better?"

Yes, that was definitely better. She had leverage now and she had every intention of using it to her advantage. She bobbed and sucked and lapped. She probed the tiny slit in the head and swirled her tongue around the surrounding flesh. He moaned and twitched, but didn't come. She sucked harder, worked him deeper.

"So good, Edie mine," he groaned as he pumped into her mouth. "I could fuck your beautiful face forever."

She didn't have forever. Her jaw was aching and she was tiring. She knew she could give up. Let him win. It didn't mean anything. It was just a silly game but she couldn't get his expression out of her mind. That drive to dominate. Even if she wasn't planning on staying his mate forever, she wasn't going to be a second-class citizen to his will, and giving up now would definitely make her that.

Her tooth caught on the flared head of his cock. His whole body jerked. She paused, remembering his reaction when she'd bitten his chest. Very slowly she drew back until his cock slipped almost out, then tilted her head so she could catch his fat cock head on her lip. His disappointed moan was music to her ears. She let his cock pop free of her mouth before catching it on her chin. Holding his gaze, she smiled. Then just as slowly ducked her head, still holding his gaze, and worked him back into her mouth until the broadest part of the spongy head lay nestled between her lips. Very deliberately she pulled her lips back, letting him see the teeth that now imprisoned him. When his breath caught and his nostrils flared, she bit down.

His hips slammed forward, driving her back into the wall. His shout sent whorls of stream fleeing. His hand on her neck held her still as his cock surged past her resistance and into her throat. There was a sensation of extreme pressure. She couldn't breathe but there was no pain. Deuce held her there for a heartbeat—impaled on his cock, groaning as his hips jerked. His shaft pulsed against her lips and in her throat. As if it took everything he had, he pulled back, his cock leaving her throat with a reluctant snap, and then her mouth was flooded with his seed. Her pussy clenched as she hung in his hands, sucking his big cock. The coiled tension exploded into savage bliss as his seed filled her mouth and his scent filled her nostrils.

With every spasm of her orgasming pussy, she drew more and more of his hot seed in as he shuddered and gave her all he had. When she couldn't coax another drop out of him, and the spasms in her pussy had died to gentle waves, she simply held him in her mouth, hanging limply in his arms, too drained to move.

Deuce's breathing slowed from labored to normal. He released her arms and let her drop to her knees, but kept his hand on her neck. He pulled her face between his legs. As water poured over her head, he ordered, "Kiss my balls."

His tone left no room for resistance. She pursed her lips, pressing delicate kisses over the soft skin. There was a metallic squeak and the water stopped. He spread his legs. "That's it. Nice and soft." He directed her attention to the left one. "Now, let me feel your tongue."

She slid her tongue around each orb, working between them. His hand twisted in her hair, pulling her mouth up into his balls, directing her attentions with his touch. She could feel the tension in his grip as she opened her mouth and took one of the soft-hard balls inside. It was a totally submissive posture, and it was turning her on like hell.

His "Good" was a rasp of sound. His "Do the other" barely understandable.

She did, enjoying the knowledge that she was pleasing him. It was her turn to moan as he pulled her away. He stroked her cheek. She looked up at him. His cock rose anew against the backdrop of his hard abs. She licked her lips as a bead of come welled in the tip.

He shook her head slightly to get her attention. She reluctantly switched her focus to his face. "Women of the Chosen attend their mates this way after mating and when a need to pay tribute is required by their mate."

The haze left her world. "Pay tribute?"

"It is an ancient custom."

She sat back. Out of the heat of the moment, it sounded barbaric. "One we'll be breaking with."

His grip on her hair tightened. "It keeps peace among the Chosen mates and reminds all of the natural order. Without it, there would be strife."

"I don't think so."

"On what do you base your objection?"

"It's demeaning."

"Chosen women are honored above all others. They in turn honor their mates this way."

"I don't like it."

Deuce could not believe she would deny this part of her. "You lie."

As if he'd struck her, Edie jerked away. He held her easily, controlling the move so she did not wrench her abdomen. "I do not."

She did. Her pleasure scented the air around them. He did not know why she denied it. "You liked it and would have come again from it, had I allowed you that pleasure."

Her face paled to deathly white and she stared at him with a wounded look in her big blue eyes that said her world had shattered. "That's not true."

He rubbed his cock along her cheek. She shivered in a purely involuntary reaction to the dominant gesture. "You are naturally submissive. It is my pleasure to attend to the needs that brings."

He caught her hand before she could land a punch. "You bastard."

"I do not understand your hurt. It is good that you are this way. It will allow for harmony in our home."

"Because you like to be the one to give the orders?"

That might have been sarcasm in her voice. It did not matter. It did not change the truth. She would need to accept that.

"Yes." He grasped his cock in his hand, and tilted her head back. "It pleases me to see you on your knees, eager for me." He pumped his cock through his hand, not holding back, letting more come flow to the head, noting the stronger scent of her renewed arousal. "Even now your body readies for mine, aches for my seed with as much fervor as I ache to give it to you."

"No."

He could not tell if she was denying him or the reaction of her body. It did not matter. "Yes."

He pulled her closer, close enough that even with her weaker human sense she had to scent him. A quick glance down showed her nipples drawn up diamond-hard. "When you are balanced and it is safe, I am going to spend weeks pleasuring you." He could not wait. Her gasp and the strong scent of arousal told him she couldn't either. "But for now, you will see to this new need you have created."

If human looks could kill he'd be dead. He ignored her displeasure and lifted her into his arms. Bohdan said she could take as much as she needed this time. So far, her body had not protested. It was encouraging.

Her weight was as nothing, a precious burden he could hold forever. She glanced at the window as soon as they cleared the shower stall. He felt her guilty start, followed quickly by a surge of determination as he crossed into the bedroom. She thought to run again. Anger, primitive and wild, rose within, breaking through his forced calm, smashing his patience to bits. She was his. She would accept this, and she would not run.

He dropped her on the bed. Before she could bounce to her feet, he placed his palm on her chest, stretching his fingers up the slope of her breast, pressing in, the round indentations satisfying his need to mark her in a way she would recognize. With his other hand, he turned her head, holding her steady to the angle of his cock. "Taste me."

She kept her lips firmly closed. Water from her hair soaked the pillow, creating a halo of deeper color around her head. He bent his knees slightly, drawing the tip of his penis from one corner of her lips to the other, coating her lips with his seed until they glistened in the low light, one more mark of his possession. He stood, letting his shaft bob against her cheek. With his thumb, he pressed the silky liquid between her lips. Her eyes closed as they always did at the first taste of his seed. Her shudder and the goose bumps that sprang up on her flesh were dead giveaways to her pleasure. "Open your mouth."

She barely parted her lips.

"Wide enough to receive my tribute." Her eyes popped wider than her mouth. "Did you think only women paid tribute?"

Her narrow-eyed glare spoke volumes. He shook his head at her lack of understanding. All things required balance. Even mating.

"I am forbidden to spill my seed other than for your pleasure. Not by my own hand, or by another's, can I be delivered relief from the desire you create. In this way I honor you." He tapped her lip with the tip of his penis. "Stick out your tongue."

As she did, slowly and suspiciously, he told her, "You will not move through this. You will remain still and obedient, and accept my tribute with the respect it should be given." He rested the head of his cock on the tip of her tongue. "Do you understand?"

She nodded. His cock fell to her chest. He let it linger on her breast a moment, dark to light, hard to soft, male to female. He took her hand and brought it to him. "Replace my cock."

Her hands slowly wrapped around his sensitive shaft, each finger feeling like a red-hot flame as she brought him back to her mouth. His cock looked huge as it rested in her hands, even bigger as it settled on her tongue, almost obscuring his view of her temptingly perfect mouth.

"Keep your mouth open," he warned as her lips instinctively closed around the tip. She shot him another glare that was belied by the shiver that took her from head to toe. His mate burned with this act of submission, the flow of her desire perfuming the air around him, filling his balls with the seed she anticipated. He pumped his cock faster, tightening his grip, rushing his climax, eager to fill that hot, anxious mouth with his come, to mark her again in a way that would broadcast to all to whom she belonged. He stroked harder, twisting on the upstroke, rewarding her obedience in the face of her hungry anticipation with a small taste. Her eyes closed and her body shuddered, setting those delectable breasts into an erotic shimmy. The memory of how they'd looked coated with his come sent a shudder down his own spine.

"Open your eyes, Edie mine." She did, slowly as if in a daze, the lids remaining lower than normal, signaling her liking of this. "Watch me."

Her heavy-lidded gaze dropped to his cock. Her breath caught and staggered.

"You will learn to do this for me in time," he told her, grunting as her teeth grated the sensitive head as she nodded. His balls pulled up tight and the base of his spine tingled. His climax could not be delayed long.

"Do not move," he ordered.

She stiffened. Her breath drew in and held as he pressed forward. She opened her mouth wider. The restless shift of her hips spoke of her need. The spicy edge to her scent told how close she was to coming. He pushed deeper, until the sensitive head of his shaft hit the back of her throat. He held his cock there, enjoying the caress of her muscles as she fought her need to gag, satisfaction blending with lust as she followed his orders over instinct and did not pull away. He backed off, releasing a shot of his seed on the retreat, groaning as she moaned but didn't move, just let his come coat her mouth as her gaze clung to his, a plea in their smoky blue depths. His cock dropped to her chest. He touched the corner of that sweet mouth, took the smear of come, pressed it between her lips and gave her the permission she required. "Swallow."

Her lips closed around his index finger, and her lashes fluttered down in delight as she swallowed. More satisfaction nudged aside his frustration as she gasped in a hard breath and eyed him warily as the hormones in his come whipped through her

166

system. He was her mate. No other could give her what he could. She would accept their union.

Her scent took on a desperate edge, the unique aroma signaling her need and agony, calling to everything in him as he grabbed her ankles, the strength of her summons driving him crazy. In two quick moves, he turned her so that her legs were over his shoulders and her pussy was level with his face. For one moment he just stood there, breathing deeply, imprinting her scent with all its nuances into his being. Everything about her was a pleasure. Everything about her made him insane with emotions he did not understand. With the last of his reason, he ordered. "Do not come yet."

As much as he would love to wallow in her scent, drink her dry of her essence, his control would not survive that. With the tip of his tongue, he separated her labia. She whimpered, and her juices creamed his chest. Her little clitoris stood swollen and aching, peeking out from beneath its heavy hood. He could see the throb of her desire in its distension. Edie was very close to coming. Very needing of her mate's attention.

He stepped in, forcing her higher and opened his mouth over that pleasure point. Her flavor filled his senses. His beast roared its pleasure. He welcomed it, embracing its power and its demand. She would accept the joy he could give her. She would see where she belonged. "You may come now."

Very carefully, he caught the nubbin between his upper and lower fangs. Before she could do more then gasp, he gently bit down, piercing the plump nubbin the tiniest bit. Her scream was muted but her convulsions almost tore her out of his arms. He held her close, cupping his hands under her buttocks as she jerked with the strength of the climax rolling over her. A few drops of blood flowed into his mouth, encouraging his possession. He clamped his lips around her, nursing her orgasm on from one wave to the next. The bitterness underlying her flavor reminded him of what still had to be done. One more pulse, one more breathless scream, and then he released her.

He lowered her hips, the lingering spasms of her orgasm rippling against his palms. With a regretful kiss, on the straining bud, he ducked his shoulders out from under her and let her slide down his body, her tender pussy skating the ridges and hollows of his torso, leaving behind her own mark. One he welcomed. As her hips hit the bed, he leaned over her, braced his left arm alongside her head, cupped her swollen pussy in his hand and whispered in her ear, "You are mine."

The shudder that took her body at his claim ended between her legs. She was so aroused, with three strokes of his finger she was ready to come again. He held her there on the edge of orgasm with his nail on her clit, one twitch shy of shattering, and opened the bedside drawer with a thought. Cold metal settled in his right hand. He stepped forward, forcing her calves up over his shoulders, splaying her legs high, wedging her between the mattress and his body. Her legs quivered under the strain. Her breath came in short, tight pants, but she didn't object, just stared at him with an air of acceptance that soothed a bit of his prowling rage.

The thick gold hoop lay in his hand, catching the faint light in the room. He tilted his palm. The light danced across the ancient joining words, magnifying the strength in the carvings, in the tradition that was older than his parents' memories. A tradition that had lost favor in recent joinings. He closed his fingers over the ring. Too many things had been lost lately. Too many traditions abandoned along with that most precious commodity—hope. He concentrated on the hoop, warming it to his touch, imprinting it with his energy, whispering the joining words in his mind, his lust and joy rising with every syllable. The correctness of the decision settled amidst the turmoil. This was his mate. This was right.

His "Do not move" came out more growl than speech as he slipped his hands under her soft hips. His palm shaped effortlessly to her thigh, as if created for no other reason than to please this woman. Edie tensed as he pinched the hood of her clit between his fingers, jerked as his nails sharpened and clenched on the delicate skin. He felt carefully, finding the spot he wanted, close enough to the nerve bundle that the weight would be a constant stimulus, but not so close as to create irritation. Before Eden could process his intent, he pierced the layers of skin, squeezing her clit between his thumb and index finger at the same time, milking it hard, hurtling her into climax. She arched high off the bed, her scream a mix of pleasure and surprise. He did not block all the pain of the piercing, letting some of it blend with her orgasm, knowing it would drive it higher, wanting this moment forever engraved on her memory. Deuce waited for the last shudder to settle to a quiver.

"Watch." She shook her head. He leaned in, curving her spine, tipping her hips inward, compelling her with thought as well as command. "Watch, my heart."

Her lids lifted slowly. Her tongue slid over her lips, wetting them with lingering seduction. He opened his hand. The ring glowed from within, pulsing with the energy he'd fed it. He opened the hoop. Edie's eyes widened and flew to his. He held her gaze as he threaded the hoop through the opening he'd made. Her hips bucked as the thickest part stretched the piercing. The swollen bud of her clitoris leapt under the pressure. Her scent saturated the room. She was such a miracle.

Deuce held Edie in place with his hands and leaned back, lapping the sensitive nub, sending pleasure chasing her shock. Her scent lured him lower, seducing him to linger longer than he had intended. She tasted of blood, woman and heaven. Of perfection incarnate. The hoop brushed his cheek. He gave it a nudge, treating her to a sample of the delights to come. She bucked up into his mouth, her moan as enjoyable as her responsiveness. He kissed her weeping folds gently, lovingly before rising over her, easing the pressure on her back. The hoop lay heavy and large against her delicate pussy, dominating the area.

His cock throbbed. Never again would she move without the memory of the joy he could bring her. Never again would another look at her and think her available. She was his Chosen mate. She bore his mark. It was as it should be.

He healed the wound before heating the ring, chanting the permanence ritual, protecting her flesh from the worst of the heat, but not all. There was a great deal of feminine delight coming through the uncertainty swirling around her as the heat transferred to those ultra-sensitive nerve endings. When the hoop fastener sealed smoothly, and she hovered on the brink again, Deuce slid his finger through the center, for the first time ever, taking control of his mate in the ancient way. The weight, the feel, the way the ring glowed against her delicate flesh—it all pleased him deep inside. It was a hoop of substance. Worthy of a woman of substance. He tugged gently. Eden jumped a foot, the lightning bolt of sensation projecting outward, snagging his lust and tossing it higher. She caught her breath, and he caught her gaze. "You are mine."

He tugged again, a little harder, holding the ring out a second longer the next time. Her head thrashed side to side. Her fingers dug into the comforter as her body drew taut while fine tremors quivered down her legs.

"Deuce!"

"Come for me." He jiggled the ring, ending with a series of sharp jerks as he thrust his finger deep into her grasping pussy.

She came, screaming his name, filling the room with the scent and sound of her satisfaction.

He brought her down gently, circling her swollen clitoris with soft as air brushes, maintaining his presence high inside her for a moment longer before withdrawing. When she sagged, he didn't hold her, just let her feet slide down. Two discordant thuds punctuated her heels hitting the bed rail. Her hands went between her legs to touch the heavy ring. A small moan disrupted the staccato pants of her breath as she explored the prominent hoop. Deuce pulled her limp body to the edge of the bed. Her body was sated, but she still hungered. Only the slightest of direction from his hand was required before he felt her lips brush his balls. And then her tongue. The Maker, she had a sweet, tempting tongue. Too tempting.

He stepped back. His cock dropped in front of her face, hitting the mattress with a soft thud. Eden opened her mouth, giving him a glimpse of her teeth and the hot wet promise of heaven. She welcomed him in with a delicate suction. Though everything inside him demanded that he fuck her hard, he gave her control. She was still in shock over the piercing, her mind alternating between delight and horror, as she experimented with the pleasures of the joining ring. He slid his index finger alongside hers, touching the warm gold, tracing the ornate carving of the joining words before hooking his fingertip through the thick hoop, letting the weight of his hand rest against her thigh, heating the metal as he encouraged her passion.

"Take what you need, mate." He cupped her head as she engulfed his aching cock in the tight heat of her mouth, suckling gently on the tip, drawing his orgasm from him in delicate sips that burned up from his groin until he thought the top of his head would explode. Time after time, when he knew he could not bear another moment, she demanded he give her that much more — more pleasure, more of what he was, taking him higher than he thought he could go, sapping his strength and his anger with the searing heat of her mouth. Tentatively blending her soul to the edge of his until his knees gave out and he collapsed on the bed above her, his cock jostling free, the last of his seed spilling on the side of her breast.

He gasped as she moaned, cocooning the small splash in his hand, letting the warmth from his palm and his seed meld their flesh together. He met her tired gaze with his, conviction welling with the truth. "I will never let you go."

Chapter Twelve

৪০

"I think you cured me."

Deuce smiled at the sleepy, brave boast and gently lifted another section of Edie's nearly dry hair to the heat coming off the fire in the fireplace. "That would be good."

Improbable, but good.

He let the hair fall, watching it slide over her shoulders to flow like liquid gold as it puddled on the burgundy throw he'd spread on the white carpet. She adjusted her cheek on his naked thigh, her breath a tantalizing stroke along his balls. His cock stirred with renewed interest. She pressed a tiny kiss on the receptive flesh of his inner thigh as his gaze followed a natural path over her still peaked breasts, down over her stomach to the ring of gold that glowed between her labia. The shadows from the flames danced over her slim body in intriguing patterns, reflecting off the ring, glinting stronger at the edge of the deep carvings.

Her gaze followed his. Embarrassment, trepidation and pleasure flashed across her face before she buried her it against his hip, her nails digging into the muscle as she wrestled with her reaction to the piercing.

"Why did you do it?"

He ran his hand down her hair, the waves turning to spirals toward the ends as the strands dried, catching on his fingers. "I am not always as civilized as I would like."

She did not lift her face. The moistness of her breath sent goose bumps up his leg. "Meaning?"

"The Chosen are very possessive of their mates. The rings are a traditional marking."

One given up except by the most possessive, but she did not need to know about that. She would find his mark easier to accept if she thought it a common practice.

"It won't come off, will it?"

"No." Nor could it be cut off by anyone but him. Along with the ancient joining words, he'd carved in the strength of his wishes. Eden shifted, her white teeth sinking into her lower lip as her movement disturbed the ring's position.

"It's very distracting."

"It is as it should be."

"You did it because I tried to leave, didn't you?"

"Your actions precipitated the marking sooner than it would have been."

"But you intended to 'mark' me all along?"

He pulled her up his body until her cheek rested on his forearm. He did not hide from her gaze as he answered her question. "Yes. Beneath our layer of civility, all Chosen are prey to baser instincts. When it comes to you," he touched the corner of her slightly swollen lips and confessed, "I am more so than most, which is why it would be wise for you not to challenge me again in the future."

"I didn't challenge you. I left."

"By leaving you deny all that is between us."

"You want me to be some sort of puppet?"

"I want you to be my mate, to share your hopes and fears with me as well as your joy."

She had nothing to say to that. He grazed his knuckles across the fat hoop, pulling her closer as she shivered, her arousal rising along with his, as it should between mates. He kissed her forehead, not wanting to see her expression as he asked. "Do you truly object to wearing my ring?"

"Honestly?" Her gaze searched his, not allowing him to hide from her.

"Yes."

"I was pretty much primed for a ring on my *finger*."

He arched his brow at her. With a thought, he sent the hoop swinging. "Where would the pleasure for you be in that?"

She hitched herself higher, her thighs shifting against his as her passion spiked. Her fingers intertwined with his larger ones. Her hand felt so small in his as she pressed his knuckles into the ring. The wet folds of her swollen tissues opened around his flesh, accepting him into their moist embrace.

"Nowhere near where it is," she gasped.

Her honesty humbled him. She didn't have to give this to him. With her mind closed he could only guess at how she felt. She could lie to punish him for his insistence on the tradition, but she didn't. Wouldn't. No matter what the Coalition had done to her, they had not touched her inner core, which was as pure and as decent as the Maker could create.

He brought her hand to his lips, kissing the back before catching and holding her gaze. He turned their joined hands slowly, deliberately, so that the remnants of her pleasure teased his nostrils. His tongue touched the back of his hand, precisely over the spot where her scent was strongest. Her eyes closed. She bit her lip as if in pain.

"You need to let me go, Deuce."

"Why?"

"So Jalina can be safe."

"You will explain."

She tensed and then seemed to sink into him. "If I get away, convince them she died, they'll stop looking for her."

And start experimenting on her again. She didn't need to say it for him to understand.

Her gasp alerted him to the fact that he was squeezing her hand too tightly. He relaxed his grip. "That is unacceptable."

"My grandfather, Clay…" She pushed her hair off her face. "He's a very powerful man with a lot of connections, but no one other than he knows about Jalina. If I can get back, get close, I can put an end to it all."

There was only way to put an end to Clay Lavery's obsession. "You plan to kill him."

"More than plan, I intended to succeed."

To protect her daughter. He could not fault her courage, just her plan.

"Others would continue the research. Your sacrifice would be for nothing."

"I only need to kill him for any reference to Jalina to be erased from the face of the Earth."

That was interesting. "Are you sure that no one else knows of your pregnancy or Jalina's birth?"

"That would be a loose end. Grandfather doesn't leave loose ends."

"And this is why you left? Not because you feared our mating, but to save our daughter?"

She nodded, her lip back between her teeth. "I knew you wouldn't let me go. It goes against everything you believe in."

The hard knot in the pit of his stomach unraveled. For the first time since she'd slipped out the bathroom window, he felt he could breathe normally. He smoothed the pleat between her brows with his thumb, pressing her into the shelter of his larger body, needing her softness to soothe his beast that howled in protest at the thought of her putting herself in danger. "It is not the Chosen way to barter our mates."

"But for our daughter's sake…"

"For any reason." He did not like the set of her chin. Eden could be very stubborn. He tipped her face up to his. "You will leave the safety of my family where it belongs. With me."

Tears washed the blue of her eyes, magnifying their brightness, catching flickers of the flames in their depths, for a split second giving the illusion of her being Chosen. Her nails snagged on his collarbone and her lids lowered. The illusion disappeared. "You can't let them get her."

Adrenaline surged through her system as memories swarmed her calm. Deuce checked the chemical flow and stroked her back, easing her tension. "I am a Chosen warrior, leader of my people with an army of Chosen and Others at my command. Who do you know better than the supernatural to protect her?"

She ducked his gaze. Her hand clenched into a fist. "She's an outsider."

He had to remind himself that she was human before he understood her point. "Any child of any race can approach a Chosen or Other and ask for sanctuary, and it will be given. Jalina differs only in that she does not have to ask."

Edie shifted against him again. "Thank you."

He brushed her hair back from her face, kissing her eyes closed, frowning when she could no longer see. The disharmony was beginning again. It had taken longer this time. Hopefully, a good sign. He sat up, taking her with him.

Bohdan, come.

He rested his hand on the small of Edie's back, increasing the heat of her body before reflecting it back to ease the tension he could feel there. Her ribs and spine were nothing more than fragile impressions against his palm, lacking the density of a Chosen woman's. With the smallest fraction of his strength, he could smash them to powder. She was small and delicate and totally unaware of her vulnerability. He traced her lower rib with his thumb. She thought of herself as strong, yet even a human male could kill her with a blow. He would have to guard her very carefully.

The first shiver started deep within, more of a sensation of cold. Beneath his hand, she stiffened. He couldn't blame her. He wrapped the comforter around her and cradled her in his lap.

"Oh God."

Her fear tore at him. He should be able to spare her this. "It will not be so bad this time." He would not allow the statement to be a lie. The next shudder had her head snapping against his chest.

Her accusation of "Op...tim...ist" broke into three syllables under the force of her shudders. The reaction might have started later, but it was coming on stronger.

Deuce pulled the comforter up over her shoulders. "Bohdan will be here soon."

Her fingers dug into his shoulder. "Don't let him do that to me again."

"We must."

She shook her head and another quake hit her. "It's wrong."

He looked up as Bohdan came through the door, the healing bag swinging ominously in his hand. The contents of the bag were only required in the most dire of circumstances. "It was what was done before."

"Nothing they did could be right."

"You conceived under their care."

"A fluke." Another shudder. Deuce caught her jaw in his hand to keep her neck from snapping violently. Her "It had to be" was muffled by his hand and the stress being put on her body.

He didn't argue with her. He was more concerned with the results.

"You did not allow her more than she could handle?" Bohdan asked, putting the bag on the table beside them.

For the second time in his life—for the first time since he had lost Edie last year—Deuce felt shame. "I did not think so, but my control is not what it should be with her." She had only to be near him and a host of emotions he could not control, and could not predict, swamped him with powerful, alien demands.

Bohdan opened the bag and took out the syringe. "How much?"

"She took me twice."

"Did you take her blood?"

"Only a couple drops."

He was glad Eden could not understand the swear word that tore from Bohdan's mouth. "I should take her from you."

"You would die trying." It worried Deuce that he meant it. While he'd always known he would be bonded to his mate and responsible for her care, he had not expected the primitiveness of his reaction to her presence.

Bohdan gave no sign that he'd heard the threat. He knelt beside Edie. "I am sorry your evening is not going well."

"Me, too."

Edie's irrepressible humor, even in her misery, drew a lightening to Bohdan's stern mouth.

"I need to touch you."

"I know."

The calmness of her response did not communicate the terror Deuce felt pouring into her.

"You will concentrate on me and relax," Deuce told her. "I will not allow the pain to touch you."

"No." Her fingers dug into his arm. "Too much."

Too much for whom? He could and would do whatever it took. She was his. "It is my duty."

Bohdan reached for his arm. The needle flashed in the firelight. Edie slapped at Bohdan's hand, almost stabbing herself in the process. The curse Bohdan muttered was not polite as Edie shoved the needle away. "No transfusion."

Bohdan glanced at him, a question in his dark eyes. Deuce shook his head, steadying Edie as she twisted for better leverage, apparently operating under the assumption that her muscles were a match for his brother's. Her heart was beating too fast. Adrenaline pumped into her system at an alarming rate. Deuce reduced both before saying, "You will do what Bohdan commands."

Edie shot Bohdan a glare, set her chin in that stubborn line, and then turned her glare on him. "No."

Deuce tipped her face up to his, the tremors shaking her body traveled through his hand. How she expected to win this argument he had no idea. It was taking all her strength to keep from shaking apart. "I will force you if I have to."

Her eyes narrowed further, her anger projecting as clearly as her dare. He ignored both. Her displeasure was nothing in the face of her loss. He nodded the go-ahead to Bohdan, turned his arm out and said, "I will not lose you, my heart."

Bohdan slid his hand under the quilts. The implied intimacy had Deuce's fangs springing into his mouth before the thought formed. Bohdan paused, casting him a questioning glance. Deuce beat back the animal inside that raged at the sight of Bohdan's hands touching his mate, even for the purpose of examination.

It took four steadying breaths through his nose to find calm, focusing all his energy on mastering the primitive demand that he sever his brother's hands for the affront. Finally the rage settled under the force of his determination, and the soft touch of Edie's hand. At the arch of his brother's brow, he nodded his consent. He would control his impulses around Edie. And she would not die.

Edie fought. To her credit, despite the shock her body was enduring, despite the turmoil inside, she fought hard enough to make Bohdan's assessment difficult.

Allow her some pain.

Every instinct screamed no. Despite the logic of the move, despite the fact that doing so could save her life, he could not do it. It was as if he were two men, one rational and one primal, when it came to Edie. Of the two, the more primitive was the stronger. The logic of Bohdan needing her mental resistance weakened by the distraction of pain did not matter. It was impossible to send any amount of agony to that delicately made, vitally important body.

I cannot.

Bohdan did not waste time arguing with him or censuring him. He nodded. Deuce felt his understanding a second before his brother's mind went blank. In the next split second, Edie screamed as pain raced up from her thigh, racing from her mind to his. He caught it, managed it and took it into himself even as he sliced at his brother with his claws, going for the throat but meeting air instead for the simple reason that Bohdan was no longer there. Deuce lay Edie on the floor, and sprang to his feet, placing himself between her and the threat. Bohdan stood ten feet away, frowning down at Edie as she lay on the carpet. The only indication that he was prepared to battle was the way he balanced on the balls of his feet, and the slight surge of power shimmering around him in challenge.

Deuce bared his fangs. "You will die for that."

Bohdan shrugged, his frown deepening as Edie shook and moaned on the floor. "I did what you could not."

Knowing it was necessary did not appease Deuce's rage. Bohdan looked up. The depth of sympathy in his eyes and his next words tore the rage from Dusan's soul and replaced it with terror.

"She is dying, brother."

"Impossible." He went back to her side. "She was better after this morning."

"And now she is worse." He motioned with his hand. "The blood sustained her organs, but now they collapse at twice the rate. She cannot accept the change as she is."

"I gave her too much." Guilt rolled through him in an agony of condemnation. He had lost control, let her seduce the beast to prominence. He touched her cheek, his finger starkly dark against her unhealthy pallor. He could feel her fear and desperation through her despair, felt her jaw muscles tighten with the effort to control the shaking. Deuce met his brother's gaze. "If she goes, know I will follow."

That certainty came from deep within. The bond was not complete, but strong enough that there was no question. He would not allow her to pass to the other side alone and unprotected.

Bohdan nodded, as calm as ever. "It is expected."

Edie's nails sunk into Deuce's wrist. Her *No* slammed into his mind while a hoarse hiss of sound passed her lips.

"The baby." She struggled to sit up. "Promise."

He knew what she wanted. She wanted him to promise he would live for their daughter. He could not. Their bonding was too new and the emotions too strong for him to promise he would survive the despair of her loss this time. He lifted her shoulders off the floor, shocked at the strength of the muscle spasm that shook her. Much harder and her joints would be in danger. He could feel her strength of will, her determination to wrest this one promise from him before she gave up. He would not allow her to give up. "I cannot give you what you want."

Deuce closed his eyes and sought the link between them, matching his heart rate to hers, his soul to hers, his life force to hers. In the final moments, he would mate his mind to hers, completing the process.

Bohdan knelt beside them, his voice a stroke of calm amidst the turmoil of Edie's agony and her body's collapse. "It is my privilege as Jalina's uncle to see to her safety in the event of your loss."

Eden looked from him to Bohdan. Her protest came from her soul, the agonized scream of a mother whose last hope had been torn away. A mental cry that had even Bohdan flinching. The need in Deuce to see to her anguish was equally primal. The only thing that kept him from responding was the even more aggressive demand that she not die. He would use anything that he could to keep her with him. Even if it meant letting her believe her daughter would be defenseless in the wake of her death.

Edie's nails raked his forearm. The scent of his blood filled the air.

His hair slid over her shoulder to land against her chest. She grabbed it and pulled his face to hers. "You...have...to live." The order hit his face in disjointed puffs.

He cupped his hand behind her head and supported her when she would have dropped back. Her breath was shallow and rapid. Her pulse laboring. "Then you must live."

She grimaced. "The baby."

"Will either have both of us, or neither of us."

"Unfair."

He shrugged, his strength draining right along with hers. A Chosen would have recognized what he had done. His mate had no idea.

Bohdan's "If you are done establishing who dies when, maybe we could talk about her life" snapped his head up.

"You said she is dying."

"She is. She cannot sustain a slow conversion."

"There is no other way."

"There is one."

Deuce would do whatever it took. "How?"

Bohdan touched Edie's cheek, the gesture uncommonly tender for him. "A total drain."

"It is forbidden."

"Yes. For good reason." Bohdan's hand dropped to the floor. "Rarely does anyone survive."

Any chance was a chance.

"Deuce?" Edie's voice was weak, but still there. That was all that mattered.

"What?"

Her hand slid down his arm, her fingers fumbled with his, bumping and tangling before slipping between his. The squeeze he had no doubt she meant to be strong, was barely felt. He curled his fingers around hers. His gaze met hers. There was nothing fragile about her determination. "Do it."

"It is dangerous."

"I'm…dying."

"Painful."

"Still dying." That twist of her lips was a caricature of her normal wry grin.

Bohdan interrupted the discussion with the unvarnished truth, shielding neither of them from the reality. "It may not work and in the end you still might die after great suffering."

Edie cut him a wry glance, gritted her teeth as she shivered and groaned. "Like this…is a…picnic."

"This is not a joke."

"I dis…agree. Getting bad enough to become…one."

Bohdan shook his head and touched her hair, admiration in the light contact, regret heavy in his voice. "The choice is your mate's."

She moaned. Deuce caught her close as she buried her face in his chest. Her "Make it" was a high-pitched squeak of distress. Her pain was getting too deep for him to shield her from without penetrating her barriers. Which would kill her.

He had to shift her in his arms, the continuous shaking making her a stiff weight. Soon the shudders would escalate to convulsions. She had borne so much. Her fingers tightened on his as her head dropped back. Her eyes closed. Deuce looked at the fragile stem of her throat, the white skin, delicate muscles, and felt the burden of his duty.

It was his responsibility to make the best choice for her. He could let her die in relative peace. That would be kind. Or he could make a desperate play for life, putting her through what legend said was unbearable pain to more than likely have her die anyway, with her last moments unimaginable agony that he had inflicted.

Choose life.

He glanced across Eden's unconscious body at Bohdan who stared back at him.

"She would choose to be with her daughter."

"She does not know how it will be."

"She survived the Coalition's torture, freed her daughter and climbed a mountain in a storm to get her to you. She would not care."

"I cannot help but care. Logic does not enter into it."

"I know."

Deuce held Eden closer, cherishing the signs of life despite her unconscious state. "What does the drain involve?"

"You will take her blood to the point of deprivation."

It could not be that simple. "And?"

"Her blood is tainted. It might kill you."

"It will not." He would not allow it. Not with her life being the price for failure.

"You will purify it in your body, then give it back."

"How will she survive without blood?"

"I will keep her alive."

He could not imagine the toll that would take on Bohdan. Tales were much longer of the healers who had died trying to support two lives with one force, than those of the ones who had succeeded. "You are too valuable to our people to risk."

The pause in Bohdan as he stripped out of the confinement of his clothes was infinitesimal. "Who else has a chance of succeeding?"

No one. There was no other healer with Bohdan's skill and strength. The worry for Eden mushroomed into worry for his brother. Bohdan had been growing more distant of late. He suspected Bohdan was willing to do this for no other reason than that he did not care if he saw another moon rise.

"Our people cannot be without both of us."

Bohdan took the sacred candles from the bag and laid them out in the pattern of healing. "Then we had best not fail." He waved his hand. The candles lit and the familiar scent of rasha drifted into Deuce's turmoil, instilling calm.

"You will need help." To succeed in this Bohdan would need a steady supply of blood, monitoring. Possible intervention.

"The Chosen await your decision."

Deuce did not doubt that his people would support him. They would do so for the same desperate reason that he would let them. They could not bear another loss, and the joy and hope his daughter brought to their long desperate lives was unimaginable. They would fight to their last drop of blood to keep that hope alive. Edie moaned and shifted as Bohdan began to chant. Her hair fell across Deuce's arm, the long tangle of curls wrapping around his wrist, binding them together in a vibrant shimmering link. That primitive corner of his soul that came vividly alive in her presence roared for life despite the preponderance of logic that said to let her go in peace. He sighed and increased the depth of her breaths. "When you were with *her*, did you feel like there was another inside you?"

Bohdan pulled out the red ochre paint and very carefully put it on the floor. Too carefully. "Yes."

"And he ruled?"

"Sometimes." He closed the bag with care, as if by controlling the things around him, he could control the pain inside. "Being human, she seemed to understand that part of me better."

"Your mate was human?" He had not known that. Only that she had died so Bohdan could live. It was a hard gift for his brother to live with.

"Yes."

"Would you do this?"

Bohdan's gaze met his, for once doing nothing to hide the ravages the loss had left in his soul. "I would risk anything to hear her laugh again."

"Even if it hurt her?"

Bohdan took a breath. His answer flowed with the calm of logic when he released it. "We are taught that life occurs in many dimensions on many levels, and passing from this one brings us to another." He dipped his fingers into the paint, ritualistically painting the prayers for hope and strength on his forearms.

"I know the teachings."

Bohdan arched a brow at him as he drew the simple, powerful images on his right pectoral. "Do you believe them?"

Dusan shrugged. "I believe in what I see, and am willing to wait on the rest."

Bohdan completed the figure eight on his left pectoral before commenting. "Yet you bonded your life force to hers."

Deuce nodded. Edie was all that was precious in the world. All that would ever be good in him. "She cannot go unprotected to the other side."

"If it exists."

Deuce conceded the point. "If it exists."

Bohdan replaced the lid on the ochre jar and met his gaze dead-on. "Then your decision is which life do you believe in more? This one, or the next?"

Deuce kissed the wildly independent curls on Edie's head, breathed deeply of her unique scent and pictured her smile as it had been a year ago—full of life, hope, innocence and the beginning of love—and had his answer. "How do I begin?"

Chapter Thirteen

ഇ

If this was heaven, she wanted to give hell a try.

Eden bit back a moan as another searing pain sliced through her skull. She buried her face deeper into the softness of the pillow, jerking back into the pounding of her headache as her skin screamed in agony. She froze in place, panting as the wave of dizziness swept over her, afraid to move. Afraid to find out what else was going to hurt. But mostly she was afraid to open her eyes and see where she was. What she was.

"You could not be anything other than what you were born to be."

The pain fell behind a cloud she recognized. "Deuce?"

The mattress dipped. His arms came around her. Her bracing was instinctive but unnecessary as he pulled her against his naked chest. There was no pain and her headache was now only a memory. She nuzzled her cheek into the soft dusting of hair. His scent surrounded her, wonderfully comforting. She inhaled more, taking it deeper into her. There was something so intriguing about the way he smelled. She touched her tongue to his flesh. Tasted.

"Who else would be in your bed?"

She wasn't going there. "Turn on the light." Muscle stretched under her cheek. A double click and then brightness against her lids. "Thank you." She took a deep, steadying breath and ordered. "Give it back."

"What?"

She cautiously cracked an eyelid. "My pain."

Even this close, he looked good. All that golden skin and rippling muscle with that sexy dusting of hair was pure eye candy.

"You know that is not possible."

"Not only is it possible, I'm demanding it." She didn't really want to experience that god-awful pain again, but to let someone else suffer it for her was more horrendous.

"It is not the Chosen way for a woman to make demands."

"I'm not Chosen." Eventually he'd catch onto that. She cracked her other lid. The view just got better for having the whole picture. Damn, he was big.

"You will accept my caring for you as I see fit."

"You really need to get rid of that tendency to spout orders." She rubbed her head. "How long was I...sleeping?"

"Three days."

Three days? She took a breath and risked tilting her head back. She couldn't prevent her gasp. "You look terrible!"

He did. His face was haggard and worn, with dark circles under his eyes that were almost as black as the pupils.

He rolled her to her back, propping himself above her with one elbow. His hair fell about her, curtaining her off from anything but him. "Your conversion was not as easy as we had hoped."

Considering they'd worried she'd die, "not as easy" must translate into something pretty bad. She touched the deep lines of strain carved beside his mouth, her eyes burning with tears. He'd gone through hell for her.

"I'm so sorry."

"Your tears are uncalled for."

"I'm not crying."

His smile could only be called indulgent. Weary, but indulgent. "Though you have not let your tears fall does not make them any less real."

She bit her lip, gathered her courage, and asked, "Did it work?"

His thumb brushed her cheekbone. "Although it has yet to be confirmed by Bohdan, yes. Your body is healed."

She ran her tongue over her teeth. Nothing felt unusual. "Is it night or day?'

"Night." His fingertips brushed her cheek on their way down. He surrounded her. Mentally, physically, and emotionally. She should feel threatened, but right now she just felt amazingly safe.

Deuce touched his nose to hers. "You will always be safe with me." He pushed back, much of his usual grace lacking. "What is the question you wish to ask me, Eden?"

"How do you know I want to ask you a question?"

"I can feel the need and anxiety within you."

"Am I...different?" Images of every horror movie she'd ever seen flashed through her mind. Deuce shook his head.

"You are tired and your body heals from the trauma of conversion, but you are as you always were."

She must have been projecting again. "Except for the fact I'm your mate now."

"Yes." He managed to pack a wealth of satisfaction into that one syllable.

"Which means?"

"I supply your every need."

Eden laid out her biggest fear. "Am I going to want to gnaw on strange guys' necks?"

No smile accompanied his "No".

She hazarded a guess. "Just yours?"

He nodded. "Yes."

His hair slid forward on the affirmative, stroking across her nipples with a silken glide. The sick traitorous puppies they had to be to think about pleasure when she knew she felt like shit, immediately perked up, sending messages of delight to her core. Eden brushed those tantalizing strands of hair to the side.

"Why am I never dressed around you?"

Deuce shrugged, his dark eyes painting the half-peaked buds with the caress of anticipation. "You are beautiful, and it pleases me to look upon you."

A woman had no defense against a look that hot. Eden reached for the comforter with some half-baked idea of using it as a shield. "You said I was too skinny."

"I said I did not like that you had lost weight." His fingers left her cheek, trailed down her throat, rode the rise of her collarbone before angling down to cup her breast. Her breath caught, her ribs expanded, pressing her breast harder into his hand. Her womb clenched in anticipation as his thumb hovered over a straining peak. "I would like to see our children at your breast."

Eden blinked. That was not what she'd thought he was going to say.

His thumb tapped the tender peak, centering her attention on his touch. His hand shifted. His fingers flattened against the sides of her swollen breast. He slowly brought them up, compressing the flesh, milking delight from her before engulfing the hard tip in the heat of his mouth. He drew slowly on her nipple, holding her gaze, suckling strongly.

I would taste your milk.

Oh God! She wanted him to. She wanted to give to him in every way she could. She arched into his mouth, moaning as she reminded him, "I don't have any milk."

He dragged his teeth along her nipple as he withdrew, taking her shudder against him, pressing her nipple deep into her breast with his tongue, drawing out the pleasure. *Next time.*

Next time?

She blinked. She hadn't finished with this time yet. She moved his hair off her aching breasts as he propped himself above her. "How is Jalina?"

"She thrives."

Thank God. She owed him so much. "Thank you for taking care of her."

"She is my daughter. Thanks are not necessary."

"I want to see her."

"Marlika will bring her in after you feed."

They needed to get something straight between them. "I don't feed, I eat, and I have other needs to see to first." Her bladder was uncomfortably full.

His hand slid over her stomach to cup her lower abdomen. "You need to urinate."

The blush started at her toes. She shoved his hand away. "For God's sake, you don't just say those things!"

His right eyebrow arched, and despite the embarrassment eating her alive, she couldn't help but admire his aplomb. "You do not have to?"

"Whether I do or not is immaterial. It's private and *not* a subject for conversation."

She could tell from his expression that he wasn't taking her seriously.

"You are embarrassed by your bodily functions?"

"I'm embarrassed by your insistence in talking about them."

"It is my duty to see to all your needs."

"Trust me, there are some things a woman has to do herself."

"Like vomiting?"

Eden pushed Deuce back and slid out from beneath him. "Exactly."

The room spun as she sat up. Instantly, he was beside her, his arm around her waist, drawing her into the shelter of his body, lending her his strength. "The urinating you can do yourself. The getting there I will help you with."

She rolled her eyes, pretending she wasn't burning up with embarrassment from the inside out. "You just don't get it, do you?"

"No. But you have forever to teach it to me."

Now there was an intimidating thought. He opened the bathroom door for her and gave every appearance of planning on escorting her right up to the toilet. That was so not happening. She braced herself against the door. "I can take it from here."

"You are weak."

She was, but she was a long way from dead. And that's what she'd have to be to want a too masculine, too sexy for his own good man—Chosen—put her on the toilet like a toddler. She stepped through the door and started to close it. "Not that weak."

The door stopped when it ran into the barrier of his hand. "It pleases me that you think of me as sexy."

She rolled her eyes. As if the man needed his ego stroked. "Stay out of my head."

She shoved it the rest of the way closed. He really was too much. She braced herself on the vanity as she inched her way across the floor, the hoop swaying with every step reminding her of Deuce's will. She couldn't ever remember feeling this weak. She sat down on the toilet with a weary sigh. Thank goodness the bathroom wasn't one of those big fancy modern affairs with more floor than utility, or she would never have made it.

Two minutes later, she realized getting down was definitely easier than getting up. Getting up took everything she had and left her shaky. She leaned on the vanity while she caught her breath. Sitting in front of her was her toothbrush, reminding her that her mouth tasted like the inside of a shoe. She reached for the brush and glanced in the mirror. Her scream almost shattered the glass. The door slammed open and then Deuce's reflection was behind hers, looking impossibly big from this perspective.

She put her hands over her face, as if covering it hid the reality. "Don't look!"

Deuce's arms came around her again, one settling across her abdomen, pulling her back into his chest while supporting her weight. The other tucked across her shoulders. "You screamed because of your face?"

"Of course I screamed. Anyone would." She was hideous, her eyes beyond bloodshot and swollen with blue-black bruising all around. The same for her nose and mouth. She peeked through her fingers. The flash of red that was her eyeballs was enough to have her snapping them closed again. She shuddered in horror. "Why didn't you warn me?"

He had not warned her because the most beautiful thing he'd ever seen was her opening her eyes. "The bruising is temporary. I will heal it after I feed."

"I'm not going to be stuck like this?"

"No."

One hand twisted to cover her eyes, the other flicked at his reflection. "Go. Feed. Quickly."

The laughter caught him by surprise. Despite his exhaustion, despite the tearing burden of her pain and his own, she had managed to amuse him. "First, we will see to your comfort."

"*We* are not doing anything."

"You are too weak to support yourself."

"Call me shallow, but no one is seeing me like this."

She could not be shallow if she took classes. "I have already seen you." His logic did not appear to soothe her.

"Then I hope you looked your fill."

He tapped her fingers in a silent request to drop her hands. "Think you a bruise or two would matter to your mate?"

She pushed his hand away. "This is a hell of a lot more than a bruise."

"I do not like your swearing." He turned her around. Edie did not make it easy and she did not uncover her face, just dug those pointy elbows into his abdomen and was as uncooperative as she could possibly be. He was hampered by his need to support her. He would levitate her but that would take more mental strength than he could spare. But he would, however, spare the energy to take away the worst of what caused her horror.

He finally had her turned and anchored with his palm at the middle of her back. He arched her backward, smiling when she caught her hand on the vanity behind her, leaving her mouth vulnerable. As if he would let her fall. He brushed his lips over hers, using the connection to accelerate the draining of the blood and fluid, repairing the damage, his lips lingering on hers after the job was done. He did the same with the rest of her face.

She held absolutely still while he did so. Only the steadily increasing scent of her arousal and the little pulsing breaths meeting his indicated her emotions. Of his, there was no doubt. He stepped back, letting gravity drag his cock down before closing the gap between them, his cock nestling between her legs, snuggling against the center of the joining ring, touching the hot crevice beneath. There was nothing little about her gasp this time.

Her "There is something seriously wrong with you" was as disgruntled as her woman's flesh was wet.

He touched her lip with his tongue, testing her flavor. Such an intriguing mass of contradictions. Sweet and hot. Shy and bold. Sass and compassion. "I am your mate. Always will you be attractive to me."

She peeked at him from under the edge of her hand. "As much as I realize you think that's comforting, getting a hard-on for what I saw in the mirror—that's just…sick."

Deuce shook his head at her silliness. His hair fell over his shoulder, blocking his view of her breasts. He flipped it back impatiently, losing his balance as he did so, bumping her against the sink.

"Deuce?" All play left her voice.

He straightened, blinking back the dizziness. "I'm sorry." He eased Edie up, centering himself. "I should not have healed you just yet."

She touched her lips, frowned and slid her arm around his waist. It was only when she stepped to his side that he realized she had the absurd notion of supporting him. He caught her hand and brought it to his lips. "I am fine, mate."

"You almost passed out." He could feel the fear beating at her with that realization. She tugged him toward the door. "You need to lie down."

He went because even though she could not feel the pain her actions were costing her, he could. And one of them needed to be lying down for him to manage it. Another wave of dizziness hit him halfway across the room. He stumbled. Edie twisted around in an effort to support him, tripped and fell. He yanked her back against him and spun so he took the brunt of the fall. Her knee dug into his groin, jarring a moan past his control. Eden leapt to her feet, using his groin as a springboard, forcing out another moan, and backing away from him as soon as she hit her feet.

"Oh my God! This is it. This is absolutely it."

She rushed to the door, without explaining what "it" was, and yanked it open before he could remind her of her nudity. Dak stood on the other side. The only thing that kept Deuce from marking him for death was that, after that first glance, his eyes never left Edie's face as she grabbed his arm, her worry coming in a breathless, urgent rush.

"Oh God, you have to help him." She was yanking on Dak's arm, dragging him into the room as she spoke. "He almost passed out."

Deuce was going to have a serious talk with her about exposing herself to other men. He didn't like the way her breasts bobbed with every jerk on Dak's arm, or the view the other man had of her ass as she came to kneel beside him.

Dak intercepted his glare, smiled, and grabbed the comforter off the bed and wrapped it around Eden on his way over. "Deuce?"

"I am fine."

Edie was shaking her head before he finished, her wildly bouncing curls drawing the werelion's eye. "He's not."

"If you ask me neither one of you looks like you should be out of bed."

Deuce wrapped the throw more carefully around Eden as she knelt beside him, her hands touching his face and shoulders as if she didn't know what to do, but was determined to do something.

"He needs Bohdan," Eden said, placing her hand on his forehead, holding it for a second while the sheer novelty of having someone fuss over him kept him sitting where he was while her soft hands stroked his shoulder in agitated little pets that had the Pride leader giving off waves of envy. Deuce caught Eden's arm and pulled her down to his side. Dak had been getting restless lately, showing all the signs of mating hunger. He did not want to lose a friend to a moment of frenzy.

"I am fine."

Edie shot him a look of pure disgust. "You need Bohdan."

"No." Bohdan was not recovered. He was still deep within the earth. Deuce could feel his life force in its muted, almost disconnected state. He lived, but it would take days for him to recover enough to see if there was permanent damage.

Dak knelt down, his rifle thumping the floor with a muted clank. Deuce could feel his impatience with Eden's drama. Dak did not think Eden was worth risking two leaders of the alliance and had spoken against the healing, though when he addressed Edie, his tone was totally neutral. "Bohdan is not available."

"He left?" Eden asked, shock freezing her in place.

Dak shook his head. "He is not well either." His amber eyes missed nothing as he looked at Deuce. "You need to feed."

"Yes." Eden's revulsion was immediate. He squeezed her hand reassuringly.

"You are too weak to hunt safely." At the word hunt, Eden's revulsion turned to horror. Mental images of monsters tearing out faceless humans' throats whirled out from her mind.

Deuce glanced over at Dak. "Your terminology needs work."

Dak merely shrugged, his thoughts hidden behind his impassive expression and flat catlike eyes.

Deuce tightened his grip on Eden's hand, preventing her from indulging the need to move away that pushed at her.

Dak glanced down at his hand and then at Eden before meeting his gaze. "It is dangerous for her to remain so ignorant."

"My mate is none of your concern."

Dak inclined his head. "True."

"What don't I know that I need to?" Edie asked Dak, clearly seeing him as the weak link in the wall of silence around her.

It was a measure of their friendship that Dak remained silent. As the leader of the Pride, he had more than just Deuce's feelings to consider.

"Dak is concerned that your disobedience will bring harm to the compound."

"Disobedience? I'm not some child who needs controlling."

No, she wasn't. She was human and not used to working within the strict hierarchy of his people and the Others. "You would prefer that I use the term independence to describe your behavior?"

She yanked her hand free to slam it on her hip, her fear turning to the more comfortable outlet of anger. "And what's wrong with independence?"

The move sent a wave of pain to his already overloaded senses.

Dak frowned, no doubt scenting the weakness. "Be silent and still, woman."

Eden reacted immediately, jumping to her feet, challenging the Pride leader. "Who the hell are you to tell me what to do?"

Deuce used all of his waning strength to manage the flood of physical anguish pouring from her body to his.

Dak's lip lifted in a warning snarl any female of his Pride would have recognized. He stood, towering over Eden. "Though it is not my joining ring you wear, I am the one you will listen to."

Edie gasped and turned red, but didn't back down. Deuce got to his feet. The spike of healthy fear surging through her at the lion's threat should have sent her behind him. Instead, it drowned under a wave of fresh anger. Along with that wave came something else, something he couldn't identify. Dak snarled again and Deuce yanked Edie behind him. She bounced back like a ping-pong ball, hitting Dak in the chest with her hands, knocking him slightly off balance as she snarled back, "I suggest you save those fangs for someone who's more impressed with them."

Her foolishness defied description. No Chosen woman would ever endanger herself so.

Between one breath and the next, Deuce grabbed Eden and shoved her behind him. With a flash of his fangs, he ordered, "Stay." He turned back, ready to battle if Dak wanted satisfaction. "My apologies for my mate's behavior."

"She is impulsive," was all the Other said in the face of the tremendous insult Eden had just delivered, his power banked again behind the mask of placidity.

"Yes." Deuce ignored Edie's disgusted snort. "Do you demand satisfaction?"

"Satisfaction?" Edie asked, outrage evident in her tone.

Dak glanced around Deuce. Deuce looked down to find Edie peering around his side, maintaining her challenge of the Pride leader's dominance.

He pushed her farther behind him.

The way the other man's arms folded across his chest in combination with the smile playing on his lips told him Dak wasn't done provoking Edie.

"When a female touches a male of the Pride, it is an invitation to her bed, and if she is mated, an invitation to fight her mate to prove his worthiness."

Edie blinked and stepped a little closer to Deuce's back. What in hell had she gotten herself into? From the set of his shoulders to the placement of his feet, Deuce stood like a man issuing a challenge, throwing off waves of testosterone like it was candy at Halloween. In front of him stood Dak, a muscle ticcing in his cheek, tossing back the same invisible challenge to Deuce. Were they about to come to blows?

"Good God! You can't be serious?"

Dak smiled a smile that did nothing to ease her nerves as it showed the edge of his fangs and his personality. "I am debating my options. You are not displeasing. And you display a ring well."

She blocked the urge to put her hand over the heavy hoop. There was nothing for him to debate. "I don't want you in my bed!"

"Then you should not have made the invitation."

Good God! Had she stepped back to the dark ages? She pulled the comforter tighter around her. "I was warning you off!"

His eyebrow rose in a habit that she was finding annoying. "From what?"

"Hurting Deuce."

Dak stared at her for second, disbelief, surprise and at last humor spreading across his face. He shook his head, met Deuce's gaze, and jerked his chin in her direction. "I have decided not to accept her invitation."

Deuce nodded as if Dak had done him a huge favor, though he didn't relax. "Thank you."

Eden wanted to kick him in the shin. She settled for glaring at Dak, who shifted the gun on his shoulder. The twitch in his cheek turned into a smile as he motioned to her. "She is too hard on the ego."

She couldn't see Deuce's face because he kept blocking her attempts to get around him, but there was no mistaking the amusement in Deuce's voice as he said, "Fortunately, she compensates in other areas."

She did kick him for that. Not hard, but enough to hurt her toe, and have him grab her wrist and anchor her to his side as she rubbed her toe against her shin.

Dak took in the exchange and laughed out loud. "May the Maker spare me from a human mate."

"She will learn."

"No doubt." The glance Dak cast her let Eden know he was well aware of her distaste at being so discussed. The faint lines by his eyes expressed his amusement with her reaction more clearly than words. He turned his attention back to Deuce and his smile faded. "You are not in good shape, my friend."

"I will heal."

"Quick enough?"

"Quick enough for what?" Neither man paid her any attention.

"As fast as I need to."

"You need blood."

"Yes."

"I offer you mine."

Edie felt Deuce's shock in the tightening of his body, and in the thickening of emotion in the air. "The offer is generous."

Dak inclined his head. "I have my moments."

"It is not without risk." Deuce's tone was cautious, but she could feel how much he wanted this. There was more than just a food chain going on here. She looked between the two men. Dak didn't look any more civilized than Deuce for the fact that he was wearing khakis. Both were males in their prime. Both wore the mantle of authority as if it were made for them. And one was offering his blood to the other.

"The trust must be complete if we are to succeed."

Deuce nodded, acknowledging the point. "The Chosen are honored by your sacrifice."

"I'd prefer no one but you and I know of this."

"Agreed."

Dak held out his arm and with the claw that suddenly appeared at the end of his finger, slashed his wrist. Blood welled and pooled. Beneath her hand, Deuce went rigid. "Mate, go shower."

"I don't want to."

The eyes Deuce turned on her were wild, the black pupils swirling with flickering shards of red. His "Do as you are told" reverberated in her ears, in her mind. She went, the order too dark, too compelling to ignore. She closed the bathroom door behind her, but before she pulled it all the way shut, she looked back. Deuce advanced on the other man, the way he moved, the way he held his head was that of a predator stalking his prey. Dak stood as he'd been when she'd fled, relaxed, waiting. She shuddered and shut the door. There were parts of this mate business that were going to take some getting used to.

Chapter Fourteen

ร❧

Halfway through her shower, Eden's mental and physical strength gave out. She sat down and let the water pour over her head and body. Too weary, too overwhelmed to do more. She was married to a vampire, had a half-vampire child, and was living among vampires and werepeople. Her family was gone, everything she'd thought her life to be was a lie, and there was no going back. Ever. From here on out she lived as the Others did. On the fringes of society. Hated or revered, depending on the mindset of the person feeling the emotion, but never accepted. In her wildest dreams as a child, she'd never anticipated her life going like this and honestly didn't know if she could accept it.

Steam swirled as the door opened. "You will accept it."

Eden looked up through the water pouring over her face, mixing with her tears for all that she'd lost, and saw Deuce. He was stronger now. She could sense it. See it. He'd gotten that way by sucking another man's blood. "I thought vampires bit people's necks."

"Vampire is a human term. I am Chosen." He opened the shower door. "And that is a pleasure reserved for mates."

"Great. Can't wait."

He held out his hand. She didn't take it, just stayed where she was, weighed down by the enormity of change. "I don't think I can do this, Dusan."

He stepped into the shower and sat down in front of her. "It is already done."

Water bounced off his shoulders and splattered her eyes. "Maybe the right term would be I can't accept this." She pushed her hair off her face. "Good God, you just sucked the lifeblood from your friend."

"I was honored by his offer."

"I was repulsed."

"That is to be expected, but in time, you will understand."

"That's what I am trying to tell you. I don't think I will."

His sigh was not unsympathetic. "It is my duty to see that you adjust."

"I don't want to be your duty." Why couldn't he see that? "I don't want to understand. I don't want to be weak. I don't want to be hunted." Her voice rose with every syllable until her "I just want to be normal" ended on a muted scream.

"I know." Deuce's calm flowed over her agitation, muting it. His hand slid behind her head, pulling her into him. "It is my duty to give you whatever you want, but of all your wants, the only one I can help you with is to make you strong." He tipped her chin up. "Will you let me do that?"

She searched his eyes for some sign that he was holding back. Hiding a secret. She found nothing but compassion. "Do you have to?"

"Your pain tears at me."

"Then give it back."

"I cannot."

"You told me you could do anything."

"Anything but hurt you."

"I don't have the same restraint."

"It does not matter."

But it did. It seriously did. "We are so different."

"Not in the ways that matter."

"I almost got you killed!"

"My powers are beyond your comprehension, Edie." He cupped her shoulders in his palms and let them slide down her arms. "The Pride would not have taken you."

"Because he was teasing?"

"Because I would have killed him."

"He's your friend." He lifted her and drew her forward, draping her hands around his neck.

"You are my mate."

She balanced her hands on his shoulders and straddled his thighs as he lowered her onto his lap, the hard ridge of his huge cock sliding in the folds of her labia, surging through the wet cleft, catching on the ring, tugging attentive nerves to vibrant life. Her breasts swelled and pushed outward. Her pussy ached and pulsed in answer to the throb of his cock. The hot steam from the shower intensified his scent and then hers, until they blended together—the way her body wanted to be blended with his. So tight and so solid that not a degree of separation remained.

"A pretty dumb mate." She dropped her forehead to his chest. "I all but propositioned your friend."

Deuce smiled and opened his hands on her back. "Your ignorance of custom was known."

"Then why the big deal?" She arched her back and slid her torso side to side, teasing her breasts with the light abrasion of his chest hair on their sensitive tips. She was scared and she was confused, and she just wanted to forget about everything that she had to accept.

"He is the leader of his people. Protocol could not be ignored."

"Your culture is so backward."

"I have often had that thought about yours." His fingertips grazed her skin as they traveled the path from her buttocks to her waist, raising goose bumps in their wake. Desire slammed into her with the intensity of a brand, strong, unmistakable and familiar. So blessedly familiar. She leaned into his chest. His arms came around her, holding her close to the heat of his skin while the warm water poured over her back. She shuddered at the sheer bliss of being in his arms. She'd dreamed of it the whole time she'd been trapped in the makeshift lab, made all kinds of promises to God if he'd just allow her to feel Deuce's arms around her one more time. She'd needed him so. Which brought up something she needed to deal with.

When she'd first met Deuce, she'd thought he was human, and she'd loved him enough to consider marrying him. When her grandfather had used her to trap him, she'd loved him enough to die for him. And now that she'd found him again, she needed to know if she could love him enough to live for him. In his world and on his terms. She slowly inched her hands up his chest, over the swell of his pectorals. Across the ridge of his collarbone until she could wrap them around his neck. She pulled herself hard against him and tucked her face against his breastbone. "Do you remember that last date we had before everything went bad?"

"Yes."

"Do you remember how I was?"

His whole body jerked and his cock surged up against her, putting pressure on the ring, leaving her no doubt that he remembered how close she'd come to surrendering everything to him that night. "It is one of my fondest memories."

"Can you make me feel like that again?"

His hand left her hip. Light as down, it settle cross the side of her head, protecting her face from the spray. "Yes."

"Will you?" His index finger traced her jawline from her ear to her chin. She didn't wait for him to apply pressure to lift her face, and didn't wait for him to ask the question she could see in his gaze. "For tonight, I want to forget about everything that's happened. I want to forget about everything I've lost and everything I've got to face. I just want to go back to that one night and live it like I've regretted not doing every day since. Would you be willing to do that?"

His "Yes" held its own wealth of regret and nuance of hope. She touched the corner of his mouth with her fingertip. "Good."

He kissed the pad of her finger and sucked it gently. She felt the edge of his fang against the side of her finger. Her first instinct was to pull back, but she stopped herself. This was her man, her mate. She needed to start as she meant to go on, and running scared wasn't on the agenda. She left her finger where it was and concentrated instead on the brush of his tongue on the sensitive tip. The tingle started in her finger, spread out to her hand, balled and gathered energy before shooting down her arms, shards of the tingling energy stroking every nerve ending on the way, until her entire torso strained for more. She'd probably go to her deathbed wanting this man.

He'd go to his grave wanting her. Almost had once, but she was here now, with her heart open, asking him to give her his fondest wish. A night with no past, no future, just the here and now and what they felt for each other. Deuce looped Eden's arm back around his neck, keeping his fingers locked around her wrist, sliding them over her arm until the width of her forearm forced him to open his hand. Her flesh was soft and smooth, the fine hairs decorating her skin providing a tantalizing caress to his palm. He would give her everything she asked for but first they had to deal with something else. "Before we can put it all behind us, we need to face one more thing. "

She pulled back slightly, a frown between her brows. "What?"

"You need to feed."

"You told me I didn't need to drink blood."

"You need my blood to make you strong."

She groaned and dropped her head to his chest. "That's really going to put a damper on the evening."

"Not if you let me shield you."

"You want to start our lives by playing let's pretend?"

"There is nothing to be proven between us."

"I've always believed in starting as I mean to go on."

"Trusting your mate to see to your comfort is not a bad thing."

"Needing him to is."

"It is right that you need me."

"Not like that."

He brushed his lips over her eyelids, closing them. "Any way you need. Whenever you need it. I am your mate."

"Forever." She said the word with an edge of fear, without the rejoicing a Chosen would feel.

"Why does that scare you?"

"I can't even conceive of that long."

He could, and those endless years had stretched before him with no end and no relief when he'd thought her dead, but now that she was here, he could not see it being long enough. "Then in this, you will allow me to guide you."

"That sounds suspiciously like an order."

"It is." Her only protest was a token shift of her body.

"You need to feed. Feeding will make you strong. If you do not, all that was done will be undone."

"Oh God."

Her stress levels increased. He caught a flash of an image, of her face grotesquely distorted to that of a monster, mouth gaping open with red-stained teeth and blood all around. He sighed. She feared turning into someone like she saw on TV. "That will not happen, Edie."

"I went crazy before."

"Your body was unbalanced then. You are balanced now."

"How do you know?"

He slashed his chest. The blood flowed. He felt the leap of interest inside her. Her body's understanding of what it needed, but there wasn't the insane urge to feed they had battled before. "I am not holding you and you have not fallen upon me."

"But I want to." Her eyes never left his chest, watching the blood flow, her expression one of horror and desire.

"The urge to feed is stronger because you have gone too long without, but you can control it."

The shower washed the blood away as fast it poured, sending it in pink rivulets down the drain. "Let me help you, my heart."

She looked up at him. The confusion in her eyes hurt him in ways he didn't know a Chosen could be hurt. He took her hesitation as an answer. Sliding between her uncertainty and her desire, he clouded the moment, bringing her mouth to his chest, barricading everything from her knowledge except his order to drink and the pleasure she gave him as she did so. As her mouth met his chest, he curved his index finger through the joining ring, completing the connection.

Her lips and tongue sucked at his flesh, stroking him softly, not with the hard edge of a Chosen woman but with a delicacy that worked his lust into a fever pitch. He tugged the ring with the same delicacy, nurturing her desire and his own. By the time she'd had her fill, his hands were shaking and he was on the verge of coming.

He needed her. Needed to touch her, to make her his so no other could ever take her away.

He closed the wound with a brush of his hand, sliding his thumb between her lips, groaning as she sucked it with the same delicacy. He stood, taking her with him, shielding her from the spray with his body as he turned off the water. He carried her out of the shower, her weight barely registering. Such a small, frail body to house such a huge spirit. He put her down in front of the sink. With her mind still fogged, she swayed. He steadied her, helping her rinse her mouth—he did not want the lingering taste of blood to spoil her plans for the evening—before wrapping her in a towel and freeing her.

She blinked, clutching the towel to her. "Is it over?"

"Yes." He took another towel and rubbed her hair. The strands went from dark to light, regaining their curl as he got most of the moisture out. He touched a long spiral next to her cheek. It wrapped around his finger. "Your hair is beautiful."

Her right hand came up immediately, squashing the curl he toyed with. "It's the bane of my existence. "

An image flashed of her desire to cut it short.

"It is the joy of mine. You will not cut it."

She sighed and shook her head. "It's my hair."

"And my pleasure." He closed his hand around the curl. "Would you deny me that?"

She bit her lip, her gaze dropped. Then her chin came up and she shook her head. "Not tonight."

He released the curl, hearing what she hadn't said. "And tomorrow?"

She smiled, the edges blunted with uncertainty and determination. "Tomorrow doesn't exist."

"So we agreed." He tossed the towel on the floor. "Are you feeling stronger now?"

"You know…I am."

"Your surprise is insulting. I told you feeding would strengthen you."

"Call me a skeptic."

"Another mate would take offense."

"But you won't." She let go of the towel and linked her hands around his neck, pressing her soft breasts, with their silky hard tips into his abdomen. "Not tonight."

The towel fell, wadding up between them, preventing him the full impact of her damp skin against his. "No. Tonight is for us."

"The way it should have been..."

"From the beginning." He flicked the towel away and pulled her tightly against him. Damp and moist, rich with her scent and the promise of completion, her skin melded to his. He ached to his back teeth with the desire to make her his. Now. No more waiting, no games. He slid his hand through the tumble of curls, letting them ensnare his fingers the way she'd already ensnared his soul. She was a wild, sweet, courageous bundle of suspicious passion, and she was his. From now until the last breath left his body, she was his. The back of her skull fit his palm as if sculpted to be there. Everything about her was perfect from her wild curls to the tips of her small toes. Perfect for him. He tapped the inside of her ankle with his toe. "Spread your legs."

She parted them a few inches. Another tap, this time on the opposite ankle gained him the last few he needed. He stepped back, letting his cock trail down her belly. When it reached the tip of her sex, he stepped forward, sliding it down along the crease until his groin met her stomach. Her nails bit into his forearms as he arched her back, pressing her clitoris into the wiry hair surrounding the base of his aching cock. Her gasp whispered into the quiet of the bath.

"Do you like the feel of my cock between your legs, Edie mine?"

"Yes."

He nudged her legs a little wider and thrust slightly. "How much?"

Her "Very much" was more squeak than words.

"You are going to have to show me."

He bent her back farther until the clean line of her throat was exposed. Her hair fell away from her face, revealing her bone structure and the confusion in her blue eyes. "Uhm, don't take this wrong, but I don't know what response you're looking for."

"The way your sweet pussy is creaming my cock is a good start." The faint pink on her chest flared to a bright red. He ran the edge of his tongue over the heated flush as it rose up her neck. She swallowed hard, the underside of her chin, pushing against his tongue as he trailed upward. He kissed the rounded point of her chin and shook his head, his hair falling forward to tangle with hers. Light with dark. Male with female. "Now, that was not."

"What?"

"You held back." He tested the little crease beneath her lower lip with his tongue. "I do not approve of your holding back."

"You don't?"

He smiled at the breathless little question. He let his mouth hover above hers, so close a piece of paper couldn't slide between, but not quite touching, prolonging the moment before contact, drawing out the anticipation. Her heartbeat went from gallop to thunder, her vaginal muscles clenched and released, the slick, wet heat of her labia stroked his cock with a feminine entreaty that everything male in him roared to answer. He held her like that for an endless moment, letting proximity and her own imagination heighten her senses. She sucked in a deep breath. Her pupils dilated and then contracted. "Do you want my mouth, mate?"

"Oh God!" Edie sagged in his arms. He did not allow her the respite of distance, just held her there with his hand behind her head, and his arm across her back.

"That was not an answer." Her body was already giving him his answer, her need so strong he could taste it on her scent, but he wanted the words to come from her. Needed them to. For all the times he'd heard them in his dreams, this time he needed to hear them in reality.

"Please."

"You do please me." He lowered his mouth to hers, gently, carefully, fitting edge to edge, seam to seam, sealing their lips the way he wanted to seal their bodies, until even the concept of separation was unbearable. She responded deliciously, her hips lifting to his, her head twisting in his hands. He clenched his fingers around a fistful of the damp locks. Her soft cry at the twinge of pain pelted his mouth at the same time that her delight swamped his senses. Desire, hope and embarrassment rolled from her to him in desperate waves. She wanted more, but was shy.

He touched his tongue to her lower lip. "There is no shame between us. You but need to ask, and I will give you anything."

He pressed gently until he came in contact with the inner lining. Her unique flavor rolled through his mouth in an addictive incentive to pursue more. "Just like you'll give me anything, will you not?"

"Yes."

"Open your mouth." He caught the plump fullness of her lip between his teeth and bit down gently, taking her gasp as his. "Let me in."

She didn't have a choice. Eden opened her mouth and her soul to his. She might have been able to hold out if Deuce had been rough or selfish, but his gentleness and patience in the face of the violent desire shimmering around him touched her in ways she hadn't expected. He was bigger than her, a different species than her, capable of doing things she couldn't even conceive of. Despite the danger that lurked around him like a dark cloud, his touch on her back was gentle, controlled, as he slid it down to her buttocks, his fingers sinking into the soft flesh, pulling erotically on the cleft between as he drew her up and into his kiss.

He was a creature of the dark, but when he held her in his arms he created light—pure, clear, brilliant light that started behind her closed lids and exploded through her head, her body, until it consumed her in the a fiery heat that left her dizzy. He kissed like a lazy summer day, heat and warmth seducing her into a complacent lethargy. Between her thighs, the ring heated, adding fuel to the fire in her blood. She slid her hands up over the swell of the hard muscles in his arms to his broad shoulders, pulling herself closer to the flames.

He pulled her mouth away. She shook her head. "More." She needed more. More of his energy, his heat and the pleasure he held out like a shimmering enticement.

Deuce bent, swung her up in his arms and strode out of the bathroom. She turned her mouth into his chest, finding his nipple, licking it, sucking it, catching the small, flat nub between her teeth and biting down. He stopped dead halfway to the bed, his head dropping back, his hair swinging against her arm. "Edie."

She looked up. "What?"

He looked down. "You should not push me this time."

His expression alone should have scared her witless, but it didn't. Knowing she aroused him to the same level that he did her was heady and restored her sense of balance. "If you don't hurry, I'm going to finish this without you."

His head jerked back and he looked down the length of his nose at her, every century of living packed into the arrogance of that look. "You will not come until I give you permission."

"Then you'd better hurry."

He took a breath. She lapped delicately at his nipple, nudging it with her tongue. She could feel him reaching for control, and knew he found it as the heavy lust that swirled about her abated to a dull roar.

"Be easy. I'll give you what you want."

But not fast enough. She could tell he had no intention of giving her what she needed as fast as she needed it. She'd spent years being good, years being what her grandfather wanted in gratitude for him raising her, tamping down her natural impulses so he would be proud of her. She wasn't going to start that again with Deuce. She wasn't going to be a good little girl who buried her desires behind a façade. She was his mate. If Deuce wanted her for his mate, he was going to take her as she was, whether that fit his plan or not.

"I don't want easy. I want you."

He took the last four steps to the bed and held her above it, his black eyes deeper than midnight, swirls of red glinting through the opaque surface. "You will have me."

"Now."

"You are not ready now."

If she didn't think he'd enjoy it so much, she'd bite him for that display of arrogance. "I've waited forever for you."

"And I have waited even longer for you, so we will do this my way, and I will determine when you are ready."

The slide down his body was pure torture. Every hard ridge of muscle teased her sensitive thighs and stomach, tugging at her new ring, the proud thrust of his cock settling to the outside if her thigh. As soon as her butt hit the mattress, she reached for it, levering it up and in until it was level with her mouth. Just a dip of her head away from pleasure. Fat, thick and hungry, it throbbed. For her. She pushed her hair back off her face and licked her lips. "Maybe I can hurry you along."

Deuce caught her head in his big hands. "It is not about hurrying."

"But I ache!" From her knees to her breasts, she pulsed with a relentless need.

"This is our joining night, mate. It needs to be done right."

She kissed his cock, sucking the tip into her mouth, sucking harder when his salty taste greeted her efforts. Her clitoris swelled in delight. She squeezed her thighs together, twisting the ring between them, trying to appease her clit's relentless howl for attention. Her effort to take more was thwarted by his hands on her head, pulling her away.

His cock popped free of her mouth. The broad head glistened in the lamplight, harder than before. Redder. She looked up at him to find him staring down at her with an intensity that would have terrified her if she hadn't been feeling the same way.

"At least part of you has the right idea," she grumbled.

"You act like I will leave you wanting."

"You already have."

Deuce stroked his thumb over her lips, a slight smile on his own. "You have not yet begun to want."

Chapter Fifteen

ॐ

"Lie back on the bed."

Eden propped herself up on her elbows, eyeing Deuce cautiously. He looked a little too comfortable standing over her, handing out orders.

"Spread your legs."

Way too comfortable. "Why?"

He arched that eyebrow at her in that way that set her heart to pounding at the same time it encouraged her to smile. "I want to see you."

There was no doubt what part of her he was referring to. Her breath caught in her throat and swallowing became impossible. From where she sat, she could appreciate the way all that muscle flowed from narrow to wide, cut to bulge from his waist to his shoulders. It was both arousing and intimidating. He was the one man her body wanted above all others, but he'd never looked less human than he did in that moment, his eyes flaring black with intermittent swirls of red, the emotion coming off him too powerful, too intense to be human. Too intriguing to be ignored.

"Now, Edie."

Blinking slowly, she took a deep breath, and parted her ankles. His nostrils flared and his gaze left hers to linger on her legs. Feeling incredibly daring, and a little like she was baiting a bear, Eden separated her knees. Deuce's breath hissed in. She didn't hear it leave. She got as far as her upper thighs before her courage ran out. She glanced at his face. Every angle was drawn tightly into sharp planes with the force of his desire. Pure, unadulterated male desire. For her. It still wasn't enough to get her past that last barrier of modesty.

His gaze flicked hers. "You are disobedient."

He didn't sound upset by the knowledge. The thick muscles in his upper arms flexed. His touch on her ankles had her jumping. She wanted this, wanted him, but she had a horrible feeling she was out of her league. She snapped her legs closed. "Deuce?"

His fingers encircled her ankles, pulling her feet apart. "Yes?"

She let her knees fall together, foiling his attempt. "It's not that I'm being difficult."

His "You are not?" was skeptical.

Okay. So maybe it did look like she was being a little difficult. "Not deliberately."

The chain of his fingers slid up her calves, opening and gliding around until he cupped the curve of her calf muscles in his palms. "Then why do you hide yourself from me?"

Good question. "It's just not that easy."

He paused. "You fear me?"

"More like your reaction."

That stopped him cold. "Why?"

"I have all sorts of weird thoughts running through my head."

"Show them to me." A jerk of his chin punctuated the order. His hair fell forward over his shoulder with the force.

"No. Absolutely not." Some things were meant to be private.

A sound distinctly like teeth snapping together had her setting her own chin.

Deuce shook his head, sending strands of his thick hair brushing across her knees and thighs. "You will get over this resistance to sharing with your mate."

"I am entitled to some privacy."

"This privacy is a human concept."

She shrugged. "Go figure. It must matter to me because I'm human."

He shook his head at her. Pressure from his fingertips had her knees parting a hairsbreadth, whether she wanted them to or not.

"Wait."

"I have waited long enough."

She squeezed with everything she had. "Promise me one thing first!"

Again he paused, but his impatience was palpable. "What?"

"Don't be shocked."

His fingers twisted on her calves, sending tingles of desire up the inside of her thighs. "You think seeing your pleasure could shock me?"

She shifted her hips to alleviate the pressure, but it didn't help. Her body clamored for his attention. "You just make me so crazy."

"That is as it should be."

"Please?"

Deuce paused. A quick glance at her face proved the truth of his senses. She was truly worried that she felt too much, whereas he thought she could not feel enough. Her scent was so strong, so pleasing he felt almost humanly drunk. He stared up her thighs to the patch of pale yellow curls protecting her mound. The glimmer of gold drew his eyes, not only because of what it symbolized, but because of the fully engorged nub it framed. The previous taste he'd had had been too short and tainted, but this time when he loved her she'd be as she should be. His completely. His hands shook with the anticipation. Her muscles—those dainty little muscles she thought prevented him from anything—flexed in his palms, reminding him that she was awaiting his promise.

"This promise is given." She didn't seem any more relaxed for receiving it. Her breathing was becoming erratic and along with desire, fear was pumping adrenaline into her system again. "Take a breath, Edie."

She did, sucking it in deep, but forgetting to let it go as he pulled her thighs apart. He backed off her adrenaline and the stress that had her breath lodged in her throat. "What do you fear, Edie mine? Do you think you are ugly to my eyes?"

Her groan confirmed his suspicions. He parted her thighs farther. Her head dropped back and her eyes closed. "You are beautiful, my heart. Delicately made, lushly inviting, and perfectly wet."

The last drew a strange squeaking sound from her throat. He glanced up to catch the blush racing over her torso.

"I like you like this. Wet and eager and hungry for the touch of my fingers…" He parted her labia with his fingers. "My breath…" He leaned in until his mouth was a scant inch from her clit. "My tongue."

He touched her shy, sensitive little clit with the tip of his tongue. Her scream echoed in his ears as he nuzzled his way under the heavy ring. The carvings of the joining words lay against his tongue as he pressed the sensitive nubbin, imprinting the rightness of the moment into his mind.

"Oh God!" Her sob of "Too much" reached out to him.

It was not enough. Her hands fisted in his hair, tugging at him. She didn't have a prayer of getting him to move. Not when he finally had her under him, her scent in his nostrils and her juices on his tongue, and all the time in the world to enjoy all three. He circled her clit lightly, feeling the spark of delight shoot through her. Followed quickly by a shot of fear.

He kissed the straining little bud gently. Glancing up her body, over the fluttering muscles of her abdomen and between her heaving breasts, he studied her expression. Beyond fear and desire, he saw confusion.

"Edie?"

Her grip tightened in his hair. Her "What" was cautious.

"I am trying to make you lose control."

"I figured that."

He dipped his finger into the copious cream coating her pussy and thighs and brought it up to her clit, sliding his finger all over the little bud, coating it thoroughly. "Then why do you hold back?"

"Because I'll do something incredibly stupid and ruin everything."

He rubbed his lips over the freshly slicked area. She shuddered and strained toward him, her body understanding what her mind could not accept. "There is nothing to ruin, Edie mine. Just relax and trust that I know where I am taking you."

"That's what my grandfather told me when he took me on my first roller coaster ride."

"And?" There was always an "and" with Edie.

"I threw up all over him."

He squashed the snort of laughter that threatened his control. "You will not throw up tonight."

"But if I do?"

"Then the fault will be mine."

"How so?"

"With six-hundred-fifty years of experience, I should have this down pat."

She stared at him, her breath lodged in her lungs, her mind straining to reach for him but smothered by her will, and finally nodded. "Okay."

"You will relax?"

"Yes."

He kissed her little clitoris again, smiling when she jumped. "Because you know you can trust me?"

He felt her weigh the lie and then sigh with the truth. "Because I don't seem to have any choice."

"No. You do not." And neither did he. He had to have her. Her scent, her taste, her passion. Her joy. "Come to me, mate."

He cupped her buttocks in his palms, frowning at how little of them there was left. He would need to remember to make her eat. Her gasp as he squeezed the soft mounds jostled another smile from his desire. His mate had a sensitive ass. That was good. Very good.

He lifted her pussy up into his mouth. Keeping her suspended on the platform of his hands as he traced the swollen outer lips of her pussy, licking at the cream there, rolling her unique flavor through his mouth, catching the ring between his teeth and tugging gently, as he pulled her buttocks apart, stretching her anus ever so slightly, savoring the reality.

This was his mate who tossed beneath the lash of his tongue. His mate who panted with anticipation as he rimmed the opening of her vagina. His mate who screamed and pulled at his hair when he plunged his tongue inside. His mate. Forever and in all ways, for all that she still did not accept it. But she would. Before the night was over she would accept all of him. And not just his body. He lapped at her clitoris, teasing her with the stiff strokes. Her muscles tightened. Her body stiffened. Her head thrashed from side to side. Her scent changed subtly. He sucked her clitoris into his mouth. Edie screamed and thrashed on the bed, denying herself and him her orgasm. He growled deep in his throat, deep in her mind.

You will not deny me this.

"I can't bear it."

His fangs exploded into his mouth. She would do more than bear it. She would come for him. On his command. He increased the pressure of his tongue, adding little nips between the strokes, gradually increasing the force until she stopped pulling away and began thrusting up into his mouth.

He took his hands away from her buttocks. She fell to the bed. She stared at him uncomprehendingly, her blue eyes dark with her passion, her lips swollen and red from her biting, almost as swollen and red as her other lips.

"Present yourself to me."

The flush on her chest intensified, and then with a little whimper that went straight to his cock, she arched her back, thrusting her breasts out and her hips up. Her body swayed slightly as she offered herself to him.

"Higher."

Another whimper and her hips lifted that fraction more that had her legs quivering and her sex parting, exposing the tender flesh between and the gold hoop resting above.

He reached out, placing his finger at the top of her labia, dead middle of the hoop, centering it over her clitoris. She shuddered and her whole body went stiff as a board. "Do not come."

"I have to." It was almost a wail.

"No."

Her glare was pure frustration. He ignored it. He palmed the pad of her vulva, massaging the heel of his hand into the slick prod of her clitoris. Edie whimpered and shook, but didn't fall.

"Deuce…"

"Not yet."

Her vagina fluttered helplessly as he traced the opening with his index finger. Once, twice, he circled, drawing her need, focusing her attention before he nudged the opening. Her hips dropped. Her moan projected outward, flowing through his mind with addictive pleasure. "Yes. Show me your delight."

The ring of muscle kissed his finger in a tiny clench and release. He rimmed her vagina again, tempting more cream from her body, more moans from her throat and another kiss from her hot channel. He eased his finger inside, biting back his own moan as her heat surrounded him. He pushed in farther. She cried out and her muscles clamped down with everything they had.

The Maker! She was tight. Incredibly tight, and her muscles strong. If he took her now he'd be lucky if he did not come on the first stroke.

"Do that again, little one. Let me feel your power." She did, another broken whimper gouging at his control. "Can you take more without coming?"

She shook her head no. "I think so."

The contradiction made him smile. "What part are you not sure about? Taking more or coming?"

"Coming." She arched her hips a fraction higher, her thighs trembling with the effort. "I can't tell that part."

He blinked and looked at her. "You cannot tell if you are going to come?" She shook her head, her pussy clenching and releasing on his finger in pre-orgasmic entreaty.

"How could I? I've only done it with you."

It was inconceivable. His Edie was a woman of passion and heat. Accepting pleasure should be as natural as breathing for her. He kept his finger in her and brushed his thumb over her clit. "You had never come before I loved you, not even by your own hand?"

She could not blush any brighter without exploding into flames. "You saw my grandfather's house. There were video cameras everywhere. Even in the bathrooms."

He had not realized the surveillance went to private areas.

"He was obsessed that I keep myself pure."

"For me." He had not meant to say that last aloud. More evidence of how she affected his control.

Her hips stilled. "Yes. Apparently, you Chosen are picky."

"When it comes to our mates, yes."

He could feel the resentment surge in front of her desire. "Quite the double standard you have there."

"It matters not who comes before — but after — you are mine."

The desire that had been raging in her body now hummed at a low level. He eased his finger out of her pussy, giving it a reluctant little pat. "Relax."

Her hips went down but her head popped up. "I'm sorry."

"For what?" He circled her belly button with his index finger, waiting for her answer. Her stomach fluttered as her breath sucked in. He glanced up. She stared back at him from the bed, her torso propped up on her elbows, her small pink nipples still peaked, her breathing still labored and her eyes full of regret. "I go crazy thinking about all the women you've known."

He cupped her breast in his hand as he knelt on the bed over her. "I cannot change the past. I can only promise for the future."

Her lower lip slipped between her teeth. Her gaze ducked his as her fingers drew into a fist. "I don't know enough to compete."

He pinched her nipples between his fingers, compelling her gaze to his. Her breath squeaked off to a gasp. She jumped, her flush slowly dying away, the residual heat tempting him to taste the rich blood that lingered on the surface. "This is a mating, not a competition."

Despite his reassurance, she did not look at him. "What if I'm a dud?"

Other women would have whispered the fear. Edie threw it out like a challenge. Deuce opened his fingers on her breasts, cupping the softness in his palms, unsure how to address her insecurity. No other woman had the power over him that she did. No other woman could match her importance, yet she saw herself with human eyes. As one of a crowd when in reality, she was the center of his universe.

"You are the other half to my soul. My match in all things. There is no failure between us."

Her nipples were small in his grip, but sensitive. Very, very sensitive. He rubbed them lightly while she struggled for her voice. "If I'm not doing something right, do you promise to tell me?

"Yes." The promise was easily made as it was natural for him to give orders, in and out of bed. "Now may we proceed?"

This time she did meet his gaze, bravado almost but not quite, masking her fear. "Yes."

He slid his hands up the sides of her soft breasts until his fingers snuggled under her arms. He lifted her up. She grasped his shoulders as he lay her down on the pillows. She lay there all pink and white, innocence and heat, tempting his beast to roar. He beat it back. This was her night of fantasy. He would not disappoint her. He came down over her, sheltering her body under his. "Put your arms around my neck."

Her arms were soft, her body softer, calling softness from him that he hadn't known he possessed. He kissed her lips, running his tongue along the parted seam. Every bulge, every crevice was a miracle, luring him to explore further. His hair fell around her face, obscuring the light. He could see easily, but she squinted, trying to make out his face. Her tongue came out to touch his, coaxing, teasing. He granted her request, slipping into her mouth, exploring leisurely, slowing the pace, calming her passion. She was too impatient, seeming not to know there was pleasure in the journey. He wanted her to experience the journey.

He cradled her head in his hand, kissing her cheek, the end of her nose, her lips. "You please me, my heart."

"I haven't done anything."

"You gave me happiness, gave me my life, a child, and now you give me yourself." He shook his head, so amazed that she could not see the truth. "The statement would be better phrased as 'What have you not given me?'"

Her fingers wrapped around his wrist. Her eyes met his—determination where there had been shyness. "I'd rather give you the best night of your life."

"You already have."

"Not the way I want." She bit her lip and her voice filled with the determination he could see in her face. "Tell me how to make it good for you."

He turned his head and kissed her palm. "You will not worry about this tonight."

"What if I want to?"

"Then your pleasure will wait on mine."

She didn't give him the argument he expected. Instead, she pushed his hair behind his shoulders. Her blue eyes searched his face as if memorizing his features one by one. "But later you will show me?"

"Yes. But now I will show you how a Chosen man makes love to his mate the first time."

"Dare I hope that's fast?"

The element of hope in her voice made him smile. He discouraged it with the shake of his head. "Slowly. Very slowly."

She let go of his hair and fell back on the pillows. "You're just determined to torture me, aren't you?"

He nibbled on the side of her neck, lingering on her faster than normal pulse, tasting the banked promise of her passion. "Yes."

She threw her arms wide. "Then do your worst."

He shook his head and chuckled through his passion. She was such an intriguing combination of play and seriousness. He captured her wrists in his hands, pinning them to the bed. Her eyes popped wide open, inspiring another chuckle. "I like you like this."

"You would." She tugged at his hold, her efforts insubstantial against his greater strength.

"It is good you are beginning to understand me."

"I don't think I'll ever understand you."

He traced the "u" where her collarbones met with his tongue. "You have but to open your mind."

"So not happening, Deuce."

"It will be my pleasure to teach you." He stretched her arms wider, arching her torso up. The point of her nipple brushed his chin. He ducked his head, capturing the small point. Her cry was the sweetest music. Almost as sweet as the way her nipple melted on his tongue and her breathless moan caressed his ears.

Eden tugged at her wrists again. Deuce didn't let go, just held her hostage to his pleasure, taking as much of her breast as he could, sucking gently, then harder as she thrashed beneath him. He slipped his thigh between hers, drawing his knee up until it grazed her pussy. She shuddered and wiggled down. He gave her what she wanted. More suction, more pressure, his cock jerking in an agony of its own, wanting the warm nest he could sense opening for him.

She bucked under him. "Oh God, Deuce. I need you."

He released her breast. "What do you need?"

She arched her back, her nipple prodding his lips. "I need you in me."

"What part of me?" he asked, letting the words shape the caress of his mouth.

"You know."

Her shyness was sweet, but he wanted a woman in his bed. "No, I do not."

"Do you need me to beg?"

"Yes." He nudged her with his knee. "Let me hear how much you need me."

She sobbed and ground down with her hips. "I need your cock, all right? I need it in me now."

He had not thought she would say it, but he should have known better. His Edie was a woman determined to go after what she wanted. Inside he smiled. It was good she wanted him.

"Then you shall have it." He nipped her nipple sharply, absorbing her start with his torso, enjoying the hard clench of her pussy against his thigh. "When I come inside you, I want you to do that again."

She hesitated before nodding. He slid his other knee between hers. "That is all I want you to do."

He levered his cock to the top of her cleft, teasing himself with the brush of the joining ring, the solid proof that she was his. "Do not move, do not help, just concentrate on how it feels when you accept your mate for the first time." Her eyes darkened as his cock slid down the slick crease, nestling with precision into the well of her opening. Her pupils dilated as he pressed in, panic mixing with desire. "Be easy, mate."

Her whimper broke off in a gasp as the broad head eased her open. Her respirations shortened to pants. Her muscles tightened. Deuce drew a hard breath and halted his forward movement. He caught her face in his hands, brushing his thumbs against the corners of her closed eyes. "Look at me."

She blinked and lifted her lids halfway, more of her attention focused inward than outward.

"I will not let you hurt, Edie."

Her teeth sank into her lower lip as she nodded, every muscle pulling tight. He sighed and ran his tongue along the smooth surface, tracing the edges, her small squeak as he stroked under her upper lip bringing a smile to his face. "If you believe this, why do you tense?"

"You're so big." Her lower lip went back between her teeth.

"Which will only bring you pleasure." He kissed his way to the corner of her mouth—easy, gentle kisses designed to lower her defenses. He feathered his tongue in the tiny crease between her lip and cheek. She gasped again. Her lower lip popped free. He caught it between his, sucking it into his mouth, seducing her past her anxiety with a gentle suction. "I will not turn into a beast because you give yourself to me."

He levered himself over her, kissing her lips gently while everything inside urged him to plunge into that hot, willing channel with all the hunger clawing at his control.

Her "What if I turn into one?" pulled him up short. He leaned back to better see her expression. "This is your fear?"

"Among others." Her fingers on his chin were shy, delicate and very welcome. "I really don't think you have any idea how crazy you make me."

He snuggled his cock a little deeper into her, stopping the minute she tensed, taking the edge off her awareness. "You could show me."

Red color flooded her face. The heat in her chest and cheeks drew his lips. "No way in hell."

"Your swearing is not acceptable," he whispered against the curve of her cheek. He switched her hands to one of his, smiling when she blinked at the speed of the maneuver. Her back arched naturally with the pressure, presenting her breasts for his delectation. He opened his fingers, stretching them out to encompass her fullness into the cradle of his palm, following her back as she sank into the mattress, sliding his fingers up until they encompassed her nipple. He pinched it lightly. Her cry whipped past his ear as he ordered, "You will cease to do so."

Her breath sucked in on a retort. He caught her earlobe in his teeth, biting down slowly, gently. Her breath hissed out on a sigh of bliss.

"Can you feel yourself opening for me?" he whispered in her ear, encouraging her muscles to spread farther with a steady pressure. She nodded. "Does it feel good?"

"Scary," she gasped. "You're too big."

He shook his head at her foolishness. "You will come to appreciate it."

He nudged forward. Her body tightened on him as if to resist, but her strength was nothing compared to his, and on his next bite, the tight ring of her vagina closed behind the head of his cock.

"Oh God." She tried to move. He held her down with the weight of his body, easing her stress with a thought, taking the pain of the stretching into himself, needing a break as he assimilated the feminine distress into his own raging need.

"Be easy, mate." He pulled her arms a little farther up, feeling the spike of her desire with the increased restraint. "Let yourself feel me."

She didn't have any choice. Eden arched beneath Deuce, into the heat of his body, the stretching in her arms somehow magnifying the stretching in her vagina, pulling the two sensations into an ache she had to satisfy. She ran her tongue over her dry lips, tasting Deuce as she felt him, needing more. She dug her heels into the mattress, and pushed up, accomplishing nothing more than adding the strain in her calves to the strain in the rest of her body.

His chuckle burned into the curve of her shoulder and neck. She felt the brush of his fangs and the scrape of his nails as he pinned her down. She was helpless beneath him. Completely open and vulnerable. Her body wept with her pleasure. "Deuce…"

"Do not try to move." The order vibrated down her spine, spread to her center, to end on a flutter in her womb. "Just feel me."

She couldn't do anything else as he pressed forward, his cock a huge alien presence in her narrow channel. She had the impression of pain, but no sensation of it. There was only the overwhelming reality as his big body took slow possession of hers.

And then he stopped. Above her his chest expanded and glistened with perspiration in the low light. His head tilted back. The strong muscles in his throat jerked as he took a breath.

"What's wrong?"

He looked down. She didn't think he saw her until he blinked. "You are very tight."

"I told you we wouldn't fit." She tugged at her hands. He didn't let go, just caught her gaze with his, all the hunger she felt throbbing in him, swirling in his eyes as he surged deeper. Her breath caught in her lungs. The pressure increased to incredible proportions. The smallest of smiles touched his lips as his hand skated over her stomach and drifted over her pubic mound, bumping the ring so prominently placed. Sharp stings of delight drove down to her core. A sharper tug left her gasping as he slid his finger through the center, drawing it out in exquisite torment as his other finger came to rest against her swollen clit.

"I was not complaining, mate."

She just bet. She shifted beneath him to relieve the pressure. The red in his eyes flared. His pleasure spilled into the air around them. He groaned, jerked and gave her more of himself.

"Oh God!"

"I have you, Edie."

No he didn't, and that was the problem. There was simply no more room inside her, but he didn't stop, just kept pressing forward, and her body, her stupid body kept encouraging him with hungry pulses of entreaty and a steady flow of thick cream—not remembering or caring how he got thicker toward the base, seemingly equally hungry for the pressure and the pain.

She bit her lip and closed her eyes, letting the wave flow over her, the foreign sensations taking charge, moving forward with a surety she could only envy, taking her to a destination only they seemed to understand.

Go with it.

The order filtered through the distraction, trembling on the edge of her mind. Had he spoken, or mentally whispered the words?

A sharp tug on the ring centered her attention lower and the question was lost amidst a new swirl of sensation. Deuce's thumb brushed her clit, inching higher before a steady draw centered her pleasure firmly in his hand. All thought ceased as he rubbed and tugged her into acceptance. His cock slid deeper. Pain speared hot and high, riding her pleasure, weaving through it, making it more than it was, more than she could bear, more than she could resist.

Deuce's "Is it too much?" wavered in and out of her consciousness. She didn't know how to answer. She didn't know whether to scream or beg. He stretched her to the point of pain while pleasuring her past the point of bearing, but it wasn't enough. She needed more—something more to make all the sensation buffeting her coalesce into something she could understand. She shook her head and bit her lip. Her reward was another tug on the ring and more of Deuce's cock.

"Wrap your legs around my hips."

She lifted her right leg. His cock shifted within her, inspiring another stab of pleasure-pain. She hesitated, absorbing the reality that to complete the move would allow him deeper access.

The flesh above her clit pulled tight in a new way. The angle and pressure changed. He was twisting the ring. The knowledge as much as the sensation had her nearly weeping with an agony of need.

"Now the other." She was moving before he completed the order, logic buried beneath primitive need. She wanted to belong to him. Needed to give herself to him as he wanted. Needed to take all of him. Her left leg wrapped around his waist. One ankle hooked over the other, leaving her wide open, her hips tilted for maximum penetration.

His cock sank a fraction of an inch deeper and the glory inched a bit higher. "Yes. Accept me. Take me."

She did, shards of liquid lightning sparking to life, ricocheting through her pussy before shooting straight to her womb as Deuce rubbed her clit between his finger and thumb, drawing it away from her body as he pulled on the ring, catching the pain of his increased possession and melding it into the pleasure, making it more than it was. More than she could stand. Something had to give somewhere. She couldn't take this.

"Squeeze down, Edie."

She tried but she couldn't tell if she was succeeding.

"Harder." She gave it everything she had, gasping with the effort and the sensations it caused. She could feel every pulse of his penis, every vein. Every whisper of movement.

"Now hold it." The order blended with desire, driving it higher just as he pulled back, taking away the painful fullness she needed.

"No!"

The pressure changed direction, driving her swollen clit down onto the smooth flesh of his hard cock, forcing that engorged point to ride the surface of his shaft, as with one forward lunge he took her past her shyness and inhibitions, leaving her suspended on the peak of anticipation.

"Clench."

He wanted too much from her. She groaned and refocused, trying to hold him when he pulled out, taking his thrust as he forged back in. His big cock rubbed her raw with its presence, delighting her beyond belief when it drove in, creating despair when it withdrew.

Deuce picked up the pace from slow to easy. "Accept me, Edie."

His possession was wild and thorough, nothing like she'd expected and more than she'd dreamed. With every thrust of his hips, Deuce pushed her harder than she'd ever been pushed, but soothed her when she took that little bit more, teasing her on the withdrawal, whispering to her of all she could have if she'd just take a little bit more. Just that much more.

With every thrust he forged deeper, with every pulse that flowed from him to her, the bond between them strengthened. His desire called to hers. His body called to hers. His mind called to hers. As the joy spiraled higher, pulled tighter, it became harder and harder to hold back. He commanded all that she was, his demand that she join him riding the edge of her desire, fueling it. Through the haze of approaching euphoria, she felt his mind reach for hers, and felt her resistance fall away as another thrust spiked higher, tighter. He drove into her over and over. Pleasured her again and again. His fingers on her clit tightened, squeezing hard, throwing her into the storm she was struggling to avoid.

"Come to me, mate." The order reached through the confusion like a lifeline. She clutched it hard as reality threatened to splinter. "Now, Edie."

She threw open the doors to her mind, inviting him in, only to be overwhelmed by his thoughts, emotions and the pure carnality with which he relished his possession.

No!

The cry shot through her pleasure, landing in the center of her desire, scattering the pleasure to the far corners of her mind. Foreign, feminine, but incredibly strong, it offered her a choice. A reminder. Eden latched onto that strength, slamming shut the door she'd just thrown open, pulling back into herself as Deuce's climax crashed over her with the force of a tidal wave, his displeasure as tangible as his pleasure as she separated her mind from his. She wrapped her arms around his neck and held him close as he shuddered and shook, feeling his cock pulse as he filled her with his hot seed, turning her mind from his even as she stroked his back, her thoughts her own, her body still aching for the release she'd denied it, fear rapidly replacing complacency. What had she done?

When he recovered, Deuce pulled himself up over her and looked down. His finger under her chin forced her gaze to his.

"Why?"

Chapter Sixteen

❦

Deuce was not happy.

Eden slid out of the big bed, well aware that he watched her, knowing without having to feel his thoughts that he wanted a do-over. Equally determined not to give him one. He was too dangerous. When he took her in his arms she totally lost all her senses in a way that put them all in danger.

She made it one step from the bed before he spoke.

"Where do you go?"

She looked over her shoulder. He was propped up on the bed on his elbow, his hair falling around his shoulders. He didn't look any more relaxed after coming. Every muscle in his torso appeared to be carved from stone. His cock, glistening from their lovemaking, lay across his powerful thigh, only slightly softened. It twitched beneath her look. Her womb clenched in sympathy, aching with unfulfilled desire. "To the bathroom."

His gaze was as knowing as his expression was solemn. "You will not find relief there."

She wasn't sure if that was an order or a statement of fact. It didn't matter. His seed tricked down her thigh. "Actually, I thought I'd clean up."

"You are running away."

"If I were running away, I'd plan on making it a lot farther than the bathroom."

Not by a bat of an eyelash did he let on how her flippancy had to annoy him. His gaze dropped to her thighs. His nostrils flared. "If you wash off my seed, I will only replace it."

"Now, that just sounds gross." She continued to the bathroom as if his displeasure wasn't beating at her.

His "You will not deny what's between us, and you will not run from it" followed in her wake.

She looked over her shoulder at him. His head was tilted back in that arrogant way he had that just irked her to no end. He was too damn fond of issuing orders. She opened the bathroom door. "I'll do whatever the hell I want."

It felt good to close the door on the click of his teeth. Let him be frustrated. It was only fair. Her body was aching for the satisfaction she couldn't have without giving up her soul.

She washed her hands and face. Looking in the mirror, she heard again the "Voice" in her head that she'd heard at the last moment. Deuce hadn't been able to shield her. They'd found her. She.didn't know whether the woman was friend or foe, but the fact that she'd found her meant the Coalition would not be far behind.

She glanced into the mirror and gasped for an entirely different reason. Her hair was a rat's nest of curls flying all over the place. Her lips were red and swollen and her eyes haunted. She looked exactly what she was. A woman on the edge.

She touched the red mark on the top of her left breast. A remnant of Deuce's passion. She glanced at the door, and the panic she'd been beating back since the "Voice" had burst into her mind returned full force.

In a minute, she had to go out there. She had to deny Deuce and herself. Again. She honestly didn't know if she was strong enough. The more she stayed with Deuce the more she bonded with him. Which, she was beginning to believe, might be what her grandfather wanted and why she'd been allowed to escape. It had seemed too easy when she'd broken free, but trap or not, it hadn't mattered. All that had mattered was getting Jalina to safety. But now she had to think further ahead. She had to explore the "whys".

What if she'd only been let go to be used as a weapon against Deuce? What if they needed her to bond with Deuce in order to find her? Or worse, to further their experiments? As long as she stayed, both Deuce and her daughter were at risk. She had to accept that, to be strong enough for everyone. She took a deep breath and rested her head in her hands. She had to.

She wasn't prepared for the arms that came around her and pulled her back against a warm chest. Deuce. The man could move so silently when he wanted. He turned her. "You will tell me why you are upset."

She propped her elbows against his torso, her body naturally relaxing into the planes of his. "I have to go."

"You cannot leave."

"I can't stay with you, bond with you."

His hand opened on her spine, at once soothing and possessive. "It is already done."

She fought the urge to melt into his chest. "Not all the way."

"No. But it shall be."

She touched his nipple with her finger, the way it beaded against her nail a tiny distraction from his silent demand that she look at him. "No. It won't."

His fingers tangled in her hair catching in a snarl, sending pings of sensual pleasure through her scalp. He tugged harder until he tipped her head back. "You cannot run from me."

"I have to."

"Why?"

"They've found me."

The only indication of his surprise was the total stillness of his body. "You know this how?"

"When we were…" she waved her hand. Even standing here naked in his arms with his cock pressing into her stomach, she couldn't bring herself to say the words.

"When we joined?"

"Yes. At the last minute, I heard her."

"Who?"

"The woman who finds me."

His hand on her back tightened. "You will explain."

"They have someone who can find me. You said that you can shield my thoughts but you can't—couldn't—and she found me."

"How do you know?"

"She spoke to me."

"What did she say?"

"No."

His left eyebrow arched up. "Just no?"

"Yes."

"What was she denying?"

She shrugged. "It doesn't matter. It'll be just a matter of hours before they get here. Once she finds me, they always come." She opened her palm over his chest, feeling the strength of his heartbeat. "You have to leave here and take Jalina with you." She glanced up. "Now."

His thumb brushed her cheek. "If there is a need, we will all go."

"You can leave one of the Others with me and go. I'll catch up later."

His thumb touched her mouth. His mind reached out to hers. She fought it back.

"Separation is not an option. There is no life for you without me."

But there would be life for him and her daughter without her. She pushed his hair off his face. She brushed the hard line of his shoulder. "I'll be okay, Deuce."

"I know." He lifted her up to sit on the edge of the vanity. "I will see to it." He nudged between her thighs. "As I will now see to your need."

He pulled her hips forward. She caught herself on her hands. His cock pushed between her legs, finding her aching core, promising her the relief she couldn't accept. "I can't."

He pressed against her. Her body flowered around him, responding to the enticement of his, taking it in and amplifying it back, ignoring the dictates of her mind.

He had no compunction about using her weakness against her. He palmed her thighs, sliding his fingers around until he sank them into her buttocks, pulling her to him. "You will."

Desire, lust and fear shot through her with the force of a bullet, tearing through every defense she had. She needed him. Oh God, she needed him.

I will always be here.

Heat flowed into the promise, sinking through her pores to settle into the cool metal of the joining ring, setting it to vibrating with the power of his determination. More heat radiated outward from his palms, tempting her to come closer, to wallow in him. "We can't do this."

"There is no can't between us."

The vibrations of the ring intensified sending aching pulses of lust pouring into her resolve, drowning it in a tangle of desire that was so much more. She needed Deuce. So much. Eden opened her hands, and pushed him away. "You have to let me go, Dusan."

He pulled her face into his shoulder as he pulled her onto his cock. Her body opened on a cry of ecstasy as her mind exploded with a nauseating swirl of bright color. His "Never" echoed through the chaos, pulling the edges of the kaleidoscope into the center. Streaks of yellow flashed the dark perimeter, adding to the mental confusion.

"Wrap your legs around me, Edie mine."

The order welled out of the center of the spiral, dispersing the colors outward again. She pulled away, losing her bearings. Color swarmed her mind, listing to the left and then the right as she struggled to find a pattern in the morass.

"Hold onto me."

She did, as hard as she could, with her legs, her arms, her mind. His voice was the only thing solid in the careening landscape in which she found herself. He pulled her hard onto him, surging so deep it felt like he pierced her soul, the colors paused and shimmered with the same breathless anticipation that froze her as she ached around him. He was too much, it was too much. She shook her head. "No."

"Everything, my heart.

She found a thread of her voice. "I can't."

With relentless purpose he pulled back and thrust deeper, forcing her past what she thought was possible. "You will."

His tone brooked no denial. His cock accepted no resistance. Her body offered none, her mind couldn't find any. Even tied in the lab she hadn't felt this helpless, this out of control. "Oh God, Dusan. Please help me."

"I am here." The assurance echoed off the different colors, leaving small sparks of light lingering in its wake.

"I don't know what to do."

"Just feel me. Feel me in you."

As if she had any choice. "You're too much."

"I am what you need."

"They'll kill you."

"They cannot."

"They'll take Jalina."

"They will not."

"You're her only hope."

"You will trust me." He thrust the last two inches into her. The scream tore from her throat as red poured over the colors, drowning them in a churning sea. In the distance a black cloud formed, racing toward her, turning the waves it covered from red to burgundy. "More Edie. Take all of me."

There was a pain in her throat, followed by a strong suction and then a surge of pleasure that ricocheted through her so fast it snapped her head back. She ground her pussy into his groin, needing more. He pulled her thighs wider, granting her wish, until it was too much. She fought but he wouldn't let her get away, just held her there and forced her to accept what she couldn't. The pain in her throat abated. The black cloud spread and slowed. Her pussy ached and throbbed. Her clit strained. The ring bounced and burned.

"I take you into my protection, mate. My heart for yours. My life for yours. My soul for yours. Through this time and the next." She had an impression of black eyes staring at her from the black cloud, holding it back, demanding something from her. She wanted to give it. Whatever he wanted, she wanted to give it. "I don't understand."

"Do you want my seed, Edie?"

"I don't know." She didn't know what she needed. She ached and throbbed with an emptiness she couldn't stand and a need she couldn't define.

"You know." His desire swamped her. She could feel how hungry he was, how his cock ached for her, how full his balls were. How he burned for her.

"Yes."

"Yes what?"

The eyes grew in size. The sense of urgency grew. The ache intensified. "I can't."

"Tell me what you need."

"I need your seed?"

"How much?" The cloud shimmered along the edges with glints of silver.

She wrapped her legs around him, and pulled him closer, moaning when her raw flesh protested. "All of it. All you can give me."

The eyes flashed as red as the sea in her mind, and then she was empty. Before she could protest, he was back, driving into her harder than before. His desire tangled with hers as his mouth lowered to hers. "You shall have it."

His kiss was as wild as the pace he set, his tongue thrusting deep as his cock drove hard into her slick channel, accepting no refusal. And she offered none, opening her legs and accepting him as he needed. Taking what he offered, until with a harsh groan, he buried himself to the hilt. His fingers dug into her buttocks as his cock flexed within her and then his rich seed poured into her channel, burning and soothing at the same time.

She twisted in his arms. The cloud seethed and rolled. The sea churned. The eyes grew and swirled with red. She couldn't breathe, couldn't move. His hand pressed low on her abdomen.

"Relax."

Something deep inside softened as he continued to come. He shifted against her, pulling back before pressing forward cautiously, as if searching. The eyes glowed. The cloud coiled and tensed. There was a sharp pain that spread into an ache. "Dusan?"

"Be easy."

His voice was uncharacteristically harsh. She was not reassured. There was something wrong. "I don't think…"

"It is as it should be." He held her steady with his hands as he eased forward. An incredible pressure surged outward. His cock slid deeper, but it was different. Wrong.

She tried to push him away. Her strength was no match for his. It hurt, but at the same time, she wanted more. She clawed at his shoulders, trying to pull him closer. The scent of blood joined the scent of sex and sweat. He swore in his own language. With one hand he held her anchored, not allowing her relief. The other slashed his chest. His order to feed was a guttural bark of sound in her mind. She did, horrified and elated as the sweet taste of his blood filed her mouth.

"Yes." His head dropped back. "Take from me." His hand gripped her buttock, pulling her right hip forward into his, sending shards of pain and pleasure through her. "Accept me."

She had no choice. With a steady push that felt like he was splitting her in two, he gained what he wanted. Muscles she couldn't identify clutched at his cock, every spasm causing splinters of delight to whip through her, burying the pain under an avalanche of pleasure so intense she screamed. It was too much. She wouldn't survive. His cock jerked, tugging at her sensitive flesh. More come soaked her deep inside, feeding her hunger yet satisfying her need. The storm clouds gathered and whirled. The eyes glowed red. Wind churned the waves to a high froth. The tension built to intolerable levels. The cloud swept forward, promising to destroy all in its path.

Dusan's "I am here" fell into the turmoil, separating the colors, calming the waves. She threw herself into the huddle of calm, reaching for him with her heart and mind. His arms came around her. She wrapped her left around him. The jarring drove his big cock deeper that fraction of an inch she needed and the black cloud detonated into a shower of light as her body convulsed violently against his, pleasure so piercing she couldn't bear it taking her out of herself, her only anchor Dusan's soft whisper of "Come to me."

* * * * *

Eden came back to herself slowly. She was lying on top of Deuce as he lay on the floor. His hard body labored beneath hers, rocking her with the force of his breathing. Calmer now, she was aware of the incredible fullness in her abdomen. Before she changed positions, Deuce's hand on her buttocks held her in place. "Do not move."

His fingers slid into the crease of her ass, sliding along slick flesh until he reached the tight ring of her anus. As if he anticipated her start, his other hand pressed down. His finger probed as she felt his cock jerk. The pressure within her increased.

"Oh God." He was still coming. "What have you done?"

"We are mated the Chosen way."

Internal feminine muscles clenched. He groaned and jerked. Pain and pleasure blended as his cock danced deep within. "What does that mean?"

He didn't answer verbally, but an image of his cock sliding through her cervix flashed through her mind.

"That's not possible!" Horror built in the aftermath. Her mind denied the reality, but her body knew the truth.

"Be easy."

"You'll kill me."

"I pleasured you and will do so again if you but allow me to finish."

"You're finished."

He cupped her cheek. "This is an intimate time between lovers when our bodies are joined, and I fill you with my seed." Another jerk of his cock and more fullness.

"Deuce…"

His hand closed over her breast. His thumb stroked her nipple. Her muscles clenched and her womb spasmed. Deuce's groan was immediate. His fingers dug into her hip "Lie against me mate, and be still. Do not provoke further joining until this one is done."

She didn't want to provoke anything. She lay against him, both horrified and fascinated as he stroked her hair while his big cock pulsed within her. Her throat ached. She brought her hand to the spot. "You...fed from me?"

Red lights flashed in his eyes. His smile was pure male satisfaction. "Yes."

"Why?"

"The bond must go both ways to be strong."

She didn't know enough about the process to argue. Besides, other parts of her were getting distinctly uncomfortable. "How much more?"

"Relax." His finger pressed against her anus. "Many Chosen women enjoy this time to the point of climax."

"I'm not Chosen."

"But you are my woman." He groaned as she twisted, and pressed in with his finger. She arched against him as his finger pierced her anus. He jerked and the sense of fullness intensified dramatically. "You are a greedy woman," he said with a slight smile.

"I am not."

He shook his head at her. Sweat beaded his brow and he closed his eyes. "Your body calls the seed forth from mine."

"Does it hurt you?"

He cracked an eyelid and smiled gently. "It is extremely pleasurable to meet your needs."

She felt her inner muscles clutch at him. More seed poured from him. Her womb cramped on a sharp pain. "Deuce!"

"Be still."

His cock jerked as his hand cupped her abdomen over her womb. There was a moment of unbearable pressure and then a relaxation inside. "Your body but stretches to accept what it demands."

"I don't want this."

He pulled her down to his chest. Beneath her ear she could hear the accelerated beat of his heart. His voice was strained. "Many women are fearful their first time."

"What if you puncture something?"

"Never has such a thing happened."

Something brushed her hair. She knew it was his lips the same way she knew he was enjoying this.

"Lie against me and let yourself feel what is happening between us."

She did because she didn't have a choice.

Deuce held Edie as she lay tensely against him, keeping his grip light, his thoughts soothing as she clenched around him again, milking more of his seed from him, her womb stretching to handle the flow. Her fear pushed at him to the point that he would have stopped this if he could have, but the joining was determined by things beyond his control.

"Have you done this a lot?" Edie's question ended on a sharp cry as a spasm of her cervix sent bolts of fire up his spine and a hard jet of seed from his cock. He could feel her confusion as pleasure teased the edges of her consciousness.

"Only mates know this sharing," he answered when he could get his breath.

Her "Oh" was a soft exclamation.

Her muscles rippled again, squeezing him and stretching her. Seed poured from his body in a burning rush. Her eyes flew wide with panic and pleasure as her womb stretched, putting pressure on the nerves connected to her clitoris.

He kissed the top of her head. "Let the pleasure come."

"I can't take any more." The last word ended in a gasp.

"Your climax will signal the end."

"Pull out."

"I cannot without damaging you."

"Oh God." The scared little cry came as her body worked his penis. He held her close, keeping her as still as possible, not sure himself how much more she could take. She was not Chosen. He was taking it on faith that this would not harm her.

He slid his hand between them. Her stomach bulged with what she had already taken. She struggled as he pressed, nature fighting for what it wanted, wiggling her hips, jostling him within, drawing more semen from his balls long past when he thought he should be empty.

The urgency increased between them. Eden panted and moaned, her nails digging into his chest as she grasped his cock with strong muscles, her scent, her need, demanding he satisfy her.

He was helpless to do anything but give her what she needed. The tension in his balls spread outward, hardening his muscles into a solid knot of desire as he battled to keep the flow light, trying not to overwhelm her. The next clench of her womb tore the last of his control from his grasp, squeezing him so hard and long that the dam broke, and he arched beneath her, mindless with the primitive need to answer her call, his body bucking against her as she screamed and climaxed above him, milking him to the last drop, eager for everything he could give.

She fell against him as he bucked one last time. His cock vainly tried to give her another drop, another piece of himself. She groaned and braced her hands on his chest, as if to pull away. He grasped her thigh before she could do herself damage. He caught her hand in his and brought it to her stomach. "You did well."

She knelt stiffly above him. His cock still firmly embedded in her womb, too big to withdraw, the echoes of her climax rippling through them both.

He felt the distress shudder through her. "What is it?"

"Your hand." She bit her lip and closed her eyes before admitting. "It's too much."

He was not surprised. She had taken more than he would have expected. He gentled his touch but could not resist curving his fingers on the convex curve of her stomach. A seeded woman was a thing of beauty. "You are beautiful."

She looked down, shock in her eyes and voice as she saw the small distension caused by their union. "I'm a bloated cow."

"Any Chosen man who saw you now would be instantly in rut." She cast him a glance that indicated he'd lost his mind.

"There is something beyond beautiful in a seeded woman to the point that many of our women wear clothes to imitate the state."

"You have got to be kidding me."

He stretched his fingers wide and then pulled them back, soothing her discomfort as best he could. "It is much the same as the padded bra you wore when we first met."

She blushed. He traced the heat as it raced over her skin, up her chest and to her neck where the bruise from his bite remained. "I would show you off now."

"I don't think so."

He laughed, biting back a moan as his cock softened and slipped a little. "I do not know of another woman as greedy for her mate's seed. I am feeling quite proud."

She shifted.

"Unless it is your intent to mate again, you would do well to sit still and allow my cock to soften."

"You could do that again?"

"I am Chosen." He pushed her hair off her shoulder, tracing her collarbone to her breastbone, following it down to the softness of her midriff, irresistibly drawn to the bulge of her stomach. "I can do that as often as you require." Desire and heat flared anew. He hooked his finger in the joining ring that glistened with her pleasure and lifted his gaze to hers. "It is no hardship."

The tiny answering clench of her pussy froze her stiff. "Please, Deuce."

He shook his head at her ignorance. "I was but teasing, mate. I cannot seed you in succession." Though he wished he could. He would love to see her abdomen distended with his come, love to parade her past the Others with a belly so round she would have to waddle as Chosen had in days of old, her stomach marking her so much his that none would dare to trespass.

"You mentioned other women."

"Yes."

"Where are they?"

"With their mates."

"They're not here?"

"No."

"Their husbands don't want to risk them being hurt by the Coalition, do they?"

"Our females cannot be risked."

"That makes sense."

He still felt her hurt and despair. She was a social woman. A woman who took pleasure in people and came alive at parties. To be viewed as a pariah, even for the most logical of reasons would bother her. "It will not always be like this, Edie."

"I know." She stroked his chest. "It's not your fault."

She forgave him too easily. "It is, but I will correct it."

She didn't say anything, just lay above him, for once quiet, her weight off to one side to accommodate his possession. There was silence while he stroked her back. Her ribs rose and fell under his hand. Peace reigned for a few minutes, then there was a hitch in her breathing and a transition. He waited for the question he could feel building.

"How will you get it out?"

"You will relax and bear down, and I will gently withdraw."

The way her nails cut into his arms let him know relaxing wouldn't necessarily be accomplished easily. She was very nervous about this. He was soft enough to pull out now, had been for several minutes, but he liked being joined with her. "We could do it now."

"It's going to hurt, isn't it?"

"You will not mind."

He cupped his hand low on her stomach, shaking his head as her panic began. He adjusted her breathing and adrenaline levels before ordering her to bear down. She did, yet managed to clench at the same time. He rolled her to the floor. He braced himself over her and settled his thumb on her puffy clit. He stroked it gently as he withdrew. "Bear down, Edie mine."

She did. The way her eyes flew wide told him she had expected pain, but the pleasure took her by surprise. His fingers slid easily over her sensitive nubbin, rubbing gently until her breathing came in hard gasps. He pulled harder, pinching her clit as his cock head popped free. She cried out, taking the pain as pleasure. Her pussy was swollen, almost raw from the unaccustomed activity. The extra heat bathed him in residual pleasure. Deuce bent his head to her breast, sucking her nipple and nipping the taut crest as he milked her clit until she climaxed. Her hands fisted in his hair, yanking hard before she arched her back and screamed, her mind accepting the embrace of his—at last.

As the last of her climax rippled away, he heard what she did. A strong female voice screaming, *Run!*

Chapter Seventeen

⌘

He could not trace the source.

A woman connected with the Coalition had a private path to his mate, a path so strong she could block Eden and his child from his senses while she could communicate at will. He did not like it at all. He held Edie still beneath him and tried to find the connection point, but the woman ducked his efforts, anticipating what he wanted to know and moving on. She was very skilled. And she wanted Edie to run.

As she retreated he built barriers around Edie's mind. They would not keep her out forever, but they would slow her down.

As if she heard his thoughts, Eden pushed at his shoulders. "Let me up."

Deuce caught her before she could slip from beneath him. "Remain where you are."

"I have to go." She wiggled down and to the side.

He stopped her by simply resting his elbow on the floor. "There is no need to run."

She froze.

"You heard her?" Surprise pitched her voice to an octave above normal.

"Yes."

"How?"

"We are mates." He touched the pleat between her brows, an indication of the worry tensing her muscles.

"That's your excuse for everything."

"It is not an excuse."

"It's not a reason either for invading my privacy." She shivered. "Stay out of my head." The order lacked strength.

"No." He lifted her away from the coolness of the floor before gliding to his feet. She swayed. He pulled her to him. The taut swell of her stomach against him reminded him of her fragility. He cupped her cheek in his palm. "I have said they will never touch you."

Shadows haunted her blue eyes. "They know where I am."

"That is not certain."

Edie pushed away his arm, rejecting his touch. "She would never tell me to run unless they were close."

He caught her wrist, drawing her up short. She winced as she took a step, the delicate muscles between her thighs protesting movement.

"Who is she?"

"I don't know."

"They use her to find you?"

"Somehow." She cast a glance at the door.

"Yet she protects you."

"I think so." She took another step and winced again.

"She is connected to you."

"I don't know how."

He would—soon.

"But you trust her enough to run on her order?"

"Yes."

"You will do so no more."

She took a deep breath and closed her eyes, but shielding her gaze could not hide the turmoil putting the tremble in her hands and mixing the scent of desperation with the scent of satisfaction. "I don't know what to do."

"I do." She flinched on the next step. He slid his arm under her knees and swung her up against his chest. She lay against him, neither cooperating nor fighting.

"I can walk."

"You are sore."

"Whose fault is that?"

He lay her on the white comforter, "Mine, which makes the healing my responsibility."

He brushed her hair off her cheeks. She seemed to glow from within as she lay on the bed, her skin whiter than white and her hair brighter that gold. Her breasts were still swollen, would stay that way as long as his seed sought fruit. He trailed his fingers down her throat, over the mark of his possession, down into the damp center of her cleavage, to her upper abdomen, until he reached the well of her navel. He circled the rim before dipping his hand to cup the evidence of their mating. He knelt, brushed the small mound with his lips, and breathed deeply of her scent. "You are the mother of my child, the keeper of my future."

Her hands slipped between his mouth and her skin. "Will this go away?"

He glanced up, running his tongue between her fingers, sensing the shivers that ran up her arm, giving her more. "If you do not conceive, yes."

He knew she heard the hope in his voice, the excitement at the thought of her pregnancy, by the shock in her voice. "You want me to conceive?"

"It would please me."

"It wouldn't please me."

Her unease was strong. He had flashes of the baby and a sense of danger. "Because you see the future as uncertain."

"Because I've just had a baby."

That was not the reason, though it might be if things had been normal. "You are uncertain."

"Aren't you?"

"No." He wanted another child with her more than anything. He wanted to be with her from start to finish, to guard her, ease her through the changes, watch them both bloom. He touched her stomach. The comforter rustled as she shifted uneasily. He leaned in until he could cup her stomach. "Another child would be a gift."

"He'd be hunted."

"It will be a girl."

"How do you know?"

"Chosen and human matings always produce girls."

She shifted again. "That must piss you off."

"I do not like your swearing." He stood and moved to her head. Her confusion and frustration consumed her emotions. He would lessen both if he knew how. "And why would you think any child would be a disappointment?"

"Men always want sons." There was resentment in her voice that he could not understand.

"Any child gifted to the Chosen is valued by all."

She shifted up. He caught her under the shoulders, helping her past the last of her weakness. "So pretty much, I'm just a baby machine to everyone these days."

He accepted the lash of her bitterness without correction. "You are my mate."

"You didn't want me until you knew Jalina was yours."

"I wanted you."

"I could tell by how fast you came for me."

Pain overwhelmed the bitterness in the words, the dual emotions lashing out from within the residue of her satisfaction. He had an impression of hope gone dry and a hell beyond endurance. His grip tightened on her shoulder as guilt flowed from his center. "You believed I would come?"

Her gaze dropped from his, as if there was shame in a woman believing her mate would do anything less. "It was stupid."

"It was not stupid." He did not know if he would ever learn to live with the ways he had failed her, the marks her body bore because he had grown complacent. Marks he would not heal as they served a warning to him of how dangerous complacency could be. "I did not come because I thought you dead, but never again will I accept less than proof from my own eyes."

She shrugged, her breasts rising and falling on the lie. "It was just one of those things."

He tipped her chin up. Her eyes did not follow, remaining instead locked on her clenched hands. "You will not hide behind polite words. Your faith in me was broken."

"I didn't know you well enough to have faith."

He touched her too thin cheek, drawing her gaze. "You hoped."

"I was desperate."

"You still are." Her start betrayed everything she sought to hide. "Do you think I do not feel your turmoil?"

Her big blue eyes widened further. He brushed his thumb over her parted lips.

"It is the way it is. In this life and the next, I am bound to you. We cannot be parted without death." He slowed her heartbeat and breathing. Her mental panic evaded his efforts. "You will tell me what upsets you."

She grabbed his wrist. Her nails dug deep as she gasped, "They'll come for me."

"I am anticipating it."

"You don't know them." Her grip tightened and her breath caught. "They won't give up."

"It does not matter."

She was shaking her head before he finished the statement. "They'll keep coming until they get me."

He cupped her throat in his hand. His thumb rested against the mark from his bite. "They will never take you from me."

"But if I leave, they will follow."

The thought of her out there alone trying to stay ahead of the men who hunted her made his blood run cold. "You will not leave."

She tugged at his arm. Her strength barely registered against his. She was so weak. So human. She took a breath. Her fear of being captured again was so strong it flavored the air. She grabbed his wrist with both hands, her arms shaking with the need to make him understand. "You and Jalina have a chance to escape if I can lead them away." Hope lifted her voice. "You can take her so far away they'll never find her."

On the edges of her consciousness he felt the subtle probe. Was the stranger responding to Edie's distress or taking advantage of it? "Your plan is unacceptable."

She shook his arm. "It's good if you stop thinking in terms of keeping me."

"Since the day I found you, there has never been another thought."

Her lips pulled back from her teeth. If she were Chosen, her fangs would be flashing in the lamplight. "Goddamn you!" She yanked away from him. "Why can't you understand?"

She shoved her hair off her face, holding it against her head, pressing in with her palms as memories fed into the stream of her panic. "They can't take Jalina. You can't know what they'll do to her, what they'll put her through trying to become immortal."

"They will not touch her." Instead of soothing her, his calm unleashed her fury.

"Damn you!" She took a swing at him. He caught her hand before it could connect with his face. Her "You have to protect her" was a feral snarl flying in the wake of her blow. She swung at him again. He caught that one too, gentling his grip when she winced. He pulled her close as a subtle stirring began in her mind. The probe strengthened, giving him a path to follow. Deuce lashed out at the next foray, blocking the stranger before she could connect. Satisfaction at the faint echo of shock from the intruder filtered through his guilt and rage. Good. Let her run and tell the Coalition his mate was no longer unprotected. Let them fear the retribution of the Chosen.

He stroked Edie's hair off her face, following the waves down her back, into the hollow of her spine where he lingered, pressing her into him, wanting to give her his strength, knowing he didn't deserve her trust but needing it anyway. "Be calm, Edie." She pressed her forehead into his chest as he said, "Jalina is safe and so are you."

She shook her head, her forehead rocking on his breastbone as her hands opened on either side of her face, the fingertips stretching away, as if through sheer force of will she could undo all that was. Her tears left damp patches on his chest. "She'll never be safe as long as I live."

He could not bear her torment. It tore at his calm, bringing forth emotions as primitive as hers were strong. Dangerous emotions he could not control. He pulled her closer, her stomach pressing into his thighs, a small reminder that they had a future. "Your death would not stop anything."

"If they can't find her, they can't hurt her."

She clutched that plan with an unreasonable fervor. "You have thought on this for a long time."

"I had nothing but time to think." Her hands relaxed into his chest, one knuckle at a time as if she were forcing herself to calm. He wished he had her ability to manage the emotions that raged from her to him.

"That plan was made when you were alone, but you would do well to remember you have a mate now."

"You can't fight them all."

"Dak is right." He tipped her chin up and wiped the tear from the corner of her mouth. "You are hard on a mate's ego."

He did not get the smile he'd been looking for with his joke. Her chin trembled a second before the muscles in her jaw bunched. The faint grind of her teeth proceeded her, "Chosen or not, you're just one man. They are hundreds."

"You are not alone and neither am I. You are one of the Chosen, and we will guard what is ours."

"Jalina?"

"In six hundred years, no Chosen union has been blessed. And only one Other family has conceived. Jalina is more precious than you can understand. She is our hope for the future. She will not be taken while a Chosen draws breath."

"I want to believe you."

"You have no choice. If the Coalition knows anything about the Chosen, they know that all they need to do to get me is to capture you."

She gasped. "You can't let them take you!"

"Then you cannot allow me to think they have you."

"But you would know…"

He shook his head, his hair brushing her cheeks before settling amidst the blonde strands of hers on the top of her chest. "As the woman you hear in your head can block me, I would not know. And I would not chance thinking a truth a lie."

"But Jalina—"

"Is only safe if you are with me. And you cannot leave me."

Eden leaned back, her instinctive trust that he would not let her fall settling some of the anger surging at her insistence on leaving. "You keep saying that."

"You need to feed regularly or you will die."

Beneath his hand, her spine pulled taut. "How regularly?"

"Daily."

"Good God! I can't be away from you for more than a day?" Her shock at this announcement left her totally dependent upon his strength.

"Your discomfort would become unbearable after two."

She shoved at his hold. "You mean I'm a junkie, and you're my drug?"

He held her easily, not trusting her apart from him as she absorbed this. "It is as it should be."

"You never told me that."

"I told you it was forever."

"But not that I would be addicted."

"Bonding is not an addiction."

"So says the man who can walk away."

"I can no more walk away than you can."

"Right."

Dak was right. Her ignorance was dangerous. "My life force is bonded to yours. If you die, I die. It is that simple."

She slumped against him. "Oh God, you totally messed things up."

If ever a plan needed "messing up", it was hers. "I set things right."

She had nothing to say, just lay against him, her despair prodding his beast to roar in frustration. There was nothing he could say to ease this for her. A Chosen woman would rejoice at coming under a mate's care. His independent human viewed it as a fate worse than death.

He changed the subject. "This woman who speaks to you, can you block her?"

It took her a minute to switch subjects. A small shake of her head preceded her "No".

"But you can block me." He made it a statement of fact.

She looked up and bit her lip, the natural red color receding under a wash of white from the pressure of her teeth. "She can. I can't do much on my own."

"Unless I touch you?" The woman had to be a very strong telepath, her connection to Edie just as great to accomplish so much from afar.

She nodded and shrugged as if it didn't matter. "I don't know why."

Neither did he, but he would. "The reason will be discovered. In the meantime, it will be my pleasure to touch you often."

Touching her was his greatest pleasure and biggest distraction. He needed to talk to Dak and Nick. Security needed to be updated on the new threat. He needed to feed again before dawn so he would not awaken weakened. He needed to do many things, but instead he stood there, his discipline subdued as if it were nothing as he savored the texture of her skin, the scent of her pleasure, the gentle beat of her heart. His hand drifted to her belly again.

She sighed and stepped back. "You are obsessed with my stomach."

He followed her, cupping his hand over the curve. "You are beautiful like this. Has your discomfort eased?"

"It's no worse than my time of the month."

Excitement surged through his body like a streak of lightning. "I had forgotten that humans bleed."

She rolled her eyes. "The proper term is menstruate."

Menstruate, bleed, he would not quibble over a term. "When is your next time?"

"Far enough away that we don't need to worry about it."

"I was not worried."

Her blush heated her chest and face to a fiery red that made her hair glow like spun gold in contrast. "We are so not going there."

He was definitely going there, but he did not need to argue about it now. "I need to advise the Others on the security issues and to feed."

She stepped back. "Go ahead. I'm fine."

She was far from fine. Too much had happened, too fast for that, but she was as good as could be expected. "I will have food and Jalina brought to you."

Her initial response was joy, quickly buried under a flood of desperation that dissolved under a wash of love so intense that he didn't know why she thought she could ever stay distant from her daughter.

"So much for our one night."

"There will be others. Many others."

Her doubt swept over him in disturbing ripples. Deuce paused before opening the door. A glance over his shoulder showed her slipping back into another too big T-shirt and shorts. He needed to get her more clothes. Clothes that defined her beauty. Clothes that left no doubt to all Chosen that she was mated. Maybe then he could get the wildness she inspired in him under control. He would ask Marlika to shop for her.

He drew himself up to his full height, sending his senses out, scanning the area for threat, blinking as he absorbed the information flowing back. The enemy gathered. "You are not alone, Edie. Those who have harmed you will be punished. Those who think to harm you will not succeed."

"Deuce?"

Edie stood staring at him, the dark blue of the borrowed shirt highlighting the wariness that developed in her eyes whenever she saw him as too different. He paused halfway through the door. "Yes?"

"What does your name mean?"

He met her gaze without flinching. "Lord and judge."

Chapter Eighteen

၈၅

The sun was just coming up over the trees, the bright light piercing the gently stirring leaves to strobe across her eyes and face. Eden hitched Jalina up on her shoulder and sat down on the top step of the porch, dragging the comforter around them both against the chill. Deuce's shorts and T-shirts weren't much in the way of insulation.

She tilted her head back, as the light touched her skin. It felt incredibly strong for winter, but welcome. Oh so welcome. She felt like she'd been in the dark so long. She shifted on the cold wood of the porch and turned the baby in her arm. She carefully pulled the blanket away from her little face. "See that, baby girl? That's the sun."

Jalina stared ahead of her as if fascinated. Eden didn't know if she was staring at the sun or the scenery. Truth be told, she didn't know if she saw like a human baby or if her vision was enhanced by her Chosen blood. It was simply enough that she was in the light of day, breathing the freshness of the air, listening to the sounds of the daylight world waking up.

Eden kissed the top of her head, whispering against its downy softness, "Remember how this feels, Jalina."

She felt rather than heard the presence of another behind her on the steps. It had to be the Other, Harley, who'd been assigned to protect her. The man irritated her. He was too damn male, too damn arrogant and too damn sure of himself. And there was that little incident when he'd tried to scare her off. She was still holding a grudge on that.

"You shouldn't be out here."

"I know."

"Deuce isn't going to like it."

"I know." In truth he was pushing at her to go back inside, an insistent nag at the back of her mind.

"I'm afraid I'm going to have to insist you come in."

A quick glance showed he was serious. As tall as Deuce and very heavily muscled with a bandanna wrapped around his head he was an imposing figure. He was probably counting on that to make his "insistence" enough.

"Not yet."

Harley sighed. "I was afraid you were going to take that tone." He soundlessly walked down the steps until he stood on the bottom one directly in front of her.

"You're blocking my light."

"I'm also blocking the sight line of anyone wanting to get a shot at you."

She shook her head. He so did not understand the nature of her enemy. "You might as well take a seat."

He hitched the gun up on his shoulder. His coat parted, revealing the broad expanse of his chest. "I'll stand."

"I'm no use to them dead."

"I'm not putting anything past the sons of bitches."

Jalina jerked in her grip. Her head bobbing against her chest with baby uncoordination. She seemed fascinated by the belt buckle of the big man before her. She made a funny hiccupping sound.

The harsh planes of Harley's face softened as he looked down. "She's just a bit of a thing to have so many hopes hanging on her."

"Yes." But the weight of those hopes was ballast against her own fears that the Others would eventually resent the danger Jalina brought them. She had high hopes that the fear of extinction would keep them fighting in Jalina's corner. "I'm sorry for the trouble we're bringing you."

Harley looked up, his amber eyes crinkling slightly at the corners. "There's nothing to apologize for. In case you haven't figured it out, Others and Chosen are predators at heart. The need to kick up a fuss now and then is what gives the Coalition an edge."

"You fight among yourselves?"

He shrugged. "In that way, we're not so different than humans." He tilted his head at her in a gesture that took in more than just her location "This change is hard for you."

"It takes some getting used to. Especially with Deuce being such a…" She bit her tongue on the words "pain in the ass".

"A polite term for the phrase you're looking for might be protective."

She blew out a breath. "That'll work. He doesn't understand how smothering his care is."

"The Chosen are very close to their mates."

"And the Others aren't?"

His smile broadened to wry. "Nope. We're a hell of a lot more reasonable. We're content to just tuck our mates into our back pockets."

"I bet." She'd noticed that the Others had more modern speech patterns than the Chosen, there wasn't a thing about them that made her think they were open-minded when it came to their mates. For one thing, they still referred to them in that archaic, possessive term — mates. "Could you please step aside?"

"My job is to protect you."

"If you don't let me see the sun rise, I swear I'm gong to lose my mind, and where will that leave you with Deuce?"

He cocked his head to the side. "That bad?"

"I haven't seen the sun for days and the only time I've breathed fresh air I was too busy freezing my butt off to care."

Harley whistled. "I can see where that would leave a sun worshipper in a bad way."

As he stepped aside the sun broke over his shoulder, hitting her full in the face. Jalina bucked in her arms. A quick glance showed her little face screwed up.

In one smooth move, Harley flicked the blanket over her eyes. "Must be she has her daddy's sensitivity to light."

Eden took a breath. "Does everyone accept that she's Deuce's?"

He paused halfway back to straight, his shadow covering Jalina. "Is there a reason they shouldn't?"

"No."

"Then why bring it up?"

"Because if they don't, she won't be accepted."

Harley straightened to his full height, forcing Eden to arch her neck. "She's Deuce's daughter, by his decree and Bohdan's. There will be no question."

Relief almost swamped her. Immediately, Harley reached for her. Almost as quickly, he was shoved back by an angry force. Unbelievably, he laughed.

Eden blinked. The man was primitively devastating when he laughed.

"That's one possessive Chosen you have there."

She shrugged, ignoring Deuce's mental prod to *Come inside. Now.* "He's going to have to learn to adjust."

"Uh-huh." Harley turned and scanned the surrounding area as he said, "If I were you I wouldn't count on him backing off too much that way."

"Why is that?"

"Did you ask him?"

"Yes."

"And?"

She shrugged. "He just says we're mates as if that explains everything." The sun was rising in the sky, getting stronger. It warmed her skin like midday in the summer rather than early morning winter.

"I imagine to him, it does."

She brought her hand up to shield her eyes. "Can you explain it better?"

"I'm not Chosen, so no."

"How is it for Others?"

"We're incomplete our whole lives until we meet our mates."

"Like humans."

His hair rustled against his leather coat as he shook his head. "Unlike humans who get along, seemingly oblivious to the fact that part of them is missing, Others know from the minute they are born that they are only part of what they should be."

"Makes me glad I'm human."

"The hunger is hard to live with, but the resolution is a gift beyond price."

"Are you married?"

"I haven't met the right woman yet."

"Then how do you know?"

"A wolf is born with the knowing." He took two steps to the left, his lips quirking as his shadow shifted.

"What are you doing?"

"Balancing out your color."

She touched her right cheek. No wonder the sun felt so strong. "I'm burning?"

"A side effect of marrying up with the Chosen is an increased sensitivity to the sun." He motioned to Jalina. "You should get her back inside."

She leaned over to kiss the top of her daughter's blanketed head as she accepted the truth. Jalina was never going to play in the park with other kids, splash in the ocean as waves sparkling with sunlight washed around her, laughing with other children as she built memories during long summer days to cherish for a lifetime. "I just wanted her to know a little of my world."

She knew he'd heard the catch in her voice by the gentleness in his tone as he said, "She might build a tolerance over time."

"Or she might get worse and not even be able to bear a single ray. Like Deuce."

"It won't change how she feels about you."

"She won't even know me. We'll have nothing in common, no similar experiences, no common pleasures."

Oh God, now she was going to blubber like a baby in front of a man who looked like he could take on a whole motorcycle gang and walk away unscathed. A white handkerchief appeared in front of her face. A werewolf dressed like a biker who carried a clean handkerchief? The laugh that burst from her throat caught her by surprise. "I think I'm losing my mind."

Deuce's probe was not subtle. She closed her eyes and concentrated on blocking him.

When she opened them Harley's expression was knowing. "You should let him comfort you."

"By letting him take over my mind?"

"Sharing is not the same as taking."

"As my mind is the only thing I have left that's mine..." She stood. He caught her arm, steadying her on the step. She turned away. "I think I'll keep it just mine."

The porch boards creaked as Harley followed her to the door. "Punishing him won't change anything," he said as he reached around her to open it.

"I'm not punishing him, just holding onto me."

"Uh-huh."

The house was dim after the bright light. She stubbed her toe on an end table. "Do you think we could open some curtains?"

"You can ask Deuce when he gets up. With Chosen living in the mansion, we have to take precautions."

Jalina whimpered. No doubt she was hungry. Eden changed her direction to the kitchen. "How sensitive is a full-blown Chosen to light?"

"It burns them like acid in a matter of minutes."

So much for her hope that the new sunscreen clothing might allow them a more normal life. Her slippers made a slight swishing sound as she went down the hall. Noise came from the kitchen. As she got closer, she recognized voices. She stopped. Harley drew up beside her. "It's just Dak and some of the Pride welcoming back one of our members."

"A Chosen?"

He cocked an eyebrow at her as if to ask if that made a difference. "No. Other."

"Oh."

She wasn't ready to sit in a group of Others and try to pretend everything was normal and that she wasn't sitting in the middle of a bunch of freaking actual living, breathing werepeople.

"They won't hurt you."

"I know."

Harley shifted the gun strap on his shoulder. "Then why are you standing here in the hall?"

"Believe it or not, I'm having a bit of a dramatic moment contemplating so many figments of my imagination at once."

"You don't think we're real?"

"I didn't used to."

"And now?"

"I'm trying to take it all in."

"C'mon. I'll introduce you."

She didn't want to be introduced to a bunch of strange men. Especially the newcomer. The knowledge hit her with the force of a sledgehammer. She backed up. Harley caught her arm. She pulled away. He frowned and then dropped his hand.

"How about I get the little one's formula and some of whatever they've cooked up and bring it to the living room? You can eat it while watching TV."

The living room was only a few feet from the kitchen. Not much of a safety zone, but it was something. "Thank you. That would be good." Harley turned on his heel. The nervousness inside her built as he got near the door. He reached for the kitchen doorknob. The panic built to intolerable.

She took another step back. One, two, holding Jalina closer with each step. As his lean fingers closed around the door handle, she knew the living room wasn't far enough. "But I think I'll have it in my room."

Harley's only response was a lift of his brow and a nod. She bolted for the stairs, knowing nothing more than that she needed to be out of sight before that door opened.

As soon as she reached the stairs some of the unreasoning panic faded, but her sense of urgency increased. She raced down the dozen steps, practically throwing the bedroom door open. She closed and locked it behind her, looking around the room, seeing Deuce sprawled on the bed, his body in the same position as when she'd left, the sheet she'd twitched over his privates still in place. She leaned against the door and held Jalina against her. Her heart pounded in her ears and her mouth was so dry it hurt to swallow. She moved toward the bed and Deuce. Even though he was comatose, he was at least big enough to give the impression of safety. She sat carefully on the edge. The mattress dipped. Jalina whimpered again, a soft cry that built in volume to the end. "It's okay, baby," she whispered as she patted the little girl's back, "we're safe now."

Her words hit her like a slap in the face. She was actually cowering in her bedroom, huddled up against Deuce's unconscious body, because—why? There were Others about? There was nothing new in that. The only thing new was that one of *them* was new. To her anyway. There was no reason for her to be reacting this way, unless...

She looked down at Deuce. Unless someone was putting the idea in her head. The only one she could think of who was so inspired was the man supposedly dead to the world.

"Damn you!" She slapped his shoulder. "Can't you even leave me alone when you sleep?" Deuce didn't answer, didn't move, but she thought she felt a flutter of concern at the edge of her mind. She ruthlessly blocked it. "You're so helpless right now I could do anything to you and you couldn't prevent it."

She could leave, stay, hurt him, their daughter. It was hard to believe, but at this time, he was truly vulnerable, all that big muscle and bone useless against anyone who would harm him. She paused, the realization coming to her that he actually had a vulnerability. One that her grandfather could take advantage of. She touched his arm. He didn't move, but the sensation of comfort came to her again. He was Chosen, a different species, but he cared for her. Took care of her like no other and as much as it irritated her, she liked the thought that if she needed him, he would be there.

Always. The reassurance whispered into her mind. So he wasn't totally out when he slept, but he was still weak.

The Others are here, also.

She should have known he would have that angle covered. She leaned over and touched her mouth to his. It was so hard to be cold and aloof when he gave to her so effortlessly. "Thank you."

She sensed rather than felt his smile, but that didn't diminish her reaction to it. Part of her delighted to bring happiness to him. The other part of her did not like the strangeness of him lying so placidly. She was used to Deuce taking charge, aggressively staking his claim. Having his lips so calm under hers created a sick feeling in her stomach.

There was a surge of power around her and his black eyes opened. "You do not sleep."

How could she explain that lying next to what in essence was a corpse creeped her out? "No."

"You worry." There was a tightness to his voice that she wasn't used to hearing. Signs of strain around his eyes.

"Is it hard for you to be awake now?"

"Yes."

He turned onto his side, touching Jalina's cheek with his fingers, a smile on his face and in his voice, everything about him softening. There was no doubt he loved his daughter. "Hello, my little light."

Jalina stilled, her fussing dying off to a happy coo at her father's attention.

"Why do you not rest?" For a moment father and daughter stared at each other. Deuce glanced up. "She is hungry."

"Harley is coming with a bottle."

He touched her cheek with the same gentleness with which he'd touched their daughter's. His frown did not bode well for the man. "He is supposed to be guarding you, not running errands."

"He would be if you hadn't indulged your jealousy and given me a panic attack."

Signs of his weariness vanished. His fingers curled under her chin, lifting her face to his. "You will explain."

"You gave me a panic attack when I was going to go into the kitchen where the newcomer was."

"I did not."

"Well, I don't have panic attacks!"

"But you experienced one?"

"Yes."

"When, exactly?" His eyes narrowed and she felt his probe. She blocked him, and felt his surprise.

"Do you even know that you do that?" she asked.

"What?"

"Probe my mind."

His thumb brushed her lips. "Not always. It is natural for mates to blend thoughts."

"But not for me."

"No."

There was absolutely no inflection in his response, but she sensed his frustration. Between them, Jalina fussed. He rolled to his back and propped her on his chest. She rested there, a happy sigh sliding past her rosy lips as a weary one passed his. He closed his eyes. Jalina did the same. There was something so intriguing about the big powerful man cradling the tiny baby that it scared her. Mostly because she wanted to be a part of that circle and she couldn't. Deuce's hand wrapped around hers, keeping her close to the temptation he presented. His weariness traveled from him to her. She wanted to resist him, and at the same time soothe him. She settled for curling her fingers around his.

His "Tell me about your panic" was calm, almost disinterested, but she wasn't fooled. She had his full attention.

"We were going to the kitchen to get something to eat. I heard men talking, and I started to get uneasy. I tried to ignore it, but I couldn't. I had to get out of there before he saw me."

"Before who saw you?"

She paused. "I don't know." She hadn't realized it until that moment, but she didn't know who she didn't want to see her. Nor why it was so important that she leave. "And before you ask, I also don't know why."

"But you had to run away?"

She bit her lip and relived the emotions, sorting through the impulses to the message beneath. "Not away. To you. I had to get to you."

"And this is why you accused me?"

"It seemed logical."

He squeezed her fingers, his eyes glittering through his lashes. "Later you can make amends for the insult."

"In your dreams." She was not Chosen and she'd be damned if she'd behave as if she was. Especially when it came to that.

He brought her hand to his lips, the confidence of his smile flicking her on the raw. "You will."

She yanked her hand free, resenting the tingle that sprang up in the wake of his touch. "Don't hold your breath."

"I will not." Deuce tugged and she fell against him. His arm curled against her back, tucking her into his side. "But I will enjoy it all the same."

Logic said to pull away. Emotion said to slap him. Desire had her pussy clenching in anticipation and her body softening against his. She was truly a sick individual to get turned on by his utter assurance that she'd submit to him. Even sicker that she didn't care.

Her cheek fit naturally into the hollow of his shoulder. So naturally, she left it there.

His warmth surrounded her along with his satisfaction. She watched as he stroked Jalina's back with the tip of his finger. He was so in tune to the little girl that the slightest tensing of her muscles had him adjusting his touch until with a little sigh, Jalina closed her eyes.

"She sleeps."

"You really don't mind Jalina and I landing on your doorstep, do you?"

He turned his head. In the dark room, his eyes were little more than vague glitters of light. "From the time he is born, a Chosen male prepares for the day he finds his mate and prays for the blessing of a family."

"I mean...you don't mind that you got me?"

"I am content with what the maker has given me."

He was content? "You waited six-hundred-fifty years just to be content?"

"Yes."

She sat up. "I've only waited twenty-five, but I know I want a hell of a lot more than that."

"You are angry."

Yes, she was. She turned on the light. "Of course not."

His hand trailed down her spine, raising goose bumps. "You are not happy that your mate is content?"

"Contentment wasn't the emotion I thought to inspire in my significant other."

He shifted his hips back, being careful not to disturb the baby. "You think I am displeased?"

His level of enthusiasm was underwhelming. A knock on the door saved her from having to answer. She stood up. "That will be Harley."

"It is."

She paused at the side of the bed. "How do you know?"

"I recognize his step and scent."

"You can smell him from here?" She looked at the door and tried a sniff. Nothing.

"Yes."

She surreptitiously checked her underarms. Nothing seemed untoward but that didn't mean it wasn't to him. His laugh snagged her blush and brought it to her cheeks. The swat he delivered to her butt sent her forward a step. "You worry needlessly. Let Harley in. Our daughter is hungry."

She shot him a glare and rubbed her stinging buttock. "Aren't you supposed to be unconscious?"

"Later, I will have no choice. Now, I would talk to Harley."

And later her. He didn't say it but she felt it in the intensity of his gaze as she crossed the room. No doubt as soon as Harley left, he would be grilling her. She glanced over her shoulder before she opened the door. Deuce lay there propped on the pillows, the sheet barely covering his hips, their daughter snoozing on his chest. A big, powerful man who could be incredibly gentle. And she made him fucking content. She opened the door with a quick jerk.

Harley stood there, a tray in his hands, but no smile on his mouth. "Are you feeling better?"

She nodded. "I'm sorry for earlier."

"No explanations necessary."

"Deuce disagrees."

His gaze sharpened. "He's awake?"

She opened the door fully and stepped back. "Yes."

He handed her the tray. "Good."

Her "Thanks" drifted in his wake. Deuce sat up, propping Jalina on his shoulder. A human male would have ignored the sleeping baby, but Harley acknowledged her first, his touch on her arm a light expression of joy. There was no doubt that the Chosen and Others loved children.

She couldn't hear what the men were saying and as soon as she got close enough to excuse herself and reach for Jalina, they shut up, watching her with those patient expressions that irritated the heck out of her as she took the baby and the bottle. "I'll go down to the living room so you can talk."

"You may stay."

How nice of him to offer since they were no doubt discussing her. She tucked Jalina into her chest. "It's all right. I'll watch some TV while I feed her."

Deuce's gaze narrowed. "I would prefer you stay where I can see you."

She hitched Jalina a little higher. "In case you haven't noticed, there's been a whole woman's movement that's gone on in the last sixty years. The times of a woman jumping to fulfill a man's preferences are gone."

"Chosen women accept the guidance of their mates."

"Not me."

She couldn't see Harley's face, but that sound he made could have been a cough. Or laughter. She cut him a glare and then turned her back on Deuce. "When this whole bad guy thing is over, we are so going to talk about your habit of giving orders." She dropped into the overstuffed chair by the bathroom door hard enough to bounce. Jalina startled and began to cry, almost drowning out Deuce's "We will definitely talk".

She brushed the little girl's mouth with the nipple. She latched on, her tiny belly rumbling as the first swallow hit bottom. They certainly would. She was not spending eternity heeling whenever Deuce snapped his fingers.

Jalina sucked steadily on the bottle, no longer hesitant about eating. She was turning into quite the little piglet. If Eden just lowered her focus to this moment in this room, she could pretend all was right in the world and she was like any new mother, happy with her baby — fearful of meeting her needs, but determined to do so in the most successful manner possible. If it weren't for the waves of reassurance Deuce was sending her way, she could indulge in a bit of "let's pretend", but the fact that he was worried about something to the point that he was reassuring her in advance, made pretending impossible.

The men's voices were a low murmur. She could tell from the set of Harley's shoulders that he wasn't pleased by what he heard. She could see very little of Deuce's expression, but whenever she caught a glimpse of his face, it had the controlled calm look that she was coming to understand meant he was containing whatever he felt inside. If she were to extrapolate from the high level of calm in his expression and the reassurance he was sending her, he was very agitated.

Jalina finished the bottle. Her face screwed up into a ball. A sensation of hunger reached out to her. Eden froze. Not even breathing as she recognized the mental touch of her daughter for the first time. She wanted to respond so badly, but she couldn't. Couldn't risk giving the Coalition a path to her daughter. Instead, she leaned down and kissed Jalina's cheek. The touch intensified. Confusion and frustration wove into the blend. Eden resisted the call, tears burning because she couldn't make her daughter understand the rejection.

A weight settled on her shoulder. Deuce stood beside her, unselfconscious in his nakedness. The door clicked closed behind Harley. She hadn't heard either of them move.

"How do you move so quietly?" she asked, not looking higher than his bare chest.

"Chosen and Others are in harmony with nature."

She stroked Jalina's cheek, ignoring the child's frustration with her refusal to respond. "And that means you can avoid making wood floors squeak."

"When we want to, yes."

His fingertips slid over her shoulder and up her neck. "Do you avoid looking at me because you fear my disapproval?"

She traced Jalina's pale eyebrows with the pad of her index finger. They were silky soft. As perfect of the rest of her. "No."

His fingertips pressed under her chin. "You are right to keep separate from her right now."

That did snap her gaze up to his. "You know?"

"That she calls to you? Yes." He curved his hand down behind her head. Pure reflex tipped her head back as he applied pressure to the base of her skull. His black eyes were flat and hard. "And I feel the pain that eats at you that you cannot respond."

"I don't want them to find her."

"It will not always be this way, my heart." His thumb brushed her jawline. "Soon, it will be better."

"I don't care about soon. I care about now." She stood, shoving Jalina into his arms, unable to bear it a minute longer. Jalina's and Deuce's surprise hit her like a slap. "Make her confusion go away."

Bond with her. The resentful thought was so petty and spiteful, she couldn't believe she'd had it, but damn it, that was her daughter. Her daughter who called to her. A daughter who'd wanted her mother, and instead she'd get her father. Her big perfect, able-to-communicate-with-her father. The father who loved her more than she thought any father would.

Deuce touched Jalina's cheek, his head bent to hers, her profile a softer version of his. The baby's fussing transformed into an expression of concentration. Eden bit her lip and turned away. This was what she wanted.

"But not what I wanted."

She spun around. Deuce stood right behind her, Jalina cradled to his chest, her cheek resting on his shoulder one tiny thumb stuck in her mouth.

"You were in my mind."

"You were projecting."

"I don't like it."

"I know." He took another step, his need to comfort reaching her before he got close enough to touch. "Your pain needs soothing."

"There's nothing to soothe."

"You have not failed Jalina, Edie. "

Yes, she had. She looked at Jalina, the soft one-piece pink sleeper highlighting her rosy cheeks that flexed softly as she sleepily sucked her thumb She was a healthy little girl, one any mother would be proud to claim, but she couldn't. Couldn't claim her, and couldn't touch her in any way the child valued. Jalina was so fragile and innocent, and what the Coalition would do to her so evil that she couldn't bear the thought. "I failed her the day I conceived her."

Deuce shook his head, his long hair falling about Jalina like a protective cloud. "She is a miracle of the Maker's creation."

"They created her in a lab." It was foul and it was bitter, but it was reality. "And since when did you find religion anyway?"

Deuce didn't flinch or back away. Instead, he seemed to cradle the baby closer, as if to shelter her from the harsh words. "I have always had it." He delivered the statement without reprimand, his quiet assurance scraping her own lack of conviction raw.

"I'm surprised Chosen and Others believe in anything. Why bother when you have the power to simply change it?"

"The Chosen are a very old people, bonded to our world." He rubbed Jalina's back, his hand spanning the width of her small spine, the power in his hand sheltering rather than threatening. "It is not our way to challenge the design laid out by the Maker, but to embrace it."

God, he said that so easily, so acceptingly. She knocked his hand away from her face and stepped back, the helpless rage surging past her restraint. "And you think your Maker wanted me locked up in a room, surgically raped and impregnated?"

Deuce caught her before Eden could take another step away from him. Her rage and the pain it covered clawed at his calm, gouging deep furrows into his soul. They should never have been able to take her. Should never have been able to lay one finger on her for a second, let alone for a year.

"I failed you, not the Maker," he told her as he pulled her into his side, taking the cutting lash of her pain as his due. "But it will not happen again."

Her nails dug into his chest and back. "Let me go."

"Never."

Blood flowed as she dug in. Her nails tore at his skin as the pain tore at her in deep dark waves that pushed her away from him, away from herself. "Let me go."

"No." He dragged her to the crib, letting her go for the split second it took to put Jalina in the bed, which was a mistake. From one heartbeat to the next, Eden was at the door. He leapt to cut her off, the shock on her face telling him she hadn't seen him move, her human senses too slow to register the maneuver. Before she could bolt, he had her, chaining her wrists in his hands, pulling them up his body to his shoulders, linking them there, ignoring her efforts to push him away, keeping her pinned against him as he slid his hands down her back. He hooked his hands under her buttocks and lifted her up. She grabbed his shoulders reflexively. He bent his head to the crook of her neck, breathing in her scent and her pain. "I am sorry."

Three little words that were so inconsequential, so inadequate against all he could sense whirling inside her. He deserved her anger, her scorn. He had failed her when she had needed him most. But she didn't hit him or scream. Instead, her hands crept around his neck, her fingers threading through his hair. Dampness touched his cheeks. She was crying.

He wrapped her legs around his waist and headed for the bed, pushing back the day weariness that called him. "Do not cry."

He tried to lay her on the bed, but she clung to him, demanding the one thing that was always hers. His strength.

"I waited for you," she whispered into the curve of his neck like it was some dark secret too shameful to be spoken aloud.

"I know."

"I cried for you." Her nails gouged crescents into the nape of his neck.

He opened his fingers over her spine in a vain attempt to siphon off all the memories and the pain they brought. "I know."

"I needed you so badly." She pulled herself harder into the shelter of his arms.

"I know."

Her hands yanked on his hair as he cradled her in his arms and sat back on the bed. "I don't want to need you like that again." Her tears soaked his skin in a burning flow of truth. "I can't."

He tipped her face up, looking straight into her red-rimmed eyes. "You must."

Chapter Nineteen

അ

She didn't move, didn't speak. Just stared at him, her big blue eyes awash with tears. Her too thin cheeks were blotchy and her full mouth trembled as she shook her head. Her "Don't ask that of me" was a broken hiccup of sound.

He wiped a tear from her cheek. It shimmered on his finger like an accusation. "I am not asking. I am demanding."

He felt the impact of his words in the flinch of her mind, her body. She was afraid, not knowing what to believe, where to place her faith. Such indecision could be deadly. "You must choose to believe in something."

Her lips flattened to a determined line. "Maybe I'll choose your Maker."

He touched the corner of her mouth. "You do not believe in him."

"I don't believe in you either."

He closed his eyes and absorbed the pain of her words before shoving it aside, opening his eyes, and bringing forth the truth. "You do or you would not have brought my daughter here."

Her cheek pushed against his finger as she grimaced. "I was desperate."

He shook his head at her attempt to distract him. "You are a logical person, Edie. You think and you plan. Desperate or not, you would not have brought our daughter here if you did not think I could keep her safe." She sucked in her breath and tried to pull away. He did not allow it. "The time for hiding is over, mate."

She shook her head, still holding that breath and his gaze, as if to release it was to take a step there was no coming back from. And he guessed in a way, there wasn't. "Breathe, Eden."

She did, letting her breath out on a hard push that told him she was fighting for control. He released her chin and pulled her face into his neck, wishing he could soothe her fear as easily as he could soothe the rush of adrenaline that flooded her system. But she had to take this step alone. He brushed his lips over the top of her head as she pressed her forehead into his collarbone. "I will not fail you again."

"I know that in my mind."

He could hear the "but" as loudly as if she had spoken. "You need to accept it in your heart, for our daughter's safety as well as your own."

He rubbed her back, keeping her against him when she would have pulled back. It was selfish, but he did not want to see the doubt in her eyes as she fought with herself.

"I know that, too." She patted his chest. He had the strangest notion that she was comforting him. "I just need time."

"You are out of time."

"I know." She shrugged, the delicate muscles in her back flexing under his palm. "It's just that knowing is not helping."

"Maybe the loving will." She went absolutely still against him, even her breathing suspended. "You loved me a year ago, Eden."

"A lot has happened in a year."

"But you still love me."

She shook her head. "I don't know what I feel."

Her doubts beat at him, but he couldn't let them sway his certainty. "I do."

"How?"

He touched his mouth to hers. "Because we are mates. Your feelings cannot be less than mine."

Again that stillness that could mean anything. And then a very soft, very tense "Are you saying you love me?" breathed against his lips.

He rested his forehead against hers. "You have been my all from the first moment I saw you."

She shook her head, her fingers spreading over his chest. "You wanted me when you first saw me?"

He smiled, remembering the flood of alien emotion that had shaken his control that first time. "That, too." He gathered a handful of her hair and pulled her head back. "I have pledged my life, my happiness and my soul to you, and still you doubt my feelings?" He could tell from her expression that she did. It was the why he did not understand. "Explain."

"I don't want to."

"You need to."

Her stomach rumbled in the silence. "I'm too hungry to concentrate."

He doubted that. "Then you must eat."

Her little start of surprise was well concealed, but their minds were too linked for her to hide it entirely. He sighed and shook his head. "I have told you often enough mate, your needs come first."

"Unless they go against your wishes."

He reached for the tray Harley had left and moved it to the bed. "That is untrue."

Her full lips thinned to another flat line of disagreement. He released her hair and smoothed it back from her face. "It is only when your wishes endanger your safety that I must insist on obedience."

He leaned back on the bed, giving her some space. She eyed him warily and cautiously reached for the sandwich. "You're the one who gets to determine what's safe?"

"Yes." The soft T-shirt clung to her unfettered breasts, enhancing their roundness and the softly peaked nipples. "You do not wear a bra." He patted her back as she choked on the mouthful of sandwich, easing her through the spasm. "Swallow."

She did, cautiously, clearing her throat, the redness in her face increasing rather than subsiding. She blinked the tears from her eyes. "I'm sorry." And then red-cheeked, she said, "Marlika's didn't fit.

"There is no harm done." He cupped her breast. "You are still swollen."

Her head dropped back even as she pressed her torso into his touch. "Oh for goodness' sake."

"What?" The softness of the cotton shirt could not equal the softness of her flesh, but it was close.

"That's not something a man should notice."

He laughed despite the day weariness tugging at him. "That is the first thing any Chosen would notice."

"You are a sick man."

"No." He weighed each breast, rubbing his thumb over the tips and corrected, "I am a very appreciative mate."

Against his groin, through the cotton of her shorts, he felt her pussy flex. He brushed the tips again. Her moan drifted through his mind as the scent of her arousal rose to embrace his senses.

"You need." Her stomach rumbled. "And you hunger."

She leaned harder into his hands. "I'll eat later."

He caught the hand holding the sandwich and brought it to her lips. "You need sustenance now."

She shook her head and her blue eyes narrowed. Her blonde curls tumbled over her shoulder to wrap around his wrist as she tilted her head. "If you think there's any way I can eat now, you have another think coming."

The plumpness of her breast, the silky smoothness of her hair binding him to her, called to his lust. His cock ached and strained against her pussy, pushing up, meeting the downward press of her hips. This time the sound of her pleasure filled the room. He gritted his teeth. "You strain my control."

She pushed her breast into his hand, not backing off even through she winced. Her "Screw your control" contained the pleasure-pain of the caress.

"I would much rather screw you." He eased her back with a hand on her shoulder. Her mental wail of protest mourned the separation. "But you will eat first."

"No way."

He smiled at her determination. If he wasn't touching the too thin curve of her shoulder, he might have let her persuade him, but with the reminder of her condition under his hand, he would not be swayed. "I must insist."

She put the sandwich back on the plate and grabbed the hem of her shirt. Her "Insist away " was only slightly muffled by the thin material. It caught on his hands, creating a moment of peekaboo when it stretched, exposing her stomach and the undercurve of her breast.

Eden tugged. He let go, and then there was nothing between his eyes and her breasts. Nothing except his duty to see to her welfare. It was a sad realization that his resolve wasn't what it should be in the face of baser needs. Not when she sat before him, her beauty enhanced by the fullness of her breasts, the hungry red color of her distended nipples and the seeded curve of her abdomen.

The smugness of her expression as she watched him watch her was the only thing that kept his desire under control. A mate's desire was a gift, but one a Chosen mate was duty-bound to control and not allow to interfere with her health. Especially a newly seeded mate who had no experience with the hormones flooding her system. It sounded so easy when lectured about. It was a lot harder to remember when said mate cuddled his cock to her heat and her scent enclosed him in a haze of demand.

"You will eat."

She leaned toward him. "Later."

"If you wish the pleasure of my cock, you will eat now."

She cupped her breasts in her small hands, lifting them to him. "What if I want the pleasure of your mouth?"

Lust rolled over him in a debilitating wave. He tightened his grip on her shoulder, the bone pressing into his palm reminding him of his duty. "Then you will eat."

Her fingers slid up the high curves, tightening as they reached the pouting tips. He could not take his gaze away. Desire shot through his blood in staccato bursts that hammered with insidious query. What would it hurt if he satisfied her need first and then insisted she eat?

She squeezed the tips, too hard, too soon. Her flinch and surprise anchored his desire and his purpose. She did not know what she was asking.

He brushed Eden's hands aside when she would have tried again, shushing her protest with a mental touch as he cupped her breasts anew, pure pleasure at the feel of her skin and heat sliding through him in a culmination that had his hips arching up into hers. He fought for his voice when he would have much preferred to project his feelings.

"You need to learn patience, mate." He thrummed his thumbs lightly over her nipples. Her cry was sweet to his ears. As sweet as her scent. "Pleasure is not rushed."

He thrummed her nipples one last time before turning her around. Her foot caught awkwardly. He held while she pulled it free, then gently, ever so gently, he settled her firm buttocks against his erection. She'd dressed in another pair of his shorts. The loose cotton was no barrier. His shaft slid neatly between the tempting globes. The drive to take her immediately almost overrode his common sense. Almost. He grasped her wrist in his hand, the fine bones making him aware of his much greater strength and her vulnerability. "No more tempting me until you finish eating. "

She tossed her head, her curls flying in his face. "Uh-huh."

She wiggled her ass on his cock. The gesture almost as defiant as the toss of her head. He tipped her chin back, the arch of her throat a seductive curve that beckoned his lips. "Eat so we may play."

The back of her head settled into the curve of his shoulder. "I thought Chosen had to sleep during the day."

"We do." He ran his lips over the whorls of her ear, feeling the hitch in her breathing as he did, pulling her just that much closer, unable to believe she was here when he'd lived with the agony of her loss for so long. "Which means if you do not hurry up and eat, I will be too tired to play."

"All the more reason to play first."

He skated his lips down the soft skin of her neck, listening to the pulse beat in her throat, enjoying the heat from her skin, smiling as it increased beneath his caress. Most of all enjoying the knowledge that he was whole once again. "You will need your strength."

"So will you."

"That fades as the sun rises."

She looked at the heavily draped window, harrumphed and took a bite of the sandwich. Her cheek flexed against his as she chewed. He traced the slide of muscle with his lips as she swallowed. He caught her hand before she could put the sandwich down.

"Again," he whispered against her throat.

"Bully."

He smiled at the sass in her tone. He'd missed it too much to reprimand her for it. "Mate," he corrected.

He knew she felt the eager twitch of his cock as she took the next bite. The way she rocked her hips demanded a reprimand, not the encouragement of his hands but he gave it to her anyway, his control as nothing against her wishes and needs. She was his miracle, his salvation. He could deny her nothing. He waited in an agony of controlled anticipation as she ate the sandwich. At first, he wasn't sure, but by the time she was on her fourth bite he knew. Edie was deliberately dragging out the meal, each bite getting smaller, each swallow taking longer.

"A woman who teases her mate asks for trouble," he informed her calmly, as if his primitive side wasn't salivating with lust.

She took another miniscule bite, chewed it and swallowed before answering. "According to you, everything I do 'asks' for trouble."

There wasn't a hint of fear in her voice, or in the gentle clench of her buttocks on his cock. He pressed up into the hot crease. "You are very disobedient."

The glance she sent over her shoulder had his heart picking up the beat to match hers. The slow squeeze of her buttocks on his hard cock an enticement that had his fangs exploding into his mouth. "Do you know what you are asking for?"

"I don't see why I should suffer alone."

"So you admit to your teasing?"

She squeezed him again, sliding her hips up and down his length as she took the last bite of her sandwich. Her eyes flashed blue from under her sun-tipped lashes as she smiled at him over her shoulder. "I haven't been trying to keep it a secret."

"Good." He pushed her forward on the bed, stroking her back as she caught herself on her hands. Before she could push up, he came over her, capturing her in the entirety of his embrace, her back arched into his chest, her ass pressed to his hips, her thighs trapped between his. "I need you."

I need you.

The calm whisper breathed against Eden's ear, shivered down her spine, the deeper timbre stroking her desire in an invitation as silky as the cool swathe of Deuce's hair falling over her shoulders. He was so big around her, his body dwarfing her, his erection pressing firmly between her buttocks in a dark demand that should have frightened her, but instead sent every nerve ending leaping in excitement.

"Deuce?"

His lips were a brush of fire on her shoulder, her neck, her cheek. "Yes?"

She felt something sharper graze her hip. There was a tug on the waistband of her shorts. The mattress dipped as his weight shifted, then there was the same tugging on the other side. The soft material fell away from her groin and dangled between them, trapped by the pressure of his touch and the sweat of their bodies.

He backed his hips from hers. The air felt cool against her flesh. She shivered and gathered her courage. "I want it all this time."

He stilled. The torn shorts slid to the bed. His big hand touched her shoulder with incredible gentleness, before sliding down her side. "I do not understand."

"You've been holding back when we make love. Sheltering me." She arched her shoulder into his palm, needing his touch as much as she needed her next breath. "This time I want to feel everything."

Her desire for him waged war with her fear of being vulnerable to him. His hand cupped her stomach, tracing the small remaining bulge. So light a touch to convey such hope and feeling. "It is too soon."

Damn it, how was she supposed to hold herself apart when he did things like that? She turned her head until she could see his face. His expression gave away nothing, but she knew, just knew he thought she couldn't handle it. "You can't ask me to trust you when you hide things from me."

"It is my duty to protect you."

"Not to the extent that you interfere with my experience." She turned beneath him, catching his hair in her hands as she fell back on the bed, taking him with her. "You need to let me make my own choices."

He came down over her. Thigh to thigh, hip to hip, chest to chest. His hair settling around her face as he blocked out the rest of the light and there was only his scent, his touch, his lips on hers. "I cannot let you hurt."

"Are you planning on hurting me?"

He rested his forehead against hers. His breath hit her face in a carefully controlled rhythm. "You are so small."

She walked her fingers down his side over the hard pad of muscles protecting his ribs, smiling as they expanded with his next breath. She turned her hand and dragged the backs of her nails around his waist, gliding into the hollow of his hipbone, aiming for more intimate territory. "And you're so big." She curled her fingers around his cock. It leapt and pulsed in her hand. His breathing stopped altogether. "I've always heard that's a good thing when it comes to making love."

He grabbed her wrist. There was a moment when she thought he was going to pull her hand away. She stopped him with a simple "Please?" His fingers slid around hers. His grip tightened and then relaxed.

"I cannot deny you."

He didn't sound happy about it, but she was. "I'm glad."

"We will try it your way, but—" His agreement melted to a groan as she squeezed gently. He pulsed in her grip, his cock somehow soft and hard at the same time.

"But what?"

"I will decide if it is too much."

She shook her head. "No way." She brought her knee up between his thighs until she could press gently against his balls. "You're going to have to trust me."

His denial was instant and silent but she felt it anyway. She cupped his cheeks in her hands, squinting to see his expression in the low light. "You promised to give me what I need."

His fingers tightened on her hair, pulling the strands, sending fine tingles through her scalp that reverberated down her spine. "I will."

The tingles flared to shocks of anticipation. Her nipples drew to hard points, and her pussy swelled and flared open in a blatant invitation. She took a breath, inhaled his scent, and forgot to let it out. Dear God, he was potent. His mouth opened over the top of her breast.

She arched up, pushing the hardened nubbin between his lips. The pressure of his teeth was just enough to send her breath skittering from her lungs.

"I need to have a say in all this." For a moment, she felt the sharp points of his fangs. Before her whimper could dissolve in the air, they were gone. "Please, Deuce."

Her answer came in the shift of his hips that had his cock pressing against the opening of her body. He was huge. She sucked in a breath.

"Come to me, Edie."

She knew what he wanted. "I can't."

"Trust works both ways, mate."

He was right. "What about *her*?"

She didn't want this time ruined by the intrusion of the strange woman.

"She will not touch you."

"You can do that now?"

"I know her path."

"You're sure?"

"I have said so."

So he had. Which meant she was free to let go. For the first time ever. She flicked his flat brown nipple with her thumb as she milked his cock slowly. "So I'm free to enjoy you?"

His big body shuddered against her and his cock swelled in her hand. "Yes."

"I might like this."

The bed bounced as he dropped to his elbow, bringing his nipple within range of her mouth. "I am glad."

She bet he was. A simple bend of her neck and she had that small protrusion between her lips. His hand cradled the back of her head, supporting her as she nibbled on the sensitive nub. His groan was a deep whisper of sound. "Do not stop."

It took her a second to realize he meant the slow pumping of her hand on his cock. His shaft jumped and pulled in her grip while his upper body held absolutely still, with a desperate edge. A quick glance up as she laved his nipple with short strokes of her tongue showed his face drawn into harsh lines of pleasure. A shot of pure pride went through her as he shuddered on her next stroke. And suddenly it wasn't enough to have him in her hand.

She angled the fat head of his cock down to the shallow well of her vagina. "Make love to me, Deuce."

Was that throaty siren's voice hers?

"You are not ready."

She laughed outright and arched up. "I'm on fire for you."

It was true. If fire came in a liquid form, it would be pouring from her body right now, spilling over the head of his cock. "I need you."

"Be easy."

She couldn't "be easy", not with his cock teasing her, hovering just beyond her grasp. She lifted her hips, coaxing him closer. "Please."

He nodded slowly. "Come to me."

She felt the brush of his mind. As gentle as the touch of his hand on her cheek. "I don't know how." The confession shuddered out on a hoarse sigh that didn't begin to communicate her frustration.

"Reach for me, Edie." The order came from within and without. "Relax and reach for me."

She locked her gaze on his shadowed one, and braced herself for the flood of foreign emotions. Then, tentatively, she opened her mind. Or at least thought she did. She didn't have a clue as to what she was supposed to be doing. Deuce pressed into her body. Her muscles strained under the pressure. Her mind followed her body, flinching away from the reality. His palm cupped her cheek. His mouth brushed hers.

"Do not try to control it. Just open for me."

His "Come to me" breathed against her lips with a comforting rush. She slid her arms over his shoulders and linked them around his neck. Deuce shuddered against her. His pleasure shimmered around the perimeter of her consciousness. Her body wept its eagerness as her mind fought to stay apart. It had always been so much easier to keep to herself. To believe that if she maintained her control, her separateness, she could control everything. But she couldn't, she knew she couldn't. But she didn't know if she was strong enough for this. To surrender her mind, her identity, and give herself over to Deuce. Strong enough to trust him.

His breath hissed between his teeth, blowing tendrils of hair off her face. "You are not wrong to trust me, Edie."

She opened her eyes as his chest settled against her breasts, the soft mat of hair prickling lightly. "I was projecting again?"

"Yes." He kept the slow rotation of his thumb on her clitoris as he kissed her forehead. "I do not mind."

She just bet he didn't, considering the array of images her aching pussy was transmitting to her brain. Wild, crazy things she wanted him to do to her. Impossible things.

His smile let her know he was reading her mind. "You are a wild woman."

She wrapped her legs around his lean hips. "Are you going to try to convince me that you don't like it?"

His laugh was pure pleasure to hear. He so rarely laughed. "No."

She cupped his cheeks in her hands, savoring the remnants of his laughter with her palms. "I liked it before. It was more than I expected, overwhelming, but it was wild, passionate and the most incredible thing." She traced the crease between his dark brows with her index finger. "I want it again." His whole body jerked. The air thickened with his scent, his need. "Give it to me, Deuce."

"It might hurt." He angled his cock into the well of her vagina, the deliberate gesture at odds with the concern in his voice.

"I won't care if you make it feel good, too." She lifted her hips into the descent of his cock, taking his hand and bringing it to the ring he'd given her, knowing how it turned him on to see it, feel it. "Make it feel good."

"I will."

Chapter Twenty

ℬ

Make it feel good.

Deuce threaded his finger through the hoop, tugging firmly, urging Edie's hips up, letting her impale herself farther on his cock, pushing himself deeper into the heat he craved, her pleasure floating to him on a shimmer of pain, both emotions so intertwined that he couldn't sort one from the other. He tugged the hoop harder, feeling her startled wince, followed immediately by a surge of delight so intense she lost her breath. He looked away from her face, down over her flushed breasts and damp belly to where she hung suspended from the hoop—his mark—her desire strung as tightly as her body, her need carved as deeply as the ancient words that bound them together.

"You look good like this, Edie mine. Open and needy, your body begging for my cock."

Her fingers scraped across the sheets as she arched her back, pressing her pussy higher. "Then why don't you give it to me?"

"Because it pleases me to see you like this." He twisted the ring again, harder. Too hard to put her over, hard enough to make her pause. He pulled her higher, twisting the ring gently this time. She cried out. Cream poured from her body. Her chest flushed and her pussy pulsed. "You are almost there, aren't you?"

Her teeth bit into her lower lip as she nodded. "Where are the colors?" she gasped, pressing up.

"What colors?" He moved with her, keeping the pressure on the ring steady as he extended his fingers between her plump labia until he touched the tautly stretched skin surrounding their joining.

"Before, everything was red, blue and swirling black."

She was talking about the interpretation her mind had superimposed over the alien violence of the stranger's battle to keep him out. "Only you and I are here now. They will not come back."

More hot cream flowed with a slight twist of the ring "Good." Her scent flooded the room, her pleasure mixed with his, thickening the air around them, driving him wild with the demand that he claim her hard and fast, take her as her body demanded, with no further consideration.

He'd planned to love her with consideration this time, to keep his primitive side carefully hidden. Prove to her he could be as tender as any human male. He'd intended to control his passion for once, but she made it impossible. With every beat of her heart, every flex of her pussy around his cock head, she called to his primitive side, demanding her satisfaction. With a stroke of his thumb, he gave it to her. "Come for me, Edie."

She did, in a screaming, quivering rush, taking him with her as her pussy milked his cock in hard, rhythmic pulses, his shout echoing off the walls. When the violent wave subsided, he cupped her breast in his hand, gentling his touch when he felt how hot, full and hard it was. He squeezed the base, plumping it up to his mouth until her breath caught and she clenched around him again. He held her there with a steady pressure that had her body grasping at him, weeping in soft, hot pulses of entreaty. She was so soft, so delicate, but her soul was so strong. He wanted her to come again.

He laved the hard point of her nipple with the flat of his tongue, knowing from the bite of her nails in his shoulders that it wasn't enough. He caught the sensitive nubbin between his lips, grinding gently as he rolled her clit between his fingers. Her shriek reverberated in his ears. Her juices flooded his cock. He curved his fingers in, scraping her clitoris with the sharp edges as he pressed her engorged nipple between the points of his fangs. Deuce gave her a little of what she wanted, biting down gently, piercing her flesh that first tiny bit, the sweet taste of her blood bleeding into his mouth as she arched, one breathless moment, one tiny lave short of completion.

He didn't give it to her. He released her instead.

"You are so beautiful like this," he whispered against her areola, smiling as she turned in his arms on a half-formed curse, seeking to reestablish the connection of their bodies, "hot and hungry with desire."

"I need you, Deuce."

And he needed her. Her scent, her desire, her broken breath all tore at his restraint, but he'd waited so long for his mate, he wanted to draw out every moment, every nuance. He wanted to savor her. He nibbled at her neck, teasing himself with the heat of her skin and the pulse of her life force. This time he would not settle for less than a true mating.

"Come to me."

She whimpered and then stilled. He ran his fangs over her skin with the utmost delicacy, pulling back when her shudder would have caused a nick. He rolled to his back, pulling her above him so she sprawled across his torso, her cheek pressed against his breastbone, her legs dangling limply along his sides. She lay above him, her ribs pushing at his in short heavy lurches. His Edie was very close to coming.

Deuce eased her hair off her face, smiling as her curls tangled around his fingers in a silken demand as imperious as the call of her soul to his. His cock lurched against his stomach, responding to the hot, swollen need of her pussy. He brushed the edges of her mind with his.

She glanced up at him. In her big blue eyes he saw the confusion weaving through the desire. But she didn't pull away or throw up barricades.

He brushed his finger over the curve off her cheek. "Earlier you said you waited for me."

She blinked. Shock quivered along the edge of her consciousness.

"Needed me." He held her to him when she would have rolled off.

"Cried for me." He let her push up as far as her arms allowed. He didn't flinch from the resentment in her gaze. "And I did not come."

"Why are you doing this?"

He would never adjust to hearing that pain in her voice. He stroked her shoulder blade with the tip of his finger, soothing her tension. "Because I am here now, Edie. And I want you."

The resistance in her expression bled into her tone. "You have me."

"Not as I want."

That pulled her up short. "What do you want?"

He shifted her left elbow out of his ribs. Her breasts swung with her exasperation, the nipples dangling like sweet berries, the right one beaded with blood. He touched his fingertip to that droplet and worked it into the velvety soft tip. He held her gaze as he gave her the truth. "I want my mate." He opened his hand, nestling that tender nipple deep into his palm, cradling her breast the way he wished she'd let him cradle her. "Not a woman I've seduced past her resistance."

She stared at him for seconds that seemed to stretch for hours, her frown more prevalent than her desire until she withdrew. Once again, that pain that only she could deliver sliced through his control and wakened his beast. He kept his reaction from her, wrapping it in layers of calm, smothering it under sheer determination. "You have made a decision."

"Yes." Her glorious hair fell forward with her nod, pooling on his pectorals before sliding to the side in a gliding caress. He wanted nothing more than to bury his hands in it, flip her onto her back and hold her as he drove into her, over and over until she admitted what they were to each other.

Her "Why don't you?" took him by surprise.

She could not mean what he thought. The arch of her brow belied the natural innocence of her expression, driving him to ask, "Why do I not what?"

"Why don't you make love to me until I admit what you want?"

Shock held him perfectly still. "You shared my mind."

"And you didn't even notice." She sounded incredibly smug. And well she should. It was not often a Chosen was taken off guard, but he had been too busy shielding her to guard against her.

He trailed his finger up the delicate knobs of her spine, relishing her body's shivers as he slipped his hand up to cup her head in his palm. "A mate should not boast of this."

"I have to take my moments when I can get them." She did not sound repentant, and truthfully, he did not want her to be.

He pulled her mouth to his, letting her breath mingle with his, holding her gaze as his mind brushed hers. Her flinch was not well-concealed. "What?" he asked against her mouth.

"How do you stand it?"

He frowned and rolled her beneath him, keeping his mouth close to hers, his mind locked to hers. "Explain."

Her palms brushed his as her fingers pressed against her temples. "There's just so much coming at me from so many angles, I want to scream."

She didn't know how to filter. He adjusted the flow of information from him to her as he pushed her thighs apart and brought his cock into precise alignment with her hot pussy. "Better?"

She nodded and bit her lip. "Much." Her hands slipped to his shoulders and a hot little whimper broke from her lips as he pressed his cock into her receptive body. Her head fell back over his hand. "Oh God, you feel so good."

She gave him the gift of her trust, her pleasure. He would not abuse it. He tasted her skin above the pulse in her throat with his tongue. She was hot and salty and incredibly feminine, calling to everything masculine in him. "You are mine."

She shuddered and her thighs wrapped around his hips, rocking him a little deeper. "Yes."

"All of you. Your body, your heart and your mind."

She shuddered and turned her head, offering him her throat. "Yes."

"Before I rest this day, I'm going to mate myself to you in all ways." He projected the images into her mind, his cock tunneling into her mouth, her pussy, her ass.

The last brought panic.

"You'll never fit!"

Along with her panic, he'd also felt her excitement and her guilt at feeling that excitement.

"Not only will you take me there, you will enjoy it." He scraped his fangs over her throat, teasing them both with the promise of pleasure.

Her mind touched his, awkward in its attempt but welcome, very welcome in how it spoke of her acceptance. Beneath her embarrassment and fear he heard her question.

"Yes. I will come in you there. As often as you can take."

Another of those broken whimpers burst against his lips, into the silence of the room. The tender muscles guarding her vagina stretched under the steady pressure of his insistence. Warm juices spilled from her body in a moist welcome. Beyond the tight ring of muscle, the incredible heat of her body beckoned. She shuddered and whimpered again, her thoughts and scent taking on a desperate edge.

"You need to come," he murmured.

She nodded, her chin bumping his head. "Please."

"So do I." He needed the release of bonding with her also. "Relax for me and accept your mate."

Her vagina fluttered against his cock in a purely feminine moment of indecision, before she took a deep breath and allowed her tense body to sink into the mattress. He followed her down, kissing her throat as she tilted her hips up. As before, her discomfort hit him first.

Her quietly whispered "Don't" halted his instinctive move to block her pain. Her soft hands stroked his shoulders, comforting him through the initial moment when her body took his. Then she surged up against him, taking a fraction more, her breath hissing out on an "Oh God, yes" and he was no longer anticipating her heat, he was part of it.

Edie moaned as Deuce came to her. Her whole being centered on the reality of his possession. He was in her. His thick cock stretching her to the edge of exquisite pain, but not taking her beyond, just leaving her hanging there, suspended on a breathless moment of anticipation.

"Do you accept me as your mate?" The mattress shifted as Deuce propped himself on his elbows. In the dim light she could feel his stare. In the depths of her mind, the seriousness with which he asked the question. "Do you accept me, Edie, as the keeper of your heart, your happiness and your welfare?"

She'd promise him anything in that moment. She could not survive the emptiness. "Yes."

"Then take me." His passion rolled over her mind with the same irresistible force that his cock surged into her pussy. His emotions overwhelmed her own, leaving her tossed on the waves of his desire, scrambling for security. Through the pounding surf, she heard his whisper. Calm and strong it stretched through the waves and offered her a familiar lifeline. "Come to me."

She clutched it to her soul, as she arched into him. Taking more, demanding more, because she needed to be closer to him, couldn't bear for a breath of air to separate them. She followed the lifeline he provided back to the center of the storm, to a place of sheltered unity where she was part of him and he part of her.

"I have you."

And he did. Mentally, physically he had her, safe and protected from the fears that would drag her under.

She relaxed into his arms, opening her eyes to find him staring down at her with that fathomless black gaze, and saw the truth. If he had known she hadn't died, he would have come for her. Nothing, not even the devil himself would have kept him from her. To him, she was all that was important to him in a way it was a struggle for her to comprehend. He was pledged to put her above his happiness and his needs. It was a matter of honor as much as it was a matter of heart. And Chosen or not, he was a man of honor. The last remnant of her defensive wall collapsed, and everything she'd felt for this man, everything she'd tried to suppress rushed before her, spilling into the quiet void, churning the waters anew. She cupped his lean cheeks in her hands, and stroked her thumb across his lips. "I love you, Dusan."

His pleasure washed over her, mingling with his satisfaction. He caught her finger in his mouth, sucking it into the moist heat as he pulled back, the broad head of his shaft tugging erotically at nerve endings straining for any stimulation he could provide. He released her finger. His expression changed, became more intent, more primitive. She held on to his shoulders, enjoying the flex of the hard muscle, under her hands as he powered back into her. His teeth scraped her throat as his hand skated between them. She couldn't breathe, couldn't think. His fingers brushed the top of her hoop, marking her with his touch the way he'd marked her with the gold. As his.

"Deuce."

"Come to me," he repeated.

And this time she went, heart slamming, nerve endings screaming, she went into his embrace, welcoming his touch, his guidance, feeling betrayed when he pulled out of her, leaving her empty and aching, just short of completion. He turned her over, bring her to the edge of mattress, pressing gently between her shoulder blades as he drew her knees up to her chest, raising her and opening her for his possession. Featherlight, his fingers traced her spine, dipping between her buttocks, tantalizing her with a forbidden desire. "Stay."

She did, feeling the mattress rise as he stood, listening as the drawer opened, stiffening as the distinct sound of metal links sliding against each other punctuated the closing of the drawer.

"Do not move."

The only thing keeping her in place was the pleasure from the last time he'd ordered her still. His hair kissed her first, brushing her ribs with promise, following it up with the heat of his breath, his lips, his touch until he was once again surrounding her with his passion. His tongue traced the edge of her shoulder blade, adding first moisture, then fire to the mixture, tempering her ragged desire to a fine edge as he rode the trail of goose bumps up to her shoulder. She felt the graze of his teeth and the soft press of his lips. His hair slid over her shoulder, falling onto the back of her hands. She wrapped her fingers in the thick strands as something cool and wet pressed against her anus. Her "I love you" melted into the soft rasp of their combined breaths.

"As I love you." It felt right to hear him say that now. As right as his finger entering her there, pushing past her natural resistance, lubricating her receptive flesh while opening a well of desire she'd never known she had.

"I want you."

She knew what he meant. Knew why. He needed her submission, this proof that she accepted him in all ways. His dominance was as much a part of him as his honor. She bit her lip, closed her eyes, and arched her back, taking a leap of faith as she echoed the words he so often used with her. "Then take from me what you need."

The links rustled again. His hands on her hips moved her forward. He reached between her legs. There was a tug on her ring, a steady pressure, and then a soft click. She opened her eyes and looked between her legs. A chain of brushed gold glittered from the top of her pussy, to fall over the edge of the mattress. She shuddered as the reality of what he'd done licked over her skin. "You chained me to the bed."

His cock aligned with her anus, nuzzling in as softly as his kiss on her ear. "Yes."

"Why?"

"For your pleasure and mine."

She glanced again at the glittering chain and then over her shoulder, catching only a fraction of his expression. His power surrounded her, bore down on her, demanded her compliance. Deuce was a good man, a strong man, but he was entirely too used to getting his way. "I don't think so."

She reached between her legs and unhooked the chain, the arch of her spine pressing his cock harder against her, tempting her to relax. To let it go. Just this once.

He caught her hand in his. "It is my wish."

Of that she had no doubt. It was his nature to dominate everything around him, and if she let him, he'd dominate her. With the best of intentions, but with the worst of results.

She opened her fingers. The delicate chain dropped to the bed, clinking lightly before slithering to the floor with a metallic hiss. "But not mine."

Deuce didn't move for a minute, but she felt his power build, bear down on her. He was not happy. She turned in his embrace, falling backward onto the bed. He was going to have to adjust. The mattress bounced as he propped himself on his elbows above her.

"You will explain."

More power reached out to her, subtly probing her resolve. His brows drew low over his eyes, red lights swirled in the black depths. He wanted her. Wanted this. She put her hands on his shoulders. His skin was hot and hard beneath her fingers, his scent a potent lure, the throb of his cock against the inside of her thigh a metronome for her own desire to the point that she wasn't fighting just him, but herself. Sometimes he was too incredibly masculine for either of their good. "It can't be like that between us, Deuce."

His frown deepened. "Is it because you fear to be taken that way?"

She closed her eyes, shook her head, counted to three and then opened them.

He traced the blush on her chest, dragged his finger up over her breast, and flicked the hard nub cresting the tip before wandering over her collarbone to settle against the pulse in the hollow of her throat. "I would understand."

She wrapped her legs around his hips and linked her ankles, straining to keep her breathing even as her core pulsed a welcome to his. "I'll love you, wear your ring, submit to you any way you need, but I won't be chained like a dog or otherwise treated with disrespect."

He frowned. "There is no disrespect. It is common for Chosen to love their mates this way. Chosen women enjoy the feeling of helplessness."

"I have enough areas of my life where I'm helpless." She touched the frown between his brows, smoothing it with a stroke, hoping he'd understand and whispered, "I just don't want to feel that way with you."

He caught her hand in his. His frown disappeared to be replaced by an intensity that drew her in. She couldn't look away from his gaze as he brought their linked hands to the bed beside her head. "Then you will not."

She couldn't believe it. "Just like that?"

The corner of his mouth twitched. "Just like that."

A featherlight brush of his lips over hers kick-started her arousal.

"You don't…need that?"

Intensity faded to gentleness. "I need you."

The second brush of his lips closed her right eye. The third, her left. "If you raise your legs, I would love you now. As you wish. No chains. No restraints. Just the pleasure of my body joining with yours."

"Uhm, about that…"

He worked his arm under her thigh and raised her ankle to his shoulder. "You will like it, Edie mine."

"I'm prepared to."

"But?"

"I think you're being very optimistic about the fit," she pointed out as he lifted her other ankle to his shoulder as he stood straight, his height pulling her hips off the bed, the width of his shoulders stretching her inner thighs.

He leaned forward again, letting her legs slide down his arms until they hung up at his elbows. His hands came down over hers, his fingers threading through hers, locking them together. "I will bring you great joy."

She squeezed her fingers around his as he brought his shaft into alignment with a shift of his hips. "I'm holding you to that."

Her body had none of her mind's caution, rejoicing in the dark possession, fighting at first, and then accepting the foreign invasion. Deuce pushed and she surrendered, her body gradually opening under the insistence of his. She shook her head. It was too fast. Too much. She pushed at his hands, using the resistance to steady her panic.

"Slow down." She needed time to adjust. Her heartbeat thundered in her ears, her breath rasped in her lungs, stealing her voice. She closed her eyes as he pierced her that first inch. Pain and pleasure blossomed together.

"Open your eyes, Edie mine."

It was incredibly hard to do so.

"Look at me."

His "I wish to see you as you accept my cock this time" sent a shot of white-hot desire straight to her womb. Her muscles clamped down hard on his shaft, squeezing and releasing, milking tiny spurts of pleasure from his thick length. He moaned and she clamped down harder holding him so tightly she could feel the echo of his heartbeat, slower than hers, but harder. Much harder.

"Relax."

His voice joined the wild rhythm strumming through her body, the burning ache in her rear transcending pain to something more primitive, more elemental, threading between her caution and her need, creating a quilt of desire so complex that she couldn't sort passion from pain, desire from fear. She just knew she needed him to feel whole. All of him. As much as he could give her for as long as he could.

"Love me, Deuce."

"I do." The burn dissipated to an ache as her body adjusted to his size. "Better?"

"Yes."

With a squeeze of his fingers, he freed his hand and bent over her, his cock inching deeper as he did. "Good."

Moist and hot, his tongue traced the whorl of her ear, sending shivers down her spine. Shivers that promptly shattered into long, streaking sparkles of delight. Sparkles that exploded like the Fourth of July as he slipped his finger inside the hoop and tugged. She lunged upward as her muscles surrendered in defeat and his cock head shot into her ass, yanking to a stop as his knuckle pressed down into her engorged clit, the tension prolonging the sharp stab of sensation, holding it centered on her core, giving her time to get past the surprise, to the delight. Above her, Deuce continued his assault, pressing steadily inward, not giving her time to adjust or protest, keeping her in an agony of suspense, filling her with his passion until she couldn't tell where his left off and hers began.

"Push out, Edie."

She did, but only because the strain on her clit was too much. "Oh God, Deuce." She wrapped her fingers around his wrist, digging her nails in as the ring heated and vibrated. "I can't take this."

It hurt so much, but it wasn't enough. None of it was enough. She leaned forward as he pulled back, finding the searing bite of the hoop instead of respite. She twisted against him as her womb clenched and her pussy grasped at air. She was helpless, a prisoner to her own needs and the desire he raised in her so effortlessly. He forged back in. Too fast. Too hard. She couldn't control it. She curled away into the mattress. He didn't back off, just kept coming, tugging the hoop, stroking her clitoris, keeping her pressed between reality and threat. No matter what she did, she couldn't escape the desire winding tighter, coiling deeper. She held on, waiting for a reprieve, needing it. When it came, it wasn't what she expected. Deuce's withdrawal didn't give her pleasure, just left her aching and empty with nowhere to go with the emotion surging inside. She needed Deuce. His direction. His passion. His power.

"Oh God, Deuce, I need you."

He growled into her ear, "Where?"

She leaned forward into the ring, the symbolism in the piercing catching on her passion and dragging it out into the open as she answered, "In my ass. My pussy. Just you. Wherever you want."

He released the ring. The mattress dipped as he shifted his weight to the other side. "You hunger."

"Yes." She did. So desperately. For him. His fingers untangled from hers, trailing steadily up her arm, down over her breasts and belly, following her curves until he came to the top of her mound. There he lingered, playing in her damp curls, sliding his fingers between the hoop and her flesh, cupping her intimately. Protectively.

"I have you."

She needed more than his protection. She needed his possession.

"I don't want you to have me. I need you to take me. Make me so much yours that I can't see myself as anything else *but* yours."

Against her cheek, she felt his smile. In her mind, she felt his surprise and satisfaction. In her body, the hard thrust of his cock as he gave her what she asked for. All of him, all the way, until there was nothing between them except the strength of their love.

Chapter Twenty-One

∞

Deuce awoke for the first time in his six-hundred-fifty-eight years with a sense of pleasure. Exhausted from his demands, Edie sprawled over him, her moist breath caressing his skin, one thigh thrown over his, her arm stretched across his chest. As if she feared he would disappear. In time, she would lose that fear. Until then, he would hold her as close as she needed, for as long as she needed.

One of her wild curls tickled his chin. He caught it between his fingers, rubbing the thick silken strands against each other. She was doing better, responding properly to the rituals. Her cheeks were flushed and a small smile curved the fullness of her lips. Beneath the fan of her lashes, faint dark circles marred the perfection of her face. Those were his fault.

He'd meant to be easier with her, but she made it very difficult to remember her frailty. As difficult as she made it for him to take care of her properly. He could feel the soreness in her muscles, the rawness between her legs. Everything in him demanded he soothe her pain, but he could not. His little mate forbade it, claiming she liked the physical reminder of what was between them.

He carefully pulled her into his shoulder, kissing the top of her head. There was so little he could give her right now that he was unable to deny her request, no matter how illogical. He eased her down onto the pillows. The little smile that accompanied her sigh of satisfaction tugged an answering one from within.

The Chosen were not prone to high emotion, but Edie made him want to laugh and cry and roar with the pure male satisfaction of having her in his arms, his bed. She snuggled her face into the palm of his hand in a purely unconscious gesture. If this were any other time, he'd slide back into bed and hold her while she slept, cherishing the peace she brought, but tonight there was no time. Bohdan had risen, and the enemy was near.

* * * * *

He found Bohdan near the pass, a dark shadow in a darker night. His energy was not what it should be, but not as erratic as when he'd first risen. "It is good to see you."

Bohdan glanced up from the young man he was feeding from. He closed the wounds on his prey's neck before letting him drop unceremoniously into the snow. He inclined his head. "And to see you. Eden survived intact?"

"Yes."

"You are mated?"

"Yes."

"Good."

It was very good. Deuce motioned to the man sprawled in the snow. "He was not to your liking?"

Bohdan didn't spare the man a glance. "He is one of them."

Deuce had known Bohdan was going to say that. The compound was too remote for tourists and the winter too severe for recreational skiers. "Did you get anything from him?"

His brother shook his head. "What he knows is the story they have concocted."

"Which is?"

"You kidnapped the woman and child. Lavery is simply trying to get her back since the police have bungled the recovery. He has been hired to accomplish that goal."

"He is what they call a mercenary?"

"Yes."

Deuce glanced at the man. He was not one of the men from Eden's memories. "I would not say a very good one."

"Lavery would not want someone too smart involved. They might ask questions."

"I did not think mercenaries asked questions."

Bohdan stepped away. "It would be a mistake to think all humans lack honor."

He knew that, but lately, it had been getting hard to remember. "I know."

Bohdan walked around the camp. "This pass is one of the few alternate routes off the mountain."

Deuce crossed to the small orange tent. He sliced through the side and looked within. Supplies were meager. Only enough for a couple of days.

"He was not planning on staying long." Cold prickled up his spine as he looked across the barren, snow-covered land. "One man could not hope to block the pass."

Bohdan motioned to the crushed communications device attached to the man's shoulder. "But he could serve as an alert."

"In case a human woman and child chose to leave," Deuce finished the thought. A gust of wind blew Bohdan's hair across his face. Deuce reached in his pocket and handed his brother a leather tie.

"Thank you." With the efficiency that marked everything Bohdan did, he tied his hair back, the severe style highlighting the strain of his ordeal. "Is your mate still planning on leaving?"

"I have convinced her of the benefits of staying."

Bohdan raised a brow, the doubt in his expression a reflection of what he'd felt previously in Eden. "You are sure?"

Deuce heard again Edie's sweet cries, felt again her body's demands on his. She might be scared and uncertain, but she was trying. "Yes."

"If they are not planning on her leaving voluntarily," Bohdan said as he leaned down to check the pulse of the human he'd fed on, "they have something else in mind."

If they were, they were doomed to failure. "They will not breach the compound."

Bohdan straightened. "You have given the alert?"

"Yes. Others and Chosen are prepared."

Bohdan brushed off his hands and frowned. "It does not make sense that they would try and take her from the compound. It is too heavily guarded."

"That occurred to me." Deuce stepped back from the tent, restraining the urge to deliver a death blow to the unconscious human lying outside it. The Chosen did not kill without reason. "The Coalition is devious and cunning, but never stupid."

"Then they must have something else in mind."

"But what?" The feeling of unease increased. Even with their abilities, they were a good fifteen minutes from the compound. *Edie, you are well?*

He had to wait for her response, and when it came, it was a clumsy endeavor, but that she tried soothed him, considering how sensitive she was about sharing thoughts.

Yes. Marlika and I are having coffee.

Coffee is not good for you.

Her *Don't even think of messing with my caffeine* shook a smile past his worry.

It is not your place to give orders.

Another awkward pause and another staccato effort. *I'm giving this one.*

You are being disrespectful.

Deal with it. The lack of concern with his displeasure in the stuttering reply twitched the corner of his lips. His little human was very bold, courting his discipline. He would have to deal with her when he got back. His body hummed pleasurably at the thought. In the interim, he needed her to be alert.

Be careful.

Is something wrong? Worry shrouded her laughter.

Yes.

What?

I do not know, but do not take chances.

I never do.

For once, I would like that to be the truth.

Her love touched him with a soothing stroke. If she uttered an apology it was lost in her efforts to communicate. But he took the light touch as one, anyway.

I will accept your tribute later.

Her *Fat chance!* spurred a chuckle past his control.

"She is well?" Bohdan asked.

Deuce ran his palm over his hair as he faced his brother. He should not be smiling, but she did amuse him with her natural independence. "She is having coffee with Marlika."

"Coffee is not good for her."

Deuce dropped his hand to his side, shrugged and tried to wipe the smile off his face. "So I told her."

Bohdan's weary expression lifted with his own amusement. "She was not impressed?"

"No." She was neither impressed with the fact that he was her Chosen mate, nor with the laws he laid down. It was irritating and intriguing at the same time.

"It is good that a human mate brings so many other pleasures, because I have not found obedience to be one of their strong points."

"The Maker knows it is not one of Edie's." Deuce agreed, noting the thread of nostalgia trailing behind Bohdan's words. "Your mate did not obey well, either?"

For a second Bohdan froze, and Deuce feared he'd gone too far, but then Bohdan sighed and shook his head, staring off toward the mountains. "She was just a little thing, small even for a human, but she didn't seem to know it. She was always testing limits and challenging authority."

They had never spoken of Bohdan's loss. Perhaps, it was time. "She must have given you much stress."

Bohdan shrugged. "None that I minded."

"I am sorry that you lost her." For the first time in three hundred years, Deuce felt comfortable saying those words to his brother.

Bohdan nodded, his expression hardening to granite. "Thank you."

Tiny slivers of the pain Bohdan lived with leaked past his guard. Deuce wanted to drop to his knees from the enormity of what his brother suffered, but he didn't. Couldn't. To speak of the pain would be to make it real, and he didn't know if Bohdan could survive a living, breathing recreation of the agony he suppressed.

"Maybe she will come in again." It was the only solace he could offer.

Bohdan gave him a perfectly polite agreement that emphasized how hopeless his situation really was. "It is a hope."

Not a huge one, Deuce knew. Though legends of mates reborn littered the stories of the Chosen, he couldn't think of a single time it had ever happened. "It is a hope we will hold onto."

He couldn't fault Bohdan for the eyebrow he cocked at him. He never gave orders to his brother, but he would not surrender him to despair. If ordering him to hold onto hope kept him alive one more second, then he would give orders until all the Chosen passed over. Bohdan stepped over the man and stumbled. Deuce caught his wrist.

"You are still weak." He extended his arm. Bohdan was shaking his head before he could present his wrist.

"You cannot afford the weakness." He jerked his thumb in the direction of the human. "There are more of these about."

It bothered Deuce that the human had been so near and tempting. The Coalition knew what comprised the nature of the Chosen and Others. Knew their habits and weaknesses. Not all, but enough to set a trap. "I find that fact too convenient."

Bohdan paused in searching under the tent. "You think they are setting a trap?"

"Not with anything you can detect."

"It is widely known that the Chosen hunt. And that they hunt alone."

Bohdan eyed the man. Deuce could feel the energy churning his thoughts. "It would be natural for us to assume their sentries are easy pickings."

"And for them to count on that."

"But what could they gain by that?"

"I can only think of one thing." The unease Deuce had been battling surged to the fore. "Complacency."

He headed for the edge of the clearing, reaching for Eden with his thoughts.

Bohdan took the realization to the inevitable conclusion as they launched into the air. "They are not worried about breaking in, because they already have someone inside."

"Yes." The delay waiting for Edie to respond stretched to eons. Deuce swore and strove to keep his thoughts calm. Where was Edie? Waiting on her answer was an agony. As soon as he got back, he was locking her thoughts to his and to hell with the privacy she put such stock in. He called to her again. This time her response was immediate and crystal clear. Everything he could have hoped for. With the skill of one long used to telepathic thought, she projected across the miles.

A crystal clear, perfectly tuned, terrorized primal scream of his name.

* * * * *

Marlika reached across the table that had been set up in the suite to touch the dimple in Jalina's cheek as the little girl waved her hands and cooed. "She likes her new carrier."

Eden gave the brightly colored plastic carrier a rock with her toe. "Thank you for bringing it. And thanks for getting some clothes for me."

"Deuce was not pleased with my choices for you."

And that still tickled Marlika's sense of humor. Eden could tell from the way she smiled. The clothes Marlika had picked were bright, sexy and formfitting. In other words, what every other woman her age was wearing. And she loved them. "He needs to come out of the dark ages."

"All Chosen do."

Eden couldn't argue with that. The brightly patterned tunic she wore now was as comfortable as Deuce's T-shirts, but much sexier. Deuce hated the low neckline. She loved it even more because of that. And jeans, well even new jeans were like old friends to her body. "At least he liked what you bought Jalina."

Marlika finished off her coffee. "Next time I go back to that store, I'm taking a lot more money. There are so many cute things she must have."

Eden raised her brows and took a sip from her own cup. "Must have?"

Marlika's smile spread to a grin as she met her gaze. "Absolutely. Our little princess cannot do without."

Eden propped her chin on her hand and put the cup down. "Since when is she a princess?"

"Since the day the Others found out of her existence. In case you haven't noticed, there's a line of people out the door wanting to spoil her."

"I noticed. It really has been a long time since the Chosen or the Packs have had babies."

Marlika's smile faded. "Too long, and the last few, I'm told, were so sickly it was painful to see them, and impossible to make them smile." She chucked Jalina under her little chin. "But Jalina is so healthy and happy, she brings joy with just the sight of her."

"And to think I was worried you all would resent her."

"You cannot know what Jalina means to the Chosen or The Others. She's hope, happiness, and pleasure."

"I know what she means to Deuce."

"He is truly a doting father. You will have your hands full when he decides it is time to find her mate."

"There's a long time between now and then."

Marlika shook her head. "As fast as she's growing, maybe not so long."

"She's sprouting like a weed all right." Try as she might, Eden couldn't detect anything about the woman to indicate that she was a werewolf. She'd been discreetly studying her through two-and-a-half cups of mediocre coffee, and so far not a stray hair, fang or claw had made an appearance.

"If you give me a hint what you're looking for, maybe I can help."

Oh good God, she'd been staring again. And this time she'd been caught. Just her luck. "I'm sorry. I just find it incredible that you're one of the Others."

"Would you be more comfortable if I wore a sign?"

"Seriously? Yes."

Marlika drew back. Before the other woman could totally take what she said wrong, Eden clarified. "It's not that I care, but unlike everyone else in this place, I'm the only one who can't tell Chosen from Others, human from Chosen." She dropped back into her seat and waved her hand dismissively. "Forget about choosing between the *types* of Others."

Marlika's even features relaxed into a small smile. "You're stressed and out of sorts."

Trust a woman to understand. "Absolutely."

"By any chance is it near your time of the month?"

"I've decided that's never happening again."

"I'm sure Deuce will be disappointed."

"Which is the whole reason I've decided to go on some sort of forever Pill."

"You do not want him to have the pleasure of your flow?"

"I'm just having a really hard time thinking of it as a pleasure. About the only emotion humans associate with 'that time of the month' is ick!" She cut the other woman a pointed glare at her chuckle. "And that's a capital I on ick!"

As if she could read her mind, Marlika said, "You are mated to a Chosen. Anything associated with blood is erotic."

"Great. Just another of the great 'grossities' I have to get used to." She grabbed up her coffee cup and swirled the pale contents. "And no, it's not 'that time of the month'." Thank God. She had no idea how they would work out that discrepancy in taste.

"Dusan is your mate. He'll find a way to make you comfortable with the idea."

"Maybe I don't want him to work this out."

Marlika snagged a doughnut off the table. It was her tenth one so far. "You want to leave him?"

"No, I just want him to work with me sometimes rather than presenting everything as a *fait accompli*."

Marlika took a bite of the doughnut, chewed and shrugged. "That would be hard for him."

"Why is it so hard?"

"Because his whole life he has trained for two things." She waved the doughnut for emphasis, powdered sugar sprinkling the air like fairy dust as she elaborated. "To lead his people and to defend his mate. Being a warrior, he's more inclined to action than to talk."

"Being human, I want talk." She brought her cup halfway to her mouth, took a deep breath of the fragrant aroma, and then replaced it on the table, untouched. If she had any more, she'd only succeed in proving Deuce right that the caffeine would make her sick.

"Do you need more coffee?" Marlika asked, brushing the powder off the wood tabletop.

"Nah. Any more and I'll be dancing around the room." Right after she heaved it up. She pressed her hand to her stomach. That third cup had definitely been a mistake.

"Which would be why Dusan did not want you drinking any."

"He so doesn't get the allure of caffeine."

Marlika nodded and took a drink of her own coffee. "The Chosen do suffer from a few drawbacks."

Marlika's dry sense of humor was just one of the things that Eden had come to appreciate about her. That and her willingness to risk her life so she wouldn't have to be alone. "I want to thank you for volunteering to keep me company."

Marlika shrugged, her smile an open expression of friendship. "It's not like it's been a hardship. I've had a cute baby to play with and made a new friend."

"Being with me is dangerous."

"We're in a compound bursting its seams with testosterone-laden Others and Chosen who're just itching for an excuse to fight. I wouldn't call the risk high."

"High enough that other women avoid me like the plague."

"Don't hold it against them. They're humoring their mates, but it won't last much longer."

Eden's heart made the jump from her chest to her throat. There was only one reason she could believe the men would stop worrying. "You think the Coalition will make a move soon?"

Marlika shook her head, the long, delicate gold chains dangling from her ears swinging, catching the light, reflecting it back in mesmerizing flickers. "I think the women are going to revolt." She reached for another doughnut.

Eden watched in amazement as she made short work of it. "How can you eat that much and stay so slim?"

Marlika smiled and wiped a smear of power from the corner of her wide mouth. "One of the perks of being Pack. Fast metabolism."

"I have so gotten the short end of the stick when it comes to this whole Chosen, Other thing." She grabbed a doughnut. It would serve Deuce right if she got so fat she couldn't fit through the door.

Marlika took the doughnut from her hand and dropped it back into the bag. She touched her finger to hers. "You have a daughter and a mate who honors you above all others. From now until the day you die, you will never know loneliness or want. Do you really find your situation so bad?"

The sadness in the other woman's voice reminded Edie why this woman was allowed to befriend her. She had no mate, and if Deuce was to be believed, even if she had a mate, children were very unlikely. In comparison, she had everything.

"I'm sorry. That was totally uncalled for."

"Don't be sorry." Marlika shrugged. "It is up to the Maker to provide a mate. If he does not, I will pass to the other side and wait for my mate there." She said that so calmly, as if they weren't talking about a life stalked by loneliness and a death with no memories to carry over.

"Just a curiosity, but how long do Others and Chosen live?"

"Chosen and Other males live indefinitely if they do not lose a bonded mate or die in battle."

"I thought it was only Chosen who lived forever."

Marlika laughed and rocked the little seat as Jalina fussed. "The Chosen and Others share many characteristics, but while Others have learned to blend with humans, the Chosen have a love of the old ways that interferes with their blending, giving birth to many legends."

"That and the fact that they are nocturnal."

She nodded. "There is that."

Eden motioned to Jalina. "Is she asleep?"

"Like the angel she is."

"Ha! You're only saying that because you didn't hear her pitching a fit after dinner this evening."

"I'm sure she felt her reasons were valid."

Eden rolled her eyes. "I can see I'm going to have to keep an eye on all of you. "

"I have no idea what you mean." The abundance of innocence in Marlika's expression told Eden she knew exactly what she was referring to. The other woman's sense of humor matched her own. It felt good to have a friend. One she knew hadn't been paid to steer her in the direction her grandfather wanted her to go.

"I know you've said it's no hardship, but thanks again for being so good about all of this."

Marlika waved off her gratitude. "What are friends for?"

Eden pretended to wipe crumbs from the table and blinked fast. Twenty-five and her first genuine offer of friendship. Damn, if she cried, she'd have to shoot herself. She brushed the crumbs into her hand. "Thank you." As she wrapped the crumbs in a napkin, it hit her. "You mentioned that the men live indefinitely. What about the women?"

"We live perfectly healthy lives until…"

The "until" trailed the end of the statement. Eden grabbed hold of it and dragged it into the open. "Until what?"

"Until we either find our mate, or we reach one hundred years of age."

"What happens at one hundred?"

Marlika shrugged. "We die."

Eden blinked. Not sure she'd heard her right. "Say again?"

"Without a bonded mate, we die."

Eden knew she was staring, but she couldn't believe it. "Just like that?"

Marlika nodded, the only indication that the subject disturbed her was a tightening around her deep brown eyes. "Just like that."

Good God! She crushed the napkin in her hand. She couldn't imagine such a thing. No wonder her grandfather had been hitting dead ends. He thought the women held the secret to immortality. Another thought struck her. "How old are you?"

"Ninety-nine."

"Just turned or well into the year?" It was a stupid, painful question, but she had to know.

"Just turned."

The relief that swept over her was overwhelming, taking the depth from her voice and the breath from her lungs. They had time. "We have absolutely got to find you a mate."

Again Marlika offered that smile that soothed and saddened. "It is not that easy."

The woman was stunningly beautiful, kind and courageous. And she thought there'd be a problem? "How hard can it be?"

"We are not talking a sex partner, Eden. We are talking mate, the one chosen for me from birth. The only one who will complete me."

"If he's out there, we'll find him." The alternative simply didn't bear thinking about.

Marlika shrugged. "I have decided 'if' is a very big word."

"Have a little faith, Marlika, unless you want us humans labeling you a wuss."

"I certainly wouldn't want that—"

A knock at the door interrupted Marlika's response.

Be careful.

Deuce's warning hung in her mind. She caught Marlika's arm before she could open the door. "Who is it?"

"It's Pietre."

She didn't know any Pietre. "Who?"

"He's one of the Pride," Marlika answered, frowning at her.

Eden shushed Marlika with a flick of her hand as a wave of foreboding came over her. She grabbed Jalina's carrier and moved her away from the door, into the corner. Marlika gave her a sharp look and moved between the door and them, before calling out, "What do you need, Pietre?"

"I have a message from Dusan."

"A mate does not need a message delivered."

"He does when his mate is human and fearful of thought-sharing."

It was possible that Deuce had been trying to reach her and she'd blocked him out, but she didn't think so. Still... Eden took a step forward. This time, Marlika was holding up her hand. "Where's Nick?"

"He took a break." From the way Marlika stiffened, Eden got the impression that Nick wasn't the type to desert his post.

Marlika motioned Eden back toward the baby, every nuance of her body language screaming danger, but the tone she used dripped helpless apology. "I can't open the door, Pietre. Harley was very explicit in his orders."

"My orders are to deliver this message in person."

Eden got a sick feeling in her stomach. This wasn't right. Marlika's worried glance indicated the same sick feeling. She glanced at the intercom. "So slip it under the door."

"It's not that kind of message."

"What the hell kind of message is it then?" She made it two steps toward the wall panel.

The door swung open with utter silence. "This kind."

Chapter Twenty-Two

ဢ

Eden would have felt better if the door had crashed open. If the man standing in the entry had sported a grotesque mask or at least a creature feature or two. She'd have been ecstatic if Nick wasn't standing just behind him with a blank look on his face, hands lax at his sides, if Marlika wasn't standing with that same unnatural stillness, watching him approach. Doing nothing. Saying nothing. She'd feel a lot better if the man flat-out wasn't there.

In a perfectly normal, perfectly conversational voice, Pietre said, "I want the baby."

It was the scariest thing she'd ever heard. With everything she had, she mentally screamed for Deuce, reaching for his strength as she moved forward, placing herself beside the silent Marlika. "You can't have her."

His smile was more of a shift of mood than a shift of muscle. "There's no one to stop me."

She glanced over at Marlika. She was staring straight ahead. Her face expressionless as if she couldn't sense what was going on, but Eden could feel the waves of hatred rolling off her. "What did you do to her?"

"She, like the others, are thought-bound."

He'd frozen the entire compound this way? Was that even possible? "Is that anything like being tongue-tied?"

She couldn't believe she was cracking jokes, but stalling was the only thing she could think to do, and if cracking jokes gained her two precious seconds she'd take it. Too bad Pietre didn't have a sense of humor.

"Yes." He looked over her shoulder. "Get out of my way."

She didn't like the way he was eyeing Marlika. She folded her arms across her chest. "No."

A force hit the side of her face and the room spun out of focus. Eden caught herself on her hands. Reality centered in a splash of red against the pure white carpet. Blood. Her blood. She touched her lip. And then her cheek. She couldn't feel pain or the touch of her own fingers. Considering the force of the blow, that wasn't such a bad thing. She turned her head. Pietre was in front of Marlika. His hand stroking her cheek. As Eden watched, he dragged it over her cheekbone, lingering on her jaw in an oddly tender gesture.

Was Pietre in love with Marlika?

She pushed herself to her feet, receiving the answer to her question as a trail of red appeared on Marlika's cheek in the wake of Pietre's caress.

He wasn't in love. He was just one sick son of a bitch.

"Leave her alone."

"You will be silent." He said that with a complete expectation of obedience. She was getting damn tired of these men barking out orders. "What is it with you Others? Did the lot of you miss the women's movement entirely?"

"Be silent and still."

She wasn't going to be either. *Deuce, where are you?*

There was no answer. In the corner of the room, Jalina stirred. Adrenaline surged as Pietre glanced at the carrier. No way in hell was he touching her baby.

"Leave her be."

"My orders are to bring her back."

"You, your orders, and the delusional cowards who hired you can all go to hell."

"I do not work for the Coalition."

Trust an Other to split those kind of hairs. She inched closer to Marlika, angling her steps so that she was between Pietre and Jalina. "Must be the way you blindly follow their orders that confused me."

"I am merely repaying a debt."

"That's what they all say."

"I told you to shut up."

She refused to cower before the lowering of his brow and the menace he projected. "And I told you to get out of here." She shrugged. "Doesn't look like either of us is going to get what we want."

She never saw him move, but suddenly he was in front of her, his hand locked around her throat, cutting off her air as he lifted her off her feet.

"Why do you not shut up?" The puzzlement in his tone clued her in to what was bothering him. The man had actually expected her to shut up.

"Is my natural resistance to telepathic persuasion inconveniencing you?" she croaked out, keeping her own surprise that he couldn't control her buried under bravado.

His hands tightened, shutting off the last of her air. "Not in the least."

It took everything she had not to give in to her instinctive urge to kick and struggle, but she'd had a lot of practice in the last year, enduring. She could endure this too. For her daughter, because every second he spent choking her was one more her child was safe. Deuce was coming. She couldn't feel him or sense him, but he'd promised her he'd come and she was holding him to it.

Pietre held her like that until she couldn't stop herself — she clawed at his hands and saw spots before her eyes.

"Too bad they want you alive." He dropped her to the floor.

She closed her eyes on a wave of relief. *Thank God!* She dragged air into her lungs. Horror distorted her efforts as Pietre approached Jalina.

"What did they do for you that you owe them enough to betray your people?"

He paused and turned so fast his hair flared around his shoulders. She had no doubt if he were in lion form, his mane would be bristling. "My people have been playing second fiddle to the Chosen for too long."

She propped herself up on her elbows. "And you've come to this conclusion how?"

Human form or not, Pietre could pull off a snarl. "Others were meant to rule. After today, all will see that. I have seen to it."

She really didn't want to know, but she had him talking instead of walking, so she asked, "How?"

This time his smile was impossible to miss, slashing as it did across his square features. "By learning how to level the playing field."

God help her, she didn't know what he meant by that. "Dak is the leader of the Pride and he doesn't have a problem with how things are."

"Dak is old-fashioned, accepting what is rather than exploring what could be." She was once again facing his back as he headed for Jalina. She had to stop him.

"In other words, he's not a glory-seeking, power-hungry ass like yourself," she retorted, getting to her feet.

Her insult bounced off Pietre like a ping-pong ball hitting a wall. He didn't stop and didn't look back, just headed for her daughter.

Deuce, help me!

Eden threw herself after the man, leaping for his back. He turned with amazing speed, catching her desperate hope for success and tossing it aside as easily as he tossed her. She hit the floor hard. Air exploded from her lungs as she slid. She came up against something unsteady. She grabbed hold. Denim under her hand, the curve of muscle over bone. A leg. Marlika.

She dug in with her fingers, watching in horror as Pietre reached for her daughter. "Shake it off," she hissed at the other woman, willing her to hear, willing that damn blankness to leave her face. "Goddamn it, Marlika, shake it off!"

To her shock, the woman blinked. Eden grabbed her leg with the other hand, fought for a mental connection and threw every bit of willpower she had behind it when she screamed, "Wake up!"

Marlika blinked again and looked down. Her earrings glittered and swung in the light. Memory wiped the blankness from her face, and before Eden's shocked eyes, those features shifted. Elongated.

In the next instant, she was leaning up against the leg of a wolf. A big, major league, pissed-off, fang-sporting wolf.

Marlika sprang for Pietre, and Eden headed for the door. She needed help. She cut across the floor, feet slipping, stumbling in her panic, terrified she'd feel Pietre's hand on her shoulder. Terrified that he'd stop her.

Behind her there was a snarl and a roar. Furniture crashed. Glass broke. Eden blocked the sounds and kept her goal in sight. She slammed into Nick, latched onto his shoulder and screamed. "Wake the hell up!"

He blinked. A high-pitched yelp echoed around the hall.

"Oh shit. Oh shit." Marlika was in there alone fighting that sick son of a bitch. She needed reinforcements fast. Eden grabbed Nick's face so hard her nails bit into his dark skin. "Wake up!"

There was another crash and a howl from the room, then a god-awful silence.

Nick moved her aside, his gaze looking where she didn't dare — into the room where her daughter sat with a killer. One blink he was there, and in another he was gone. And the noise began again, fiercer this time. Eden forced herself to turn around. To look.

A wolf and a lion fought, blood was everywhere. She couldn't see Marlika in any form. And just past the fighting Others, her daughter screamed. Eden's heart thundered in her ears and her mouth dried to parchment. She had to get Jalina out of there.

"Oh my God. What do I do now?" She hadn't expected an answer, but one came. Strong and calm, a port in the middle of the horrific storm, the "Voice" said, *We fight.*

Fight? She didn't know how to fight. She'd been raised to throw parties, not fists. But that was her daughter in there, and that was one fucking ugly werelion trying to take her away. It was either fight or give up. Eden wasn't giving up.

Jalina screamed again. The two Others crashed to the floor next to her in a flurry of gnashing teeth and ripping claws. She had to get her daughter out of there, now. Pietre and Nick leapt to their feet and faced off over Jalina's carrier. Blood flowed from both, coating their fur and the floor. Teeth bared, they circled each other, jockeying for a better position in relation to the baby. The lion feinted in. Nick leapt between the carrier and Pietre. Teeth snapped and more blood flowed. Nick was fast, but was on the defensive, his attention split between fighting the lion and guarding Jalina. He was taking heavy injuries as a result. Eden didn't see how he could possibly fight much longer, not with all the blood he was losing. Something needed to be done.

She slipped into the room, pressing back against the wall just inside the door. To the right Marlika lay crumpled on the floor. She was still in wolf form. A growing pool of blood spread around her. Eden closed her eyes against the atrocity, offered a brief prayer for strength, and then opened them again. As bad as this was, as horrifically surreal as this was, it was still something she had to take care of.

She made it five feet into the room before Nick went down. As the lion dove for his throat, she grabbed the marble lamp off the table and swung for all she was worth. The lamp collided against his back with an arm-jarring thud. He grunted and looked up, blood dripping from his jaws, eyes flat and eerily unemotional.

He took a step toward her. She took one back. And then another, drawing him away from Nick. And Jalina. He snarled. She pulled the lamp back, ready to swing. He stared at her, those gold eyes holding hers. Drawing her in. The eyes blurred, changed, grew larger, shifted higher. She blinked. He'd changed back to human form.

Blood poured from a bite on his shoulder. The flesh hung from the gash on his cheek. He smiled. The flap of skin stretched into an obscenity. "Looks like I'm done here."

She wanted to run. She couldn't. Couldn't move. Could barely breathe. Whatever protection she'd had was gone, and Pietre now held her thought-bound. This was not good.

Deuce! Goddamn it, Deuce! The scream came from her soul.

The only answer she received was the mocking echo of Pietre's laughter. "Scream for him, human. It'll give you something to do."

He crossed the room with that particular glide of the Others. No board squeaked to mark his progress. Out of her peripheral vision she saw him grab his clothes off the floor and step into them. How could he look so normal getting dressed when all around them people were dying? Jalina screamed a high, warbling cry that lashed her fear into panic.

Why didn't Deuce come? Why didn't *someone* come?

There was a stirring at the edge of her mind.

Deuce?

No answer. But then she could move her eyes. As Pietre snapped his pants, she scanned the room, the floor the walls, looking for something. Her gaze lingered on the swords on the wall above the table to the right of Jalina.

Pietre came back to her, his shirt tucked in, his belt buckled, looking perfectly normal except for the blood darkening the black silk, and the dripping gash on his cheek. He touched her face. Jalina screamed. "I should leave my mark on you. A present for Dusan."

Hatred like she'd never known before swept over her, followed by a calm that was equally alien. She felt his nails. His tainted energy. Her gaze remained locked straight ahead, giving her no choice but to view his gloating expression of regret. "Too bad I can't."

He turned in dismissal. Bent over Jalina. Reached for the carrier handle.

"Die!" The scream ripped through her brain, as her body leapt into motion. Like a passenger on a thrill ride, all she could do was marvel as she leapt into the air, and launched off Pietre's back as he tried to turn. The cool metal of the sword felt alienly familiar in her hand as she ripped it from the wall, tossed the scabbard and brought it down with a skill that would have had her mouth gaping had she control of any part of her body.

Blood spewed in a high arc as the werelion's arm separated from his body. She stood in the spray, sword held before her in a defensive gesture, legs braced as she stood before Jalina. She didn't know how she was doing what she was doing, but she was profoundly grateful that she was doing it. Especially when Pietre screamed and backed up two steps, blood spraying in a new angle. Eden was morbidly glad she wasn't in control of her body, because for sure she'd be on the floor heaving up her guts.

"Touch the child and die." It was her voice, her thoughts, but she hadn't thought to utter the words.

Pietre answered with a snarl. His muscles bunched, he closed his eyes. The spray of blood ceased. When he opened his eyes again, it was to smile. "They will win in the end."

"They won't win today." Eden hoped whomever was running the show had the knowledge to back up that declaration.

"You cannot stop me."

The way he said it, the calmness with which he said it, scared the shit out of her, but didn't seem to faze the woman connected to her. "I will try."

"You will fail."

"Don't count your chickens before they're hatched."

Pietre's laugh skittered across Eden's raw nerve endings in an eerie prelude to the stillness that dropped over the room. He stood straight, chin up, eyes slitted, hands open. Energy shimmered around him, growing in density as it collected. Inside her, Eden felt the stranger collecting her own energy, drawing it around her in a buffering shield, working faster as Pietre's laugh built in volume, a dark reflection of the strange field all but obliterating the satisfaction in his flat yellow eyes.

The ball of energy throbbed twice before swelling outward until, with a searing burst of light it exploded. The rippling shock wave hit the perimeters of her consciousness with a scalding burn before slicing inward. Her mind's eye flared red. Pietre roared in agony. The field around Eden shuddered and wavered before strength not hers surged forward. Energy she recognized. Deuce. More strength surged in. Bohdan. Her knees gave out, and then there was nothing. No pain, no light, just a blessed drift toward the center of a swirling darkness backlit by a woman's sob, and Bohdan's anguished shout of "No!"

* * * * *

Come to me, Edie.

The order reached into the black void, catching her on the edge of the precipice, holding her when she would have pitched over.

Deuce?

I need you, mate. You will come to me.

She didn't know if she could. *I can't let go.*

Of what?

She didn't know, but if she let go, she'd lose a part of her forever, and she couldn't do that. *I don't know.*

I will come to you.

She shook her head. He couldn't come with her. *You have to stay where you are.*

Not without you.

There was no mistaking his resolve. Turbulence shook the air around her.

You can't. He couldn't go where she was going. It wasn't his time.

You go nowhere without me.

The tug of the precipice increased. She didn't know what to do. She couldn't go over and she couldn't let go.

You will come to me now.

I can't.

There was a pause during which she hung suspended between the choices, then Deuce was back, his calm spreading over her panic. *I have brought Bohdan.*

Bohdan? Why? Am I dying?

Be easy, my heart. You do not die.

Then why is Bohdan here? Wherever here was. The pressure in her head increased. The energy pulled her toward that edge of no return. Fighting her, fighting to be free. Maybe she should just let go.

No. The order slammed into her mind, waves of agony swelled as Bohdan's will shoved through hers. She fought back. He was too strong. The agony tore through her mind, threatening her sanity.

Deuce held Edie tighter as her body spasmed in his arms. Fresh blood leaked from her nose and ears. He caught her head with his hand before it could slam into the floor. The psychic blow from Pietre had been near fatal, leaving her unconscious and on the verge of death. She only lived because the stranger who protected

321

her had taken the majority of the blow into herself. Now Edie's life and the life of the stranger hung in the balance. If he could not bring Edie to trust him, both would be lost.

No. The stranger you fear is my mate. Eden must not let go.

Deuce looked across the floor to where his brother squatted, his expression intense. The stranger was his mate?

"Back off, Bohdan."

His brother's eyes were hard and flat when they met his, but in their depths swirled the red of primitive emotion. "She cannot let her go."

"You cannot make her hold on."

"I will do what I must."

That was what Deuce feared. Bohdan was at his most primitive right now. Reacting on instinct, protecting his mate at all costs. "If she dies, we lose them both."

"I will not lose her again."

"And I will not let you kill my mate."

Bohdan took a deep breath. His muscles tensed. Deuce braced himself. If Bohdan did not find reason, then he would have to kill him. Bohdan shook from head to toe. Edie spasmed in his arms again. "Let her go, Bohdan."

Bohdan looked her over, not relinquishing his hold on her mind. "She is afraid."

"If fear were something that stopped Edie, I would not be alive and she would not be here."

"I cannot chance it."

"Can you chance the other feeling the threat to her and taking the choice away?"

Bohdan stilled. His hair fell over his shoulders as he bent his head. His hands clenched into fists on his thighs, every muscle rock-hard with the battle he waged with himself. His answer was a flat "No" revealing nothing of the agony Deuce could feel tearing at him. His hold on Edie dissipated.

Edie relaxed in Deuce's arms, her hand falling to the floor, her head lolling, her life force further away, flickering with indecision.

He followed the flickering light to the deepest corner of her mind, feeling Bohdan behind him, repairing ruptured blood vessels in his wake.

Come to me, Edie. He whispered it in her ear, in her mind, keeping his voice calm through sheer force of will. She was so weak. Too weak. The other was draining her.

Now.

She struggled to find the path, her *Help me, Deuce* a soft plea.

I am here, my heart. He touched his soul to hers, guiding her closer, wrapping as much of her as he could in his hold. *You will hold onto me, and you will listen.*

I'm listening. Exhaustion imbued the two words with lethargy.

Bohdan is here.

Her withdrawal was immediate. *No!*

Deuce held her mentally. Soothed her, pulled her back from that dangerous edge. *He needs your help.*

Why?

Bohdan's voice crossed his, a calm brush of strength. *You hold my mate.*

Your mate?

The woman who speaks to you, helps you, is my mate.

You said your mate was dead.

She is reborn.

I hold her?

She took the blow for you. She is injured. Her link to you is all that keeps her here.

Shit.

I do not like you swearing. Deuce gave her the reprimand as a distraction. Edie's *Tough* lacked most of its usual force. Her strength was failing.

He shot Bohdan a warning glance. He needed to keep his anguish from Edie. She was not an experienced telepath. She couldn't filter.

Bohdan nodded his understanding. *I need to get to her.*

You're going to tell me you need to mess with my mind, aren't you?

Bohdan glanced at Deuce. Deuce nodded. There was no way to keep that from her.

She is linked to you. I can only reach her through you.

You could at least sound apologetic about it.

I am sorry.

Deuce.

I am here.

Hold me.

He would, with everything he had, ignoring the Others filling the room, the sounds of battle outside the window. Edie was all that mattered. *I have you.*

He felt her mental bracing. He shook his head. *It will not work like that. If the other thinks you are in danger, she will sacrifice herself.*

Oh God, you want me to be calm.

I need you to be very calm, Bohdan inserted.

I can't do that. Eden's agony ripped at Deuce. *It hurts too much to be calm.*

You will trust me in this.

Deuce didn't know if she would, or could. Their relationship was so new. He'd had so little time with her. It was his duty to protect her from moments like this, not throw her into the middle of them.

Oh, get over yourself. I'm not that fragile.

Deuce touched the gold of her hair, sinking his fingers into the curls. *You read my mind.*

It's only fair if you get to read mine.

He caught the frantic rush of adrenaline as she prepared herself, and evened it out.

There was a short pause in which he felt her indecision. *What if I fail?*

I will not let you fail.

Her fingers twitched on his thigh. He caught her hand in his, bringing it to his cheek as her breath, that precious sign of life caressed his neck. He whispered in her ear, "Trust me."

She took an uneven breath, her body caught between unconscious and alert, defense and acceptance and then she relaxed. Her mind reached for his, falling open, giving him blanket permission to do with her as she willed.

Go for it.

He did.

* * * * *

It didn't hurt. Eden opened her eyes, the dragging sense gone, the memory of Pietre heavy on her mind. Deuce was staring down at her, the lines by his eyes the only indication of his worry.

"Jalina?"

"Our daughter is safe. Nick and Marlika have been taken to heal."

She glanced to the right, saw Pietre's mangled body and flinched. She turned her head back and caught Deuce's gaze. "Others like him should come with a warning label."

"Others like him should not exist."

"Can anyone else from the Pack or Pride do what he does?"

His lips thinned. "No. He has been altered."

She closed her eyes, accepting the truth. "By my grandfather?"

"Yes."

"I'm sorry."

His lips brushed the back of her hand. "You are not responsible for his actions."

"But if it weren't for me—"

"I would not be a happy Chosen."

She took another quick glance at Pietre. "Is he dead?"

"Yes."

"Who…" The question drifted off. Deuce brought her hand to his chest. Beneath her palm his heart beat steadily.

"He touched you. Threatened our daughter. He knew the price."

Deuce had killed him. With great joy it would appear from the blood splattering the walls of the room. "I don't think he expected to be on the losing end of the deal."

"He was a fool." Only Deuce could pack that much disgust into a sentence, reducing something she regarded as fraught with complexity to something so simple.

"If you had zapped him mentally there wouldn't be such a huge cleanup to do."

"He was killed according to custom."

She did not want to know the details. "You Chosen have a ritual for everything."

He nodded, his hair falling over his shoulder onto her breast, where it pooled in a dark spill. "Yes."

She glanced at the glistening puddle surrounding Pietre's head. "For all your longevity, you are a rather primitive bunch, aren't you?"

Deuce stiffened infinitesimally as a soothing brush of calm surrounded her. "Yes."

She didn't fight his hands sliding under her shoulders. "You don't have to try and shield me, Deuce. It's not as if I hadn't already figured that out."

For the first time ever he didn't meet her gaze. "You have?"

Did he think it was a well-kept secret? "The first hint might have been when you started with the mate business, then got all feisty because I wore another man's jacket and the fact that you can't stand to lose the edge in bed…"

He lifted her against his chest. "I would prefer that you had not experienced that part of me so fully."

She caught his hair and gathered it into a ponytail at the base of his skull. "The one thing you should understand about humans, Deuce, is that we really get off on emotions."

"You are not upset at the killing?"

"Are you kidding? That freak hurt Nick and Marlika and tried to take Jalina. Killing was too good for him."

"Would you like the details of his death?"

She shuddered. "I understand the need for his death but details are not necessary."

His lips brushed her ear. "You are bloodthirsty...but squeamish?" She suspected that hitch in his breathing was a chuckle.

She nodded, cuddling her cheek against his chest, listening to his heartbeat, breathing deeply of his scent. "We humans are funny that way."

"I am thinking not all humans, but maybe just *mine*." His free hand slipped under her knees.

The emphasis he put on mine did not escape her notice. "Maybe just yours." If he hadn't been holding her so tightly she might have missed his stillness at her agreement. She let go of his hair and opened her fingers over his shoulders. "Take me out of here, please."

Without the slightest of jostling, he lifted her. "You feel well enough to move?"

"Yes." She could be near death, and she'd feel well enough to be out of here. She kept her eyes on the pulse in his throat, ignoring the darker stains on his black shirt, knowing instinctively what they were, and asked the one thing she feared most. "Did we lose her?"

Dusan shook his head. "No. Bohdan has her."

"Physically has her?" As impossible as that seemed, she wouldn't put much past the Chosen after what she'd experienced.

"No. But he holds her life."

She linked her arms around his neck. "The way you hold mine?"

"No. He has to find her first for that."

Remembering the desperation, combined with the determination with which Bohdan had torn through her mind toward the woman, she didn't have any doubt that he would. "What if she doesn't want him?"

She could easily see Bohdan scaring the pants off any woman with all that intensity.

"She is his mate. There is no choice."

She didn't know much about the woman who had been speaking in her head, who Bohdan now claimed was his mate, but she did know one thing—she was not a pushover. "I don't think that whole mate thing is going to hold much water with her."

"Bohdan will see to it."

"Or she'll see to him."

Deuce paused and glanced down, his right brow arching in that endearing way. "You fear for him?"

"He has a few likable qualities."

Deuce's lips twitched. "No doubt his mate will find a few she likes also."

If she didn't kill him before she discovered them. "I hope so."

A shift of energy in the room had her stiffening. Deuce turned. Dak stood in the doorway, his broad shoulders filling the expanse. His clothes were torn. Blood smeared his hands and the gun he held. Three slashes marred his left cheek. One glance was all he spared Pietre. The disgusted curl of his lip indicated how he felt about the lion's plans for a takeover. "The invaders have been eliminated."

From the number of dark stains on his clothing and skin, Eden figured the Others were as primitively ritualistic as the Chosen when it came to dealing with traitors.

"Casualties?" Deuce asked.

"None." He jerked his chin in the direction of Pietre's corpse. "The rest were not strong psychics like that one. With the Chosen's help we were able to defeat them easily."

Dak said that as if it was over, but Eden knew better. It would never be over. Not as long as Clay Lavery lived.

"He won't give up, you know."

"Who?" Dak asked, running his gaze over her. Maybe she didn't look as bad as she thought because with a quirk of his lips, he relaxed.

"My grandfather. His biological clock is ticking. He'll just keep creating more and more monsters until he finds what he needs to get what he wants."

"And what does he want?"

"Immortality."

"We will not give that to him." Calm as always, Deuce had given her the answer she'd dreaded.

"I think he just plans on taking it."

"He is welcome to try."

Dak shifted the gun to his shoulder, stepped back and motioned two Others into the room toward Pietre's body. "We will be ready for him."

There was no getting ready for what a man of her grandfather's intelligence and determination could create. "You need to just kill him."

"Not all of his discoveries were evil," Deuce pointed out.

Jalina. He was talking about Jalina. "Surely your own scientists can find out what he did and recreate it on their own?"

"We cannot risk that they won't."

"So you're going to let him live?"

Deuce nodded, his lips a hard, flat line. "For now."

Eden tightened her grip on his shoulders. There was one option they were all overlooking. "He might take a trade."

To her surprise, it was Dak who shot her idea down before Deuce could utter the denial pouring through his body. "We do not trade our mates for secrets."

"It was just a suggestion."

Deuce's grip on her tightened to the point of pain. "If ever the suggestion is made again, you will discover the discipline a Chosen mate delivers to his woman."

"There's no need to get huffy."

"I am not huffy, I am displeased. We will find the solution, but we will not trade the lives of our people for a shortcut."

Dak nodded. "Agreed."

"So, my grandfather gets to live." It did not seem a fair trade.

"On borrowed time, but for now he has a reprieve."

She arched her brows. "But you do have someone working on it?"

He nodded. "Yes. Many someones."

She rested her cheek against his chest. "Good. Now, could you get me out of here?"

"With pleasure."

Chapter Twenty-Three

&

Deuce was gloating. Eden stood on the porch, looking out onto the moonlit yard, Jalina in her arms, and knew it was true. It wasn't readily apparent to the naked eye, but the man was on an out-and-out gloat fest. He said something to Dak. Whatever he said shocked the Pride leader as his eyes widened briefly before resuming their steady stare. Or maybe it wasn't what he'd said but the fact that Deuce had been smiling when he'd said it. Eden knew Deuce wasn't much of a smiler.

Before today I did not have much to smile about.

You still don't as far as I can see.

I have my daughter, my mate and the trust of each. It is a very happy day.

The ping of resentment that he'd listed Jalina first took her by surprise. Deuce loved her. She had no reason for her insecurity.

Immediately, she was enfolded in mental comfort. *I love my daughter, but you are my soul.*

Peeping Tom.

His laugh stroked her nerve endings with its note of promise. *Later I will peep, now I am just observing.*

She stuck her tongue out at him. Dak, who'd followed the direction of his glance, laughed out loud. Eden hitched Jalina up on her shoulder and rubbed her back. As far as she could tell, not much had changed, but to Deuce it seemed as if the world had shifted.

"Your mate is a happy man."

"Marlika?" She turned, tamping down her shock. "Should you be out of bed?"

"The Others heal fast."

She must, since Deuce had told her that Marlika had suffered a severe concussion, lacerations to her face, and two broken ribs. All that remained of the lacerations were faint lines where five hours ago they had been gaping wounds. "More benefits of a fast metabolism?"

Marlika shrugged slightly, her right shoulder moving more easily than her left. "Since I was feeling better, I thought I'd see how everyone was."

She used the word "everyone" but her eyes were on Jalina, and a strange glimmer of energy surrounded her. "Thanks to you, she's fine."

"My help was not much."

Now, Eden recognized the note in her voice and that glimmer. "You are so not going to tell me you're feeling guilty?"

Marlika's gaze ducked hers. "I underestimated Pietre, and he almost succeeded."

"Good God, no one could estimate Pietre." The Coalition had altered him, making him a strong telepath. Unbalancing his mind in the process.

Marlika touched the soft curls on Jalina's head, apology in every nuance of her posture. "I should have been more careful."

"That's ridiculous."

Marlika flinched and now Eden was the one who got to feel guilty.

"I'm sorry, but I've lived with my grandfather my whole life. Even when I had no idea of what he was doing and operated under the delusion that he loved me, there were two things that always stuck out about the man." She kissed the top of Jalina's head. "He's brilliant, and he's ruthless about getting what he wants."

Marlika glanced uneasily over Eden's shoulder. "The Coalition is very determined."

"They are not as determined as the Chosen," Deuce said, coming up behind Eden. She leaned back into him as his arm came around her waist. She put her hand over his, holding him to her. She didn't remember much about her time in that black void, but she remembered one thing. She hadn't been alone, and Deuce had been her anchor, keeping her safe. She tilted her head back to see his face. "Tell her she didn't fail us."

His hair brushed her cheek as he inclined his head in that arrogant, unconsciously regal way he had. "The Chosen are forever in the debt of wolf Marlika and her blood. We offer our eternal gratitude and protection."

That wasn't what Eden had meant. Men were so obtuse.

Marlika didn't say thank you. She didn't even seem to breathe. Then she collected herself, and nodded her head, her aura as regal as Deuce's. "On behalf of myself and my blood, I thank you."

The words were nice, but Eden knew only one way to express her confidence. "If you are feeling up to it, would you mind watching Jalina while she naps? I need to talk to Deuce."

The formality left Marlika's expression to be replaced by shock. "You want me to watch her?"

"As far as I'm concerned, you're family, and I wouldn't trust her to anyone else."

A smile replaced the shock as Marlika reached for Jalina, taking her in her arms as if she were the most precious of gifts. Her smile softened further with the love she felt for the child. She glanced up, her beautiful dark eyes misted with tears. Her "Thank you" was equally damp. "I will take very good care of her."

"I know you will." Jalina was the child Marlika never expected to have. She'd almost given her life for her tonight, and would do so again in a heartbeat. When it came to babysitters, there was no one Eden trusted more.

Eden turned in Deuce's arms as Marlika took the child and headed into the house. "We need to find her mate."

"Harley has been working on it."

She touched her finger to the slight dent in Deuce's chin. "You need to put the Chosen on it full time. I'm not having my daughter's godmother dying on her."

Deuce's hands slid down to her hips. Against her stomach she felt his cock stretch in greeting. "Godmother?"

"It's a human concept." She rested her cheek against his chest. Surrounded by his arms, his heart beating under her cheek, it was easy to believe all things were possible. She tilted her head back.

"Basically, I have chosen her to be Jalina's mother if anything happens to me."

Deuce frowned. "That is not wise. Marlika's time approaches."

Despite the calmness of the words, Eden could feel the pressure and anxiety in him. "Well, I'm human and I believe in miracles, and I want one for Marlika, so I'm doing it."

"We are all hoping."

She unbuttoned the top button of his shirt. "Now, there's the difference between you and me. I'm not hoping, I'm believing."

His hand caught hers as she would have unfastened the second button. His knuckles under her chin tipped her face up. "I would give you anything to make you happy, mate, but I cannot promise to give you this."

"I don't need you to."

He raised his eyebrow. "You don't?"

She shook her head, meeting his black gaze dead-on. "I've gone over your head."

He frowned.

"I've asked your Maker, my God, to do this for her."

"And you believe this is all it takes?"

"It's my experience that miracles are ten percent faith and ninety percent perseverance." She unbuttoned the second button of his shirt. "I can be very stubborn."

He didn't argue with her and he didn't stop her work on his shirt, but let her undo the buttons one by one until his shirt hung open. She reached for his pants. He caught her hands in his. "You play with fire."

She smiled and rubbed her cheek against the hair-roughened skin of his chest, loving his scent and strength and the way he was instantly hers at a touch. "I didn't realize I was playing."

"You wish me to take you here in the yard in front of the Others?"

"Pervert." She slapped his chest, trying to suppress the thrill of excitement, the thought of being claimed so openly created. "You could at least try to sound appalled at the idea."

"Why?" When she would have stepped away she ran into the barrier of his hand. "I would have no trouble seeding you here in front of them all if that is your desire."

The serious expression left her in no doubt that he meant what he said. "Well, I would have a major problem with it, so just get the idea right out of your head."

His hand slipped to her now flat abdomen. "Too late."

There was a tugging at the waistband of her jeans and then a slow loosening until gravity peeled the heavy material off her like the skin of a banana, cut from her body by his razor-sharp nails. The simple act of him putting his hand over her mound cut off her shriek mid-birth. "The idea excites you. You are wet."

"I'm always wet around you." Embarrassment made mincemeat of her voice, leaving more air than disgust in her tone as she retorted, "That proves nothing." She pushed against his chest. He didn't move. Her only consolation was that the tunic she wore fell to her thighs, preserving her modesty.

His finger slipped through the center of the joining ring, gliding along the sensitive flesh, curving slightly as he pulled back, giving her the pleasure of his nail gently scraping the receptive flesh until he reached the edge of her clitoris. Then he stopped, holding her there on the edge of anticipation.

"Deuce?" He made it so hard to think.

He bent his head, his hair shielding her from others as he whispered in her ear, "You owe me tribute, woman."

But not here, not like this. The only thing that came out of her mouth was a breathless "Please".

He reached down. Two more slashes of his nails and her jeans fell away entirely. One arm slid around her back and the other curved under her knees as he answered her thoughts, not her words. "No. Not like this."

He straightened, holding her in his arms as if she were nothing. She loved it. His laugh brushed her temple. "I am glad my strength pleases you."

Her "Stay out of my mind" was pure reflex, because she was getting more comfortable with him there.

"But it is such an interesting place to be right now."

She just bet. "Well, I'm not comfortable with you wallowing in my fantasies."

He paused in front of the door. "Who else would you have...wallow in them?"

She sighed and pulled his hair over her face. "No one. I'd just rather bring them out more gradually." She had been going to say normally, but it was normal to Deuce to read her mind so she'd settled for the alternative. She was glad she had when he pulled the hair away and he smiled that gentle smile of his, the one that transformed him from leader to lover in one sexy flex of muscle.

"You are adjusting."

"Don't look so smug."

He opened the door and stepped in. "I am not smug, I am happy."

She looped her hands behind his neck. "I have to tell you, it's hard to tell the difference."

Once inside the house, he made a beeline for their temporary bedroom. She pressed her face into his neck to avoid the eyes of the Chosen and Others they passed.

"Your shyness pleases me," he said as he stepped through the bedroom door.

"I thought my boldness pleased you," she murmured as he let her lower body slide against his on the way to the floor.

"In private, your boldness pleases me immensely." The door clicked shut. "But in public, I prefer your shyness."

She shook her head. "The old lady-in-public-whore-in-the-bedroom cliché?"

"Do you mind so much?"

She leaned her cheek into his hand, savoring the pure emotion of his touch. "As long as you're my private gigolo, I think I can live with it."

"I am glad." His eyes crinkled at the corners and his lips twitched, letting her know he was more than glad. He was amused.

She touched the corner of his mouth. She did so like making him smile.

"You still owe me tribute, woman."

She rolled her eyes. "You are so hung up on that."

His smile broadened. "It is tradition."

"Oh yeah, I'm sure that's the reason." She stepped back into the support of his hands and motioned to his shirt. "You're a bit overdressed. "

He didn't move to take off his shirt, just shrugged in an apparent attempt to look helpless and pointed out, "Undressing her Chosen for tribute is a mate's job."

She eyed him suspiciously. "Another tradition?"

With a perfectly straight face he answered, "Yes."

"We are definitely going to have to discuss your traditions."

"I am happy with them."

She placed her hands on his chest, reveling in the way all that hard muscle leapt and shivered at her touch. "I'm sure you are, but brace yourself, the times they are a-changin'."

His teeth flashed white. "So you say."

She nodded in agreement, spreading his shirt to the side so she had an unrestricted view of his chest. "So I say."

He had a marvelous chest, his pectorals well defined, expanding above the steep ladder of his abs. The lamplight deepened the gold of his skin, polishing it to a burnished temptation. She leaned in, letting her breath caress the sensitive flesh at the top of his right pec, touching him lightly with her tongue, remembering how he felt, how he tasted. His ribs expanded on a harshly indrawn breath to be released on a careful "You hunger".

His finger, with one razor-sharp nail extended, slid between his chest and her mouth. With every pulse of his blood, she could feel his desire. He wanted her mouth on him. She caught his hand in hers before he could open a vein, and kissed the knuckles. "Not just yet."

His other hand cupped the back of her head, offering support. "I do not mind."

She just bet he didn't. "Thanks."

She shifted position, angling along the other side, her lips offering the haphazard caresses here or there while her hands slid under his shirt to close over the hard curve of his shoulders. They were too broad and too developed for her to hold them entirely, but she gave it a shot, working her hands between the material and his flesh, scraping the tops with her nails, soothing the sting with slow circles of her fingertips while her mouth slid lower, closer to the small male nipple beading in anticipation. She made him wait, approaching at a snail's pace, ignoring the urging of his hands, tickling the turgid nub with her breath, her lips before gently taking it into her mouth.

Deuce's groan shimmered in her mind and in the air above her head. His breath hissed between his teeth as she lightly, ever so lightly touched it with the tip of her tongue.

"Harder," he ordered, his hands coming up to cradle her head.

"Not yet."

He might have forced the issue, but she distracted him by sliding her hands down his abdomen, raking the firm flesh with her nails, forcing another groan from between his clenched teeth that stopped abruptly when she reached the waistband of his jeans. She inched her fingers under the material, pulling it away from his flesh, denying him the sensation he craved. She fumbled with the button, sinking her teeth into the hard nub of his nipple as she did. He bucked against her, making it impossible to undo the fastening. She fumbled a second more before stepping back and away.

She liked the way he watched her as her hands slid down the front of her tunic, his black eyes swirling with red, his breath coming in shallow pants, his expression drawn tight with passion. She crossed her hands in front of her, grabbed the hem and brought it up slowly, stopping just short of exposing her pussy. Her hot, throbbing, slightly different than before pussy. She inched the shirt up, holding her breath, waiting on his reaction.

Hot and primitive, Deuce's growl filled the room. Eden widened her stance, giving Deuce a good view of her freshly shaved pussy before turning around and, with a wiggle of her hips, presenting him with the full view of her ass.

She wasn't expecting the smack he landed on her backside or the thrill of excitement that shot through her at the heated sting. She paused, legs spread, ass quivering, shirt over her head as she waited for what he'd do next. Or maybe to see if he'd do it again.

"You are supposed to be paying tribute, not teasing."

She took that to mean he wasn't going to do that again. She threw the shirt off and turned back. He caught her chin in his hand. His thumb stroked her lips. "And yes, I will do that again."

The promise burned through her veins as he kept her in position with his hand on her chin. His gaze traveled down her torso, stroking her breasts like a touch, lingering on her pussy with an intensity that had juices spilling from her body. His nostrils flared and his pupils drew to pinpoints of fire before expanding to a black reflection of infinite desire. "A Chosen blessed with such an impudent mate will have to deliver punishment often."

She shuddered as he removed his hand. He smiled, unashamedly, exposing the fangs that grew with his desire for her. Only for her, making it hard to remember her goal.

She stepped back into his embrace, letting her nipples graze his stomach. She pushed his shirt back off his shoulders, nestling against the hard bulge of his cock, rubbing up and down as she stretched to work the material off. It slid a quarter of the way down before getting caught on his biceps. She frowned and slid her hands back over his shoulders and down his chest, casting a couple considering glances at the stuck shirt while she kissed first his right nipple and then his left, lingering there longer because she'd neglected it earlier. A simple twist of her torso and she once again attacked the stubborn button on his jeans. No matter how she struggled it wouldn't let go, pressure from beneath impeding her efforts. She sighed, glanced down and noticed his boots. Those would have to come off first.

Relying on Deuce to provide support, she bent her knees, sliding her body along his, whimpering when the waistband of his jeans caught on her nipples, pausing to control the rush of pleasure before she dropped the rest of the way. A tap on the back to his calf and he lifted his foot. She tugged on the heel—nothing happened. She tugged harder. The heel slipped out of her hand.

She cut him a glare. He merely lifted a brow. Oh, he so needed a lesson. "Lean back against the wall."

The other brow echoed the first. It was amazing that he could stand there with his arms trapped within his shirt and still look completely male and completely in control. Of himself and the situation. It was also annoying.

"You think to give your mate orders?"

"If my mate wants his boots off, yes."

Deuce didn't lean against the wall, he leaned against the door. As she'd seen in the movies, she turned and straddled his calf, lifting her ass high, spreading her legs wide, giving him an intimate view of everything he craved. His growl was music to her ears. The boot did not want to come off, giving her ample opportunity to wiggle and squirm before finally slipping it free. She removed his sock and moved on to the next boot. She tucked her smile away as he snarled when it came off and she fell forward, catching herself on her hands.

He pulled his foot out from between her legs and removed the sock. She turned and knelt facing him. She held his gaze while bending down and kissing the top of his foot. First the right and then the left. Deuce reacted predictably. His breathing increased twofold and his body jerked under the lash of lust that thickened the air around them. She was learning nothing turned an alpha male on faster than an overt symbol of acceptance.

She inched closer and kissed the inside of his calf. Even through the thickness of his jeans, his strength and power reached her. She did the same to the other side, letting her mouth linger long enough to impart the moist heat of her breath. He stood stock-still, accepting her ministrations until she got to the inside of his thighs and the covered length of his cock. His fingers threaded through her hair, tugging gently, the soft stings shivering down her spine to lodge between her legs where they gathered and grew in force. She eased her hands between his thighs, urging them apart as she came completely under him.

She caught and held his gaze as she pressed her mouth to his balls through the worn material. He stood as tall and as immobile as a statue while she nibbled at his balls and struggled with the fastening on his jeans, but around her the force of his energy seethed and surged.

He was close, very close to breaking. She fumbled with the fastening of his jeans again. Letting her fingers slip. Once. Twice. When her third attempt to get the button to slip through the hole failed, Deuce's patience shattered on a harsh snarl. A loud rip punctuated his loss of control as he tore the shirt in half, freeing his arms, the moment all the more erotic for the fact that he didn't use magic, just reacted with pure physical instinct. She did so like it when he went all primitive.

His hands knocked hers aside. With an ease that left her blinking, the jeans rent down the middle. His cock sprang free into the air, the heavy weight of the head dragging it down. A glistening drop of pre-come spilled free as, with a muttered curse, Deuce grabbed handfuls of her hair and dragged her mouth up into his groin.

Eden knew what he wanted. She opened her mouth, tucking the right nut in, sucking it gently and then harder as he tugged on her hair, demanding the tribute she gladly gave. His hips rocked above her, his cock pumping air. She pulled back, ignoring his growl that ended in a sigh as she took the other ball in, nurturing it to painful hardness before catching it between her teeth.

Deuce froze, the only movement the heaving of his ribs as he waited. She held him like that, poised on the edge for two heartbeats before she delivered his pleasure in a soft bite. He came on a roar, yanking her hard against him as his cock bobbed above her, spurting his hot seed into the air. She turned her head so she could breathe and sucked his balls gently as the spasms waned, kissing both round orbs in their sensitive sac as his grip eased. His knees bent, his hands cupped her shoulders, and he leaned her torso back until his cock poised above her face. His eyes locked on hers.

"Open your mouth."

She did, closing her lips around the wide tip as he slid it between. A trickle of seed teased her desire. She swallowed eagerly as he lowered her to the floor, his knees landing on either side of her shoulders with determined thuds. His hands landed somewhere above her head and her mouth was suddenly full of his cock. He pushed it all the way to the back of her throat. "Suck it."

She did the best she could as he held her there, imprisoned between his cock and the floor, subservient to his needs as he pumped his big shaft in and out of her mouth at a leisurely pace, delighting in every break in his breathing, every twitch of muscle.

"Harder, Edie mine," he ordered when she would have faltered. "Use your lips and your teeth. Keep me hard."

She experimented with different techniques, knowing she'd hit on the right one when he groaned and his shaft firmed on her tongue.

"Yes." His hand came behind her head, angling it for better penetration. "Just like that. Ready me." He fucked her mouth steadily, wrapping her up in the intensity of his pleasure. Her jaw ached, her tongue tired, but she wouldn't stop before he did, loving that she could give him this, taking every groan and sigh he made inside herself. He rode her mouth, fucking her face in slow, easy glides, eyes slitted with the satisfaction of watching her take his cock, as if needing to reinforce his dominance after she'd taken his control.

Eden closed her eyes and relaxed, letting him have his way, understanding his nature and his need. Accepting both. Immediately, the energy around him softened. Deuce stopped, his cock bouncing in her mouth as he turned until he was straddling her shoulders and facing her feet.

His breath licked the top of her mound like fire as he whispered, "Part you legs."

Anticipation made her slow to respond. A sharp nip to the inside of her thigh had her whimpering and lifting her hips. Toward that heat and his mouth. Deuce laughed and kissed the top of her labia, his lips lingering but not moving, just teasing her with the promise of what she knew they both wanted.

Damn it, Deuce!

"What's the matter, Edie mine? Do you not like to be teased?"

She didn't even have to think about her answer. *No!*

She had waited her whole life for him, suffered for him and she just wanted him. Now.

His lips grazed lower, his soft "Shh" blowing across her swollen clit. The joining ring heated.

Oh damn. It was too much.

"You know I do not like it when you swear." The gold hoop jiggled as he nudged it aside. "Are you perhaps in the mood to be punished?"

His cock in her mouth prevented speech so she sent her displeasure to him in a short grunt. He caught it and returned it with a light nudge of her clitoris with his finger. Her grunt broke to a moan.

"You are very swollen. Very tender. Do you wish to come?"

Yes.

"Good." His tongue stroked over her labia in gentle swirls which diminished to smaller and smaller circles until he rimmed the base of her clit, flipping the ring about as the rougher side of his tongue caressed the slick, aching sides of the straining nub. Each quick lap drove her need higher. She needed more, something more. She needed him. A hot, piercing pain struck inwards from her clit, followed immediately by a searing pleasure. He'd bitten her. And now he was feeding. From her clit.

Oh God, how could anything so freaky feel so blessedly good? She was on fire. From the thought, the pleasure. Her hips jerked. Another sharp pain wrenched a cry from her soul. His cock throbbed in her mouth. She moaned around his thick shaft. He was devouring her, not leaving her any defenses, pulling her into the fire of his passion, drawing her past what she could bear. His lips and tongue fluttered around her clit, every brush, every nudge creating an answering fire in her until she dug her fingers into his buttocks and screamed as she flashed out of control. And still he wasn't satisfied. With every draw of his mouth, every brush of his lips he expressed his joy in her response, coaxing more, demanding more.

And then he started sucking. A strong hard suction that drew straight from her womb, her heart, dragging her lust past her inhibitions, leaving only a wanton woman in its wake. She thrashed in his arms, clawed at his thighs, sucked and bit his cock, lost in the spiking sensation, needing it to stop but desperate for it to go on. He kept her flying for what seemed like forever, slipping first one finger into her pussy and then another, fucking her in time with his suction, pumping his cock to the same rhythm. He took her from one peak to the next, each one higher, never letting her totally down, never coming himself, just holding her on the tip of his cock, on the promise of his desire. Pleasuring her.

When he would have driven her over for the fourth time, she shook her head and pushed at his hips. She couldn't bear it. Every nerve ending was raw with spent passion. The lightest brush of his tongue stuck through her like a lightning bolt. He had to stop. He nuzzled the joining ring as he resumed feeding in light sips. Her desire rose again. She dropped her hands to his head. His hair was cool against her palms. She wrapped her fingers in the smooth strands and pulled him closer, thrusting her hips to his pleasure, desperate to give him all he needed, not sure if she could survive the giving.

The last echoes of her climax hummed through her pussy while the beginnings of a new one started to sing right alongside. His finger slipped out of her pussy and followed the copious spill of her juices to her anus. Her breath caught as he rimmed the tight band of muscle. His cock pressed down as his finger pressed in. She closed her eyes as she shuddered from head to toe, lashing his cock with her tongue as she savored the possession. He was going to fuck her ass. With a silent pop of muscle his finger sank deep. Oh God, it felt so good. So good. She pressed down, urging him on. His chuckle vibrated against her clit. And then he was working his finger deeper. In then out. Faster. Harder. His lips took up the rhythm, then his cock. More pressure on her anus which became a burning ache, spread to a frisson of sharp-edged delight. She wanted it to last forever. She couldn't stand it another second. It was too much. He was too much.

Her orgasm hit her in a violent wave of color that swept away everything, leaving only Deuce. She wrapped her hands in his hair and tugged. *Hold me.*

Immediately he was at her side, pulling her into his arms. Her mouth felt empty without his cock. He filled it with his tongue. He tasted of blood, of her, of them. His fingers wiped the tears from her cheeks. "Be easy, mate."

Easy for him to say, he hadn't just been flung out into the universe without a lifeline.

Her hair stuck to her cheek with her sweat. Deuce eased it off, as always seemingly fascinated with the way the curls wrapped around his hand. "I am always with you."

"Uh-huh." He was smiling again. Not a big one, but a little one that teased the corners of his mouth and gave his sharply handsome features a sexier edge. If that was possible.

She worked her forearms up so she could link her hands around his neck. "When I'm recovered, could we do that again?"

"It will be your mate's pleasure to eat your pussy whenever you prove deserving."

She rolled her eyes. "Let's not go there again."

He blinked as if he didn't understand. "Go where?"

"Machoville." She waved to his pile of clothes beside them. "I think we just proved these traditions are flexible."

He glanced at the pile and then at her. His right brow arched. "Is this how you show gratitude for your mate's aid?"

"Aid, my foot."

He sat up, taking her with him as he got to his feet. "You were in distress."

She looped her arms around his neck. "I'm not the one who tore off his clothes and erupted like a volcano."

It was only a few steps to the bed. Eden moaned in protest as he set her down away from all that lovely muscle. He stood above her, shirt halves hanging from his wrists, body bare, his heavy cock glistening with her saliva. His long hair hung around his face in a heavy tangle, setting off the slight slant of his cheekbones, the determination in his eyes, and the inherent power he wielded so effortlessly. Holding her gaze, he tore one of the sleeves free. His gaze narrowed. Power radiated off him with a deadly shimmer. "Since you do not appreciate my restraint, maybe I should show you how a Chosen punishes a disobedient mate."

"You think that was disobedient?"

"Yes."

The sleeve dropped to the floor with quiet expediency. He took a step forward, and then another, clearly intent on intimidation. He was so full of shit.

Eden fell back on the bed with a smile, pulling her heels up, letting her knees fall wide. She slid her fingers down her stomach, over the bare mound of her pussy until they met the hot metal of the ring. Holding his gaze, she dipped her fingers into the slick well of her vagina, drawing up the thick cream gathered there, smoothing it over the deep carvings before cradling the anointed hoop in the palm of her hand. "I can be so much more disobedient than that."

Deuce's eyes widened and then narrowed. The other sleeve dropped to the floor, and then he was coming down over her, chest jerking with the laughter he was trying to contain. "You have no caution, my heart."

"No patience either." She shrugged and wrapped her legs around his hips, drawing his heat and power to her. "You've a long time to get used to it."

The bed sagged as he shifted his weight onto his elbows. "A very long time."

His cock nestled into the well of her vagina. Pleasure speared inward and then shot out. Eden tightened her thighs, bringing him closer. "Forever," she groaned as he pressed in, her body weeping a welcome as her muscles willingly parted.

"Forever," he repeated, his satisfaction echoing in her mind. "Come to me, mate."

And she did, opening her body to his possession, offering him everything that she was, and when his soul touched hers in that gentlest of caresses, sheltering her, pulling her close, holding her carefully, a new almost silent whisper joined the first. *Stay?*

She froze. Above her Deuce stiffened. His head angled back in that arrogant tilt that dared her to make something of the slip while in her mind that one word lingered. A request, not an order. A Chosen man calling to his mate, asking for the one thing he needed to feel whole. Her full commitment.

How could he not know he already had it? Eden caught Deuce's face between her palms, touched the hard line of his lips with her finger, and smiled. Slowly, deliberately she reached down and caught his hand in hers. With the same deliberateness, she brought his hand to his chest. He hesitated. She tapped his finger. The nail lengthened and thinned as he watched her with disbelief, and the faintest glimmer of…despair? She pressed the razor-sharp nail into the thick, heavy muscle, drawing a line.

His blood spilled between them. The gift she'd never consciously accepted. Red flames leapt in his gaze. His cock thickened and surged. His breath caught. She rose, bringing her mouth to the life-giving flow. He froze above her, every muscle hardened in agony as he waited, battling the hope he didn't want her to see, projecting an indifference she knew he didn't feel.

Holding his gaze, she drank, letting the emotion pour from her to him, following it with her mind. With the courage that was so much a part of him, he let her seek out the darkest corners of his soul, allowing her to see his strengths and vulnerabilities. Holding nothing back. She closed her eyes against the onslaught, against the hurt he harbored inside, the conviction that her human heart would always want something better.

She shook her head. That was so unacceptable. She lapped at the dwindling flow of blood before placing her hand over his heart, the beat as steady as the man himself. Deuce was everything she'd ever wanted in a package she'd never dreamed big enough to imagine. He was strength, passion. Love. So much love. It poured through her in a never-ending flow of invisible light, burning out insecurity and fear—leaving only confidence in it's wake. She was not alone. Would never be alone again.

She was a Chosen mate, forever bathed in the light of Deuce's love and protection.

And if he thought he was getting out of knowing that same security he was so mistaken. She caught the path of his emotion and forged her own inside it. One just as bright and just as strong. Into it she poured every bit of emotion she felt—her happiness, her satisfaction. Her love. Every single bit of her love.

And then she sent it back, pushing it deep into his soul, finding all the fears he harbored in the deepest, darkest corners, paying special attention to that lingering uncertainty, and burned them away. There was no room for doubt in their relationship.

She was his. Completely. Without reservation.

Beneath her hand, his muscles flinched. In her mind his joy grew, but in his gaze a question lingered. She dropped back to the mattress, shaking her head at his determination to protect her even from herself. She wrapped her fingers in his hair and pulled his mouth down to hers.

Against his growing smile, she whispered. "Just try to get rid of me."

Why an electronic book?

We live in the Information Age—an exciting time in the history of human civilization in which technology rules supreme and continues to progress in leaps and bounds every minute of every hour of every day. For a multitude of reasons, more and more avid literary fans are opting to purchase e-books instead of paperbacks. The question to those not yet initiated to the world of electronic reading is simply: *why?*

1. *Price.* An electronic title at Ellora's Cave Publishing and Cerridwen Press runs anywhere from 40-75% less than the cover price of the <u>exact same title</u> in paperback format. Why? Cold mathematics. It is less expensive to publish an e-book than it is to publish a paperback, so the savings are passed along to the consumer.

2. *Space.* Running out of room to house your paperback books? That is one worry you will never have with electronic novels. For a low one-time cost, you can purchase a handheld computer designed specifically for e-reading purposes. Many e-readers are larger than the average handheld, giving you plenty of screen room. Better yet, hundreds of titles can be stored within your new library—a single microchip. (Please note that Ellora's Cave and Cerridwen Press does not endorse any specific brands. You can check our website at www.ellorascave.com or

www.cerridwenpress.com for customer recommendations we make available to new consumers.)

3. *Mobility.* Because your new library now consists of only a microchip, your entire cache of books can be taken with you wherever you go.

4. *Personal preferences are accounted for.* Are the words you are currently reading too small? Too large? Too...**ANNOYING**? Paperback books cannot be modified according to personal preferences, but e-books can.

5. *Instant gratification.* Is it the middle of the night and all the bookstores are closed? Are you tired of waiting days—sometimes weeks—for online and offline bookstores to ship the novels you bought? Ellora's Cave Publishing sells instantaneous downloads 24 hours a day, 7 days a week, 365 days a year. Our e-book delivery system is 100% automated, meaning your order is filled as soon as you pay for it.

Those are a few of the top reasons why electronic novels are displacing paperbacks for many an avid reader. As always, Ellora's Cave and Cerridwen Press welcomes your questions and comments. We invite you to email us at service@ellorascave.com, service@cerridwenpress.com or write to us directly at: 1056 Home Ave. Akron OH 44310-3502.

erridwen, the Celtic Goddess of wisdom, was the muse who brought inspiration to storytellers and those in the creative arts. Cerridwen Press encompasses the best and most innovative stories in all genres of today's fiction. Visit our site and discover the newest titles by talented authors who still get inspired - much like the ancient storytellers did, once upon a time.

CERRIDWEN PRESS

www.cerridwenpress.com

Discover for yourself why readers can't get enough of the multiple award-winning publisher

Ellora's Cave.

Whether you prefer e-books or paperbacks, be sure to visit EC on the web at

www.ellorascave.com

for an erotic reading experience

that will leave you

breathless.